Haunted Havenport

Ruth A. Casie
Emma Kaye
Nicole S. Patrick
Lita Harris

Timeless Scribes
Publishing

Timeless Scribes Publishing LLC

Print ISBN-10: 1-945679-02-6
Print ISBN-13: 978-1-945679-02-5

Digital ISBN-10: 1-945679-01-8
Digital ISBN-13: 978-1-945679-01-8

Cover created by Jay Aheer at Simply Defined Art
Edited by Deserie Comfort of Comfort Editing
Copy Edited by Michael Mandarano

This edition published by arrangement with Timeless Scribes Publishing LLC.

www.TimelessScribes.com

Havenport Herald

*** Halloween Edition ***   *** Volume 02 Issue 01 ***

Get the latest with Candy Apples.
Gossip with a snarky, tart bite…

GHOSTS TAKE OVER HAVENPORT!

Not real ghosts, don't be silly people! Halloween is right around the corner and folks are gearing up for the annual Halloween ball at Havencroft Manor. I know I have my costume all picked out, how about you? Lets hope Mrs. X can come up with something new this year, she almost split the seams of her Naughty Nurse costume last year. Yikes!

The Witching Hour will soon be upon us—anyone think Havencroft Manor's most famous dearly departed will stop by for a visit? Such a haunting tale of love and betrayal makes this gossip columnist stand up and take notice. Keep reading, and we'll take a stroll down memory lane to find out all the juicy details.

The room above Serendipity is open for business. Looks like they kicked off rentals with a séance on behalf of our favorite philanthropist. Rumor has it, he has a ghost problem. Some say he's trying to get rid of the problem, while others are convinced he's trying to bring **The Ghost of You** back to life. With the Goddess's help, I guess anything's possible.

Sorry, ladies, but looks like our hunky veterinarian may be off the market soon. A certain divorcee was hired to spruce up his bachelor pad, but from the look of things, my money's on them turning it into a family home instead. Should be cozy with their latest rescue dog and the soldier's spirit that tagged along. So long as **A Spirit's Bond** doesn't stand in their way, should be fun to watch.

They say the new widow in town has a way with ghosts. In fact, one may have followed her into town. To help or hinder? Hard to tell. Maybe the ruggedly handsome carpenter fixing up Havencroft Manor will find a way to help out a **Kindred Spirit**.

Come to think of it, maybe I spoke too soon about those ghosts.

Don't forget to stock up on candy and have a Happy Halloween!

~Candy Apples

Contents

The Witching Hour

by Ruth A. Casie

Rachel Emerson led a charmed life. Steffen Burkett, her greatest love, was everything a woman could want and he was hers. But before the wedding invitations were sent, the wedding was canceled.

Fast forward thirty years. Rachel returns to her beloved home on Halloween eve, the day before the house becomes the property of the Historical Society. For years she mourned the loss of her locket, her only connection to Steffen. This is her last chance to find it. Going home takes Rachel on a journey of self-discovery and possibly even reconciliation.

Dedicated to ~

Staci, Cori and Ari for their unwavering support and enthusiasm. They spur me onward.

DM Comfort and her spot on editing. You've made this a better book and me a better writer.

Paul for his unconditional friendship and love. He always has my back.

Emma, Lita, and Nicole who keep me focused and on target and tolerate my bursts, the good ones and the not so good ones.

Chapter One

Rachel Emerson drew her brown wrap close and fisted the wool at her neck to block out the damp mist from stealing the little warmth she had. Crazy, that's what she was. Who in their right mind goes out at 8:00 a.m. on a New England beach road in late October? Really? No one would describe her as compulsive, but what else could explain her uncontrollable urge to come here? Now. Before the house was gone and nothing was left.

Rachel reached into her pocket and pulled out a folded note for the umpteenth time. *Meet me tonight. R.* She put the unsent note away with a satisfied sound and continued on.

Constitution Boulevard, a grand name for a small strip of asphalt, was almost wide enough for two cars. Right off the interstate, the local road cut inland through a forest of evergreens that thinned and morphed into manicured grounds of the mansions near the beach. This close to the water, tall grass grew on either side of the roadway. Rachel followed the faded double yellow line in the center of the street, which was wet from the early-morning rain.

The cadence of crashing waves in the distance created a familiar, soothing rhythm. A breeze picked up and blew down the road from the beach. She pulled her wrap closer. For a moment, she regretted her early start.

"My own fault," Rachel muttered, "for putting this visit off." At midnight, the Historical Society took ownership of the estate property and its contents. She had to be gone by then. Yeah, nothing like leaving things to the last minute.

"Come on, Rachel, one foot in front of the other," she said to no one.

This was her last chance to walk through Havencroft Manor and find what was most precious to her. Deep down, the comfort of home called to her, one last time. Finding that feeling again would warm her soul. Anything else would be a miracle.

Welcome to Havenport, Rhode Island Founded 1640, the town sign greeted her at the crossroads. Against the backdrop of an overcast sky, fingers of fog roiled at the sign's base and made it appear as if it hung in midair.

She squinted down Manor Road on the right. Visibility was poor. No way anyone could make out the wrought-iron entrance to the cemetery a quarter mile away—or the entrance to Havencroft Manor on the hill a mile past that—thanks to the mist.

As a seasoned Havenporter she knew the watery morning sun struggling through the clouds would make it difficult for the haze to clear.

Another look at the gathering mist sent a chill up her back. Rachel rubbed her arms, unable to be soothed. *Easy. Stay calm.* She cast a quick look from the short shrubs at the edge of the road to the thickening mist around her. Anyone could be hiding in this fog and she wouldn't know until they stood nose to nose.

"Breathe. Nothing's there. It's your overactive imagination."

The tall grass twitched. Her chest pounded. She dare not make a sudden move. She sniffed the air and caught the tangy order of brine, seaweed, and mucky sand. Another sniff. Some people were concerned about the coyotes and fisher cats that roamed the area. Not Rachel. Skunks terrified her ever since she was five.

"What were you thinking?" her father asked. His voice had a nasal twang probably caused by the clothespin on his nose.

"I wanted to pet the kitty," Rachel told him. *"Why are we going to the boathouse now? Doesn't the party start soon?"*

"You'll have to be brave, Pumpkin." His words were somber, but his eyes twinkled as they reached the water. In minutes, he had a fire blazing in the pit, and Mother had supplies on the outdoor table.

"Brave?" Rachel asked.

"Yes." Her mother pulled off her costume and gave it to Father.

"My costume," she cried, reaching for it. Shiny sequins covered her beautiful costume and made it twinkle in the light. *"You don't let anyone into the party without a costume."*

"Hmm…not in this Halloween costume. Unless you want to go as a skunked pumpkin," her father said, holding the smelly mess of orange fabric and stuffing at arm's length. Five-year-old Rachel watched in horror as he tossed it into the fire.

"Farewell, old pumpkin and brave clothespin." He ceremoniously removed the clothespin from his nose and tossed that into the fire pit as well. *"Life is not always a smooth ride. Sometimes it's even stinky."*

"Oh, Daddy. Don't be silly," she said with a laugh. He always made her laugh.

"Thank goodness," her mother said, sniffing her like a puppy, making her laugh even more. *"I can't smell anything. The stuffing in the costume must have absorbed the spray."*

"Can I be a witch like you, Mommy?"

"I'm not sure," her father said. *"You have to be pretty special to be a witch like your mother."* He raked the fire and made sure nothing remained of the costume or the clothespin.

"Don't give her any ideas." A special look passed between her parents. *"You know Rachel has to be at least six before I can teach her spells."*

Her mother washed her down for good measure and wrapped her in a soft towel while her father put out the fire.

"Mission accomplished," he announced. He sniffed around her. "You smell sweet as a rose. I'm sure Janet will have something for you to wear to the party."

"In the future, Rachel—"

"Edythe, she's learned her lesson. Haven't you...Hmm. I can't call you pumpkin. How about...pussycat?" Her father picked her up. "I want you to have happily-ever-afters. Rachel, wild animals are not safe. Promise me you won't go near them again."

"I promise, Daddy." He carried her back to the manor and brought her to her room where Janet waited.

"Oh, Janet. I love it." On her bed were her black leotard and ballet slippers, along with glittery, furry ears.

"All you need is a little eye pencil in the right place, and you're transformed into a black kitten."

After that incident, she had a healthy respect for skunks. Now, a grown Rachel took one step backward, and another, before turning and doubled-timing toward town. Better to wait for the fog to lift before going to the house.

"Coward," Rachel mumbled. "You didn't come this far to run away. Shush," she said, as if a reprimand would quiet her mind.

It would take her another thirty minutes on Constitution Boulevard to get to Havenport. By the time the buildings on the outskirts of town were in sight, the sun had made its way through the clouds and took the edge off the chill.

The corner of Washington Avenue and Constitution Boulevard hadn't changed. It still was a middle-class community of hardworking people who cared about one another. New England Cape Cod–style shingle houses with steep roofs and gabled fronts lined the streets. Neatly landscaped yards surrounded the houses. Cars filled driveways, and children's toys littered lawns. Jack-o'-

lanterns, with wide smiles and missing teeth, stood guard on steps and porches, ready to welcome tomorrow's trick-or-treaters. Lawn signs stuck in the ground announced the local elections. Evan Washburn. The last name was familiar. Yes, one of the families from the country club.

Rachel turned down Washington Avenue. People, busy chatting with one another, sauntered at an easy pace, and others hurried along. She passed old landmarks and headed toward the center of town.

Seasonal decorations dressed the town square and the rest of the business district.

The large white gazebo, built on a mound in the town square, provided a panoramic view of Havenport. Rachel climbed the steps, something she'd done hundreds of times. She viewed the harbor on one side and shops on the other.

Private and commercial boats bobbed in the water, tied to the new pier that jutted out into the bay. The old commercial marina at the far end of the bay was gone, replaced with footings for a new structure.

Places and people move on. Did she think they would stay the same for her? How foolish to not realize Havenport would change. She turned away from the harbor, as if ignoring progress would make it stop, and tried to swallow around the knot in her throat. What else had time changed?

Benches and trees lining Main Street gave a pedestrian mall appearance rather than the traffic-filled roadway of the past. New businesses sprinkled among the old storefronts. The Bacchanalia restaurant—it looked upscale to her—occupied the far corner where the stationery store used to be.

Pumpkins and large flowerpots brimmed with chrysanthemums and bright-yellow, red, and brown leaves along the sidewalk, creating a festive look. Ghosts, witches, and goblins hung from old-fashioned lampposts. Rich colors and trappings of a New England autumn were all around. Yes, fall was her season. Havenport was her home.

"*Havencroft,*" a voice whispered in her head. Half in anticipation and half in dread, she walked down the gazebo steps. People who laughed at the cool weather sat at the stone tables with their morning brew and Danish.

The aroma of coffee and fresh baked bread filled her nostrils. She imagined the taste of warm bread slathered with fresh butter—or better, raspberry jam—and she licked her lips. Tony's morning roll with fresh butter was legendary. He also made the best pastries in Havenport. His bakery was a daily stop for her and Pam on their way home from school. A small detour. Her mouth watered as she traipsed down Main Street, determined to satisfy her sweet tooth.

She stopped across from the bookstore, now called A New Chapter. Disoriented, Rachel looked up and down Jefferson Avenue. This was the right spot. She searched for the large white building that should be on the corner. She didn't recognize it now that it was painted bright blue. Above the gay yellow-and-white-striped awning, there was a sign: Led Zeppoli, Italian Pastries.

She jumped at a soft, playful bark from a West Highland terrier that sniffed her feet. Before she could bend to pet the pup, the dog rolled on its back, begging for a belly rub.

"I got my ticket for the masquerade ball at the bookstore. Sure, I'm out front. I'll be right with you. One minute," the woman holding the dog's leash said into her phone. "What's up, McDuff?"

"McDuff. That's a great name," Rachel said. Unable to resist the white powder puff, she bent to pet the dog. Rolling on the ground, its tail beating the pavement, this puppy would melt anyone's heart. Masquerade ball? Her mother used to host one every year at the manor.

"I just gave you a bath. Heel," the woman commanded, and put away her phone. "Sorry, no time to play."

"That's all right," Rachel said, straightening. McDuff went obediently and stood at the woman's feet, but kept his eyes on her.

The dog walker bent to pick some leaves off McDuff's coat. "They need us inside." Before they entered Wags and Walks, McDuff, more leaves stuck on his clean coat, looked back and gave Rachel a soft woof.

"Yeah, boy. I'm sorry, but I have to go, too."

She crossed the street to get a better look at the bookstore window and stared at a poster.

Edythe Emerson's Annual Masquerade Ball
October 30 at Havencroft Manor (the former Emerson Estate)
Nine to midnight (if you dare to stay to the witching hour)
Costume required
THE WOMEN OF HAVENCROFT MANOR,
available at Serendipity

An arrow pointed to the right.

It would be wonderful to go to the ball. Rachel looked at the sign. *The Women of Havencroft Manor.* Curious to see where to find the shop, she stepped back and laughed. Serendipity was next door.

A metaphysical shop. Edythe Emerson had fancied herself a witch. As a guest lecturer, her mother taught two community college courses that were always scheduled in October: *Magic, Witchcraft, and Religion* and *Witches, Myth, and Reality.* A metaphysical shop would be right in line with her thoughts.

Rachel stepped inside. With her first breath, the familiar woodsy fragrance of bay, and earthy and minty aromas of sage and rosemary, greeted her. Drawn in by the warmth, further into the shop floral notes of lavender, honeysuckle, and rose mixed and created a bouquet of fragrances. She didn't stop; instead she passed the lotions and jars and followed an overhead sign that directed her to the back of the shop. There she found a large table against the back wall with neatly displayed books. But it was the picture next to *The Women of Havencroft Manor* that caught her attention. She stared at a formal family portrait of her as a teenager with her mother.

A wave of loss rolled over her. She hadn't realized how much she wanted to hear her mother's voice, touch her warmth, feel safe at home in Havencroft.

The moment ebbed until her emotions calmed. Rachel turned to leave and stared into the eyes of a woman wearing a purple scarf.

"You'd better hurry if you're going to Havencroft," the woman said softly, and turned to leave.

How did the woman know she was going to Havencroft? What else did she know? Emotions in turmoil, Rachel followed the woman out the door and looked everywhere. The street was deserted in every direction but one. Rachel rushed in the only direction she could have gone, toward the throng of people by the town square.

Small groups, mostly women, congregated in a knot and chatted. Rachel walked through the crowd and searched for the purple scarf.

"Okay, everyone," a woman with a clipboard said.

"Shush. Ina's speaking," someone called out. Rachel kept moving through the crowd as the group quieted. She fisted her hand and smashed it into her thigh. Had the woman vanished into thin air?

"It's nine. Please line up. The bus to Havencroft Manor is around the corner."

Rachel spun around. Havencroft? Were these people all going to the manor?

"The driver will let us off at the front door. When you arrive, go directly to the assignment table in the Great Hall. You've all done a wonderful job to make this masquerade ball a sensation. Edythe Emerson would be proud."

"Ina, what about getting back into town?" someone in the crowd asked.

"Good question." Ina flipped some papers on her clipboard. "Buses will return promptly at three and bring us back here. That should give everyone plenty of time to get ready for the evening. Please remember to stay on the first floor. We've closed the upper floors for this event. If there are no other questions, please get in line."

Rachel gave one last look at the crowd. Deciding it was better to ride than walk to the manor, she inserted herself at the back of the line.

The clattering noise of a large vehicle grew louder as it approached. Finally, an old-school bus pulled up, and the volunteers filed in. She walked down the aisle of the half-filled bus and searched each face. Disappointed the woman wasn't there, she took a seat in the back.

From where she sat, the moorings were mostly empty. The boats must have been put into dry dock for the winter. The water looked a bit choppy, but it still looked like a picture postcard.

"Hurry, ladies," the bus driver called. Ina and a few latecomers took their seats. He closed the door and pulled away from the curb.

The woman with the purple scarf must have thought she was someone else or another volunteer. Rachel was sure no one cared that she had returned. Going to Havencroft was purely voluntary, or was it?

Rachel gave the waterfront a last glance then looked down the aisle.

Four rows in front was the profile of Pam Dawes. Her best friend.

Chapter Two

Seeing Pam so suddenly caught Rachel off guard. After all these years, the hurt should be gone. However, betrayal ran deep.

The Dawes had a long history that went back fifteen generations to Roger Williams and the founding of Rhode Island and Havenport. That the Dawes name was held in high regard was an understatement—they enjoyed a celebrity status among the locals. Not all family members handled that notoriety well. Most were nice and down-to-earth, but others took their privilege to cruel levels.

Rachel couldn't remember life without Pam. Born days apart, their mothers, close friends themselves, bragged that the girls were bosom buddies in the hospital nursery. More like twin sisters than best friends. They did everything together. Even fell in love with the same boy, Steffen Burkett.

Steffen. She smiled.

The week before Halloween, on her way home from an afternoon of gathering sea shells at the town beach, intent on getting her favorite hamburger and fries at Mellie's Diner, she carefully approached Water Street ready to cross.

Water Street followed the coastline and was a series of serpentine curves that led to a straightaway as it came into Havenport. The last curve, the one everyone called Killer Curve, carried a double punch. A sharp curve and steep rise not only obscured oncoming traffic, but if you didn't slow down before the drop, well, you could wind up on the beach, if the tide was out.

With nothing in sight, Rachel stepped off the curb. Out of nowhere, she found herself in the crosshairs of an oncoming car. Startled, and incapable of making sense of what was happening, she froze.

Breaks screeched, filling the air with the odor of burned rubber. Finally, Rachel came to her senses and jumped back toward the curb, but landed badly, her ankle at an odd angle, and fell to the ground. The car skidded to a stop inches away from her.

The door swung open, the engine still running, and from her position on the asphalt, she stared at a pair of muscular legs. Rachel worked to catch her breath. Her sunglasses had gone flying, and with the sun glaring into her eyes, she didn't recognize who stood over her.

"Jeez, I could have— Don't move. I'll take you to the hospital."

"Don't be silly. I'm fine." Rachel sat up and groped for her sunglasses. He plucked them from the street and handed them to her. She put on the twisted frames. Her eyes traveled from his muscular legs, up his bare, ripped abdomen and chest, to his concerned eyes. Who was he? A tourist? He helped her to her feet.

"See." Her leg buckled and she was light-headed.

"Whoa." He had fast reflexes. He caught her before she hit the ground.

He easily held her, as if her hundred and ten pounds were nothing, and he didn't appear eager to put her down. His hazel eyes were striking, but his smile...took her breath away.

Rachel sniffed the air. "Skunk?"

"Yeah. You can still smell it? My map flew out the window. When I picked it up, a skunk sprayed me."

"Don't tell me. You stopped at Constitution and Manor." She wanted to kiss that little critter.

"Yeah. How'd you know?"

"We're old friends. Did you give the critter the shirt off your back?"

He threw back his head and let out a peal of laughter. *"No, I burned it on the side of the road. I didn't want to smell up my car. I'm Steffen Burkett. My family moved to the old Dyer place. Let me take you home. It's the least I can do."* He placed her in the passenger seat.

"I'm Rachel Emerson. We're practically neighbors." It was a toss-up. She couldn't decide if it was almost becoming another Killer Curve statistic or the handsome Steffen Burkett that caused her heart to pound. She was surprised he couldn't hear it.

Yeah, she shamelessly played it up to keep his attention.

Rachel's swift intake of breath amid the silence in the bus brought her back to the moment.

The bus turned and passed the Manor Road gate. The manor wasn't visible from the road. Once through this, the main gate, one had to drive a quarter of a mile to the knoll, then another quarter of a mile to the house. Everyone stopped at the knoll for the dramatic effect, including the bus. Here you were high enough to look down on the manor and the grounds.

Audible gasps turned into soft conversation, and the bus drove on.

Havencroft Manor, last renovated in the 1920s, stood large and imposing. The Emerson family had done well in the industrial revolution—trade with China, to be exact. Not quite as well as those who built in neighboring Newport, but well enough to establish their sphere of influence a few miles down the coast.

Other Newport wannabes soon joined the Emersons and created an exclusive enclave that gave the appearance of the rich and famous.

"Havencroft Manor," the driver announced as he stopped in the circular drive and opened the bus door. He got out and helped the volunteers. "I'll be back at three. Don't be late or you'll have a long walk back into town."

The bus emptied. Only the two of them remained, Pam and her. Her betrayal still stung.

Pam wanted Steffen Burkett and did everything to attract his attention. When that didn't work, Pam developed a simple strategy. On the spur of the moment, Pam put together a surprise pool party for Rachel and invited Steffen, swearing him to secrecy.

When Steffen arrived, he found no Rachel, no other guests—only Pam in a very skimpy bikini.

Pam, a Dawes, got what she wanted. No one else mattered. Everything revolved around her, and Pam wanted Steffen, but her trick didn't work. He was already Rachel's.

Meet me tonight. S. *Rachel reread the note Steffen sent her as she waited under the oak tree.*

"Why the long face?" she asked as he came up to her.

He ran his hand through his hair and paced in front of the tree.

Her bright mood evaporated. The more he paced, the more he flexed his fists. He looked like a boxer psyching himself before a fight. What could have made him so upset? His grades from college had been great. He'd secured an internship at a prestigious investment company. All she could do was wait. A few more seconds passed.

"I know Pam's your friend." He stopped pacing and looked at her. His eyes softened and his body relented. "Rachel, I don't want to hurt you, but honey, Pam's not your friend."

He told her everything. She never doubted Steffen's honor or truthfulness. Rachel knew Pam all too well. Her little game didn't surprise her. That she would play her games at her best friend's expense, betray her...left her speechless. How many times did Rachel console other friends because of Pam's disregard for their feelings? And the countless times she spent speaking to Pam to make her understand what she'd done.

"You're going to believe him." Pam stood in front of her, arms crossed. "Over me. You know, he's not your happily-ever-after."

"Why would he lie?" Rachel wanted Pam to say it was a joke so they could go on being friends. Tell her it was a misunderstanding.

"You didn't invite anyone else. I asked. Only Steffen." Rachel's voice tightened, and she struggled to keep it even and controlled.

Pam's attention flittered from one place to another, anyplace other than on her. "Let's go to Tony's. He makes that cheese Danish that you can't stop eating, or we can go to Mellie's Diner for that hamburger and fries you love. My treat."

She forgave Pam a lot, but this wasn't going away so easily. "Why would you—"

"I didn't do anything. I would never do anything to hurt you," Pam said, but her voice didn't convince Rachel and the words sounded like a goddamn lie.

"Are you going to the country club barbecue tonight? I thought I'd wear my new dress. The one you like." Pam flashed a smile then turned away and looked at her watch.

Betrayal flashed like a neon sign in Rachel's head, and the hurt turned to white-hot anger. She said nothing. It wasn't worth the effort. Pam wasn't worth the effort.

"I'd like to stay, but I really have to go. Call me if you decide to go to the country club tonight." Pam picked up her handbag, gave her a peck on the cheek, and hurried away.

They saw each other on occasion, but Pam never came to Havencroft again. Why did she now? Rachel rose out of her seat.

"Pam?" Rachel called out, and moved down the aisle.

"I shouldn't be here," Pam mumbled. She stopped drumming her fingers on the leatherette seat next to her and smacked her hand on the empty space.

No, Pam shouldn't be here. Perhaps she shouldn't be here, either. Her best friend's betrayal was horrible, but Rachel had done worse. Much worse. Water over the dam, don't cry over spilled milk—pick a cliché. They all fit.

Without any regret, Rachel left the bus. A few seconds later, Pam followed.

"Will you be leaving soon? I need to be back in Havenport for a meeting," Pam told the bus driver.

"Sure, I'm going back now. Come on, jump back in."

Pam stared right through her, turned on her heel, and boarded the bus. Without a backward look, the bus drove away.

"She has to live with the things she's done and come to terms with it," Rachel whispered, standing outside the manor entry.

"Have you ever been inside?" Two women passed her on their way into the manor. "I can't imagine living here. From the outside it looks like a dollhouse, but the inside…this place is…"

Rachel looked up at the four-story stone Victorian structure with spires and witch's cap. Her lips turned into a smile. It did look like a dollhouse. A few deep breaths and she took a more critical look. Overall, the building and grounds appeared to have weathered the years well.

She walked into the entrance, with its impressive variety of colored marble. The further into the entranceway she walked, the more the years faded away until it was as if she had never been gone. The doors to the house were wide open. She rushed through them to get to the centerpiece of the house.

Rachel stood in the Great Hall and looked up at the massive forty-five-foot ceiling to the stained-glass skylight. Wide overhanging balconies on the second and third floors narrowed the opening to the top. The architectural trick exaggerated the height of the room.

Oak railings rimmed the balconies. How many times had a young Rachel peeked through the second-floor balusters to watch her parents' parties? And how often had her mother carried her to bed after falling asleep on the balcony carpet?

Rachel twisted in all directions to get a better view. Above the first floor's oak wood panel, faded squares outlined where pictures and mirrors once hung on the Chinese red paper. The walls looked tired and old. Her stomach dropped—the furniture. Where did the large sideboards, the velvet sofa, and central round table with mother's prize Chinese jar all go? Nothing remained except for the large grandfather clock and the flurry of activity around a small makeshift table.

Rachel came to Havencroft to surround herself with the comforts of home. That's what she told herself, but that wasn't the truth. Seeing the manor and experiencing a little nostalgia were nice, but not her mission. She went to reach for her locket, only to touch the empty spot at her throat. Lost years ago, an impulse demanded she find it. Ridiculous as it may be, the feeling persisted. The longer she put off the trip to Havencroft, the stronger the need grew, until finding the locket became a compulsion and her only thought. She'd torn the house apart when she found it missing.

It's here. There was that whisper again. After all these years, her gold heart could be anywhere.

The only way to quiet the voice was to look for the necklace. She'd start by searching each room, from the first floor to the fourth. Once she proved it wasn't here, she could leave and put this all to rest.

While the volunteers organized, Rachel stepped into the Green Salon to her right. Originally, the room functioned as a formal ladies' reception area where her grandmother received visitors and served afternoon tea. When her parents were here, it was the living room.

With the shades drawn, the room was dark. Light from the hall filtered in from behind. The stale, musty odor of years of neglect surrounded her. She grew accustomed to the dark and realized this room, too, had no furniture. A search of the floor and an investigation of the alcoves on either side of the fireplace divulged nothing. The room had been swept clean.

Back in the hall, she turned to the left and entered the billiard room, her grandfather and father's domain. They spent a great deal of time in here with their friends and their cigars. Gone was the oak and slate billiard table. The bar with the amber-colored bottles stood vacant. She searched the floor and shelves behind the bar, even her father's favorite secret compartment hidden there, but found nothing.

Rachel gripped the door handles to the adjoining library and hesitated. After a moment to collect her emotions, she stepped in. Her heart sank. Her father's grand desk and chair, as well as the leather-bound first editions that had filled the shelves, were all gone.

After running her hands over all the shelves and the few drawers, she drew back. Rachel stabbed at her eyes to wipe away the tears. The hollow ache in her chest grew until it hurt to breathe.

"I waited too long," she whispered. Closing the door behind her, she went back to the Great Hall.

"Thank you all for coming today," Ina said from her perch at the back of the room. "The outpouring of help has been overwhelming. We've gone through the lists and given out assignments. We have more volunteers than we need. However, we're holding to our promise. You volunteered to get us ready, and to show our appreciation the Emerson Foundation will give you two tickets to tonight's ball. If you don't have an assignment, enjoy the house and grounds. Just a reminder, the other floors are closed to visitors. Also, make sure you're back here by three to catch the bus and get your tickets to the ball. They won't be available in town.

"Now, if you're part of the catering staff, please go into the dining room. You'll get your instructions there.

Everyone else has their orders. Be here at three. I'm sure we can get everything done."

The hall emptied as the volunteers went to their assignments.

"You've done a wonderful job," Ina said to a man wearing a tool belt. "I have two items on my list: the front light keeps blinking, and some of the garden lights won't go on. We've changed the bulbs but that didn't help."

Ina and the electrician headed to the front of the house.

Rachel entered the ballroom and her thoughts drifted back to the days when the room was alive with people. The garden motif of the flowerlike crystal chandelier, sconces, and murals on the decorated plaster walls were still in place. Crystal lights that were strung across the pale-blue ceiling went on, to the delighted gasp of the volunteers, hers included. They twinkled and glowed, creating a starry effect.

"Dad, we don't dance like this." Rachel stood defiantly in the ballroom with her parents. A record spun on the turntable.

"Yes, I know. It's all about wiggles and bops," her mother said.

"You mean bumps and grinds," her father corrected, and moved the needle onto the record. The Debby Boone song "You Light Up My Life" played.

Rachel rolled her eyes.

"Humor me. Fathers don't dance like that with their daughters, especially at their coming-out party."

"Maybe girls had coming-out parties when you were young. I want a beach party." Rachel lifted her chin and met her mother's icy gaze. She wasn't going to let them witness her withering inside. No, stick to your plan, *her friend had told her.*

"Pam's parents can make her a beach party. We thought a nice garden party with that band you like. What was their name? Yes, The Eagles."

Rachel's jaw dropped. They were one of the top bands in the country. She and Pam talked about them for weeks. How did her parents know?

"Mom, you'd do that?" Her mom's icy gaze morphed into a warm smile.

"Don't look at me. The blame goes squarely on your father's shoulders."

She spun around and hugged her dad.

"Whoa. Not so fast. Only if I dance with you to an actual song, a proper dance, not this bump-and-grind stuff."

She held him tight with no intention of letting him go. Ever.

The garden party and the band had been a success. Rachel waltzed with her father and, later, caught a glimpse of her parents dancing a cha-cha to "Hotel California" in the dark ballroom. Her memories were warm. Even the difficult ones had softened over the years.

Was it fear of dredging up the past that made her fight coming back? Time allowed her to believe the locket remained somewhere in Havencroft, but standing in the manor now, her mind was a combination of hope and fear. *Find it*, a small voice kept saying. *Find it.* Her dreams were bound up in that locket. Her time was running out. Midnight would come quick enough.

Rachel left the ballroom for the second floor.

Stanchions blocked the wide oak staircase, but that didn't stop her. She sidestepped the velvet ropes, climbed the stairs, and walked along the second-floor balcony that circled the Great Hall below. She stood with her back to the rail, the imposing doors to her parents' suite in front of her.

Large double doors to their apartment swung open into a small foyer. A private sitting room beyond separated her mother's boudoir on the right from her father's rooms on the left. At least the rooms were set up that way. Her mother never slept anywhere but with her father. Rachel walked through the empty space. Closet and drawers gaped open. Empty. Only thin layers of dust remained, along with a few stray buttons and memories.

She went down the hall. A thorough look at the two guest rooms, also void of furniture, yielded nothing. Her room was the last to search on this floor. Rachel braced herself outside her bedroom door. There was a very good reason to suspect her room would be as empty as the others. With a deep breath for courage, she pushed the door open and stepped inside.

Soft floral paper covered the walls. Across from her, large glass French doors led to a balcony. The strained apprehension that dogged her all morning eased, but the push to move on kept building.

Nothing remained in her dressing room. She opened her closet door and let out a small cry.

A series of pencil marks etched alongside the doorjamb. Each line included initials and a date. The Birthday Chart. She traced over the markings. A tradition each birthday morning. Everyone stood against the wall to mark their height—Mother, Father, even Shotsy, their terrier. Her mother put her foot down when she wanted to measure Goldy, her fish.

Rachel returned to her bedroom and sat on the floor, her back against the wall. If the locket was anywhere in the house, it would be here. There were no drawers to look through, no pockets in clothes to rummage, no jewelry chest to inspect. Nothing.

She looked at the ceiling, as if looking into the upper floors. The compulsion drove her, pushed her. No, the locket wasn't here, but there was still hope.

On her feet now, the servants' stairs were her goal. The hall clock struck the noon hour. That left twelve hours to explore the top two floors. *Plenty of time.*

A mix of guest rooms and servant quarters occupied the third floor. Her investigation of these rooms revealed a few more buttons, some pennies, and a pencil advertising a dry cleaner. In the servants' quarters a bigger find: two metal bed frames stacked against the wall.

Satisfied there was nothing else to see, she climbed the narrow stairs to the fourth floor.

She stopped halfway up the stairs. This was ridiculous. Why had she thought the locket would be here? *Keep going.* Why was the incessant voice urging her on when there was nothing to find? The voice was silent.

She continued and reached the fourth-floor landing. The thick layers of dust in the servants' quarters confirmed the rooms hadn't been used in decades.

Only her mother's tower room remained. Remote from the rest of the house, it was her mother's perch. An urge pushed her toward the door. She reached out for the doorknob. It seemed to open by itself. Rachel stood in the doorway and imagined childhood squeals of laughter as she played some make-believe game with Pam while her mother worked at her desk.

Light streamed into the whitewashed room from the oversize oval window. Wallpaper artfully hid the door to the right of the window that led outside to the narrow walkway around the witch's-cap roof. Few knew about the door. She and Pam used to sneak into the room when her mother wasn't home and sit on the walkway. The fact that they could keep it from her mother was more reason to go out there.

Rachel stepped into the room, and her chest pounded. Her old overstuffed lounge chair, the one from her bedroom, was in the center of the room. Next to it, an open trunk partially filled begged to be inspected.

Chapter Three

Of all the pieces of furniture left in Havencroft, this chair was most significant to Rachel. Lured further into the room, the temptation to sit overwhelmed her.

Her sense of loss was beyond tears. "Why is this chair the only piece of furniture in the entire house?" Her chest hurt like an old wound that ached on a rainy day.

Nothing remained. Rachel stepped to the window and touched the fancy brass tack where her mother hung one of her crystals to catch the light. Activate it, her mother told her. Father ignored the ritual. She enjoyed the pretty prism of colors that danced on the wall when sunlight bathed the gem.

Tears welled up. She took a deep breath and turned toward the chair. She'd rest a few minutes, maybe look through the trunk so that coming here wasn't a total loss.

She picked up a manila folder that lay on the floor next to the trunk and sifted through it. Inside was a stack of clipped papers. Random things: an old list of Boston dress shops, a receipt from the print shop (the stationery store from town no longer in business), a canceled bill from a caterer, a bill from the hospital, and another from the pharmacy. She put them aside and glanced in the trunk.

Copies of the *Havenport Herald*. Rachel got on her knees, reached in, and looked through the stack. All Halloween editions, dating as far back as 1977.

She sat back on her heels. Did she want to go through these? It pained her then. How much better would it be now?

The box of Halloween newspapers had been her idea of a time capsule to be opened in the future. They should have been tossed out with the furniture. Why had anyone kept them? Her joyless laugh echoed in the room. Someone wanted her to find them.

Rachel picked up a newspaper from the top of the stack. October 31, 1977. She opened the tabloid. Below the fold, a picture of Havencroft's front door, decorated for Halloween.

"Here, Rachel, have some of your mother's special brew. She promised a special costume for dinner. Any idea what it is?" her father asked.

"No, she's been very mysterious."

Father, dressed in his dinner tuxedo, poured the ruby-red drink and plopped an ice cube into the glass that sent off a stream of fog. Mrs. Reid placed the soup tureen by Mother's plate, wearing a beautifully jeweled half mask. Everyone at Havencroft dressed for Halloween.

"Mrs. Reid, you look lovely this evening." Her father smirked over his foaming drink.

"Thank you, Mr. Emerson," she said, then left.

"Mrs. Reid has been preening with the mask all afternoon. Where did you find it?"

"In New Orleans. I knew the feathers would catch her attention." He opened the tureen and swished through the soup. "No eyeballs this year."

Father sat in his chair and took a swallow of his drink as Mother slunk in the room dressed as Elvira, Mistress of the Dark. I never thought someone's eyes could pop out of their head until I looked at my dad. He spit his drink across the table in a fine spray.

The sight of her mother, who wore her blouses buttoned to her nose and skirts past her knees, in a slinky hide-almost-nothing-from-sight dress, was compelling. She looked…wonderful.

After a quiet moment, the three burst out laughing.

"You are worth waiting for, Edythe." The tone of her father's voice sounded soft and seductive. Her parents were private people, not prone to public displays of affection, but much like they forgot the servants were in the room, they seemed to have forgotten she dined with them.

When Rachel realized that her father was…aroused, in that way, she wanted to hide. Her parents. Together. Like that. She erased the picture from her head.

Father rose and gave Mother her drink, then helped her to her chair. He took off his jacket and draped it on her shoulders. Bending beside her, he whispered in her ear. Her mother's flush started at her throat and raced up her bright face that held an innocent smile. Damn, she wanted to hear what he'd said. He had to say something swoon-worthy because Mother playfully took his face in her hands and kissed his lips.

Rachel coughed. Loud. Her father raised an eyebrow at her, a broad smile on his face. He kissed her mother's forehead and returned to his chair. Aware her parents loved each other, this was the first time she was privy to their emotions. The dress had little to do with it, although Mother looked beautiful. To have a man look at you with so much love must be wonderful. She wanted a love like that. Happily ever after. A forever love.

After Mother's grand entrance, dinner moved on as usual. Mrs. Reid's mask didn't resurface until later in the evening when the guests started to arrive.

Elvira's appearance was for Father only. Mother changed into a more respectable witch costume. Mother always wore a witch costume. It was her signature statement for the ball. Each year she found something more fantastic than the last.

Father usually wore his dinner clothes, but this year he was a dashing sheikh.

Rachel smiled at the newspaper picture. She had worn a long slender black dress with a white stripe down the back. Mrs. Reid helped paint a white streak down the middle of her long black hair.

"Rachel, come here," her mother called from the ballroom door.

Rachel dragged herself away from her friends. She made her way through the crush of people—waiters carrying drinks and women in togas serving hors d'oeuvres.

Finally through the crowd, Rachel approached her mother and her step faltered. Steffen stood with his parents. Dressed in a white suit with a black shirt, he could have stepped right out of the upcoming movie, Saturday Night Fever. *He slicked back his medium-length dark curly hair and had the twist of a pompadour in the front that fell over his forehead. The girls in the room gave him a hungry stare.*

"There you are. Rachel, I think you know Steffen Burkett. He was just telling me that he's going off to my alma mater in January, Boston University. Why don't you introduce him to your friends?"

She and Steffen walked through the room. "Do you dance like Tony Manero? You look more like him than John Travolta looked like him."

"Steffen, I had no idea you would be here," Pam crooned, and linked her arm into his. Did Pam think for a minute she could stake her claim? Rachel did a slow burn. Of course she did.

Steffen gently removed Pam's hand from his and grabbed two glasses of punch from the waiter as he went by. He handed one to Pam and the other to her.

"Pam, if you'll excuse us. Rachel and I have a lot of catching up to do." He turned to her. "It's too loud in here. Is there someplace we can go?"

It was Pam's turn to fume, but her scathing glare missed its mark. Steffen had outmaneuvered her.

"Catching up?" Rachel screamed over the music amped up to almost ear-blasting decibels. Her insides tingled and her heart flipped every time he looked at her.

"That girl corners—"

"Come with me. I know a place where we can talk without getting permanent hearing loss." Rachel scarfed down her drink in two gulps, put her empty glass on a table and led the way out the French doors to the garden. The music faded the further they moved away from the building. It turned into a soft buzz by the time they reached the far edge of the garden and turned the corner.

"That's better," Steffen said. He looked around. "Where are we?"

"In the far corner of the estate, near the cemetery. I found this place when I was ten. My parents grounded me for something. I searched for the most remote part of the grounds where no one would find me. The fact that it's next to the cemetery seemed perfect at the time, if a bit dramatic. Over the years the tree became my confidant." She was blabbering. Nervous much? Would he think her crazy?

He walked around the large tree, tested a low-hanging branch. "That girl, Pam, corners me whenever she sees me. I feel like I'm a prize piece of steak she can't wait to devour." He turned to Rachel, a wide smile on his face. "I feel better already."

There was no mocking expression on his face or tone in his voice. He interested her even more.

"I came here to meet you under better circumstances." He faced her squarely. His voice rang with sincerity. "I'm sorry about the other day in town. One minute the road was clear and the next you were in front of me. You stood in the street like a deer in headlights. I couldn't stop the car fast enough."

"It must be kismet," she said, a teasing tone in her voice. "I had looked before I crossed. I'm always careful, especially at Killer's Curve."

"Killer's Curve, eh." His lips pursed as he bit the side of his mouth. She suspected to stifle a laugh.

"It's not a joke. You can't see around the curve, and you gather speed because of the sudden dip in the road. Everyone in town knows about it."

He ran his hand through his hair. "I guess I do, too. Now."

"Anyway, I looked and the street was empty. Suddenly, you were there."

She stared into his eyes. Even in the dim light, she noticed they had changed from dark gray to a heart-stopping shade of blue. She could get lost in those eyes. They were soft, intelligent, and proud. What shade would his eyes be if he looked at her the same way her father looked at her mother at dinner? The idea made her breathless.

"Skunk," he said, looking at her costume.

"In tribute to our first encounter." Then, more solemnly, she added, "I hoped you would be here tonight."

"Skunks couldn't keep me away." He kissed her forehead and took her hand. They walked back to the garden where they sat and "caught up" on everything from their childhoods to their near-miss accident.

The music, which was tolerable in the garden, stopped. A clock chimed through the audio system.

"Cinderella?" he asked.

Rachel laughed. "No. It's the witching hour. Mother makes a big deal of it. According to her, magic is at its strongest at midnight. We should get back. We don't want to miss the fireworks. Those are at midnight, too."

"I want to see you again," Steffen said, a bit of urgency in his voice. "Tomorrow."

"At the oak tree. We can meet here whenever you like." Rachel smiled.

"How will I know you'll be there?" he teased.

"I'll leave you a note in the afternoon." Her arm linked in his, they sauntered into the ballroom.

Their connection was immediate, and she knew they would always be for each other. There would never be anyone else.

Now, at the oval window, Rachel tried to look into the garden, but couldn't see through the dirt and grime. Mrs. Reid would never tolerate this. She rubbed the window to clean a spot for a better view, but the dirt must've been on the outside.

She jockeyed around the window until she found a clearer spot and could see the end of the formal garden at the back of the house. The overgrown hedgerow hid any view of the oak tree. Bulldozers and other heavy equipment stood idle, waiting.

Her forehead on the cold glass cooled her long-forgotten emotions that bubbled to the surface. Sentiments never spoken were on her lips. She had tried to forget him, but he had been with her always.

Rachel searched the old knothole. Her heart sank to her toes and back to her chest. Meet me tonight. S.

It was the end of the summer, the night before Steffen left for Boston. She fidgeted all through a torturous dinner. Would dinner never end? Finally able to slip away, she flew across the garden. Out of breath, her smile broadened when she turned the corner. Steffen stood by the tree.

"Is everything all right? I thought you were going to stay home with your parents."

He took her in his arms. "I love you. From the very first moment I saw you. I was so struck by the feeling that I nearly ran you over. We belong together."

He took her by her shoulders and held her at arm's length. "You know that, don't you?"

Rachel stared into his brilliant, intelligent eyes and her pulse raced. Unable to find her voice, she could only nod a response. Was this just a summer fling? Pam had spent the past few days preparing her for the "kiss off." Would he go back to Boston and forget all about Havenport—and their summer romance?

He pulled her close. Her head tucked under his chin. "I love you," he whispered into hair.

"I love you." The words fell easily from her lips. She had been saying them to herself for days.

He put something in her hand. Startled, she looked in her palm. A locket.

"Forever, Rachel." With shaking hands, he put the locket around her neck as she stared at him, speechless and jubilant. Her Steffen.

"*There,*" *he said when he finished. His chest thrust out and his shoulders went back. He smiled like Alice's Cheshire cat. She stretched up on her tippy-toes and threw her arms around his neck. She smiled when she looked into his eyes. They changed to light blue when they were filled with love.*

"*I'll never take it off,*" *she murmured against his lips and kissed him, then turned to leave.*

"*Don't go back yet. Stay with me a little longer.*"

Her heart pounded.

They sat by the tree and watched the stars, his arm around her shoulder.

"*That's Orion. Can you see the three stars that make up the belt?*" *He pointed somewhere in the sky, but she wasn't looking. His lips held her attention.*

He looked at her and stopped talking. His eyes darkened and his lips captured hers. He had happily ever after written all over his face. Gentle at first, his kiss became more urgent.

She molded into his arms and never wanted him to let go. He hesitated a heartbeat then raised his lips from hers. He lifted her, carried her through the garden to the patio door.

Rachel stood there, her body in revolt. She wanted more. She wanted Steffen.

"*I don't love you like that.*"

She sucked in a quick breath, tears welling in her eyes.

"*I love you more. I want it to be right.*" *His forehead rested against hers.*

He kissed her and nudged her to the door.

She watched him cross the garden, waved when he reached the dogleg, and disappeared.

"*Was that Steffen?*" *her mother asked as Rachel came into the living room.*

Unable to get any words out, she nodded.

Her mother lowered the book she was reading. "Is everything all right?" Concern filled her mother's voice.

"*Yes,*" *she whispered, and sat next to her mother. "I'll miss him."*

"Yes, I know you will. Did he give you the locket?"

She'd forgotten all about the locket. "Yes." Her hand touched the small heart.

Mother kissed her forehead. "He'll be home soon."

Rachel didn't want him home soon. That wasn't fair, but her heart didn't want fair. Her heart wanted Steffen. She said good night to her mother, rushed into her room, and took off the necklace.

Delicate gold filigree and small diamonds decorated the outside. Carefully she opened it to look inside.

My heart is yours—Forever.

Chapter Four

Rachel moved away from the window and stood behind the chair, her hand resting on the blanket draped on the overstuffed back. Forever. Nothing was forever. Not friends, not... She sat in the chair and took the stack of papers out of the trunk.

And the locket. How could the locket be lost? She went over the day a hundred, a thousand times.

"Are you sure you had it here?" Her mother looked through her jewelry box. When she didn't find the locket, she moved on to her nightstand drawer.

"Of course I'm sure. I never take it off." Rachel pulled the linen off the bed and left it in a heap on the floor. Mrs. Reid methodically went through each fold before tossing it into the hall.

"When did you notice it missing?"

"I told you," she barked at her mother. "I stood at the sink washing my face. I didn't have my locket on."

"I'm sure Steffen will replace the locket if you tell him what happened."

"No. I can't tell him." She wheeled around. Her stomach clenched tight, she grabbed her mother's hands. "Promise me you won't say a word about this to him."

"Of course I won't." Her mother's slow, uneven tone made her stop and drop her hands.

"I could replace it. Have it engraved. No one would know."

Her mother's concern was written on her face.

"No. It has to be the one he gave me. Not a replacement from you or from him." Edythe opened her arms. Rachel stepped into her embrace and sobbed. *"Don't you understand?"*

"Shush. Everyone is looking for it. We'll find it. It couldn't vanish." Her mother moved the hair out of her eyes. *"Tell me about your visit with Pam. How late did she stay last night? I didn't see her leave."*

"Not too late. About eight."

The empty, sinking feeling flashed through her, and her loss was as deep now as when she'd realized the locket was gone. She loosened her death grip on the blanket crumpled in her fist. All that was left of his love was the locket. She had to find it.

"You've come this far," she told herself. "See it through. Go through the trunk. Finish the task. Don't give up now. Just because no one could find the locket that doesn't mean searching for it now is useless."

She warred with herself. "Listen to me. There. Is. No. Place. Else. To. Search." What perverse need drove her? There wasn't any way the locket was in the trunk. If she gave up now, she'd stop driving herself crazy, but the image of the locket swirled in her head.

The musty room closed in around her, the air sucked out by some invisible force. She tugged at the neck of her dress, without relief. She needed fresh air. Pulling on the small door to the upper walk was useless; it wouldn't budge. She rushed out of the room with the newspapers in her hand.

The image of the locket faded when she reached the second floor. She calmly came down the stairs on steadier legs. Cool air, with a hint of lemon, cleared her mind by the time she reached the first floor.

"Put this under that bottle. I don't want a pool of oil on the stairs," Ina said to Nora. At least that was the name on the tag she wore on her Havenport Housekeepers apron.

Nora took the scrap of newspaper and put it under the bottle as Ina asked.

"Good choice. Mrs. Reid always used lemon oil," Rachel said, stepping past them.

"Yes, the lemon oil is best," Ina said as Nora tested a spot on the railing.

"That's better. I knew the mahogany would shine. Stop at the second-floor landing. We don't need the rest done for tonight." Ina hurried into the dining room.

Rachel left Nora and made her way onto the veranda. Electrical cables snaked across the lawn.

"Will we have lights tonight?" Ina asked the electrician as they went down the veranda steps. He must have finished working on the lights in front.

"A loose connection and a few replacement bulbs are all you need. It's low maintenance going forward. I'm just cleaning up."

"Great. When you're done—" She pulled out her cell phone. "Yes?" Ina said, and started toward the house.

"Make sure you test the lights before you leave," she shouted over her shoulder.

"Is there anything you'd like me to do?" Rachel asked.

The woman waved. Rachel took that as a no. Ina, already back on her phone, disappeared into the house.

The electrician nodded, adjusted his earbuds, and gathered his tools.

Her grandmother's garden was renowned with the Havenport Garden Club. Her great-grandmother had founded the horticultural group. It was a peaceful place.

Rachel took a deep breath of the cool air. Overhead, the distinctive sound of honking geese drew her attention as they flew in a chevron pattern. She watched them fly until they were out of sight, then stepped into the garden.

Fallen leaves tumbled across the lawn. Bushes were trimmed and the flower beds along the perimeter of the path were prepared for the winter. Large earth-moving equipment stood idle at the back of the garden. Close to the grove of maple and cooper beech trees, the equipment looked out of place. The last time the gardener brought equipment like this into the garden, he removed large dead trees. From her vantage point, the maples and beeches looked healthy. Her oak tree was the only other large tree in that area.

They wouldn't take the oak tree down, would they?

Rachel hurried to the end of the garden and navigated past the large machines. At the turn where the garden doglegged to the right, she came to a sudden stop. This area of the property, hidden from the manor, hadn't been maintained as well as the rest of the garden. Bushes and trees had gone wild and needed trimming. That would have to wait until the spring. Leaves covered the lawn, but that didn't matter. In the distance, the massive oak kept watch over the garden and the cemetery.

She bulldozed through the piles of neglected leaves until she stood at the base of the tree. She ran her hand over the rough bark, her touch reconnecting with her old friend.

The tree and Rachel had a long history together. This was her go-to place when she wanted to be alone and work things out. The silent sentinel heard it all and didn't judge. As a child, she left notes in an old knothole. When she grew older, she left notes for Steffen. Their place. Silly, but the oak tree became special to them both.

"I should have brought something that says I was here." For a frantic minute she searched the ground but found nothing with meaning, and suddenly that was very important.

She patted her clothes and pulled the note out of her pocket. *Meet me tonight. R.*

"Of course." The note was perfect. It belonged in the tree. She tucked it into their special place.

How many times did I stand here arguing with myself? I should have put this note here a long time ago. When there was a chance that Steffen would read it.

Rachel tenderly touched the tree then stepped back. Did the day look brighter? No, but the unfinished task had weighed heavily on her mind. Now completed, there was relief and even some satisfaction.

The gnarled roots still provided a comfortable seat. She sat with the papers tucked in her lap, her arms around her knees, and savored being under the tree once again.

She uncurled and opened one of the newspapers, and stared at the 1978 Halloween revelers. Everyone looked up into the camera. The photograph must have been taken from the manor's second-floor balcony looking down into the Great Hall. One by one, she identified everyone and stopped when Steffen came into view with his arm around her shoulder.

"Should I wear the red shoes or the black ones?" Rachel asked Pam as they dressed for the ball.

"Why are you so picky? You never cared before." Pam looked at Rachel's reflection in the large mirror as they got ready for the ball.

"I've always been picky. You just haven't noticed." The black ones—they were strappy things that made her feet look sexy.

"You don't know if he's even coming. I'm sure there are all sorts of Halloween parties in Boston that are more interesting than this ball." Pam tried on Rachel's chandelier earrings. She admired them from every angle, put the earrings down, and tried on the next.

"Come on. Are you ready?" Her shoes on, Rachel stuck her head next to Pam's to get a last look before they went downstairs. *"I'll leave without you."*

Pam grabbed her arm and swung her around.

"What?" Rachel was in no mood for drama or games.

"Listen, this thing you have with Steffen is just a thing. I know the others have told you how perfect you are for each other, but be realistic. There's no such thing as happily ever after. Get it out of your head. He's a gorgeous guy in a college town full of girls who are eager to snap him up. Yeah, it's nice he comes home and sees you, but I don't want you to be devastated when he outgrows you and moves on."

Not my... Moves on? Steffen? Rachel smiled at her friend. "Not going to happen. You'll see."

Pam dropped her hand and sighed. "Don't say I didn't warn you."

"Are you going to wear those?" Rachel looked at the earrings her dad had bought her from India a few months ago.

"You don't mind, do you? You're not wearing them, and I really love them." Pam shook her head and made the tiny bells tinkle.

"No problem. Just put them back before you leave."

"Sure," Pam said as they walked out the door.

At the top of the staircase, Rachel stopped and searched the crowd for Steffen. A low wolf whistle grabbed her attention. Her wolf man stood at the bottom of the steps smiling at her.

She rushed down the stairs, leaving Pam to trail behind. In a gallant gesture, he swept her into his arms and kissed her. The scent of his cologne...

She lowered her hands, and the newspaper wrinkled in her lap. A deep breath conjured up the citrus and woodsy fragrance of his cologne. Her lips tingled from the memory of his kiss.

They were rarely apart after that Halloween. Steffen came home most weekends, and, with Boston a two-hour drive away, sometimes during the week, too. Much to her father's disappointment, Rachel passed up going to his alma mater, Columbia University in New York City, and instead commuted to Roger Williams University in Providence. Steffen continued to come home on weekends.

Rachel folded the newspaper, put it aside, and looked at the next one. Halloween, 1980. Nothing important on the front, she turned the pages. This was her favorite edition. It was worn from being read over and over. The Society page had an interview with her mother about the masquerade ball. Lower down was a picture of Pam and Huntley Andrews, her Florida University sweetheart at their September wedding.

"Rachel." Pam stuck her head in the room where the bridesmaids were getting ready. Pam and her maid of honor, Julie Andrews—no relation to the actress, but rather Huntley's sister— were next door in the bride's room.

"Julie is wonderful," Pam whispered, "but has no idea what needs to be done. Can you check on the caterer? Huntley loves escargot, and I want to make sure they're cooked to perfection. Oh, and can you check that the band has the list of songs and that they don't play 'Endless Love'? That song makes me ill every time I hear it. Here's the list in case they can't find it. Oh, and I've made some changes."

"Sure." There was plenty of time to finish doing Dottie's hair and her own, as well as put on her makeup. Pam forgot to make arrangements with the hairdresser. Rachel turned to leave.

"Oh, and remind them to play Pachelbel's Canon for the ceremony. I hate "Here Comes the Bride." Be right there," Pam shouted over her shoulder.

"Our friends—"

"Speaking about our friends, can you play hostess? You know, make sure they have whatever they need. I'll be busy with Huntley's family. You did such a great job of managing my shower. Have you thought about forgetting law and being a wedding planner? Thanks, you're a sweetie for doing this. Now go, go." Pam shooed her out the door.

Hours later, after the ceremony and cocktail hour, she sat next to Steffen.

"Are you off duty now? Or has bridezilla Pam more for you to do?" He handed her a glass of champagne.

"It's not that bad. She's excited and wants everything to be right. Every girl wants her day to be perfect." Drained from running around, Rachel sipped her drink and looked at her barely touched filet mignon and lobster tail.

"I don't think your friends are taking it so casually." Steffen nodded at the window.

"Oh no, Huntley will have a fit." She started to get up, but Steffen pulled her back into her chair. Their friends had Huntley's new Corvette covered in toilet paper. The back and side windows were full of shaving cream. Her friends had tied two trails of tin cans to the exhaust pipes.

"I stopped them when they went to put the Limburger cheese in the glove compartment. They both deserve it. You and Pam have been friends all your life and she picks someone she knows only six months to be her maid of honor. Then has the audacity to ask you to plan her shower because her maid of honor lives in Denver and doesn't know anything about Havenport. To top that off, she has you running ragged instead of enjoying your meal, or your friends, or dancing with me." He waved to someone.

The waiter set a covered plate in front of her.

"What's this?"

"I had the caterer put a meal together for you and told them to bill Pam directly. I hope they're as good as what you get at Mellie's Diner," he said as the waiter removed the cloche. She howled. Hamburger and fries.

"Have I told you lately, Steffen Burkett, that I love you?" She made herself comfortable, laid a napkin over her gown, and bit into her hamburger. He dabbed her chin with a napkin to catch a rivulet of grease.

"Thank you," she mumbled, her full mouth. He relaxed in his chair, his arm on the back of hers, and smiled. Her heart went crazy.

"You're welcome. I am here only to serve you." He bobbed his head in a slight bow. "And you tell me you love me all the time. In the way you look at me and listen to my plans. Your kisses aren't too shabby, either."

Her champagne glass froze in midair. She was willing to skip out on the rest of the wedding and go home with him, now. Until she remembered wedding coordinator Rachel had to get the cake cutting organized with the photographer.

When the bride and groom left for the hotel, Huntley's face burned red with anger. The new Mrs. Huntley Andrews whisked him away with quick good-byes, if Pam said good-bye at all.

No one understood her relationship with Pam. At times, she didn't, either. Rachel shook her head. She lowered the paper. Why did Pam come to Havencroft today? Sometimes Pam had no explanation for why she did things. Today was probably no exception. There were times when Pam was all for her, like a sister, a real best friend.

Rachel folded the newspaper and reached for the next one. It was open to the Society page. "Steffen Burkett Christens Boat at Emerson Boathouse and Wins the Prize." Rachel could recite this article word for word.

"You coming?" her mother shouted from downstairs.

Rachel turned toward her bedroom door. Mother never shouted up the stairs. It was crass. She grabbed her handbag and hurried out of her room.

"I'm here," she said, racing down the stairs. "What's the hurry? We have a half hour before we have to be there."

Rachel stopped in front of one of the Great Hall mirrors for a final check of her new white slacks and blue-and-white-striped cotton sweater.

"You look fine, dear. Your father's waiting for us outside." Her mother slipped her arm around her as they left the house, almost pushing her out the door.

"Ah, my girls." He rubbed his hands together and practically danced from one foot to the other. If her mother hadn't threaded her arm through his, she was sure he was going to fly off.

"No clothespin today." His eyes twinkled as he covered Mother's hand with his.

"I was thinking the same thing," Rachel said. "That was so long ago."

"Not to me," her father said in a low whisper.

They came down the trail and around to the front of the boathouse. Steffen worked all summer and fall on repairing the old sailboat. Now he stood in the center of a crowd of friends and family.

The boat was turned around with its stern facing the crowd. A wrapped bottle stood next to it. A white canvas covered the transom. Their friends had been taking bets on what he would name the boat. Nobody knew, not even her.

Steffen broke away from the crowd and came toward them. He held her with his eyes. God, she would love him forever.

"Glad you could make it." He smirked.

"From the look on your face, I'd say it was worth it." She kissed his nose. "Okay, I can't wait. What did you name her?"

It was her turn to bounce from foot to foot. The four of them walked to the pier.

"Come on, Steffen, there's a lot of money riding on what you named her," one of their friends shouted. Everyone laughed.

He grabbed Rachel's hand and walked to the dock. Everyone moved in to hear and see the big reveal.

"I love you, Rachel," he said, loud enough for everyone to hear.

"I know," she whispered. "Steffen, what are you doing? Not here."

He pulled off the canvas to a thunder of gasps. Rachel turned and could only stare at the name painted on the bow.

Marry Me.

She looked back at him. He knelt in front of her. Something sparkled in his hand.

The water gently lapping against the dock, and the soft murmur of the fall wind in the trees, were the only sounds, except for her heart. Surely, everyone could hear it hammering against her chest.

She bent down and pulled him up.

"I love you," he said for her ears only.

"Forever," she said, then threw her arms around him.

Their family and friends went wild.

"*Enough, you two.*" *Pam handed Steffen the covered bottle. "You're launching more than a boat, so be careful."*

Steffen gave the bottle to her. "Aim for the metal edge."

One swing, and foam and champagne exploded everywhere.

"*Congratulations.*" *Her father held her tight and looked over at Steffen. "I know you'll take good care of her."*

Steffen's parents were next. "We couldn't be happier."

But she didn't see them, her family, or their friends. Only Steffen. She wanted to be with him.

After the toasts and handshakes, her father started the small motor and ushered them onto the boat.

"*Enjoy your sail. Be back in time for your mother's ball.*" *Her father threw Steffen the lines. Everyone waved as Steffen piloted the boat out into the bay.*

They anchored the boat by the small island a few miles across from the town marina. The barren island was nothing more than a beach and a few trees.

Steffen sat in the cockpit, his back against the gunwale. She cuddled close, tucked under his arm, and stared at the ring on her finger.

"*You should have seen your face.*" *He chuckled, low and wicked. She whirled to face him. His eyes pinned her like a fly in amber.*

"*How was it?*" *She blew out her breath and licked her lips.*

"*Shocked and happy. I don't think I've ever seen you so…happy.*" *He pulled her onto his lap. "I love you. I knew it the first time I saw you."*

"*Lying on the road? That's a novel way to meet someone.*"

He held her tight. Two heartbeats passed before he whispered, "I'll love you forever." His voice deepened as the glint in his eyes darkened. He kissed the pulsing hollow at the base of her throat.

His lips covered hers like a hot brand, and she surrendered to her happily-ever-after.

They spent the rest of the day in the cabin as the boat bobbed in the water.

The folded paper lay in her lap. She leaned against the oak tree. Her vision faded, but the memory…it lingered, and she had no intention of giving it up easily.

Chapter Five

Lights flashed in the distance. The electrician must have been doing his test. An onshore breeze picked up, sending leaves into small whirls. Clouds gathered in the east. It would be a pity if it rained after everyone's hard work.

One more newspaper remained, and she wasn't eager to read it. Rachel rose, picked up the papers, and headed back to the manor.

She took the long way, past the stables and the barn, then alongside the manor. A plume of dust traveled down the drive as the back of the bus wound its way toward Manor Road. She had lost track of time.

The clouds hadn't gotten any more ominous. She hurried to the entrance, intent on returning the newspapers to the trunk. With any luck, the rain might hold off until she got away.

A black-and-orange wreath hung on the manor door. Glittery spun webs, with large cottony spiders, hung in the corners of the entryway.

The door squeaked open. Nice sound effects. Inside, the large round table was back in the center of the Great Hall covered with a black lace cloth. In the center of the table, a spotlight focused on the four-foot frosted-white urn filled with oversized long-stem black roses. A projection from somewhere on the second-floor balcony danced across the floor. Welcome to Edythe's Halloween Ball.

She peeked in the ballroom. Black drapes hung beside the floor-to-ceiling doors that led to the veranda. Full-size ghosts and witches looked into the room from every door. Hundreds of small white lights embedded in the network of suspended cobwebs twinkled from the ceiling, creating beautiful patterns on the walls and floor.

The theme carried into the dining room. Tables were set with black linens and white plates. A tall white frosted vase lit from inside was the centerpiece on each table. She flicked one of the black silhouette bats that flew along with witches among the bare white branches that filled the vases.

Around the walls, buffet stations with hot trays waited to be filled. A bar ran across the entire back wall. Hundreds of black-and-white bags with tags, treats (no tricks) from Edythe, were stacked in pyramids on either side of the veranda doors.

Rachel went to the staircase. Another Halloween masquerade ball. The day after Halloween her mother began planning the next one. Mother would approve of the dramatic decor. Rachel wasn't sure who enjoyed Halloween more, her mother or the community.

Years ago, Rachel began saving the Halloween newspapers to remember each party. She used to enjoy reading them, looking back. They became a treasured keepsake. Now, what sense did it make? Nothing could be changed, and the outcome—well, she knew all too well the outcome. Why had she put herself through this? The love and disappointment hurt as much now as before. It was time to put the newspapers away, back in the past where they belong, then she would be on her way.

Easing past the stanchion, she climbed to the second floor. A scrap of oily newspaper sat abandoned on the landing. It was from last Sunday's edition of the *Havenport Herald*. It must have been the paper Nora used under the bottle of lemon oil. Rachel picked it up.

There was a teaser about the new councilman, Evan Washburn, but the headline concentrated on the upcoming masquerade ball. It listed the members of the committee, along with sponsors for the event. Ah, now she understood why Pam came to the manor. She was the committee chair. Rachel read the list of supporters and her heart did a small flip. Burkett Brokerage headed the sponsor list, but it was the gossip item written by Candy Apples in the sidebar that made her tremble.

Steffen Burkett Returns Home. Known for his philanthropy over the years, the retired financial wizard behind the London investment group, Burkett Brokerage—

Rachel flipped the page over for the rest of the article. The information covered something about the local Girl Scout troop, but nothing about Steffen.

Halloween. He never missed Halloween. Was that the real reason she waited until today to come back? No, it wasn't necessary for her to be here to think about him. Steffen was part of her daily routine.

She spent her day reliving things they did together, his touch, his kiss, and even his love. He had been so real.

Maybe if she stayed... Her lower lip trembled as the notion took root. See him one more time. No, no, impossible. Face him now and see the hate in his eyes. That would be too much to bear.

Let things be was the only answer. Enjoy the memories. *There's nothing to be gained in what could have been.* Yes, better to let things be after all this time. Standing in the middle of the second-floor landing with the last newspaper in her hand, she wanted to cry, but the tears wouldn't come.

She sat on the top step and opened the newspaper. Halloween, 1984.

Everything was arranged. Steffen started at a new company in London the previous May and they set off on a new adventure. For the past six months, they'd traveled between London and Havenport.

Thumbing through the paper, she read their wedding announcement, as if the couple beaming at her were strangers.

They were both home for Halloween, making plans for their Christmas wedding. Addressed invitations sat bundled in the library, ready to be mailed the following day, the same day Steffen returned to London.

"If I knew you were dressing as Cleopatra I would have come as Mark Antony, my queen." Steffen dipped an elegant bow, then kissed her on her nose. "Where's your mother? I expected to see her at the door. What type of witch is she this year?"

Steffen—in a dashing pirate costume with his shirt open, showing his perfect abs—searched the decorated ballroom for Edythe. "I wanted to let her know about the arrangements with the band for our wedding and say good-bye before things got crazy. I have an early flight in the morning and won't have time to stop by."

Rachel didn't answer. She had been dealing with so much the past two weeks.

"You're going to get a permanent wrinkle on your forehead if you don't stop frowning. I won't like it in the wedding pictures," he teased, and kissed her worry spot.

"Let's go outside. We need to talk," Rachel said, her throat tight and her voice high-pitched. For days she practiced this speech, chose her words carefully. Now that the time had come to talk, the words were all wrong. She licked her parched lips. The two glasses of liquid courage she'd had earlier weren't helping. And the possibility of a last-minute reprieve she had hoped for had vanished ninety minutes ago. She wanted to hide somewhere and cry.

He leaned against the veranda's wide stone railing, his arms comfortably folded while she paced in front of him.

"What's this about? The flowers? The caterer?" *His voice—soft, male, and mellow—had her thinking of other things. Things no longer within her right to dream about.*

"No." *If only it were that simple. She stood not close enough for him to hold her. That would be a disaster.*

"Over the last few months, Mother hasn't been well." *Rachel stepped back, her eyes anyplace but on him.* Stop now. There's still time. Tell him the truth. *One deep, steadying breath. The rehearsed words flew out of her head. For a moment, she faltered and thought she couldn't go through with it. The truth was on her lips.* Do what's best for him. For Steffen, do you hear?

"We noticed it in May and thought it was overwork and not enough sleep. It progressively got worse."

Coward. *Rachel watched him out of the corner of her eye. He dropped his arms and straightened from his slouch.*

"Is Edythe all right? Should we call someone? I have contacts at the Mayo Clinic in Minnesota." *Rachel loved him more for his genuine concern.*

"We've been to several doctors. Each one gave us the same prognosis. It caught us by surprise. The decline will be rapid at first, but she'll linger for some time. They told us there is little hope for a recovery, but added that new protocols emerge every day." *Her voice trailed off. Her eyes closed. The words made everything real.*

"I can't leave her now. With Dad's heavy travel schedule there's no one but me. Once her condition stabilizes we can see about continuing our plans." *How sterile and unemotional that sounded.*

"I'll stay in the States. There's no need to change our plans." *It was an order. He sounded like he was negotiating a business deal, not their lives. No, that wasn't fair. He was fighting for them, something she'd given up ninety minutes ago when reality hit her. The war was lost. No need to keep fighting. Now he had to understand. He had to go on.*

"This is going to be a long, drawn-out process. Right now I have to take care of her, without any distractions." *She was adamant, but the hurt in his eyes was a dagger in her heart.*

"As soon as Mother's stable. It's only a delay," she lied.

She watched emotions cross his face and knew the moment he understood her meaning. She shriveled at his expression. They both were going to lose everything, and there was nothing for her to do but watch.

He gave her a curt nod. His face told her nothing. "Let's get back inside."

"I was afraid... I didn't know if you'd want to..." God, this was going all wrong. There was no way to take back the words now or tell him the whole truth. If he knew he'd never leave her.

He pulled her into his arms and held her close. "It's Halloween. I never miss an Edythe Emerson Halloween."

Every minute he held her, she died a little more. She wouldn't leave his embrace, but memorize every nuance. It had to last her a long while. There were no happily-ever-afters.

"No, you don't, and I wouldn't want you to start now." She forced a cheery smile.

"Truce?" he asked.

"Truce." He put his arm around her waist and brought her inside.

They smiled at the toasts offered for their marriage. They danced and forgot anyone else in the room. They ate with their friends and told bad jokes. The major's wife, dressed as Lucille Ball, won the costume award. Rachel's parents won the tango contest.

Rachel lost everything.

At the end of the evening, when everyone was gone, they walked to the oak tree. Steffen looked in the knothole.

"No note."

"No, I have you here with me," she said, giving him a small squeeze.

Silence.

"I'm not sure I'll be back at Christmas." He didn't push her away, nor did he hold her close. She was alone, and for the first time, very afraid. She drew in a quick breath.

"I can't come back here after all the plans we've made. Tonight was torture for me—"

"*For me, too.*"

He grabbed her by her arms. "*Was it? I don't want to be your casual friend. I want to be your husband. I won't settle for less.*"

"*I understand.*" With all her might, she wanted to tell him she loved him, but that would give him hope, and she couldn't do that.

"*Do you? Do you understand how you're killing me? And for what? Tell me what's wrong. What did I do? I'll fix it. Dammit, Rachel, I'll fix it.*" His anger broke over her like a crashing wave.

"*No,*" she screamed. "*You didn't do anything wrong. This isn't about you. It isn't even about us. This isn't what I want, but there's nothing either of us can do. Nothing I can do. Mother needs me. I can't be here and in London. I can't be with you right now. Please, please, I need you to understand.*"

"*Edythe looked fine tonight. Rachel, there's something you're not telling me. I don't know what it is or why you won't tell me. Your decision affects me, too.*"

His words battered her. She stood and took it. The seconds drew out to minutes as they faced each other. Silently, she pleaded her cause and knew he did the same.

"*All right. I'll give you your space. When you're ready for me to come back, leave a note in the tree.*" How would he know if she left a note in the tree? She let out a lifeless laugh at the irritation in his tone.

"*I'll know it's there. I promise. There's no one else for me but you. Remember I love you. My heart is yours—forever.*" He held her close.

The loud, strong pounding of his heart comforted her. A few more minutes. Please, don't leave. Just a little longer. Her shoulders shook from silent tears.

"*Shush, don't cry. I don't know why you're doing this. I know you love me—*" She raised her head to speak. "*No, let me finish. No one else will ever love you like I do.*"

"*Oh, Steffen, there's no one else. There's never been anyone for me but you. I just…*" Her head returned to his chest. "*I can't right now.*" Her voice was a whisper. She squeezed her eyes tight, wanting *to take back the words and the hurt, but couldn't.* I love you, *she mouthed.*

The walk back to the house was long and lonely and without Steffen.

Every day she went to the oak tree with a note for him, *Meet me tonight. R,* only to return with it in her pocket. There was no use asking him to come back. He was in London, doing great things, skyrocketing in the company. Proud of his achievements, she ached for him and cried for them both.

She wrote to him daily and waited for his letters. Until one day, two years later, when there was nothing to write.

Chapter Six

Rachel's ability to ignore the discussion with Steffen for the rest of that evening amazed her. Their last evening together was perfect. He was perfect. Since then, his hurt expression haunted her every day. When she walked by the oak tree, when she sat in her room, and when she looked at her locket, his face was all she saw. Doubled over, head in her hands, she wept for both of them.

He didn't come home at Christmas, or the next year. Business did well, he wrote in his letters. They made him a partner in record time. The following year, nothing was left of them as a couple. The *Havenport Herald* reported on his successes and she read them with pride, and sadness…and longing.

No longer able to deny the pain, she welcomed it, dared it to make her any more miserable. Wave after wave, memories consumed her, breaking down her controls, leaching out every emotion until she sat exposed. Empty and alone.

How many times had her lie returned to haunt her? She wanted to see Steffen one more time. Tell him the truth. He deserved that. *Truth, Rachel.* Only the truth, but was it for his benefit or for her peace of mind?

Would he even speak to her? A gasp rattled through

her. Would he turn his back, walk away? She wouldn't blame him. Perhaps his denial would help move her forward, instead of reliving, rethinking things that could never change.

What if he did see her? What would she say? What was her plan? Tell him that she knew he would stay if he knew the truth. That he would give up his wonderful job and the future it promised. He'd understand that she couldn't hold him back, wouldn't he? Was that her plan? That she didn't think he was man enough to decide for himself. That he was a shallow, uncaring person, so rather than hear it from him she'd made the decision.

The more she tried to ignore the truth, the more it persisted. Pam had taught her well.

Her mother argued with her for weeks, months, to tell him the truth, to trust him. Rachel refused. Nothing swayed her. Yet every day she walked to the oak tree and weighed asking him to come back. How headstrong and determined, and how wrong she had been.

No planning her speech now. The last time turned into a disaster. If he did talk to her, she would speak from the heart.

She stared at the newspapers and sucked in a deep breath. *Return the papers to the trunk and wait for the party.* That was her plan.

With the article and folded papers in hand, she climbed the steps.

A cool breeze rustled her skirt when she reached the fourth floor. She glanced around the hall. Only the tower room door stood ajar. The oval window didn't move.

Her brows wrinkled. Rachel stepped quietly into the room. The door to the walk stood open. Something or someone stood on the walk, but with the bright sky in the background, all she could make out was a dark silhouette. Her chest pounding, she moved into the shadows.

"I couldn't stay away. God knows I tried. I gave myself a hundred reasons not to be here. For years, I tried not to think of Havenport. I took on everything and anything to forget, to distance myself from here. But I couldn't.

"Besides, it's Halloween, and who can stay away? Everyone in Rhode Island knows Havencroft is the place to be. I was surprised when the Emersons approached the Historical Society to buy Havencroft, but I'm glad they did. Some traditions should go on, and Edythe's masquerade party is one of them. They were so much fun."

Storm clouds moved across the sky and momentarily blocked the sun.

"The times I spent at Havencroft. The times I spent with you. You were always my biggest supporter." The shadow stiffened. "Even when I didn't deserve your loyalty. How do I ask you for forgiveness when I can't forgive myself?" The shadow slammed a hand on the wooden railing.

Rachel listened, well aware of who stood on the walk.

"You understood me better than I understood myself. And how did I repay you? By taking you for granted—no, it was worse than that. I didn't consider you at all. I knew you would always be there, no matter what I did or said."

And how different had Rachel treated Steffen? Just a different end of the spectrum. A tremble vibrated through Rachel like rolling thunder. She saw that now.

The sun slipped out from behind the clouds. Beams of light blasted through the sky. One struck the oval window. The glare blinded Rachel. She shielded her eyes with her hand. Something spun in the glow. Tilting her head to the side to see what it was, she waited for the flash to fade. The cloud shifted, and Rachel stood mesmerized.

She blinked. Maybe it was the glare playing tricks on her. Another blink. It was still there. She reached out and poked it. Her locket dangled from the window's brass peg. She put the newspapers in the trunk and, in a daze, carefully removed the locket.

Her fingers traced the delicate filigree work and the cluster of small diamonds. With great care she pried the hearts apart. She let out a small sigh. Steffen's smiling face greeted her. On the other side his inscription: *My heart is yours—Forever.* She closed the locket and clutched it to her chest.

A sudden wave of keen emotion left her excited and thrilled. After so many years, it was hers once again. The heart was tied closely to Steffen's devotion—not only to her, but also to them. The idea tempered her excitement, but now, more than ever, she needed to see Steffen. He must speak to her. If he objected, she'd make him speak to her.

In the doorway, the silhouette moved, and Rachel stepped back into the shadows near the hall door.

"You were so much the better person. And I did things…to hurt you. Terrible things." A chocked laugh echoed in the room. "How many times did we have heart-to-heart talks? You were so sure you could save me. You tried so hard. But I couldn't be saved. Not then. I didn't think I was worth saving. I wish I knew why. My parents were loving, if a bit preoccupied. I had good friends, and most stood by me. I had no reason to strike out. Nothing stopped me until you left. That's when I realized. Well, it doesn't matter now."

Pam stepped into the room, closed the door, and sat in the chair, her head in her hands.

Rachel stood in the shadows and put the locket around her neck.

"The last time I saw you, I took your locket. I had just the dress to wear it with." Pam shook her head. "No, that's only partially true. You wore the locket so proudly. Did you know I went with Steffen when he bought it for you? He was so particular picking it out. The filigree had to be just right. The diamonds had to be placed just so. The inscription had to be perfect. He put so much love into that locket."

At first, Rachel didn't think she heard Pam correctly. Even she had her suspicions. Pam had been with her the night before the locket went missing. It was too much of a coincidence. Rachel was not only angry at Pam for taking the locket, but at herself for not confronting Pam.

"I wanted to show the world that I was loved, too. Stupid, right? I thought you'd say so. I never wore it. I thought it would be blasphemous if I did. Each time I looked at it, my skin crawled with guilt. Taking your locket was a betrayal even I couldn't condone. It was as if the locket demanded I return it. Before I could give it back to you, Huntley dragged me overseas."

Pam never hid her feelings about her relationship with Steffen, and after the pool-party incident, Rachel saw Pam only in large groups or alone. Pam often suggested double dating, but Steffen would have none of it. *Don't go looking for trouble*, he told her.

"Your parents had a good idea I had the locket. Your father stopped by our hotel in Italy for a heart-to-heart. Of course, Huntley was at the office. After a nice reunion of sorts, he startled me with his questions about the locket. I had the locket in my jewelry case and could've given it to him. Instead, I feigned being appalled at the accusation. I couldn't admit to him I had the thing. I had to save face with him. Besides, you were the only one who would understand…even forgive me. We didn't return to Havenport for months, and by then you were gone."

Her parents knew? She had been inconsolable.

"I treated Huntley as poorly as I treated you, and pushed him right into the arms of one of his secretaries. I blamed you. How sick is that? I blamed you for not being there for me. Me. Who was never there for you.

"I've kept the locket safe, but it's taken me two marriages and countless hours in therapy to understand love needs to be earned, then nurtured and honored. I can apologize, make amends to everyone, but I can't face you. I'm sorry for so many things."

Pam raised her head and looked around the room. "Remember when we played in here when we were children? Princess, cowgirl—even then I took the role of the villain."

"Of course I remember." Rachel stepped forward. "But I thought you wanted to be boss."

"I brought back—" Pam turned toward the window, then shot out of the chair, letting out a loud gasp. Surprise drained the blood from her face.

"Forgive me," Pam whispered, then walked toward the door. She hesitated, a confused expression on her face.

Rachel stood next to her. "I forgive you."

Pam's eyes widened, then she rushed down the stairs.

Rachel stood at the staircase. A few moments later the echo of the front door closing reached her.

Chapter Seven

Rachel stepped back into the room. The sound of a car door slamming, followed by an engine starting, drew her to the window. The taillights of Pam's car snaked down the drive and disappeared over the knoll. "I love you, Pam. Sometimes I didn't like you, but I never stopped loving you."

Her mind spun from the day's emotional ups and downs, with memories of Steffen pure and clear. "Life's not always a smooth ride. Sometimes it's even stinky. You were so right, Dad."

A long, exhausted sigh filled the room. There was no reason for her to stay any longer. Her hand touched the locket at her throat. At last, everything was peace and contentment.

A smirk stretched across her face. Common sense told her to leave, the same common sense that let Steffen go.

See him, from afar. That would satisfy her. Not talk to him or explain. Look at him one last time before she left. No more torment at what could have been. She'd spent much too long doing that.

She glanced down at the drive. The house's Halloween lights reflected in a shimmer on the damp ground. It would be a few hours before the party started.

Rachel plumped the chair cushions and tucked the blanket around her legs as her mother had done a hundred times. Comfortable and content, she watched the soft rain pelt the window, and waited.

Gravel flew as trucks and cars drove up the drive from Manor Road and woke her from a light sleep. The evening sky was clear. The rain must have stopped hours ago. Rachel stretched and, on a whim, located Orion among the twinkling stars.

Car doors slammed in the front drive while the sound of heavy trucks lumbered at the back of the manor.

The window only let her see so much. They should put the lights on around the house. Mother always lit the house and grounds like a Christmas tree.

Without a good view of the action, Rachel folded the blanket. She reached for her throat, then relaxed. Her locket was still in place. Intent on gathering every memory, she scanned the room, knowing this would be her last time here. Satisfied and ready, she moved down the stairs to the second floor.

"Testing, testing, one, two, three, four."

From her vantage point looking over the balcony railing, people ran, crisscrossing the Great Hall. The waitstaff, dressed in white T-shirts under black suits, transformed into skeletons with white-and-black makeup, and placed drinks in martini glasses on the table around the large vase. Someone else followed behind, dropping cubes into the drinks—dry ice, probably—and made them smoke.

"Sound is good. All the speakers are working." Ina, dressed in a Victorian ball gown, came into view. "Someone get to the kitchen and help set the trays of finger food on the buffet tables. Put the coatracks in the green room. It's that door on the right."

"People are here from the public broadcasting station to set up," one of the volunteers said.

"Show them to the ballroom. Let me know when you see the mayor, council, and the Historical Society. They should be here for pictures and an interview in about fifteen minutes. I don't know how Pam Dawes accomplished that. Her connections are amazing. Come with me. I want to see if the TV people need any help." Ina and two people dressed as ghosts went into the ballroom.

A Tudor princess and a Viking charged across the floor below. A moment later, two nurses and an astronaut came into view, carrying boxes. There were cowboys, vampires, pirates, even political personalities. The music started.

As she knew, sitting up in the balcony had its advantages. You heard every conversation.

"Mr. Mayor, Mr. Washburn, Ms. Dawes, this way, please." A vampire ushered the people into the Great Hall.

"Pam, thank you for hosting dinner."

"Councilman Washburn..." Pam started to say.

"Not quite yet. We'll see the results in November."

This must be Evan Washburn, Havenport's hometown hero. Evan had grown into quite a man. The woman she'd met walking the Westie was with him. They both wore pirate garb. Rachel gasped. Evan wore a real wooden pirate leg.

"Clever costume, Evan. You wear your badge of courage well. I can't help but thank you for serving and keeping us safe." Pam's words struck Rachel. Not what she said, but the sincerity of them.

"You're familiar with the house?" Mrs. Henry, the mayor's wife, asked Pam. Ina joined them.

"Yes, the Emersons are close friends since childhood," Pam said.

"Sorry to interrupt, but you're needed in the ballroom." Ina stepped up next to them.

The others went on. Ina held Pam back. "Your Gypsy costume is wonderful. Are you competing with our fortune teller?"

"No," she laughed. "I'm very happy with the present."

"I wanted to thank you for arranging the PBS interview. Everyone's excited."

"I know the company's general counsel in New York. I mentioned it, and she made a few calls. So do the social thing and keep close to her."

"I'll make sure to get her contact information and send a thank-you note next week." Ina wrote a note on her clipboard.

"By the way, I noticed you don't have all the lights on outside the house. You may want to put them on."

"They should have gone on automatically. I'll check. You go on to the others. I'll be there shortly."

Pam stared up at the balcony, a question on her face.

Rachel drew closer to the rail. "You still have my India earrings. The ones my father gave me," she mumbled.

Pam touched her ear, shook her head, then went into the ballroom.

"Ina." A volunteer ran in from the entrance carrying a large box. "There's a skunk outside and people on line are getting nervous. Can we let them in? It's only fifteen minutes until the doors open."

"Skunk? Ah, that's why Pam reminded me about the lights. Put on all the outside lights, even the ones that line the drive down to Manor Road. That should keep the critters away. The last thing we need are our quests being sprayed. Let them in, but only if they're wearing a costume. No costume—hand them one of the masks." Ina pointed to the box.

"Where'd we get these?" the volunteer asked.

"Pam thought of everything. She had these masks sent from New Orleans."

The Great Hall was the only way to the ballroom. Rachel's perch on the balcony provided a perfect view of every guest. The doors to the ballroom were open, and loud, upbeat music poured out. It didn't appear to bother anyone. They shouted over the din.

The party was in full swing when the grand clock struck ten. There was only a trickle of newcomers now.

By eleven, the volunteers at the entrance closed shop and joined the party. One hour. Had he gotten past her in the crush of guests? He had to be here. It was Halloween. He wouldn't stay away. She wound her arms around herself and tried to stop the building ache.

No sense staying in the balcony, Rachel came down the stairs. She wasn't in a costume and looked in the box for a mask. It was empty. That wasn't going to stop her. Desperate to find him, she walked up to and looked at every man. They must have thought her crazy, but that didn't matter. They ignored her and kept shouting over the music.

She had been through most of the room and stood at one of the high-top tables to gather her thoughts. No, to push down the building panic.

"I'll have one of those," the woman who stood at the table with her said to the passing waiter. To Rachel's surprise, it was the woman with the purple scarf from Serendipity.

"Excuse me—" Rachel said.

"Marta, I've been looking for you." Rachel turned and looked at a woman in a Russian Snow Queen costume.

"Come with me back to the bar. The mayor's wife is waiting for you to read her tea leaves." The two women rushed to the bar.

The clock struck the half hour. It was eleven thirty.

"Can I have everyone's attention, please?" Rachel turned. Pam stood at the microphone.

"I'd like to thank everyone for coming to Edythe Emerson's Masquerade Ball. The judges will announce the costume contest winners in a few moments. Personally, I think the pirate serving drinks is…well, maybe I shouldn't say." A roll of laughter went through the room. "I would like to thank Adam Royce from Royce Tavern. I think you want to thank him, too. He is one of the sponsors of tonight's event."

The guests hooted and hollered their thanks. Adam raised his hand in gratitude and faded back to the bar.

"This house is very special to me. I played here with my dearest friend and have many wonderful memories. This was a happy house. After a great deal of discussion, the Havenport Historical Society, in conjunction with the Emerson Foundation, has decided to continue Havencroft's restoration to its original Gilded Age grandeur. It will be a place to learn about life and art during that era.

"One year ago, the Emerson Foundation gave us a challenge. They would match donations raised by Havenport dollar for dollar. To date, the Havencroft Fund has reached a milestone, five million dollars." Everyone applauded. "At midnight, we have some surprises for you when we finalize the transfer of this wonderful manor to the Historical Society.

"As this year's committee chair I'd like to thank all our volunteers. Now here is Mayor Henry who will announce the winners of the costume contests."

The clock struck the quarter hour, a quarter to twelve.

Rachel looked frantically from one face to another. It was close to midnight. No Steffen. Her breath came in short spurts as the realization hit her hard. He wasn't coming. It was a childish notion, and life didn't happen that way. Rachel knew that better than most, but she had been so sure.

Crowded by the closeness of the ballroom, hollow and empty at not seeing Steffen, her time had run out. She hurried into the garden as the party wound down to the witching hour and the guests filtered out to watch the fireworks.

She sped through the garden, rushed to the back, turned at the dogleg, and came to a screeching halt. The manor lights weren't on here. Out of breath, Rachel stared at the oak tree shrouded in darkness against the halo of lights from Havenport in the distance.

This was her place. No lights were needed for her to find her way. Maybe Steffen never got her note. She ran to the oak tree and searched the knothole. It wasn't there. Falling to her knees, she scoured the ground and wildly sifted through the leaves. The note had to be here. Nothing.

"I wasn't sure you'd come." A male voice pinned her to the spot.

Startled, Rachel rose, her eyes closed. *Thank you.*

"Rachel?" His voice was mellow and soft, better than she remembered. He came around and faced her.

"Steffen." Her heart slammed at the sight of him until she thought she would burst.

Somewhere a clock began to strike midnight. He took her hand and they walked to the other side of the fence, near the Emerson family grave site.

"Rachel, do you love me?" She looked into his eyes and saw the passion she remembered, the passion in her dreams. It hadn't faded. He didn't hate her.

"I never stopped," she whispered. The clock continued to strike the hour.

She rushed into his open arms. They were warm, protecting, and oh, God, loving.

"I have something to tell you."

"Not now. No talking now. I want to hold you. I've waited so long." He cupped her head and drew her to his chest.

"No." She pushed away. "I've kept this secret from you too long. You've always been honest. But I've…I've lied to you."

He waited for her to continue, his face open and encouraging. The clock struck again.

"I was ill, not Mother. There was no hope." Her voice trailed off to a whisper. Time hadn't eased that pain. "I sent you away because I knew you loved me and would never leave me, and your life would be much different if you stayed. I would cost you your job and your future."

"The decision wasn't yours to make alone. There were two of us in the relationship, and we both should have had an equal say."

"Yes, you're right, but I knew what you'd do. I didn't want to be a burden. More than that, I wouldn't be able to stand it if your love turned to hate."

"Did you think me that shallow? My love for you so—"

"No. I was a coward. I know that now. For the last two days something compelled me to come here today."

"I've spent the day at the manor, going over events and decisions. I made a terrible mistake. I never doubted you. Not for a minute. I thought I knew best." Another tone from the clock.

He held her. "I know what you thought. Now it's time for me to confess. I have a secret that I've held from you. I knew that you, not your mother, were ill. The day after the

Halloween party, I sat down with your parents. They didn't want to discuss it, but I played every card I had and forced them to tell me the truth. I wasn't leaving until they did. They made me promise not to mention anything to you unless you told me yourself."

She cried for the months and years of happiness they could have had. For the comfort they could have given each other. For the love they could have shared. The clock's eighth strike of the hour.

"The hardest thing I've ever done was honor that request. I called your mother every week. When she told me you were too weak to write, that you were failing, I came to you. I never left your side. And I made you a promise."

They both looked at the grave in front of them.

Rachel Emerson. December 19, 1960, to January 24, 1986.
Beloved daughter and Steffen's fiancée.

"I remember." Her fingers touched the delicate locket around her neck. "My heart is yours—Forever." The ninth beat of the clock.

"It just took me a little longer to get here." He stood to the side and exposed the newly dug grave.

Steffen Burkett. May 25, 1959, to October 15, 2016.
With Rachel at Last.

"Two weeks ago," she said in a tone filled with awe. "How?"

"It was a heart attack. Your mother was with me. She's a mighty witch."

Steffen looked over his shoulder at the oak. She followed his gaze. Her breath caught. Rachel stared into warm, loving eyes.

"Mother. Father," she whispered.

I told you you'd find your locket. The soft warm tones of her mother's voice echoed in her head.

Her parents stood at the oak, her mother dressed in a witch's costume and her father in his dinner attire.

"Come, Edythe. It's time to go. You've done all you can for both of them." Her father wiped his eyes then put his arm around Edythe. Her mother threw Rachel a kiss. Her parents stood there a moment then turned, and walked back to the manor.

Steffen turned her to face him as the mist surrounded them. His gaze was a soft caress. Instinctively, and with great yearning, she stepped closer to him and playfully sniffed.

"No skunk," he said. The warmth of his smile echoed in his voice.

He was all she wanted, all she had thought about. The connection was immediate, as if the lost years never happened. They belonged together. She knew that now. Every part of her body screamed for him.

His hands slipped up her arms and brought her close.

She couldn't get close enough. For a moment, she fought to control the building excitement his touch ignited, but quickly relented.

With a bent finger, he raised her chin and lowered his lips a breath away from hers. Her heart hammered, her body on fire with a liquid heat concentrated between her thighs. She gasped at the sweet agony. He gathered her closer in his arms. The eleventh strike of the hour.

Nervously, she wet her lips. His chest rumbled with a deep groan. The touch of his mouth on hers sent a tremor through her. He tempted her with his tongue and teased her mouth open. Breathless, she hesitated only a moment. He swooped in, and she let him claim her mouth and quivered at the sweet tenderness of his kiss. Every nerve was live. Every touch of his lips made her dizzy with delight.

He kissed her cheek lightly, then worked his way to her earlobe; his warm breath sent chills through her. She sank into his arms.

"Forever," he moaned.

A sense of urgency drove her. The dizzying current raced through her as the wind picked up, sending the dried leaves around them. The more the wind blew, the more insistent the urgency became. In his arms, her guilt faded until only love remained.

One last gust of wind, on the final stroke of midnight, the witching hour, and Steffen pulled away. His eyes glistened with the promise of passion.

With the burst of fireworks, he led her to their eternity of happily-ever-afters.

About the Author

RUTH A. CASIE is a *USA Today* bestselling author of historical swashbuckling action-adventure and contemporary romance with enough action to keep you turning pages. Her stories feature strong women and the men who deserve them, endearing flaws and all. She lives in New Jersey with her hero, three empty bedrooms and a growing number of incomplete counted cross-stitch projects. Before she found her voice, she was a speech therapist (pun intended), client liaison for a corrugated manufacturer, and vice president at an international bank where she was a product/marketing manager, but her favorite job is the one she's doing now—writing romance.

Ruth loves to hear from readers, too, so drop her a line at Ruth@RuthACasie.com or visit her on Facebook: facebook.com/RuthACasie. She's also on Twitter: @RuthACasie. If you'd like to receive her newsletter and receive a free book, please sign up at www.RuthACasie.com. Thanks!.

Also by Ruth A. Casie

Medieval Romances

The Druid Knight Series
Knight of Runes
Knight of Rapture
Knight of Redemption – Coming Soon
The Druid Knight Tale: A Short Story Expanded

The Stelton Legacy
The Guardian's Witch
The Highlander's English Woman
The Maxwell Ghost
The Pirate's Jewel — February, 2019
The Guardian's Sword — Mid 2019

Collections

Timeless Tales – Short Stories

Medieval Romances
Mistletoe and Magick featured in Timeless Keepsakes
Whispers on the Wind featured in Timeless Treasures

Contemporary Romances
How to Marry a Stuart Brother featuring Second Chance
by the Sea & Forsaking All Others

Havenport – Contemporary Novellas
Happily Ever After featuring I'll Be Home for Christmas
& The Game's AFoot
Never Say Never featured in Snowbound in Havenport
Echoes of Betrayal featured in Legends of Havenport

The Ghost of You

by Emma Kaye

Dean Pearce once loved a ghost, but she left him a long time ago and broke his heart. Now that he's moved back into his childhood home, he can sense her once again. And it's driving him crazy. He needs to find out what she wants and how to get rid of her once and for all.

Lila Crewe left Dean for his own good, but never got the chance to say goodbye. When the Havenport coven holds a séance, she may finally get the chance to tell him how much she's always loved him before she disappears forever.

But the Goddess may have other plans. A mysterious poem at the base of a fountain could hold the key to bringing Lila back to life. Can Dean convince Lila she's worth whatever "sacrifice" the poem demands? Can he successfully perform the tasks set forth? Or will he fail, and not only lose Lila, but his life as well?

Dedicated to ~

My family. Thank you for always being there for me.

Ruth, Lita, Nicole, and Desi. This has been so much fun, it's spooky. ☺

Prologue

December 2015

"Love spells."

Dean Pearce ducked behind the stacks at the Havenport, Rhode Island bookstore. He'd popped in to buy a book signed by his mom's favorite author, Beth Alexander. The perfect Christmas present. She'd love it.

But after overhearing those two little words, he could only hope to escape unnoticed.

"Ooh, do they work?" Mavis Templesmith drooled over the book his niece's elementary school teacher waved toward the crowd with a flourish.

He grimaced. Mavis had caught him alone after a party at his sister, Theresa's, house a little over a year ago. The woman had some serious strength in those claws. He loved his mom, but facing Mavis while her mind was full of all this romance nonsense was not on his list of good ideas.

He listened closely to the words the teacher—what was her name? Janet? Jane?—read.

"'On Bringing Forth True Love.

Bring to me, what I cannot see,
I have been blind, please set me free.
A love that's true, will stand through time,
I pledge my heart, my soul, my mind.
The one I seek, so shall I find.'"

A shimmer of warmth slid down his spine and with it, a name. Lila. He hadn't thought of her for years. Why now?

His stomach twisted into a knot and a dull throbbing beat against his temples.

What a bunch of crap. If he had to listen to much more of that awful poetry, he'd lose his lunch. That Lila immediately came to mind meant nothing more than he was long overdue for some female companionship. Maybe he'd let Theresa set him up on that blind date she'd been bugging him about.

Thinking about Lila, the one who got away, was pointless. Love may stand the test of time, but what good did that do when the one you loved was a ghost?

Chapter One

"What do you think? Can you really sense her? Or am I going crazy?" Dean Pearce paced before the open door to the servants' stairs. What the hell was he thinking? Did he really expect an answer? Only an idiot would ask a psychic stripper for help, but desperate times…

Reina sat on the bottom step and pursed her lips, a mostly empty duffel clutched tightly in her lap. With her long black hair tied back in a sloppy ponytail, her face scrubbed free of makeup, and every inch of her covered in denim and flannel, she barely resembled the dancer who'd stopped in the middle of a lap dance to tell him his ghost was angry.

"She's here. What happened to make her so sad?"

"How the hell should I know?" His gut twisted. Lila was sad? The thought didn't sit well, even if he wanted her gone from his home.

Reina propped her chin on her hands and raised her eyebrow. "I think you know—deep down." She sighed. "Tell me what you can, Sugar. Knowing the history of your haunting will help me make sense of what I'm feeling here. How did you first know you had a ghost?"

He closed his eyes and thought back to the day he'd met Lila. He shivered. Cold. Mind-numbing cold right down to his bones. To this day his worst dreams were of the cold. Other people woke up sweating from their nightmares. Not him. Each shiver that had racked his body had sparked pain, but the trembling wouldn't stop. She'd responded to cries no one else could hear.

"I was eight. Kicking a ball around a playground behind my house. My older sister, Theresa, had wandered over to the swings with a group of friends. I kicked the ball a little too hard and it bounced into the street. The car came out of nowhere.

"Driver was blitzed out of his mind. Police found him a mile or so away passed out behind the wheel with the front of his truck wrapped around a telephone pole. They saw blood on the windshield, put two and two together, and realized he probably caused my disappearance. My parents had reported me missing when Theresa couldn't find me and I didn't return from the park."

Her eyes narrowed and she twisted a stray lock of hair around her finger. "How does your ghost play into this?"

"The impact threw me far from the road and I landed under a bush. Cops walked right by me, but I was too weak to make myself loud enough to be heard. Lila talked to me, sang for a while. She kept me from giving up. Then she led the police straight to me."

"She can make herself visible? Interesting."

"Yeah. So why can't I see her now?" He peered up the stairs, attempting to get even the tiniest glimpse.

Reina shrugged. "I can only sense that she's here, Sugar. She's not talking to me." She frowned, cocked her head to the side as if listening to something. "She's struggling. I think she wants to talk, but can't."

"That doesn't make any sense. She never had communication problems with me before." Until she'd pulled her disappearing act.

"She hasn't talked to you since you were a child? Was she here the whole time, or did she reappear recently?"

Kid, teenager, whatever. He wasn't going to go into his whole history with Lila so he gestured toward the back of the house. "Come on into the kitchen. I'll fix us something to eat and we can discuss it." He needed a drink.

He led the way into the outdated kitchen, flipping the light on as they entered. Empty bottles, serving trays, and trash covered every surface.

He'd dismissed the catering company as soon as the bachelor party had died down. After Reina's announcement about Lila, he'd been hard-pressed not to throw everyone out, but he hadn't wanted to ruin his friend, Dave's, night. Instead, he'd asked Reina to stay after everyone else left.

Most of the guys had been fall-down drunk and hadn't appeared to notice. With a fleet of cabs hired to make sure everyone got home safe, moderation hadn't been on the agenda for the evening. If anybody remembered one of the strippers had stayed, well, the bill had to get paid sometime. Doubtful anyone would think much of it. She didn't deserve to have her reputation trashed for trying to help him. And, gorgeous as she was, she wasn't his type.

Besides, there was way too much on his plate right now. Like renovating.

He hadn't given it a second thought before buying the family home when his parents retired to Arizona. Maybe it hadn't been such a smart move. The old place definitely needed work.

His mom had mentioned Evan Washburn's sister, Meghan, was back in town and setting up an interior design business. Haven and Hell? Nah, that couldn't be right. Something like that, though, with a play on heaven/haven. His friend, Evan, would probably be happy if Dean threw a little business Meghan's way. She'd had it rough lately and could probably use a little boost.

He'd have to get the number and give her a call. No way was he going to tackle such a huge project on his own. The labor he could handle, but the design? No way. So calling Meghan would be a win-win.

"Beer? Soda?"

"Water's fine."

He filled a glass and handed it to her. She perched on a stool at the massive island dominating the kitchen.

Getting used to the idea this was his house would take some time. He half expected his mom to come down from her room dressed in a pair of sweats and serve up a plate of freshly baked cookies as a snack. Not only weren't there any cookies, but she'd taken the cookie jar.

He'd adjust eventually. The idea of strangers living in his home had prompted him to make an offer on the old place when his parents made the decision to sell. His brother and sister both had their own homes nearby and weren't interested in taking on the headaches of another property. A single guy had no need for a mansion this size, but someday…maybe.

The top popped off his beer with practiced ease, and he took a long swig, leaning against the fridge. Cool air provided relief on overheated skin. He stripped off his sweater, slinging it on the stool next to Reina.

His T-shirt barely rode up his abs, but he yanked it back into place and darted a glance her way. He wasn't overly bothered by the scars flanking his side, but he didn't flaunt them, either.

Reina flinched. Water splashed on the counter as she fumbled with her glass. She shifted on her stool, tugging the collar of her flannel shirt closer at the neck.

What was that all about?

Shit. The reason she'd donned the messy hair and baggy clothes when the party ended suddenly became clear. *I'm a freakin' dumb-ass.* He forced his fist to relax around the neck of his beer before it shattered, then gently placed the empty bottle on the counter behind him.

Just because it was—he glanced at his watch—three in the morning, didn't mean he would take advantage of her. Too bad she didn't appear to know that. Maybe tossing his sweater away like that hadn't been the best idea.

"I'm just hot, okay? If you're uncomfortable, you can leave whenever you want. I'm not going to try anything."

Her eyes widened. A rosy blush spread across her cheeks. "I didn't think you would."

He laughed. "Right."

"Honestly, I do know you're one of the good ones. The way you made sure the guys knew me and the others were strippers, not hookers, was wonderful. We all appreciated the gesture. Most guys don't know the difference. Or, at least, they're always hopeful they'll get lucky. And sometimes they get a little pushy. That's why we bring Ace with us," she said, referring to the six-foot, two-hundred-twenty-pound mass of muscle who'd watched over them all night. She flicked a hand toward her face. "This is just habit after a show. Way more comfortable."

He nodded. "I just want to know about Lila. Now that I'm living in this house again…I thought I could handle being here with her, but I'm going nuts knowing she's around. I don't think I can deal with it. I need to get rid of her once and for all."

Dean's words pierced Lila in the heart. The fault lay with her, but knowing he wanted her gone stung. If only she could apologize, maybe he'd come to understand why she'd left. Knowing he hated her with such vehemence tore her apart. Icy tears of frustration ran down her cheeks.

Everything about her was cold—ever since she'd made her deal with the Goddess years ago. Warmth was a thing of the past—except when she got close to Dean. Being near him made her feel almost alive again.

Almost, but not quite.

Almost is a terrible way to exist.

She didn't know how much longer she could stand this limbo. For a while, at least, she'd been unaware. Time had passed, but she hadn't noticed. The reality of her existence in those years was difficult to understand. She'd been a child caught in a loop, repeating the same actions over and over.

Dean's cries for help had pulled her out of her routine and made her aware of her surroundings for the first time since her death. She'd even begun to age, almost as if she lived.

Mirrors offered no assistance, and ghosts didn't have reflections, but the changes to her body couldn't be missed. She felt solid enough, but her limbs were see-through, she could walk through walls, and moving even the smallest objects took all her concentration. She could push and pull without limit on weight, but lifting so much as a feather was beyond her ability.

Moving on scared her silly, but this partial existence had to end.

Her friendship with Dean had been wonderful. He'd been able to see her, and they'd had fun. When he'd been too weak to return to school after the accident, his mother had homeschooled him. Lila sat in on those lessons, ending up with a quality education she'd never have received in her own time. Being part of his life had been her reward for saving him. Or so she'd thought.

Until his mother explained the cost of her happiness was Dean's life.

Not his physical life or health. She'd never do anything to endanger him. No. Emotions were the problem. He'd cared for her. Loved her even. He'd have done anything for her. And she'd returned that emotion. But instead of her love lifting him up, she'd dragged him down.

Ahh. She had to stop this pointless reminiscing. Why drive herself crazy over a past that couldn't be changed?

Reina pressed Dean for more information. Despite the young woman's rather questionable manner of supporting herself, Lila liked Reina. When Lila's anger flared to life, Reina backed away from Dean immediately. Lila hadn't realized Reina could sense her presence until that moment, but she appreciated the way the woman acknowledged her presence.

The flash of jealous rage had taken Lila by surprise. The party had been going on for quite some time. Drinks flowed, music blared. A mix of beer, fried chicken wings, and scented oil permeated the air. The men were loud and obnoxious while several women danced around the room, occasionally choosing a man to favor until satisfied with the number of dollar bills sticking out of their minuscule bikinis.

Reina hadn't been the first woman drawn to Dean. But for whatever reason, seeing the beautiful woman draped over his lap, Lila's anguish had reached its peak.

Shame ate at her insides.

Her anger was completely irrational. Dean had every right to behave as he wished, with anyone he wished. Hadn't she left him so he could have a normal life, one that would involve a living woman? Lila had no cause to be irritated the moment another woman entered his life.

Yet she couldn't help her feelings. No matter how pointless.

Like when he'd pulled off his sweater, revealing the hard planes of his stomach. Her cheeks had heated in a scorching blush. She didn't have much experience with the male form, but she found his quite attractive. Staring at him caused a longing she could never ease. Hiding in her attic when he was home would have been a wise move, yet she always hovered over him, noting all the ways he'd changed through the years.

He no longer limped or favored his left arm. His dark-blond hair was cropped close. Tiny lines crinkled at the corners of his eyes when he smiled, and with too much sun, those lines became a permanent white fan that promised laughter was never far away.

"Tell me about the day she left," Reina said in her thick Southern accent. "The spirits are mysterious, Sugar. Why one stays and another goes, we may never know. Something small to us may cause larger ripples in the spiritual world. Nothing can be discounted out of hand."

"I was seventeen, an eternity ago. My parents were pushing me to decide on a school. My going to college was about the only thing they agreed on in those days. Anyway. One day Mom asked me to run an errand, and when I got home, Lila was gone. I couldn't sense her presence. Nothing. Gone—like that." He snapped his fingers. "No explanation. No good-byes. Nothing. I begged her to come back. And when I got no response, I begged her for answers. Why? Why had she left me? What did I do wrong?"

Lila choked back a sob, her hand over her mouth. She whispered through her fingers, "You didn't do anything wrong. You were perfect. You deserved so much more than I could give you." She'd heard his cries, tried to go to him to explain. But once the Goddess took action, there was no going back.

Lila had thought leaving Dean was the only answer, and the Goddess had agreed. Only Lila hadn't known the Goddess would take such decisive and immediate action.

Lila had assumed she'd have time to tell Dean her plan to leave him for his own good. He couldn't live his life for a dead woman.

Love was for the living.

Reina reached across the center island and covered Dean's hand with hers. "Sounds like you had some feelings for this ghost of yours."

Lila's breath caught.

Dean nodded. "I did. But I got over her a long time ago. No easy task. That's why knowing she's still here but not talking is so infuriating. What does she want?"

"I don't want anything." Lila stood next to him. She smoothed the lines creasing his forehead, then cupped her hand along his jaw. Warmth leached into her fingers. She couldn't touch him, but when she got close like this, some of his heat seeped into her.

Dean gasped and reared back. He held a hand to his face right where she'd touched him. His head swiveled toward her. Goose bumps covered his arm.

She cradled her warm hand to her cold chest and stared into his beautiful eyes. But there was no reflection in those gold-speckled green orbs.

Darn near broke her heart. "I know I've hurt you, Dean. I'm so sorry."

A few days after his talk with Reina, Dean sifted through the mountain of paper on his desk. The damn thing grew larger each passing day. He ran a hand through his hair and sighed.

"You really need to hire someone to help you with all that."

His older brother, Jeremy, leaned against the doorjamb. "Knock much?"

Jeremy held a ring of keys. "Still have my key. You should change the lock if you don't want family barging in on you."

"Stupid of me to think you'd respect my privacy." He smiled to take the sting out of his words. He could care less if his family barged in on him. Unless, of course, he had someone with him. Hmm. Maybe he needed to reconsider the locks. He suppressed a snort. Right, like he'd had that problem lately.

"True." Jeremy slouched into a seat across from him. "What happened with Reina last night? I was surprised she stayed. Didn't think you were her type."

"Nothing happened. I needed to pick her brain."

"She's in the Havenport Coven with Christa, you know." Jeremy gave him a serious look. "I wouldn't want to mess with her, if you know what I mean."

Surprise, surprise. "No, I didn't know."

Jeremy raised his brows and made a skeptical noise in the back of his throat.

Dean rolled his eyes. "Seriously, I had no idea. Reina's not interested in me anyway."

"You and Reina?" Christa strolled in and headed straight for him.

He jumped to return her kiss and hug hello. True, Christa had pissed him off for abandoning his older brother for the better part of a year without a word, but after everything that had happened on the Fourth of July, he'd come to realize she'd had cause.

Now she was back and he'd never seen Jeremy in such good spirits. The man was disgusting with the width of his smile these days.

Dean couldn't be happier for them. And Christa had grown on him. "So, what's up? Why are you breaking and entering today?" He reached for his pen and frowned when he came up empty. Hadn't he dropped the pen on top of the paper awaiting his signature? He checked his desk and found it at the far corner. Out of reach. "Dammit, Lila." It was an old game they used to play when they were kids. One of Lila's favorites. He could almost hear her laughing.

"Lila?" Jeremy leaned forward in his chair with a scowl.

"Don't start." A warning hand halted what was sure to be a tiresome tirade against Lila and the existence of ghosts in general. He tipped his chin toward Christa. "You haven't convinced him yet?"

She shook her head with a smile. "Your brother can be as stubborn as an ass."

Jeremy sat tall. "I'm not stubborn because I don't believe in ghosts."

"Your wife's a witch."

"That's different." He grabbed Christa around the waist where she perched on the arm of his chair and yanked her into his lap.

She laughed and tilted her face for a kiss.

Thankfully a short one. He wasn't in the mood for one of Jeremy's passionate public displays with his fiancée.

"She's alive. We can see her." Jeremy buried his face in the curve of her neck and ran his hand along her side. He inhaled loudly. "Smell her. Feel her."

Dean leaned back to study the ceiling. "Yeah, I get it. Get a room already."

Christa giggled and struggled out of Jeremy's grasp and into her own seat. "You may not be able to sense Lila, but I can. I believe she left the room when we came in."

Dean gave Jeremy a piercing glare and gestured toward Christa. "See. Told you."

"Not as strong as that first time I had dinner here, but she's still around." She fell silent, staring into space. Then snapped her fingers and whipped her attention back to the present. "Reina."

"What's she got to do with anything?" Jeremy asked.

"She has a *very* strong tie to the spirit world. We can hold a séance and call Lila to us. Then we can figure out what's keeping her here."

The idea of a séance made his skin crawl. Did he want to see Lila again? Yes. But if he were honest, the thought also freaked him out. He didn't know what to expect, and he hated the uncertainty. She'd given the appearance of aging along with him, but could a ghost truly age?

He'd often wondered in the years since she'd been gone. How old would she appear? The same as he remembered, or would she be his age? Or would she have reverted to the nine-year-old she'd been when she came to him the first time?

"I'd be able to talk to her again?"

Christa must have picked up on the pathetic note of hope in his question. She reached across the desk and squeezed his hand. "Maybe. But only for a short time. Hopefully long enough to find out what's keeping her here and figure out how to set her free." She and Jeremy exchanged a look. Something unspoken passed between them. "You know she can't stay, right, Dean?" she whispered. "She doesn't belong here. She needs to move on. So do you."

He nodded and cleared his throat of the lump that formed at her words. "Yeah. Of course. I know that. It will be a relief."

Christa tilted her head. Tears glistened in her eyes. "I'll give Reina a call and set something up."

Dean nodded and returned to the mountain of paperwork on his desk. If he concentrated hard enough, maybe he could block Lila's presence, and the tight ache in his chest might ease up a little.

Chapter Two

Lila wandered the house. So many changes since she'd lived here as a child. Electricity available in every home—a wonder she still couldn't get over, even after all these years of seeing it in action. So easy. One flip of a switch and a room lit up, clear as day.

Hot and cold running water, too. At least Dean had told her the water could be adjusted to whatever temperature suited the user. She couldn't actually feel the heat.

She'd assisted her mother with boiling and hauling enough buckets of water up the steep servants' stairs to appreciate being able to access such a delightful thing as a warm bath at the twist of a knob. The concept remained elusive without personal experience.

Boxes stuffed with Dean's belongings scattered throughout every room. In her opinion, he lived in the house, but hadn't made it his home. How could he stand to live out of boxes?

She helped as best she could. If she concentrated with her limited powers she could move an object several feet at a time. Weight didn't make a difference. A sofa moved as easily as Dean's pen.

She amused herself rearranging the furniture in the living room. Dean had left everything where the movers dropped them. She switched the couch and armchairs so they sat in a comfortable position for entertaining.

Dean had left hours ago. He'd surprised her by saying he'd see her in town shortly.

In town? Surely he realized she remained tied to the house and property. Leaving was impossible. She'd tried. Often. She simply couldn't manage as well as she had when she was a young spirit.

A strange scent, sweet with a hint of spice, filled her nose. She searched for the elusive source without luck. The smell filled her with longing. She drifted toward the hall. The odor seemed stronger in that direction.

She floated through the front door. Her excitement surged. Her body responded to a power beyond her control. So much of her existence was outside her wishes. She'd grown used to the sensation.

The Goddess fountain loomed large before her. So close. A few more feet and she'd glide right past her. Lila held her breath. Ten feet. Five. Two.

Bam! She slammed to a stop. Tears of frustration welled in her eyes. She'd thought for sure…

Noises sounded in the distance. Faded, but growing stronger. She picked out Dean's deep voice. She couldn't make out his words.

The urge to leave the property grew stronger. She wanted to get to him. Needed to be at his side.

Her vision blurred. She stumbled back and hit the ground with a resounding thud.

A spark of fear chased away the disappointment from a moment ago. She'd felt similar only a few times before.

The first, when a young Dean's cries for help reached through the strange, timeless veil that separated her from the living world and yanked her free out of a desire to ease the fear in that small cry.

The second, after her deal with the Goddess cost her the ability to make herself known to others. She'd spent more than a decade in that horrible, invisible existence. Aware of all that passed in the Pearce household, but unable to take part in any of it. She'd had to sit by while Dean searched for her. Pleaded with her to return to him. Then finally cursed her and moved on.

Her chest tightened. He'd cursed her more than once since he'd moved back home. Neither of them understood why he could sense her once again, and neither of them were happy with the situation. Why didn't he simply sell the house and be done with her?

What was going on now? Was she being drawn closer or further from the living? Perhaps the Goddess finally heard Dean's wish for peace.

She raced through the house, up the servants' stairs, and curled into a ball on the twin bed tucked against the attic wall. It had been her bed once upon a time. Shared with her mother, and rarely used. The life of a servant was not an idle one.

A piercing pain shot through her temple. She gasped.

Her vision blacked out. The wind whistled in her ears. A storm the likes of which she'd never known caught her, tossing her into the air. Her bed dropped from below her as she whirled through the air. Her stomach revolted. She wrapped her arms around her middle and squeezed.

She tried to pray, but didn't know what for. To survive? What was the point?

She was already dead.

Smoke curled up and away from the white candle in the center of the table. The Havenport Coven sat in a circle in a room above Serendipity, a froufrou store that had opened over the summer. Christa raved about the place, and it had definitely come in handy when Jane Royce had used the store's inventory to perform a spell to locate a kidnapped Christa on the Fourth of July.

Still, Dean had little use for the store's main products of scented candles, soaps, and crystals. He wrinkled his nose against the strong perfume.

Jane squeezed his hand and whispered, "Close your eyes and concentrate." The pretty brunette's husband sat on her other side. Damn, the man was a giant. Dean's survival instinct urged him to pull his hand away, but he held still. Adam didn't seem to mind, and Dean hoped to hell that wasn't going to change. He found Jane attractive, but he didn't go for married women. Hopefully Adam realized Dean had no designs on his wife.

Reina had called the Havenport Coven together to help with the séance. She wanted to leverage their combined power to draw Lila in with more force than she could pull off on her own. Jane and Christa were founding members, but they'd added to their ranks the past few months.

They planned to expand their membership further, by at least one. A woman named Lauren who had only recently arrived in Havenport. Apparently she'd grown up here and come back after the death of her husband. She worked in the shop below and was in charge of the extra space above the store as a place to hold all sorts of witchy-type activities. Séances, coven meetings—you name it, she'd rent out the space. He'd expected her to take a seat at the table, but she'd made sure they had everything they needed and practically ran out of the room.

Instead, he sat next to Francine from the craft shop on Franklin Avenue. Given that they'd met only an hour ago, holding her hand was awkward as heck, but she didn't seem bothered. He'd have preferred Christa on that side, but he couldn't exactly object when Francine sat next to him instead.

Christa was one chair over, her large spell book, *On Magick Most Powerful*, open before her. Her mouth moved as she read, but she wasn't saying anything loud enough for him to hear. She'd told him the book was there to reinforce the coven's magick and aid in bringing Lila to them without attracting any other spirits.

Since Christa was here, Jeremy had come along as well. Lucky guy had escaped the dubious pleasure of sitting around the table while everyone stared blankly into space. Christa had banned him from the room right from the start. He didn't take the matter seriously enough and his "negative" energy might keep Lila from appearing. At least Jeremy wouldn't be bored. He was probably having a great time browsing at A New Chapter next door and would end up with a dozen new books before the end of the evening.

Dean, on the other hand, was tempted to put his head down and take a nap. They'd been at it for nearly forty-five minutes with zero results. "Maybe we should call it quits for today."

"Don't be silly, Sugar," Reina responded. "Have a little patience. Calling a spirit through the veil isn't easy." She pushed a lock of hair behind her ear and patted the table. "Stop resisting and concentrate."

"I'm not resisting," he grumbled. Maybe a little, if he were honest. He wanted to see Lila, no question, but sharing their first meeting in years before a group? He had so much to say to her, and he didn't relish having a crowd witness their reunion.

He closed his eyes anyway and tried not to think of anything except Lila. Not his issues with her, or all his questions about why she went away—only thoughts of the ghostly girl he'd once called his best friend.

He struggled to remember the first time he'd seen her. She'd visited him, Theresa, and Jeremy long before they could remember. Their parents had told them how, when each of them were learning to talk, they'd mentioned the little girl who sang them back to bed after waking in the middle of the night. He couldn't remember, but once he'd gotten to know Lila, he'd realized she was the ghost that used to "haunt" the Pearce family babies.

She'd haunted them for generations, apparently. Their father, their grandfather, aunts, and uncles. They'd all had this nightly visitor sing them to sleep when they were troubled.

Other than a few sightings now and again, that had been the extent of her interaction with the family until Dean came along. For whatever reason, she'd come to him when he'd had his accident and stayed for years. At a time when visits from his healthy, active friends were painful reminders of his own inabilities, she'd been there.

Then she'd left him during another miserable part of his life. Taking care of him had taken a toll on his parents' marriage. His mother had quit a job she loved to stay home and take care of him. He'd had multiple surgeries, long recovery periods, and hadn't made it easy on his ever-patient mom, who'd had to teach him everything he missed at school. His parents' marriage had been falling apart because of him. Guilt had torn him in two.

High college placement tests, a killer essay, and perfect SAT scores got him into Princeton, but he decided not to go. His parents were furious, but his decision gave them a common goal and things between them improved, so he was confident he'd made the right choice.

Then Lila disappeared. He'd struggled to put her behind him, move on with his life, and stop being a drain on his family.

But he'd always wondered what drove Lila away. He needed answers. Being able to sense Lila's presence in his house drove him crazy. He had to get his answers and send her on her way. Out of his life for good.

A shock of electricity ran up his arms. Hair all over his body stood on end. He snapped his eyes open.

A trembling, semitransparent body lay curled in the fetal position in the center of the table. A tumble of dark-blond curls lay barely an inch from where his left hand clasped Jane's. He drew in a shocked breath. *Lila?*

Jane squeezed his hand. He dragged his gaze away from the ghost.

She gave a slight shake of her head and indicated Reina across the table. He turned his attention her way, but couldn't help casting continuous glances at the figure in front of him. Lila? The girl he remembered was a teenager. Skinny, with curves she mostly hid under old-fashioned clothing. Curves he'd often teased her about when they were kids. True, he'd known she was a girl, but he'd been willing to ignore that one little flaw in his friend. His opinion had taken a definite turn toward approval as they'd reached their teen years.

The person before him was most definitely a woman, fully grown. The curve of her hip, the line of her neck. Her clothing hadn't changed. Long black skirt. White blouse buttoned all the way to her chin. She shifted, and her hair fell away from her face. He gasped.

"Lila?" It *was* her. He fought for breath.

Huge green eyes stared at him. Her lip trembled. Even for a ghost, she was pale. He could see the teenage girl he used to know in the woman before him. But man, his imagination had failed him.

Beautiful didn't do her justice.

Chapter Three

Dean could see her? Judging by the way he stared and said her name, Lila would guess yes.

"What—" Her voice came out rough, scratchy. She cleared her throat and started again. "What happened?"

Strangers surrounded her. She pressed her hands into the table, pushing into a more dignified position. The white tablecloth remained smooth where she clutched at it. Fabrics had always given her trouble. If she concentrated hard enough she would be able to move the candle she practically sat on, even move the whole table across the room, but dislodging the cloth was beyond her.

She straightened her black, ankle-length skirt to cover her legs and twitched the ruffled front of her blouse back into place. They might be transparent, but they still hid her body from view. And she had no desire to show her body to a room full of strangers.

The woman she'd seen at Dean's house the other night—Reina—sat to her left. She smiled kindly, crooked her finger, and moved to the side.

Lila followed her signal and scooted over to her edge of the table, then slid her legs off the side where Reina gave her room. Lila could go right through her, but she'd always avoided touching living people. The sensation was too strange to seek out.

"Hello, Lila. We kind of met the other night." She leaned in close and whispered, "No worries, Sugar. I don't have any designs on your man. And the feeling's mutual. I was just doing my job."

Lila flushed. She tried to think of some witty comeback about Dean's freedom to do whatever he wished, but her tongue stuck to the roof of her mouth and refused to comply.

"Let me introduce you." Reina went around the table introducing what she called the Havenport Coven. A sweet woman named Jane headed the group. Her husband, Adam, a handsome giant of a man, was the only other male present besides Dean. Lila recognized Christa, who had visited the house more than once in the presence of Dean's brother, Jeremy. In addition was an older woman named Francine, and Marcie, who worked in the bookstore next door.

Lila nodded to everyone, but her focus remained on Dean, trying to decipher his expression. Was he pleased to see her or not? His eyes were wide, his mouth set in a grim, straight line. He'd visited the house so rarely over the years—and moved in such a short while ago—that reading his mood proved more difficult than she remembered.

The veil between her existence and his had shifted. Brighter colors, louder noises. She'd seen him earlier that day, yet he looked different without the thick cloud that normally surrounded the living.

His hair was a bit darker than she'd thought. Straw-blond hair had darkened over the years to dark blond, almost brown. He kept it cut short and a bit spiked at the top. Messy, and not overly styled.

His gaze roamed over her in a constant motion, never settling in one place. If she weren't mistaken, he avoided looking her straight in the eye. "Hello, Dean. It's good to see you."

Finally his gaze rose to meet hers. He snorted. "Nice to see you, too. It's been a while."

Definitely not happy. Then why had he gone through all this trouble to bring her here?

She scanned the room for a clue as to why she'd been called. Her cheeks heated at being the center of attention. Not shocking, of course, but she'd somehow put out of her mind she was a ghost in a room full of the living who could now see and hear her every word. Being invisible and silent had become second nature.

"We're glad you've joined us, Lila," Christa said.

Lila turned in her direction. "Are you?" She darted a glance at Dean, then quickly back to Christa. "Not everyone appears so pleased. Why have you called me here?" A tall bookcase against one wall caught her attention, her interest piqued by the titles stuffed onto the shelves. The words *witch* and *earth* predominant in most. If these people were indeed a coven, then this must be where they practiced their arts.

Should she be pleased or scared? She wasn't sure. Back in her day, witches were disciples of the devil. But these women didn't appear to be evil. In fact, she got a good sense from all of them.

The teachings of her living youth were wasted in this age. Her strange existence with Dean had taught her many things about the modern world. At this point, she'd consider herself much more of a modern woman than the nineteenth-century housemaid she'd been born to.

She would simply have to put her preexisting notions of good versus evil aside. Instinct said the people in this room were good, trustworthy people.

But what of Dean?

Christa shoved Dean's shoulder. He gave her a scathing glare before staring at the floor.

"Oh, for goodness sake, Dean! Don't be an idiot. Talk to her," Christa said, exasperation heavy in her voice.

Adam pressed a kiss to Jane's hand and tucked her arm against his side. "I believe a little privacy is in order. Shall we?" He gave Lila a slight bow and turned to escort Jane from the room. The others followed.

With the door closed tight against intrusion, silence filled the room. Tension grew to almost a living thing between her and Dean. Lila cast about for a topic of conversation. Anything but what had brought them to this place. She nodded toward the door. "He's an interesting gentleman. His manner is more of my time than yours."

Dean shrugged. "I don't know him well. We met only a few months ago. He owns a tavern on the water. Nice enough. Christa thinks highly of him." Dean strode to the table and blew out the candle. "The British accent threw me off, but now you mention it, yeah, he has an old-fashioned way of talking."

This was getting them nowhere. "Why did you call me, Dean? You are clearly unhappy. If you think I know how to get out of your house, you're mistaken. I have no idea what's keeping me here or how to leave. Believe me, I don't want to stay any more than you want me to." Bad enough knowing he wanted her gone. Cruel to bring them closer before banishing her forever. She swung away to face the bookcase. Tears clouded her vision, preventing a closer inspection of the books and leaving her without a much-needed distraction.

"Is that what you think?" he asked in a rough voice. He cleared his throat. "I'm not happy to see you? All I've wanted for the past ten years was to see you again."

"I don't know what to think." Warmth spread across her back. She sensed him standing behind her. Close enough to touch, if that were possible. Of course, it wasn't.

That fleeting feeling of warmth was hard to resist. If only she could lean into him, claim some of his heat to chase away the icicles surrounding her heart.

Dean choked back a cry of frustration. He stood within an inch of Lila, knowing that trying to move in closer was an exercise in futility. He'd tried numerous times when they were kids. Playful shoves, teasing slaps to the back. The result had always been the same. His hand would pass directly through her and he'd have the sensation of plunging his hand in a bucket of ice water. Only worse. He shivered. Not only did getting too close practically cause frostbite, but the effect lasted for hours. The longer he came in contact with her, the longer he shivered uncontrollably.

He pivoted on his heels, then stomped to the opposite side of the room. A good idea to get a little distance. He'd avoid the risk of freezing his ass off and keep his anger close to his chest. "Speaking of the past ten years, where have you been? You disappeared without a word."

She gave up the pretense of reading the bookshelf and swung toward him. "That wasn't my intention. I thought I'd have time to explain my reasoning."

He clicked his jaw shut so he didn't look like an idiot. He hadn't expected to be crazy about her answer, but he'd assumed she'd at least have a decent one. Wasn't her intention? What a load of crap. "What are you talking about?"

"Nothing happened the way I'd hoped." She crossed her arms across her chest. "I wanted to help you. I never left, but from the moment I asked for help, I lost my ability to show myself." She shook her head. To his surprise, a glistening trail of tears streamed down her cheeks. "It's been horrible. And I'm so tired. I'm not alive. I'm not dead. What the hell am I? Why is this happening?"

She might as well have walked right into him. Ice flooded his veins and a deep, twisting knot settled in his gut. "I'm so sorry, Lila. I had no idea." He'd resented her all this time, and she hadn't left him on purpose? "I thought you got tired of us. That you somehow moved on or something. But lately, I could sense you in the house again. Especially since I moved home. I thought I was going crazy for a while." He ran a hand through his hair and sighed. "Until Christa showed up and sensed you, too, I doubted whether you really were back."

"You haven't seemed very happy. You didn't miss me? Do you hate me so much?"

He had to strain to hear her whispered words. "I've missed you like crazy. But you pissed me off, too."

She nodded. "I know I hurt you. I can only say that was unintentional."

"Okay." He sunk into one of the chairs surrounding the table. "I don't hate you. I could never."

"So what are we going to do?"

"Go back to the way it was? I can see you and hear you now." Even as he spoke, he knew the idea had no merit. She stirred up all kinds of emotions he didn't want to deal with. Not the least of which was the fact she'd grown into a beautiful woman. And he was no longer a bedridden, scared little kid who barely noticed Lila's gender, let alone want anything more from her than simple friendship. Or a shy teenager who fell in love with his best friend but had no idea what that meant.

Friendship was not what he had in mind when he considered her now. The ridiculous amount of lace that comprised the front of her blouse couldn't disguise the sweet curve of her breasts. He forced his head up. A rosy blush suffused her cheeks. The fact she'd recovered some of her color wasn't a good thing for him. The evidence of her modesty made her all the more attractive.

And he was a crude, insensitive idiot for continuing to stare. He pushed the chairs under the table to keep his wayward gaze from focusing on her assets.

"I don't think going back to the way we were is possible."

He couldn't agree more. He shoved the last chair in place and faced her. "I agree. Then where do we stand? What do you want?"

She gave a slight smile. "I've obviously had a lot of time." She squared her shoulders. "I must figure out what's keeping me here and find a way to move on."

"Of course." He winced. He wanted the same, didn't he? At least that's what this séance was all about. "Do you have any idea how?"

"I have a few."

"Good. Let's have 'em." He flicked his fingers in a give-them-to-me motion. At least one of them had some kind of clue on where to start.

"First, I need to figure out how I got here in the first place." She held up a hand. "I mean, I remember a little of my life before I died. My mother was a servant in the Pearce household. When not assisting her with her duties, I often helped the Pearces' nursemaids with the younger children."

"Did you sing them to sleep?" That would make a lot of sense. He'd never really asked about her past. He'd been in too much pain when she first appeared, and for years after. Then she'd become such a standard part of his life that the subject simply never came up. Besides, he'd known she'd always been around, singing to the Pearce babies for centuries.

"Yes. Why?"

"Well, you've been singing to the babies in my family for generations. Maybe you stayed because you thought it was your job?"

"I did? Did I sing to you as well?" At his nod, she frowned. "Odd. I don't remember. Little of that time before your distress woke me is clear. I wasn't entirely aware of my existence until your cries pulled me through the veil between the living and the dead." She crossed her arms and tapped her lip with a finger. "Singing to the babies was one of my duties, yes. But such a simple chore hardly seems a strong enough reason to keep me tied to the world of the living."

"Yeah. I suppose that's true." So what would keep a spirit from moving on? Some kind of unfinished business? "Was there anything you'd wanted to do but didn't have the chance?"

She gave a soft, tinkling laugh. "Everything? I was only nine years old. I had barely lived. I wasn't ready to die."

"If you don't mind my asking, how did you die?" He'd always wanted to know, but somehow the topic had always seemed taboo. He'd tried a number of times to bring up the subject, but she'd always managed to deflect his questions.

She put a hand to her head. Her forehead scrunched and her eyes screwed tightly closed. She let out a loud hissing breath. "I don't know."

Chapter Four

Lila had never given her death much thought. Anytime she did try to remember, she'd have flashes of memory that terrified her so much she pushed them away. "I don't know how I died. I have waking nightmares sometimes. There's pain and water and screaming…" Her voice froze, and her heart fluttered wildly.

Dean moved closer. "It's okay. We'll figure this out. Maybe I can do some research and find out what happened. I think we have some family history books up in the attic somewhere. I'll dig them out. If you died at the house, I'd think there'd be something written there."

Did she really want to know? Her neck stiffened, and her hands trembled. The images from her nightmares made no sense, but terrified her. Would knowing what they really meant help or hurt?

He gestured they should leave. "Come on, let's go." He pulled the door open and stood to the side.

"How?" She hadn't been off the Pearce property in years. She had no idea how she'd gotten to this strange little room. Could she simply walk out? Go where she pleased?

His eyes widened. "How? I—" He pointed out into the hall, then back at her, and laughed. It was a nervous, shaky sound. "The phrase 'I have no idea' seems to be our new motto. But let's try walking, okay?"

She returned his smile. "Okay." After a deep breath, she preceded him with hesitant steps. The air leaked from her lungs in a slow hiss.

A short hall led to stairs on the right. Muffled voices came from that direction. Was it Reina, Christa? She slipped down the stairs and into a pretty little shop with shelves full of beautiful soaps, candles, and a variety of other items. She would have enjoyed perusing the shelves, but as with everything, what was the point? Any purchase would go to waste. Such things were of no use to her. But oh, how she wished to light a few candles, fill a tub with hot water, and enjoy a bath by candlelight. She'd observed people do this on the television in the Pearce family room and had dreamed of giving it a try.

Dozens of copies of *The Women of Havencroft Manor* were stacked on a table against the wall. She squinted at a framed black-and-white photo of a mother and her teenage daughter propped against the pile. Their familiar features nagged at her memory. They reminded her of Martha, the eldest child of the Pearce family. She'd run screaming for help when…

Screams, blood, water… Lila trembled. Her heart raced. She staggered to a stop. Images flooded her brain, elusive as always, leaving the feeling of terror and sadness, but not bringing her any closer to understanding why.

She cursed under her breath. So close. Memories teased the corners of her mind, just out of reach. She struggled to grab hold of anything, but her thoughts dissolved like mist over the ocean when the sun came out.

The excited chatter of a group of women intruded on her thoughts, and she shook off the lingering effects of her waking nightmare.

A group of women huddled near the cash register. They clutched the small pieces of paper the cashier handed out. Smiles wreathed their faces. They went on so fast about costumes and dancing, Lila almost got caught up in their excitement, until she heard the word *ghost* and cringed.

She shrank back toward the stairs. What would people make of a ghost walking past them in broad daylight? She peeked out the store window to the street outside. Well, not a bright day. An overcast sky, bare tree branches bending ominously in a strong breeze. Perfect weather for a ghost sighting.

"Lila," Dean whispered behind her. "Come back up. We should probably wait until the store's closed. I'm not sure how to explain you."

She turned and raced up the stairs.

He shut the door quietly behind them. "Sorry. I didn't think…"

"That's okay. I didn't think about it, either." She laughed. "I've become accustomed to being invisible. I'm not sure why I care whether I'm spotted, but I get no pleasure at the thought of the commotion I might cause. Although the women at the counter already seemed pretty excited about something."

"I think they were picking up tickets for the Halloween ball at Havencroft Manor. It's an annual event. This year we're raising money to help with restorations, and I believe they're predicting an excellent turnout. An old friend of mine is running for city council and strong-armed me into sitting on the Historical Society board, so I'll be going. I'm actually looking forward to the party."

"You sound surprised. You haven't exactly avoided parties, as far as I could tell. I take it the lifestyle has lost some of its appeal?"

Dean leaned against the door and crossed one foot over the other. His casual stance was at odds with his wince and uncomfortable frown. "You saw all that, huh?"

She nodded. She hadn't witnessed the actual parties, but she'd observed the results. Dean had made a habit of coming home polluted with drink, falling into his bed in the early-morning hours, and generally worrying his parents half to death.

What his parents hadn't seen, that she had, was how much he regretted his actions the next day.

Not the physical effects, although those weren't easy, but the self-loathing at what he'd put everyone through.

She'd seen all this through a kind of haze. She'd been aware, but a curtain hung over her thoughts and emotions. Dimming them, putting a distance between her and what she experienced. That shadow had slowly lifted, and at times she'd desperately wished to retain the detachment she'd once felt.

"I'll admit my behavior left much to be desired. I had personal issues to work out."

"You appear to have acquitted yourself admirably in recent years." And he had. He still acted the playboy party animal, but he involved himself in a number of charitable works. He'd leveraged the financial windfall from the lawsuit his parents filed on his behalf into a fortune he used to help others.

Once he'd come of age and the trust fund his parents set up became his to do with as he pleased, he'd invested his funds and set up a number of charities to benefit victims and families of drunk-driving accidents. She didn't know the extent of his charities, but she knew he donated to juvenile diabetes research, a children's hospital, and numerous other philanthropic institutions.

Was that a blush? He truly didn't like people knowing his good deeds. She couldn't figure out why.

An adorable rosy glow spread across his freckled cheeks. She reached out to feel the warmth of his skin, but pulled back abruptly at his wince. Her heart sank.

She'd almost forgotten his eagerness to get rid of her.

Dean fought the heat spreading across his face. So she'd noticed he wasn't as bad as some people thought? He shouldn't be so ridiculously pleased at the notion. The image he presented to the world had been hard won. Even Jeremy didn't know the extent of his charitable works. Sometimes he regretted letting his brother think the worst of him.

The reputation had started honestly enough. Parties, women, and alcohol had quickly put a good-size dent in his trust fund. Thankfully he'd come to his senses before completely wiping out his accounts. He'd been stupid, but not *that* stupid.

His mother said he'd needed to get it out of his system. After being stuck either in the house or hospital for so long, when he'd finally reached a point of being able to go out relatively pain-free, he'd gone wild.

But not long after graduating grad school and watching his friends go on to start careers and families, he'd come to the realization there were better ways to spend the rest of his life and money than constant partying.

That kind of a party reputation stuck with you, though. Especially in a small town. When he'd sought to turn his life around, he'd found it almost impossible to gain anyone's trust. Volunteer organizations turned down his offer to help time and again. Until he finally opened up an organization under his mother's name and tutelage. She'd done much of the same types of volunteering he'd sought to do, and guided him along.

He ultimately came to the conclusion he didn't want his name associated with his work anyway. Too many questions, social crap, and obligations he wanted to avoid. His charities' involvement in helping kids and families similar to his naturally led people to question him about his accident. He'd gone through years of therapy and decided he'd much rather not talk about it. His past was nobody's business.

That Lila was a big part of his past made their current conversation all the more confusing.

"You know, I better go find Reina. I don't want to sit around here all day. She'll know how to get you home without freaking people out." He laughed. "Halloween is right around the corner. Cynthia over at Havenport Ghost Tours would love to have some fresh ghost sightings. Her business would go through the roof."

Her lips quirked, but fell quickly. "While that would prove highly amusing to your friend, I'm afraid I don't wish for that type of attention."

He reached toward her, but let his hand drop. He curled his fingers into a fist. "Yeah, I know. Just joking. I'll be right back." He jogged down the stairs and into Serendipity. A quick scan revealed Reina wasn't around. Lauren was still busy at the register, so he made his way through the connecting door into A New Chapter.

Jeremy squatted in one of the aisles, a pile of books at his feet, another in his hands while he read the blurb on the back.

Dean kicked him lightly in the side. "Hey, I thought you'd be long gone by now. You seen Reina?"

Jeremy slid the book back into place, then stood. "Reina left a little while ago. Christa wanted to hang around until you and Lila were ready to go. She's with Marcie, getting our tickets to the Halloween ball. Did you get yours yet?"

Shit. "Not yet. On Friday. I have to check out a tea leaf reading act we added to the party events at the last minute. They're selling tickets, too, so I figured I'd pick one up then. I'm not in the mood to stand in lines today. Did you decide on your costume yet?"

"Christa has us dressing as Elizabeth Bennett and Mr. Darcy." Jeremy rolled his eyes. "I voted for Batman and Catwoman, but got vetoed. What about you? You bringing anyone?"

"Going stag. Didn't want to deal with some cutesy matching shit." He grinned. "You know, like Mr. Darcy and Elizabeth Bennett."

Jeremy swung at his arm, but he dodged, laughing.

"Seriously, though. If you have any ideas for a costume, I'm all ears."

"Ooh, really? I have the perfect thing." Christa stopped at Jeremy's side and locked her arm around his waist. He bent toward her for a quick peck on the lips.

Dean winced. He didn't want to imagine what Christa would pick for him, and now he'd be obligated to go as whatever she suggested. "Something decent, please. Nothing humiliating, okay?"

"Don't you worry. You'll love it."

He raised his brows and waited. And waited. "Going to give me a clue here?"

She shook her head. "Nope. I think a surprise will be more fun."

Now he *knew* he was in trouble. He sighed. "Fine. But I'll need it by eleven a.m. Sunday. I have to get to the manor early. The board's supposed to oversee setup and handle publicity with the press." Actually, it was a relief to have that taken care of for him. He had absolutely no desire to go shopping for a decent costume. Who had the time? Figuring out what to do about Lila took priority. How to help her. "Lila's upstairs still. Do you have any idea how to get her back to my place?"

"Reina gave me some ideas. Let's go." She slipped out of Jeremy's embrace and headed over to Serendipity.

"I'll just buy these and meet you up there in a few. Give me a hand?"

Dean helped Jeremy transfer his stack of books to the register, then dashed after Christa. He took the stairs two at a time, catching up just as she opened the door.

Lila swung around. "I think I can get back on my own."

Christa went right in to stand by Lila. He stopped on the other side of the table. Getting too close wasn't a good idea. He'd be tempted to reach out to her, a stupid move. "How? What happened? Did Reina come up?" She must have slipped by him while he spoke with Jeremy in the bookstore.

But Lila shook her head. "No. I haven't seen Reina. It's just—" She shrugged. "I don't know how to explain, but I feel like I'm being pulled back to the house. It's taking a lot of concentration to keep myself here."

Christa closed her eyes and tilted her head. "The power of the séance is waning. The echoes of our combined power remain, but much fainter than when I went downstairs an hour ago." Her eyes popped open. "Your essence must be tied to something in the house." She lowered her voice and asked quietly, "Is that where you died, Lila?"

Lila's face fell. She frowned, her lip trembling until she caught it between her teeth. "I don't remember. I—I think so."

"We really need to dig into our family records. There'd have to be something there if you died at the house. I'm sure of it. Stop fighting to stay here. Go home. I'll meet you there."

Lila nodded. She closed her eyes. Less than a second later she was gone. Much as she'd done years ago. Here one minute. Gone the next. Would he be able to see her when he got home?

"Holy shit," Jeremy whispered from the doorway.

Guess his brother was finally a believer.

After the sickening feeling in her stomach subsided, Lila opened her eyes. The Goddess fountain loomed above her. She shivered. Something about the statue made her uneasy, but the cause eluded her.

The statue itself was beautiful. The Goddess's face kind. She remembered liking the fountain once upon a time. She and the Pearce kids would run around in the garden, and when the heat became too much, they'd sit on the fountain's edge and let the chilled water flow over their feet to cool them off.

Why could she remember that, but not what happened the day she died? Shouldn't such an insignificant memory pale in comparison to the trauma of her death?

Trauma. Was that the key? She was so traumatized by whatever had happened her mind blocked all memory of the event. She supposed that made sense. For a long time, she hadn't wanted to remember. But now she did. Shouldn't she be able to unlock those memories whenever she wanted?

She supposed life didn't necessarily work the way one planned.

Neither did death.

She turned her back on the fountain and headed into the house. Dean had mentioned the files were tucked away in the attic. She'd go find them so he could get right to searching through them when he got home.

She had no idea how long she'd taken to get home. The passage of time was so hard to follow. Best guess was her travels had taken less than five minutes. The house wasn't too far from the center of town, so Dean should arrive any moment.

Her corner of the attic had been fixed up into a room separate from the rest. She had her little bed, a set of drawers, and a nice window overlooking the gardens in the backyard. On a warm spring day, the smell of honeysuckle pervaded her small space. Dormant now, the gardener had cut back the plants to grow once again in the spring. The fragrant vine had long since taken over the evergreen bushes Lady Pearce had originally planted in the spot below Lila's window.

The rest of the attic was a mess of worn-down toys, mismatched furniture, and holiday decorations. She found the clutter comforting and irritating at the same time. That cradle against the far wall? She'd spent hours singing colicky baby Bernard Pearce back to bed when his nursemaid needed to get her own rest.

The hutch in the corner with the broken drawer? Martha Pearce had tried to blame Lila, when she was the one who used the drawer as a stepping stool, breaking it in her attempt to reach the cookie jar Lady Pearce had tucked up high to keep out of the kids' reach. But Lady Pearce knew her kids well and had made sure Martha not only confessed, but apologized to Lila as well.

Lady Pearce had been a kind, compassionate woman with little concern for society's rules and class distinctions. She made sure her kids were raised to have the same beliefs. Martha, though, had made a habit of lording her position over Lila at every opportunity. She was the only member of the Pearce family that had never been Lila's friend.

Lila drifted through the furniture, searching for the files Dean mentioned. She came across a dust-covered pile of boxes, each one labeled with a name. Martha, Bernard, Sally, and… She peered closer at the box at the bottom corner. The dust was so thick across the label, she could barely make out the name. Thomas.

She reared back. Thomas.

Images assaulted her brain. A huge shadow. The sun in her eyes. Screaming. The Goddess's kind smile.

Her stomach dropped with the weightless, nauseating distortion of traveling. She squeezed her eyes shut until the motion ceased. The sound of rushing water was the first clue as to where she'd landed. She peeked through slitted lids to confirm her suspicion. The Goddess loomed directly above her. Lila stood, brushing her clothing back into order.

The scrunch of tires on gravel heralded Dean's arrival home. "Hey. Waiting for me?" The car door slammed.

She couldn't force her gaze away from the Goddess. Memories rushed back. "Dean?" Her voice shook. She squatted near the edge, close to the wave that rolled over the Goddess's feet. A shimmer of warmth slid across her back.

"Are you okay?" Dean knelt less than a foot away.

"I remember." She brought her gaze down to the statue's knee. Her hand passed right through the wave and up the leg. She knew how it would feel. Sharp and rough. She got as close as possible. Squinted at the edges and tried to see into the cracks between. They were darkened with age. Or more? "I remember how I died."

"You died near the fountain?"

His calm voice steadied her. She pointed at a dark spot on the knee. "Right there. That's where my head hit."

"Did you trip?"

She shook her head. "No." She rubbed at her temple. "There was a man. I don't really know what he wanted. He grabbed Thomas…"

"Who was Thomas?"

"My friend. He was my age. The second-eldest Pearce child, but the first son. Maybe that's why the man came after him? I remember another boy had been kidnapped around that time. Lady Pearce had warned us not to leave the grounds." She shivered. "I was so frightened."

"How awful. You know, this actually sounds familiar. I think I may have heard the story. Your Thomas must have been my great-great-great-grandfather."

"No." She shook her head. "How could that be? All the blood. The screaming. I don't think Thomas could have survived."

"He must have. My great-great-great-grandfather was kidnapped. My mom told me. The whole town turned out to find him. They were enraged because another child died…" He trailed off, a stunned expression on his face. "Shit. I never put two and two together. My mom never said the child died here." He jabbed his index finger toward the ground. "I always thought the dead girl was another kid he'd kidnapped."

"Thomas survived?" A weight she hadn't recognized lifted off her chest. "I thought…"

"I'm so sorry." Dean paused, his expression serious. "Do you think that's why you stayed?"

"I didn't even remember him until now." Why hadn't she remembered? Was that the trauma she'd blocked? Not her death, but his?

"I guess I blocked it out?"

Dean hated the trembling in Lila's voice. "I wouldn't be surprised." He inched closer. He didn't want to make her go through it again, but knowing the whole story might be the only way to figure out how to help her. "Can you tell me the rest of what happened?"

He fought against the feeling he didn't really want to know. They were one step closer to figuring out this whole mess, and therefore one step closer to finding a way for Lila to move on. But did he really want her to?

What he wanted didn't matter in the end. What mattered was Lila's happiness. He couldn't be so selfish that he'd keep her here at her expense. Even though a part of him definitely wished he was that guy, he wasn't.

He cursed himself for even thinking it as the tears dripped down her cheeks. What good was he? He couldn't even dry her tears or offer a shoulder to lean on. He placed his hand over where hers rested on the fountain's edge. He expected the icy shock of deep, penetrating cold, but a spark of warmth surprised him.

She gasped. Her head lifted, her eyes wide.

The pain in those emerald-green depths twisted his heart into a knot. Whatever it took, this couldn't continue.

"It's okay. Tell me what happened."

He strained to hear, her words coming out disjointed, with gasps and remembered fear choking her voice.

"We were playing around the fountain when this man appeared out of nowhere. He grabbed Thomas. Thomas screamed, and Martha raced to the house, yelling for help. I remember thinking that was my job. To help the younger ones. And besides, he was my friend."

"What did you do?"

"I jumped on the bad man's back."

Dean laughed. He could imagine the girl she'd once been doing something so brave. Her crazy spirit had been exactly what he'd needed as he lay in bed, frustrated at every turn by the limitations of his broken body. "You must have given the kidnapper one hell of a shock."

She grinned, and the sight lifted his mood.

"Indeed, I did." The grin died. "What little good that did. He yelled and reared back. Then tossed me off his back like I was light as a feather. I fell against the fountain, hit my head, and everything went black. The next thing I remember was hearing your cries."

"Me?" He didn't know what to make of that. Why would his pain wake her up from a century-long sleep? "But you'd been singing to the Pearce family babies for almost a hundred years. You don't remember?"

"No." She turned her hand over.

He spread his fingers, and she curled hers up. Where their fingers intertwined, warmth returned. The sensation was so close to holding hands, he almost wept with longing. He cleared his throat. "From what I remember of my mom's story, the kidnapper got away with Thomas. I don't understand how. With you fighting him, Thomas and Martha both screaming their heads off, where the hell were all the adults?"

"Life was different back then. Kids grew up a lot quicker." She stared at the front door. "I was nine years old, but I already helped my mother. The Pearces had money, so their kids were pampered more than most, but even so, they took care of themselves at a young age. And we had wandered all the way to the fountain. They wouldn't have been able to hear us up at the house."

Aphrodite loomed over him. His gaze darted between her and the front door, not twenty feet away.

She smiled. "The fountain resided in the rose garden in those days."

"Rose garden?" He had a flowerbed out back with maybe half a dozen rosebushes his mother had tended lovingly for years and a nice, long stretch of grass where their old swing set used to be, but there'd never been another garden, that he was aware of.

"You don't own the property anymore. The playground is there now."

"Huh. I always assumed he returned the statue to its original position."

"Returned?"

"Dad bought the fountain for Mom years ago. It was something of a private joke between them, but I remember he said he wanted to return the statue where it belonged. I always assumed that meant it used to be right here." He pointed to the ground. "I guess he meant that the family owned it again. I know he got it cheap, since the town was getting rid of it."

"Why? The fountain is so beautiful. I've always loved her."

"When the town added the playground to that little park, some people deemed the fountain inappropriate." He studied the twelve-foot half-naked woman. Couldn't blame them, really. Jeremy and Theresa used to bitch every time they had friends over. Dean hadn't had to worry. He'd had few friends, other than Lila. "They were going to trash her."

Her hand flew to her mouth to cover a gasp. "Thank goodness they did no such thing. The Goddess does not take lightly to her image being despoiled in such a manner."

"What?" He'd never heard her spout any nonsense like this before. "I never knew you were such a big believer in Aphrodite."

Lila shushed him, then pointed at the figure. "That is the Goddess, not Aphrodite."

"And you believe in this goddess?" Funny they'd never discussed their beliefs before. They'd talked about everything else, but never that. He tried to remember if the subject had ever come up, but couldn't put his finger on anything other than a vague sense she avoided the subject, or stated how she attended church with the family.

"Disbelief would be unreasonable given my connection to her."

He raised his brows and waited for an explanation for that gem.

She kept her silence, running her hand along the base of the fountain over a smooth patch he'd never noticed before.

He squinted in an attempt to decipher the faint letters she traced with her fingers.

A sacrifice for love was made,
Such a spirit cannot fade.
But life will not be reached alone
And a limit on time is set in stone.
From the moment when love is sought,
Until the time when life means naught.
Freely given, hard won, hard fought,
True love's heart cannot be bought.

For one who's worthy of that bond,
The Goddess knows where love is found
This proof required for those so bound.

A test of character, with honor met
A loyal heart, in love is set.
Facing fears brings vast reward,
But seek them not on own accord.
When love is true, the heart is bold,
Sacrifice all to have and hold.

Then one last test, to see in kind,
The depth of love we hope to find.

From twelve 'til twelve, all must wait,
Time will soon decide their fate.
Will love be found, and new life made?
Or with heart untrue, endless spirit fade?
The stroke of midnight will come and go,
Only then can you truly know.

"I never saw this before."

She turned her huge eyes toward him. "That's because it wasn't here. At least not in its entirety." Her voice trembled.

"Bull. Mom must have had the fountain cleaned when they sold me the place, or something." He traced the faded letters of the second verse. "Look at this. The lettering's worn. It's obviously old. We just never noticed." She could have seen that when she was a kid, before she died.

He bent closer. "What's this supposed to mean? 'From the moment when love is sought, until the time when life means naught.' What kind of nonsense is this?"

"The Goddess is guiding us," Lila whispered in a reverent tone.

He snorted. "A GPS would have been more helpful."

There was more fire in her glare than water in the fountain. "That the Goddess has given us direction at all should be appreciated. The onus is on us to figure out the way to follow her direction."

He sighed. "Fine." He checked his watch. Seven o'clock. Nothing could be done tonight. Anyplace useful would be closed. "I'll head over to the library in the morning and see what I can find out about the fountain. Maybe there's a clue in its history." Did he really believe a centuries-old fountain contained a message for him, personally?

Then again, here he sat in his driveway, talking to a ghost. Words appearing on a fountain could be considered fairly tame by comparison.

Chapter Five

The next day, Lila sat in the rain, studying the Goddess's poem. The weather didn't bother her, except she wished she could feel the cold sting of the drops, or the exhilaration of running through a storm to reach the warm comfort of a freshly laid fire inside.

She would never experience such sensations again. The loss made her want to weep.

Tires splashed through a puddle in the drive. She peered through the rain at an unfamiliar vehicle. Not Dean's low-slung sports car. The one she'd watched longingly as Dean flew out of the drive this morning on his way to the library. She'd never been in anything faster than a horse-drawn carriage and envied the modern-day cars whizzing by from her lonely attic room.

The door swung wide and a black umbrella popped open, hiding the person exiting the car. Thunder rumbled in the distance. Reina held the umbrella high and started forward.

Lila popped up and gestured toward the house. "Go on in; you're getting drenched," she yelled. "I believe Mrs. Pearce left a key under the flowerpot to the right of the door."

Reina tilted the pot and held up the key in triumph.

Lila waited for her to open the door rather than pass ahead of her. Floating through solid objects always felt like a parlor trick.

Reina flicked the umbrella a few times, sending water droplets everywhere, some sailing right through Lila. Reina gasped. "Sorry, Sugar. I wasn't thinking."

Lila grinned. "That's perfectly all right." She held her skirts out wide. "See, not even damp."

"And your hair looks perfect, too." Reina flipped hers, which had begun to curl at the ends. "By the time this dries, a rats' nest of epic proportions will have taken over if I don't do something soon." She dug into the vast cavern of her purse and hauled out a sparkly purple brush. She used the mirror by the door and fiddled with her hair until dropping the brush back into her bag with a satisfied grin. "There. That should do it." She smiled, her teeth dazzlingly white in the dim light of the foyer.

Lila pressed her lips together. She had no idea the state of her teeth, except that running her tongue along the edge didn't reveal any major flaws.

Reina was something of a force of nature, commanding attention the way Lila avoided it. Tight jeans, high-heeled boots, and a low-cut top showed off her stunning figure. Lila resisted the urge to unbutton her top an inch or two. Nothing could make her clothing flatter her figure in the slightest.

Comparing herself to Reina served no purpose. Neither did jealousy. If she couldn't be the one in Dean's life, she supposed a kind, intelligent woman like Reina might be just what he needed. Had he asked her to meet him here?

"I'm afraid Dean is in town at the library at the moment. I'm not entirely sure how long he'll be." She pointed toward the kitchen at the rear of the house. "Would you care for something to drink?"

"A drink would be great, Sugar. Thanks a bunch."

They kept their silence until they reached the kitchen. "You'll have to help yourself." Lila swiped at the refrigerator door, and her hand passed right through.

Reina grabbed a bottle of seltzer and hopped onto a chair at the island. "I saw Dean pull into the library earlier. I figured you might enjoy some company while he's out."

A pleasant lightness filled her chest. "Oh. How thoughtful." She'd never had someone visit her before. It was almost like having a friend.

"Christa sent an email about the Goddess fountain and the poem. I'm fascinated."

"The meaning is difficult to understand." She'd spent all morning trying, sure it held the key to her dilemma.

"Well, Sugar, I've been up half the night going over it and think I have a good idea."

"You figured out the meaning?"

Reina lowered her head, studying her fingernails as a rosy blush covered her cheeks. She flipped back her hair, then brought her gaze up to Lila. "Actually, that took a twelve-year-old."

Lila wrinkled her brow. "A twelve-year-old figured out the Goddess's message?"

Reina laughed. "Hard to believe, right? I've told Mia, my daughter, all about you. She's hooked on your story, by the way. So anyway, I spent half the night trying to figure out what that damn poem could mean, and she takes one look this morning while I was making her breakfast and asks me whether I thought Dean could actually bring you back to life."

Shock swept through Lila. "Back to life?"

Reina beamed. "Yes. And I'm convinced she's right. I mean, the thought never even occurred to me. Impossible, right? But once Mia brought it up, I realized it fits." She pulled a crumpled piece of paper out of her purse. Her lips moved, and one finger slid down the page. "Here." She jabbed at the top of the paper and held it out for Lila. "'Sacrifice for love…Spirit will not fade…But *life* cannot be reached alone.' See? You sacrificed yourself. Your spirit's still here…you haven't faded. And then this line about life." Her voice rang with excitement.

Could this be true? Could she get her life back? Her gaze traveled down the page. One line caught her attention. Sacrifice all… She shook her head. "No."

Reina stared.

"That line." She pointed.

Reina glanced at the paper. The color drained from her face. "You're thinking it's referring to Dean. The one 'who's worthy'?"

At Lila's nod, Reina continued. "I'm sure it's not what you're thinking."

She tilted her head and raised her eyebrows. "Really? What else could 'sacrifice all' mean?" He would try, she knew it. She couldn't let him.

"The poem also says 'to have and hold.' He'd have to be alive for that, Sugar."

"Does he? Or does it mean he'd join me in the afterlife?" She shook her head. "I can't allow him to take that risk. I *won't*." She put her hand on top of Reina's where she clutched the paper, kept steady contact even when Reina flinched, knowing the cold would seep through the other woman's fingers. "Promise me, Reina. Promise you won't tell him what we think this means."

"Don't you think he'll figure this out on his own? I don't know him all that well, but Christa's told me a bit. He's scary smart, apparently. He'll figure it out."

She shook her head. "No. The idea's too impossible. Just like you, the idea may not occur to him. Promise me." She stared Reina down.

After almost a full minute, Reina dropped her gaze. "Fine."

Dean slammed *Havenport: A History* shut, then leaned back in his chair, stretching his arms high above his head. He'd been at it for hours. His back ached, his stomach rumbled, and the scratchiness in his throat had him dreaming of a cool glass of water.

Wilma had already come around twice to warn him the library closed in half an hour. He'd had enough of Havenport history for the day, anyway.

He gathered his pile and returned the books to their proper spots on the shelves. His mom and Wilma were good friends. He'd get an earful if he left a stack of books for the librarian to clean up right before closing. He shrugged into his overcoat, grabbed his notebook and pile of photocopies, then waved good-bye before heading out.

He made his way around the town square to walk along Water Street. Lights lit up the gazebo, pumpkins and gourds scattered along the base amid bales of hay, and an old couple huddled on the top step, looking out over the water.

He had to meet Jeremy at Royce Tavern at five thirty, then stop in to see that tea leaf lady at seven, before heading home to go over his research with Lila.

The rain had let up while he did his reading, but dark-gray clouds hung over the town. Festive lights kept the night at bay. Banners with the town crest hung on all the streetlamps, proclaiming the season. Large clay pots filled with fall flowers were placed strategically along the sidewalk. He kicked a pebble, sending it skipping down the sidewalk, and lost track when it went into the street.

The outside seating at Royce Tavern was deserted, but a few brave souls crowded around the bar on the back deck. Their voices drifted over the music and the crashing of the waves. He did a quick scan to make sure Jeremy hadn't taken a spot outside, then went back around to enter through the front.

He spotted Jeremy almost right away. Surprise, surprise, he was making out with Christa at a table in the corner. Dean hesitated.

Jeremy threw his head back and laughed at something Christa said.

He should turn around. He'd give Jeremy a call later to explain.

Dean wouldn't be missed. He started to turn when Christa raised a hand in greeting. "Dean!"

Shit, he should have moved faster. She didn't yell across the crowded restaurant, but she'd obviously seen him. No help for it.

He weaved his way through the tables and slid into a seat next to his brother. The flower centerpiece he was accustomed to had been replaced with a black, pierced metal candleholder that cast ghostly shadows across the place settings. Fake spiderwebs stretched across each corner of the ceiling with black, orange, or purple spiders clinging to them. Witches of all types were tucked into every nook and cranny.

Someone had gone overboard on the Halloween decorations.

Liz, the part-time waitress—sometimes he wondered if there was a business in Havenport where Liz *didn't* work— appeared at his side almost immediately. "What can I get ya?"

"I'll have the IPA." He raised a brow at Jeremy and Christa. "You order yet?"

Christa shook her head. "No, we waited for you, but I'm ready."

They placed their orders, and Liz sauntered off.

"How'd it go at the library? Figure out what that poem means?" Jeremy asked.

Dean sighed. He didn't want to get his hopes up, but… "You're gonna think I'm nuts—"

"Already do." Jeremy grinned.

Christa smacked him in the shoulder. "Be nice."

He smirked while Jeremy rubbed his arm with a pout on his face. Dean didn't always appreciate Jeremy and Christa's lovefest, but he certainly loved it when she smacked his older brother into submission.

"So? What did you find out?" Christa asked.

"I think there's a way to bring Lila back to life." He let that bomb hang and waited for their reactions.

Liz came to their rescue.

Dean took a deep draft of his IPA while the food was placed before them. His mouth watered at the porterhouse on his plate. He'd barely eaten a thing all day, just grabbed a snack from the vending machine at the library around one. "Damn, I'm starving. Looks great, thanks."

Liz nodded and took off. Christa frowned at the napkin she placed in her lap, and Jeremy stared at him like he'd grown another head.

"While I'm enjoying the dumbfounded looks on your faces…" He made a face of his own, mocking Jeremy's tight lips and furrowed brow. "I want to hear what you think."

"I'd like to believe it's possible, but…" Jeremy sent Christa a pleading glance. "What do you think?"

She fiddled with her knife, gazing into the distance, then sighed. "I don't like to rule anything out. We've had some wild things happen in this town." She nodded toward the bar where the owner, Adam Royce, laughed with a customer while serving a pint. "By all rights, Adam shouldn't be here. I mean, he was born over two centuries ago."

He held out a hand to stop her rambling. "Wait. What?" Two hundred years? Now Christa had gone over the edge. This made no sense.

"It's a long story, but yes, Adam was born in the late seventeen hundreds. So was Jane and her brother, Bastian, for that matter. None of this is ringing any bells? I thought you knew." She shrugged. "You remember the spell book?" At his nod, she continued. "If you ever doubted its power, don't. Jane read one of the spells a few years ago, and Adam traveled through time and showed up in her bathroom."

His mind boggled at the thought. "Okay. Another time you're going to have to tell me that whole story. Not now, though." Excitement stirred in his chest. "If time travel is possible, why can't I bring a ghost back to life?"

"Um, she doesn't have a body?" Jeremy said.

Dean waved that concern away. "She has a body, she's just not entirely solid at the moment. And she's heating up. That has to mean something."

"What do you mean, heating up?" Jeremy pushed his plate aside and leaned his elbows on the table.

"I've always avoided touching her. Contact's like submerging in ice water." He shivered at the memory. "But I touched her the other day and she was warm." He studied his hand, remembering how the warmth had seeped into him. "It was almost like we held hands." He curled his hand into a fist. "We're close. We just have to figure out the tests."

"Tests? What tests?" Christa asked.

He slid copies of the poem to each of them. "Read it again. A test of courage, a loyal heart, facing fears… Everything I have to do is listed right there." He slumped back in his chair. "I just don't know how."

Lila paced the house, singing a folk song her mother used to hum while she worked, and going over everything Reina had told her. Shortly after promising not to share her theory with Dean, Reina had run off, claiming she had to cram for an exam before she picked her daughter up from school at three thirty. Reina was working on her master's degree in business administration at Havenport College during the day while her daughter was in school.

Reina's theory made sense. The more Lila thought, the more she accepted the truth of the poem. She'd be thrilled, if not for the line about sacrificing all. *All* must mean Dean's life. And what good would that do anyone? Lila had no wish to regain her life at the expense of his.

Keys rattled in the front door. The grandfather clock showed five after seven. She hadn't expected him back for another hour, at least. She nibbled on her bottom lip and twisted her hands together, eager to know whether Dean had come to the same conclusion as Reina. If he'd figured it out on his own, how was she going to dissuade him from attempting to rescue her?

Dean's face lit. "Hey!" He dumped a notebook and a stack of paper on the catch-all table by the door. "I've got some great news." He paused in the act of removing his coat. "What's wrong?"

"Nothing. I—I'm just surprised you're home so early. I thought you had to meet with someone at seven. Did you forget?"

He must have accepted her answer because he finished taking off his jacket and threw it on the rack by the door. "No. I didn't forget. I mentioned my plans to Christa, and she insisted on meeting the woman for me. She seemed pretty excited about getting her tea leaves read. Anyway, I texted the change of plans to Marta and came home. Everything worked out."

"Oh."

He held his hand out to her, and without thinking she took it.

She nearly jumped from surprise when their hands actually connected. "What? How?"

Dean smiled as he examined their intertwined fingers. "I wondered if this would happen."

Tears clouded her vision. Warmth spread from her fingers to her chest. Her hand fit perfectly in his. He traced a small scar on her thumb, sending delightful tingles up her arm.

"I noticed this yesterday. First, there was that spark right after the séance, and then by the fountain you were even warmer, and I swear I felt the weight of your hand in mine." He brought her hand up to his mouth and placed the gentlest of kisses on her knuckle.

Amazingly, she kept to her feet, even though she'd lost all strength in her legs. She closed her eyes, savoring the moment. The heat of his breath, the softness of his lips. Oh, that living people experienced such sensations whenever they wished. She hadn't been touched in so long she barely remembered the sensation. She doubted she'd ever felt anything quite so wonderful.

"Come on." He tugged gently, pulling her after him into his office, grabbing his paperwork on the way. They settled side by side on a love seat tucked into a corner of the room facing a gas fireplace. He flicked the switch and the fire turned on.

His office was the only room in the house he'd taken the time to completely move into. While having the rest of the house in chaos didn't bother him, he preferred his work space nice and neat.

He tucked her into his side, thighs pressed together, his arm along the back of the sofa grazing her shoulders. The touch was tenuous at best. She closed her fingers too tight and they slipped through his, her body giving only a token resistance.

"You're becoming more solid day to day. Once the prophecy from the fountain is complete, you'll be one hundred percent."

She tore her gaze away from the sight of their legs so close together and met the excitement in his gaze. "No. We can't."

He reared back, his hand braced against the back of the couch rather than resting against her. "What?" He shook his head and smiled, relaxing against her once more. "Sorry, I forgot to tell you what I figured out today." He rifled through his papers until he plucked one out from the middle of the pile. "Here. This is the poem."

His left-handed scrawl littered the page. After the accident, with his right hand broken too severely to hold a pen for over a year, he'd been forced to write with his left. He now wrote with either, but tended to switch to his left whenever he had to write a lot. His right ached with too much stress.

"I discussed this with Jeremy and Christa over dinner and they think I'm on the right track." He held the paper up so she could view it with ease. "I think we activated, for lack of a better word, the Goddess's spell when we held the séance. With all those witches in one place, that séance had some punch."

She'd felt the coven's power filling the séance room. "But I thought Christa said the power of the séance had faded?"

"She thought so, but now she thinks the power settled into you and is slowly bringing you back to life. It's all part of the Goddess's poem." He rubbed the back of his neck, then shifted in his seat to face her directly. "I don't want to get your hopes up, but I think there's a way to bring you back. For real."

She missed his warmth immediately. Or did the chill that settled over her have more to do with the poem? She should have known Dean would figure it out. "And the consequences? I'm not worth it. I won't allow you to risk yourself for me."

"Not worth it?" he asked, his voice harsh, incredulous. A muscle ticked in his jaw. His eyes narrowed. "How can you say that? Would you rather cease to exist altogether? Fade away?" He leaned forward, elbows on knees, his fingers clasped so tight they turned red. "This is a chance for you to live. To do those things you've always wanted to do." He poked his chest. "To be with me. We could finally be together. You don't think that's worth whatever it takes?"

She cowered into her corner of the couch. Of course she wanted all those things. How could he question her desire for life?

No. She straightened her spine. He could be angry. Hell, he'd been angry at her for the past decade without ever hearing her side of the story. After everything she'd done for him. He didn't have to like what she had to say, but she refused to hide or cower. He couldn't hear her last time, but by the Goddess, he would hear her now.

"All I've ever wanted was your happiness. Haven't I proved that to you these past ten years? And now you think I would be so selfish as to allow you to risk your life for mine?"

He sprang off the sofa, towered over her even though she kept her spine stiff and her chin tilted to keep his gaze. "My happiness? Leaving me with no word, no idea where you'd gone. That was for my happiness?"

"Yes." She'd never told him about her conversation

with his mother. She wasn't about to do so now. But she had to make him understand. "You were giving up everything for a ghost." Her voice cracked on *ghost*. She cleared her throat and continued. "You were alive and healthy. You got accepted at every college to which you applied. You had dozens of opportunities, but you elected to throw them all away in order to stay home with me. I couldn't let you. Can't you see? Would you have done any less for me?"

He paced the length of his office. The muscles in his jaw twitched. When he finally stopped before her, his voice was thick. "I guess not. So how do you expect me to do any less now?"

"Dammit!" Dean slammed his door shut, then leaned against it. He was so fucking tired. He strode into his master bath and grabbed a bottle of ibuprofen from the medicine cabinet. His damn arm hurt like a vise was clamped on to it. He downed the pills with a cup of water, hoping to dull the pain. The throbbing wouldn't subside completely until he resolved this mess with Lila. Stress always kicked his aches and pains up a notch.

And his stress levels were through the roof lately.

He wanted to strangle Lila. What the hell was she thinking? Leaving him for his own good? What bullshit. As if she had any right to make that decision for him. Who did she think she was, his mom?

How did she even know he'd applied to college, let alone got in to some of the best? In fact, he'd only just told his parents his intention to go to college in Havenport when Lila had suddenly disappeared. His mom had sent him on errands and when he got back…

The light clicked on in his head. Mom.

He snatched his cell out of his pocket and speed-dialed her number.

"Dean," she answered, her voice cheery. "I wasn't expecting your call. Everything okay?"

"No." He hesitated. He'd been pretty pissed when he dialed, but now that his mom was actually on the phone…

Her voice rose an octave. "What's wrong? Are you okay? Theresa? Jeremy? Who's hurt?"

His dad echoed her questions in the background.

"No one's hurt. Sorry. Didn't mean to freak you out."

She repeated what he said, then came back on the line. "You scared me half to death. So what's wrong? You don't sound like your usual self."

"Lila's back."

Silence.

"Did you hear me?"

"Yes, but I'm not sure how to respond." She took a deep breath, audible over the phone. "I thought she may be, but honestly, I was hoping she wasn't."

The knot lodged in his stomach tightened. "Please tell me you had nothing to do with Lila disappearing on me ten years ago."

He didn't have to be a psychic to know the answer as the silence stretched.

"Dammit, Mom. What the hell did you say to her?"

"Don't take that tone with your mother."

"Dad?"

"You're on speaker. Now apologize to your mother."

Great, just what he needed. He sighed. "Sorry, Mom." Two seconds with his parents and he was a teenager getting his ass handed to him for sassing his mom. "So are you going to tell me what you said to her?"

"Go ahead, Sylvie. He has a right to know."

"I sent you into town to run some errands for me, and once you were gone, I simply asked her to leave. Felt like a fool, too. Until that day, I didn't one hundred percent believe she was real."

"How could you not? I know you've heard her singing, seen her move things—"

"But she never actually showed herself to me. You remember how shy she was."

Yes, he'd never understood, but Lila had always shied away from appearing before his family. She'd play with them—moving things around, singing loud enough to be heard, but not enough to distinguish the song—but she hadn't let them see her.

"So you were in town, and I made a fool of myself pleading with your ghostly girlfriend to leave you alone."

"How could you? I loved her. She left, and it was like I had my heart torn out."

The quiet sniffs and gulps of his mom's sobs came clearly through the line. His dad spoke. "Your mother was only looking out for you. You were letting your life pass you by to stay at home with a ghost. Were we supposed to sit back and let that happen?"

"My life was fine. I—"

"Bullshit," Dad interrupted. "You had already passed up a chance to spend a summer in France. You got accepted to a dozen colleges—Ivy League schools, no less—and you told us that morning you planned to stay home and attend Havenport College."

"It's a good school." Defensive much? He sounded like a pouty teenager.

"Sure. Havenport's a fine school. But compared to the others you'd gotten into, it's nothing."

"That was my choice. It's my life."

"And we're your parents," Mom broke in. "You were

throwing away excellent opportunities. Letting your life pass you by to stay at home. All because of *her*."

The bitterness in his mom's voice was impossible to miss. His anger deflated. Staying angry at her had always been impossible. Not after everything she'd done for him after his accident. She'd all but given up her life to take care of him.

"She nearly scared the life out of me when she *poofed* into view right before my eyes."

Wait, what? "She showed herself to you? You never told me."

"Yes, well... Anyway, we talked for quite a while. Broke my heart to ask so much of her, but I had no choice. Once I laid out the acceptance letters for all the schools that wanted you, she came to the same conclusion I had."

"Which was?"

"That for as long as Lila was around, you would never leave Havenport."

He couldn't argue. He'd been fully prepared to live the rest of his life right here. With her. "Well, your plan worked out great. I escaped from Havenport. Oh, wait. Where exactly am I calling you from?"

"Sure, you came back," his dad piped in. "But you got out into the world. Got your degree. Traveled with your job. Dated *living* women. You saw what life could offer."

"You needed to get out into the world," his mom said. "Your accident trapped you in that house for too many years growing up. Keeping you here was unfair. Lila agreed. We all just wanted what was best for you."

Would anyone ever let him decide what was best for himself?

Chapter Six

Lila stroked the soft fabric of the dress Christa had handed her. She loved the delicate pale-blue color. She'd gotten sick of her black-and-white servant's attire decades ago. If miracles happened and the Goddess's poem came true, she'd never go without color ever again. "I've never worn anything so lovely. I can't possibly borrow it."

"I insist." Christa studied her with a practiced eye. "Actually, Marta and my tea leaves insisted."

"I beg your pardon?"

"Remember that woman I interviewed for Dean? The tea-reading act for the Halloween ball tomorrow night?"

Lila nodded.

"She was the real deal. I could sense her power from out on the sidewalk. I'm not sure if she realizes it, though." She shrugged. "Anyway, my leaves said I planned to wear the wrong costume. That this dress"—she flicked the long, flowing skirt—"was meant for another." She grabbed a red outfit off the bed and stepped behind a changing screen.

"What makes you so sure that other is me?" She swayed side to side. The dress flowed around her legs. The style was something her grandmother might have worn in

London, before the family lost its fortune and moved to America. Empire waist; short, puffy sleeves; light, delicate color. She really wanted to wear the beautiful costume. She turned toward the mirror.

Disappointment hit her with a pang. The dress floated on its own. Her body had gained substance, yet she still lacked a reflection. Cameras couldn't capture her image, either, showing only as a hazy distortion. She may have gained some aspects of a living woman, but she remained a ghost.

She laid the dress on the foot of the bed in the guest room where Christa had dragged her over an hour ago. Dean had gone into town to pick up a few last-minute items for the big party. She hated seeing him leave, afraid of what the Goddess had in store for him as a test of his worthiness.

She snorted. As if he needed to prove anything. She wasn't a prize to be won, but if she were, he'd long ago hit the bull's-eye.

"Of course she meant you. Who else?" Christa came out from behind the screen, hands at her back, holding a gorgeous red gown in place. "Give me a hand with the zipper, if you can."

Lila darted around Christa, and with a quick tug on the zipper, Christa was all set.

"There." Christa spun around, almost knocking Lila over with the wide, caged hips of the eighteenth-century-style gown. "Oops, sorry." She swept her hands wide. "What do you think?"

"One look at that neckline and your fiancé is unlikely to let you leave the house."

Christa laughed. "Good. Exactly what I was going for. He thinks I'll be dressed as a conservative army nurse, so this should come as quite a shock." She giggled, admired herself in the mirror for a minute, and, with a satisfied nod, returned to the changing screen. She came out a minute later and picked up the blue Regency-style ball gown. "Your turn."

To Lila's delight, the gown fit perfectly. Nothing like Christa's deeply plunging, tight-fitting bodice, the light-blue material revealed a moderate amount of cleavage, but covered enough to keep Lila's modesty intact. The skirt flowed around her, whisper-soft against her ankles. The toes of her delicate heels peeked out from under the hem.

Christa clapped. "Beautiful. Oh, I wish you could see yourself." She made a few adjustments and held out a pair of long, white gloves. "Magick is a wondrous thing. Here you are a ghost, but the Goddess has seen fit to return you to a physical form."

"Not entirely." She concentrated and her hand passed through the glove.

"It's getting better, though. Before long you'll be completely restored, and you and Dean will live happily ever after."

"Do you think so?" She wished she could be so sure. She glanced at the clock. Dean should have been home. Had one of the Goddess's challenges proved too much? "Shouldn't he be home by now?"

Christa gripped her shoulder with a reassuring squeeze. "Don't worry so much. He hasn't been gone all that long."

"What if he met with one of the Goddess's challenges? What if he's hurt?"

"He'll be fine. The Goddess will want him to succeed. And Dean is a capable guy. More than up to any challenge set in his way. Especially if it means he'll be with you when he wins." They hugged. "Now come on. Let's get out of these getups before the boys get back. I want to surprise them tomorrow."

"Dean? Dean Pearce?"

Dean turned. He didn't recognize the pretty blonde jogging over, but he stopped. He'd just dropped Daisy off at the vet as a favor to Jeremy and was on his way to Faekin's Stationery on Main Street to pick up the donation envelopes the Historical Society had printed for the ball. Anything to make donating to their cause easier. A small expense if it meant more contributions.

The blonde came to a breathless stop. "Hi."

"Hello? I'm sorry, I'm drawing a blank."

She laughed and waved a hand. "No, no. Don't worry. We've never met. My name's Joey—Joanna. I go to Havenport College with Reina. She pointed you out the other day. Spoke pretty highly of you."

"Oh, you know Reina?" A guilty pang made him wince. He hadn't known Reina was in college. Still didn't explain why this girl waved him down in the middle of town. "Did you want me to give her a message or something? Because I'm not sure I have her number." He reached for his phone in his jeans pocket.

She put a hand out to stop him. "I'm not looking for Reina. It's you I wanted to see, actually." She let her hand linger on his arm.

He waited. He was eager to finish his errands and return home to Lila, but didn't want to be rude to a friend of Reina's.

"Wow, you're not going to make this easy, are you?" She squeezed his arm, then let him go. "As I said, Reina pointed you out and told me a little about you. I thought maybe we could get a bite to eat sometime?"

His eyes widened. Wow, he hadn't caught on to the clues at all. Normally he'd be all over her, probably would have asked her out before she had the chance, but Lila consumed his thoughts. He hadn't even considered the possibility Joanna flirted with him.

"Oh, well." He rubbed the back of his neck. "Sorry, I don't think that would be a good idea."

She frowned and a flush of red spread across her freckled cheeks. "Oh, well. I'm so sorry to have bothered you." She pointed down the street. "I'll, uh, just get out of your way…"

"I'm in a relationship," he blurted. "Sorry. It's kind of new—or, well, old actually, but just renewing things." He never rambled. What the hell was wrong with him?

She smiled brightly. "Sure. Okay. Well, good to know. Reina has my number if your renewal thing doesn't work out." She gave him a little wave and jogged down the street. Thankfully, in the opposite direction he needed to go.

He continued down Main, picking up his pace to make up for the few minutes he'd lost. Someone bumped into him as he waited to cross Washington. He looked up in time to see a scrawny teenager step off the curb while completely absorbed in his phone. A blue sedan slammed on the brakes in an attempt to stop.

An icy wave of panic prickled his skin. Flashes from his accident tormented him. The cold, the fear, the pain.

The car moved too fast. There was no chance it could stop in time.

Dean didn't think. He sprinted into the street, grabbed the kid around the waist, and hauled him backward, landing hard on the sidewalk with the kid sprawled on top of him. The sedan squealed to a halt ten feet past where they lay.

Searing pain engulfed his leg. The kid elbowed him in the stomach as he got to his feet. Dean doubled over, fighting to regain his breath.

"Holy shit, man. That car came out of nowhere."

The driver of the sedan jumped out of his car, yelling at the kid. A squad car pulled up, lights flashing.

Dean huddled on the concrete. He couldn't stand without help, the pain from his old injury too severe. He'd need at least a few minutes to walk it off, if he could just get off the ground.

Finally, the officer approached with an outstretched hand. He took it gratefully. "Thanks."

The officer hauled him to his feet. "No problem. Sounds like young Frankie over there is lucky you weren't texting your girlfriend like he was."

"My girl doesn't own a cell phone." He gave a shaky laugh, still recovering his breath. He took small steps, pacing to work the kinks out of his leg. He hadn't fallen all that hard. No permanent damage. He'd be walking with a limp for a few days, but nothing he couldn't handle. He searched for the kid, wanting to reassure himself Frankie would be okay. "Shit. That was close."

"You ain't kidding," the officer said. "I was a block away and heard the car slam on its brakes. Frankie would have been dead for sure if you hadn't stepped in. Are you okay? I've got a call in to the EMTs. Should be here any second."

"No need. I'll be fine." He massaged the outside of his thigh. "Old wound. Can't take much of a blow without bringing all the old pain back. I'll walk it off."

He spent a good twenty minutes giving his report to the officer, endured pokes and prods from the EMTs, then finally was allowed to continue on his way after speaking to the kid one last time.

His leg plagued him for the rest of the day. No problem. He was no stranger to pain.

The nightmares, on the other hand...well, he was no stranger to them, either, but they were much harder to manage.

Chapter Seven

Lila tilted her head. What was that noise?

Silence reigned. Dean had gone to bed hours ago. There was no clock in her little attic room, so she had no idea of the time.

There. She heard it again. A faint whimper.

Dean.

She tore down the stairs and burst through the open door to his room, only to find it empty. She'd forgotten he'd moved into his parents' larger room after they moved out.

His cries grew louder. She raced down the hall to the master bedroom and headed through the closed door.

Bam! She smashed into the solid wood. "Ouch." A sharp pain spread through her face from where her nose and chin had made contact with the door she should have sailed through. *What the…?*

She pushed the question of why out of her mind as Dean's cries grew more panicked. She grabbed the doorknob and twisted. Her fingers folded around the cold metal, and she pushed. Her hand slipped through. She took a deep breath and concentrated. The door inched open.

Moonlight flooded the room through the drawn curtains. The nearest neighbor on this side of the house was too far away to worry about privacy.

Dean thrashed around, his comforter twisted around his upper body, a pillow over his face. Muted cries so similar to those that had woken her from a ghostly slumber all those years ago sent a chill down her spine.

"Dean?" She tossed the pillow onto the floor. He hadn't had such a severe nightmare in years. They'd come frequently immediately following the accident, but had lessened. His heroics from this afternoon must have brought back all his old fears. Could she calm him the same way she had when he was young?

Worth a try.

She sat on the edge of his bed, careful to avoid his thrashing legs, and sang one of his favorite songs. No reaction. She increased her volume. His whimpers paused ever so briefly, then continued, but much quieter than before.

The jerky, wild movements of his legs and arms slowed. She kept on singing while she helped untangle the blankets. She gave a sharp tug on one corner, yanking it out from under him, then smoothed the sheet atop his chest. His skin was warm and coated with a slight sheen of sweat, the sheets slightly damp.

His body went still. The whimpering stopped. She raised her eyes and found him staring at her. His deep-green eyes wide and still cloudy with sleep. "Lila?"

She let the last note of her song drift away and nodded. Her hand rested on his chest. His heart pounded under her fingers. "I can feel your heart beating. Are you all right? Were you under that bush again, your parents nearby but not hearing you?" His nightmares had almost always involved no one hearing his cries for help.

"No," he said, his voice gravelly and a shade deeper than normal. "This was the other one."

She tilted her head and tried to remember. "Other one?" How many recurring nightmares did he have?

"The one where I'm chasing after you, calling for you, but you don't answer."

Her mouth dropped open. She blinked rapidly to keep the threatening tears at bay. "I didn't know about that one."

"They started when I was seventeen. After you left." He grabbed her hand. "Do you see why I can't just let you go? I have to try everything I can to keep you here. You say I was ruining my life to be with a ghost, but the ghost of you did far more damage."

Forget stopping her tears—they flowed freely down her cheeks. He cupped her face in his free hand, the rough pad of his thumb sweeping the tears away. "The prophecy's moving along faster than I thought. You're almost completely solid."

She snuggled into his hand. Goddess! It had been so long. Too long without the sensation of human touch. And here she sat with the man she most wanted to be close to.

Would it be so wrong if she never let him go? Selfish of her, yes. But didn't she owe it to herself, and the Goddess's plan, to take that leap of faith? Didn't she owe it to him?

Her heart fluttered wildly. "I—I bumped face-first into the door." She gave him a weak smile. "This is going to take some getting used to." Touching Dean? *That* she could get used to real quick.

He chuckled. "I'll have to make sure my camera's working. I can get some funny videos to share on Facebook."

A good smack to the shoulder was definitely called for, but both her hands were occupied. She wasn't about to pull her hand from his, and her other hand had somehow found its way into his hair. She enjoyed the feel of the short, silky strands too much to let go.

A scar wound from behind his ear toward the back of

his skull. His thick hair covered the jagged line, but couldn't hide the roughened skin from her questing fingers. So many scars, but so few visible to the eye. She'd curse the idiot that had done this to him, but the selfish side of her knew she never would have come to love Dean if the accident hadn't occurred.

The smile slowly slid from his mouth. His lips parted, and his gaze darted between her eyes and her mouth. He slid his hand from her cheek to cradle her head behind her ear. A slight pressure drew her face toward his. He stopped less than a hairsbreadth away. The light from the moon shone in his eyes as he looked deep into hers. Were she as real as she felt, she'd see her reflection in his dilated pupils, but all she saw was a depth of feeling that overwhelmed her.

Thank goodness she was a ghost already, or she'd have died from lack of oxygen. His breath fanned her face. The heat sent her pulse skyrocketing. He licked his lips, and she moaned. She leaned forward ever so slightly, and they met in a fiery kiss.

Lila was in his arms. Dean could feel her, smell her, taste her. And damn, she tasted good. He'd dreamed of this moment since he was a teen, and it was better than he'd imagined.

Her lips were soft, warm, and eager. He swept his tongue along the seam of her mouth, and she opened to him instantly. He lost all sense of time and place, consumed by the feeling of having the woman he loved in his arms at last.

A quiet moan of pleasure brought him back to the moment, enough to come to his senses. He released the pressure on the back of her neck. He half expected her to jump back, maybe give him the good slap in the face he deserved. But she pressed closer.

It might kill him, but he needed to put a stop to this. He knew her too well. She considered herself a modern woman, but her sense of self was deeply rooted in her nineteenth-century upbringing. Sex was for marriage.

Yes, he'd marry her in a flash, and would as soon as the prophecy was fulfilled and her new life began. But for her, marriage needed to precede the sex, or a tiny seed of shame would taint their first time. When they joined together in every sense of the word, he didn't want the experience to be anything less than blissful.

One last, sweet taste, then he pulled back. Held her away from him until reason shone in her eyes once more. A shame to waste such amazing passion, but he was in this for the long haul. Not one night of heaven, but a lifetime full.

"We need to stop, sweetheart," he whispered.

"No." She captured his mouth once more.

It took more willpower than he knew he had, but he pulled back with a laugh. "Oh, sweetheart. You tempt me. You really do. But you're not some one-night stand, and I refuse to treat you like one."

She sat slowly, and he pushed back to rest against the headboard. He didn't know how long his good intentions would last without at least a little distance between them.

"You don't want me?"

"Fuck." How the hell could she jump to that conclusion? She'd been close enough to have felt exactly how much he wanted her. And that wasn't a small bit, if he did say so himself. "I want you more than…no, I *need* you more than I need to breathe. And I can't believe I'm saying this, but we're going to have to wait until we're married."

Her stiff posture relaxed at his statement, but she continued to look at him with doubt. "You've been intimate with quite a large number of women. Lack of wedding vows has never stopped you before. Are you afraid you'll be disappointed in me? Because I've never been with a man?"

He couldn't let her think such a thing. "You could never disappoint me." He tucked a loose curl behind her ear, letting his fingers linger. "I may have more experience, but there's plenty you can teach me."

One eyebrow rose into her hairline and her chin tilted down.

He grinned. "Technical expertise I may have." He ran his finger behind her ear and down her neck, smiling when she shivered in response. "And I'm looking forward to sharing every last bit of my knowledge with you." He kissed the tip of her nose. "But I know nothing about intimacy. About sharing my soul." He leaned his forehead against hers. "That's something I could never experience without you," he whispered.

Chapter Eight

At a quarter to twelve, Lila hovered outside the door to Dean's office. She'd caught a glimpse of Jeremy striding in wearing a kilt, a white shirt with wide sleeves, and what looked like a dagger strapped to his waist.

Dean greeted him with, "Mr. Darcy wears a skirt?" in a teasing voice.

"It's a kilt, dumb-ass."

"Since when does Mr. Darcy wear a kilt? I thought we were all going as Jane Austen characters. How did you get out of wearing a pair of these tight-ass pants and one of these nooses Christa called a cravat?"

"She changed her mind about the costumes." His voice was so smug, Lila could imagine the annoyed scowl on Dean's face. "Now I'm some eighteenth-century Scottish warrior, and she's a World War Two nurse. They're characters from some time-travel book she loves."

"Where is she? How's her costume?"

What sounded like ice splashing into a glass interrupted their conversation. Then the clink of glasses. If it were later in the day, she'd guess scotch, but given the time, she hoped they were indulging in nothing stronger than a cold cola.

Dean didn't need to be at the party for quite a while yet, but he'd agreed to pose for some publicity photos ahead of time, and Christa and Jeremy had decided to go with him.

Christa had already arranged with Reina to hold another séance in a quiet corner of the manor to call Lila to them so she could attend the party as well. Lila had her fingers crossed everything would work out well.

"She's upstairs with Lila getting ready. I haven't seen her yet. She wants to surprise me." He paused. "Not sure what the fuss is about. She'll look fantastic, but I've seen what army nurses wore back then. Nothing to write home about. I'd much prefer a modern-day naughty nurse, but she wasn't going for it."

Lila clapped a hand to her mouth to stifle her laughter. Christa joined her in her eavesdropping, struggling to control her own mirth.

Ready? Christa mouthed the word silently.

She nodded.

Lila went first. She wanted to see Jeremy's reaction when Christa came in wearing that gorgeous dress, but Dean drew her attention, and she couldn't look away. Her Mr. Knightley was straight out of her dreams. Elegant, arrogant, and sexy as hell. Exactly as she'd imagined her favorite Jane Austen hero to look. And his *tight-ass pants* did little to hide his reaction to her costume. She smiled and crossed the room to stand before him.

The clock struck twelve.

The world went black.

❧ ❧ ❧

"From twelve 'til twelve, all must wait."

"What?" Dean spun around, searching for the source. A pair of witches walked in, and he recognized Lauren from Serendipity. Had she recited that line from the Goddess's poem?

"Time will soon decide their fate."

There. Again. He whirled toward the sound.

Marta, the tea leaf reader, smiled at him from her table a few feet from the end of the bar. She beckoned him forward with a crooked finger. Dressed as some kind of queen in icy white that contrasted with her black hair, she'd had no shortage of visitors during the ball. He'd never seen so many men flock to see a psychic in his life.

He slid into the seat across from her, his head suddenly almost clear of the fog caused by the Glenlivet he'd been slugging all night. "What did you say?" He placed his scotch carefully on the table. The glass wavered for an instant before he brought his unsteady gaze under control.

Christa had disappeared almost twelve hours ago. He couldn't believe he was at this stupid party pretending his world hadn't completely fallen apart. But his brother had convinced him there was no use in wallowing in an empty house.

He'd only agreed when he'd run out of hard alcohol.

"Care to have your leaves read, my lord?"

"No, I don't want my leaves read." The intricately folded cravat and highly starched collar of his costume threatened to choke him. He reached to tug it free, but the woman snatched his hand, shoving a full tea cup at him. She had a steely grip at odds with the delicate bones of her long, thin fingers. He couldn't break her hold without making more of a scene than he was willing to make at the moment. Better to play along and he might get some answers. He slugged down the lukewarm tea and handed her the cup with the dregs coating the bottom. He picked up his scotch and took a quick gulp. The liquor burned its way down his throat, but he welcomed the fiery sensation.

"A test of character, with honor met
A loyal heart, in love is set.
Facing fears brings vast reward,
But seek them not on own accord.
When love is true, the heart is bold,
Sacrifice all to have and hold.
Then one last test, to see in kind,
The depth of love we hope to find."

"How do you know that poem?" His heart raced. A spark shot through his hand where her nails dug into his fist. His feet rooted to the floor. He leaned forward.

Her pupils dilated to the point he couldn't make out the color of her eyes, merely a sea of inky blackness.

"Why are you here alone, Mr. Knightley? Where's your Emma?"

His hand tightened on his rocks glass. Ice shifted, clinking against the sides. Sounded like he needed another. The lunatic across from him wasn't helping. "She's gone. Again. I came alone."

"There are any number of single ladies here tonight. No need to be alone."

The idea repulsed him. "No. Without Lila…" He slumped in the chair. "Just no. I only want Lila. But I failed her. I would have done anything. Sacrificed anything." Where had he gone wrong?

She nodded. "Yes. One last test, I believe the poem said." She tilted her head as the grand clock struck the midnight hour and the band switched songs.

"Enough of the crazy talk, okay? Tell me why you're reciting that poem. Where did you hear it? What's all this about?"

"I believe you passed the Goddess's test."

He let his shoulders slump. "I don't know how you know about the test, but I didn't pass. I failed. Miserably."

"If that were true, how could *she* be here?" She tilted her chin over his left shoulder.

She? He swiveled in his seat.

People danced, laughed, ate, and drank, providing a backdrop for the most beautiful sight he'd ever seen.

Lila.

Dressed as Emma Woodhouse in a pale-blue gown with puffed sleeves, floor-length skirt, and elbow-length gloves, she weaved her way through the crowd.

Their gazes caught, and she tripped to a stop. She stared at him through the crowd from less than a half dozen yards away.

Time stopped along with his breathing. Then rushed back at a frantic pace.

He jumped to his feet, and the chair crashed to the floor with a clatter.

Two seconds and he came to a dead stop with only an inch between them.

"Lila," he whispered. His hand trembled as he reached for hers. She looked solid. Real. He couldn't suppress the icy shiver around his heart that told him his hand would pass right through her. "Am I imagining this? Are you really here?"

Her voice shook as she responded, "I'm here." She stepped in, clasped his hand, and brought it to her chest. A delicate track of tears leaked down her cheeks.

He yanked her into his arms. Kissed her until he needed to come up for air. "Oh, God. I knew it."

She smiled, her chin tilted up to look into his eyes. "Knew what?"

He tucked her against his chest, rested his chin on her head, and held her close. Her delicate, flowery scent filled his senses, wiping away the despair that had constricted his heart to a tight knot of remorse. He simply breathed and knew all was well. "That we're a perfect fit."

About the Author

EMMA KAYE is married to her high school sweetheart and has two beautiful kids that she spends an insane amount of time driving around central New Jersey. Before ballet classes and tennis entered her life, she decided to try writing one of those romances she loved to read and discovered a new passion. She has been writing ever since. Add in a playful puppy and an extremely patient cat and she's living her own happily ever after while making her characters work hard to reach theirs.

For more information on Emma, please visit her online at www.emma-kaye.com, on Facebook at www.facebook.com/emmakayewrites, on Twitter at www.twitter.com/emmakayewrites or on GoodReads at www.goodreads.com/emma-kaye.

Also by Emma Kaye

Love time travel?
Try another Emma Kaye time travel romance.

Destined for Love
Can a twenty-first century doctor find love in Regency
England with a widowed viscount.

Time for Love
A woman finds much more than she bargained for when
she travels through time to Regency England.

Echoes of the Past
Can a time traveling witch find love in present day Lobster
Cove, Maine, or will her curse get in the way?

For You
A time traveler and an earl's widow find love in Regency
London—but time may not be on their side.

Timeless Tales – Short Stories

In Her Dreams featured in Timeless Escapes
Timing is Everything featuring Granting Her Wish,
Losing Patience & To Have and to Hold

Havenport – Novellas

Baby, It's Cold Outside
featured in Christmas in Havenport
Under Her Spell
On Her Own
Tricking the Beast

The Duke's Christmas Wish

A Spirit's Bond

by Nicole S. Patrick

Self-proclaimed bachelor Dylan O'Brien is content with his new life in Havenport. No responsibilities besides building his veterinary practice, and fighting off the matchmaking women in town who see a doctor as marriage material. The single care free life is all he can handle. Except when a stray dog whose handler isn't quite out of picture needs Dylan's TLC, he discovers being alone isn't satisfying after all. He also meets gorgeous decorator Meghan LaRue and her design ideas aren't the only thing he's interested in. A date to the Havencroft Halloween Ball might be the right time for Dylan to consider giving up his solo life, in more ways than one.

Moving back to her hometown of Havenport means a new beginning for Meghan LaRue. Time for a fresh start, concentrate on raising her teenaged daughter alone, and build her interior design business. Love is not on the list of preferred designs. But when sexy, cute vet Dylan O'Brien enters the equation it might be time to rethink adding to her list of priorities to include him. Can she find the courage to have it all? Be a successful mom, businesswoman and trust in love again?

Dedicated to ~

My writing family: Ruth, Lita, Emma, and Desi. The journey continues...

Dad. Things will never be the same without you.

Chapter One

"One more pin in the knee joint and we can cast the leg," Dylan muttered under his sweaty surgical mask. The room turned into a sauna under the overheads beaming down like a french fry warmer. Granted, the new surgical lighting he'd installed at the Havenport Animal Hospital was a hundred times more efficient than the old, but talk about sunburn.

A bead of sweat dripped from his brow down a path under his mask. The Pekingese, aptly named Peanut due to its light-brown coat, was still a puppy, and fixing his broken leg could prove tricky.

"Beautiful." He swallowed before letting out a long breath. "How we doing on time, Ben?" Anesthesia, especially in a dog this small, had to be monitored.

Ben, his best tech, shifted his position by the dog's head before checking his watch. "Good, Doc."

With Ben's help, they concluded the procedure. He yanked off the sweaty do-rag and tossed it into the laundry bin beside the operating table. A-okay so far. An indication by the gentle rise and fall of the dog's abdomen. No matter how much he enjoyed performing surgery, the nervous adrenaline managed to stick around for a while.

He scratched the little thing behind the ears. "Rest up, little dude."

Oh boy, the uneven shave job Ben did on its hind leg wouldn't go over well. Augusta can work her magic as Havenport's resident grooming expert at Wags and Walks. He made a mental note to give her the heads-up.

"Doctor O'Brien, you've got a call." The new receptionist popped her head around the corner of the back room with a smile. What was her name? Valerie, or Vanessa?

"Can you take a message, please?" Cleanup had to happen first. The front of his scrubs shirt, smeared with gunk and dried antiseptic, made him twitchy.

"Um…well." She bit her lip and her grip on a chart tightened.

He closed his lids for a split second and prayed for patience. "Let me guess. It's my mother."

A flush rushed to her cheeks. "It is."

No use having the poor girl run interference. Margaret O'Brien was a force to be reckoned with. "Thank you. I'll take it in my office." Her relief was tangible, and he almost laughed, but that might make her more embarrassed.

With a heavy sigh and a last check on Peanut with instructions to Ben, he padded to his office. Guess new scrubs would have to wait. The other new receptionist manning the desk nodded to him as he passed. He'd have to suggest they wear name tags. A couple of patients sat in the waiting area, but not too many. Regardless of the number, it'd be the best excuse to cut short Mom's call.

The Havenport Animal Hospital and his practice had more than doubled since he'd taken over as director. Thanks to his staff—some he'd inherited from the former town vet who'd retired at over eighty—the former drab clinical interior turned into a sunny, more modern feel. Walls painted yellow with white moldings held framed photos of his patients with their owners. The locals loved to showcase their beloved four-legged babies. Pictures of families on the beach or at the gazebo in the center of town littered the walls. There were even a few pictures from the last Fourth of July parade.

During the height of the spring and summer tourist seasons, the animal hospital serviced nonstop cases practically every day. In autumn and winter, his patients made up mostly year-round residents, and there were much fewer appointments.

He opened the door to his office and came up short. A blinking skeleton wearing animal paw print scrubs—the only clean ones he'd left—hung from the ceiling near his desk.

One of his staff was the culprit. Avoiding plastic metatarsals in the eye, he folded into the desk chair and glowered at the hold light on the phone. Time to get this over.

"Hello, Peg."

And there went the cannonball blast of a sigh through the line. Mom hated being called by her nickname.

"Dylan Timothy, how nice of you to take time to speak with your one and only mother."

Yes, not only was Margaret O'Brien related to Mother Nature, she could've written the book on Irish guilt. "I was in surgery. You know, using those O'Brien brains you brag about to your church bingo hens."

She tsked quite loud, and he flinched. "Those bingo winnings helped buy you that first hunk of junk you drove around town."

Yes, Irish guilt, and the constant reminder of all the sacrifices made for him, his sister, and brother were her trademark soliloquy. It was all an act. No doubt Peg would run barefoot with her last dollar and a corned beef sandwich if any one of her children needed her.

"Relax, Peg. No need to fork over your jackpots anymore. I can afford my own car and house."

Dylan leaned back in his chair and stretched his legs. Running those ten miles this morning made his shins feel like someone had stabbed them repeatedly with a hot scalpel. And the weather in Rhode Island could officially be considered chilly. Winter was on its way, sooner than later. That breeze coming off the waterfront had blasted through him like a knife.

"Speaking of which," Mom continued, "I've made an arrangement."

Goose bumps broke out on his forearm. Mom's arrangements were never good. "Arrangement?"

"Your place needs a makeover," she announced.

He let out the breath he'd sucked in anticipation. Not so terrible, considering her unwavering attempts at matchmaking. Bad enough women in Havenport considered him fair game and up for auction in the love department. His mother had signed him up on a dumb dating site, which he only found out about because his sister saw his bullshit profile. *Educated, hunky vet, seeks caring animal lover for petting?* Really? *Hunky?*

"Wait, my house *is* decorated."

"Dylan, Dylan, Dylan," came the mantra, and he pictured a bobblehead. "Eternal bachelorhood with a taste of frat boy is *not* decorated."

"Says you," he said with a scoff. "Besides, you all gave my house your seal of approval."

Moving to Rhode Island and out of the O'Brien realm of Boston, had been…well…challenging. The O'Briens resided in the Back Bay for nearly seventy years, and the thought of one of the flock daring to escape—pure blasphemy. But when the opportunity arose to run the animal hospital in Havenport, he couldn't turn it down. Still, before he'd purchased his refurbished ranch, the entire family felt the need to consent their stamp of approval.

Embarrassing as all hell having your mother and two siblings show up at the bank for the closing. Christ, he'd served six years, including four tours overseas as a Navy Corpsman, yet still he'd never left the roost.

"My darling son, there's nothing wrong with the house, per se. It's what's inside of it."

"You don't like my foosball table? I'm crushed." No way was Mom putting her mom touches on his bachelor pad. He grabbed the plastic mini pumpkin from atop the computer monitor and tossed it in the air a few times for distraction. This might be a longer conversation than predicted.

"How are you going to get married and give me grandchildren if you don't make the place presentable? God only knows what that bedroom of yours looks like. No woman would be caught dead, let alone naked."

"Do not continue." *Cripes.* His ears turned fiery. Thank God she hadn't insisted on video chat, her newest fascination. His mom and his sex life, or lack thereof, did not belong on the same planet.

She harrumphed in his ear. "I'm merely trying to hurry along your settling down. I only want you to be happy, Dyl."

Yeah, right. Happy as in married with children. Her hankering for grandchildren had become an obsession. "Sell that to Shannon and Danny." Hey, it was a good argument. His siblings could easily procreate and add to the clan. They were both established professionals, dating nice people. Good idea.

"You're my first born," she quantified, as if he didn't know. "Therefore *you* need to get married first."

He almost hooted, but it would undoubtedly add fuel to her tilted logic. "I didn't realize that was a written rule."

"You wait, my dear." He heard laughter with a touch of patronizing in her voice. "The right woman will come around when you least expect it. Then I get to help plan a wedding."

That made him twitch more than the dirt and blood stains on his scrubs. *No.* Marriage, kids—not on the horizon. He'd done enough surrogate fathering after Dad hightailed it to God knew where before Dylan could even remember what the old man looked like. Mom had them all take her surname as well. So an O'Brien he'd be for the rest of his natural life, despite his father being a Duffy.

Who wanted to be Dylan Duffy anyway? Sounded like a cartoon character.

Not that he'd ever tell Mom how he felt. The last thing he wanted was to make her feel guilty for leaving him to practically raise Shan and Dan while she'd worked three jobs in order to feed them all. Truth was, Mom had been a stellar parent, still was, and for that he loved her to pieces. But if it weren't for joining the Navy, there would have been no way they'd afforded college and vet school.

"About that decorating," He lassoed the conversation to safer water, otherwise she might dust off Grandma O'Brien's engagement ring from the safety-deposit box. "When and what have you planned?"

"I've hired you a consultation with an interior decorator. They're coming to your house today." Her doorbell rang in the background. "Hang on, sweetie. Someone's at the door."

Today? He grabbed his cell phone off the desk and clicked open the calendar app. No items listed for tonight. *What luck.* He placed it back on the desk as something taped to his computer screen caught his eye.

Tickets to the Halloween Eve Masquerade Ball at Havencroft Manor, in a mere few days. He'd almost forgotten. Augusta had roped him into buying not one, but two tickets. Might want to keep that bit information to himself, otherwise Mom would insist *she* pick out a date, which he had no intention of bringing.

Solo was fine.

Augusta, too, had high hopes for his blossoming love life. Having a best friend who happened to be female *and* disgustingly in love had started to grate on his nerves.

"Dyl, I've got to run. The gas meter reader is here. I can't find the name of the consultant, but I know I set up the appointment for later today, after five, I think. Make sure you're home. Give the person a chance, if for nothing more than to please your mother."

Add another thing to the to-do list. "Only for you, Peg." He hung up.

His intercom beeped. "Dr. O'Brien, your next patient is ready in exam room two. They've been waiting awhile."

"I'm on my way." He pushed away from the desk and scowled down at his scrubs. No time to wrestle Mr. Blinking-Bones for a new scrubs shirt. His T-shirt from this morning had to suffice.

He grabbed his gym bag off the floor then swapped garments. Not the most professional attire—the dancing hamburger image from Corky's Café's last fund-raiser—but it would do. He shuffled to the exam room, stepped in, and closed the door before turning to his patient. A little dog sniffed the edge of the scale.

"Hey, Rambo. How's my buddy?" The miniature pinscher ran into his legs with a short bark, his stub tail waving nonstop. Dylan bent to scratch behind the dog's ears.

"Excuse me. I thought we were waiting to see a doctor," came a voice from behind.

Someone's annoyed. He straightened, turned, and words stuck somewhere between his voice box and tongue. "I...I'm Doctor O'Brien. Sorry to keep you waiting."

Her rather…*ahem*…full lips parted. They were shiny and pink.

"You're the doctor?" She eyeballed his shirt, then up to his chin. Heat rushed to his cheeks. He'd also forgotten to shave this morning. Usually he took much pride in keeping an impeccable appearance. Guess it came from the Navy days. This morning, however, worrying about Peanut's surgery trumped his proper grooming session.

Rambo broke the moment to climb up *her* legs. She wore some sort of one-piece pants jumpsuit thing. It hugged a killer bod—long and lean, with the right amount of curves. He'd guess she topped around the five-ten mark. Being a half inch over six-two himself, he appreciated not having to look down to converse with a woman.

Dark hair brushed past her shoulders in a riot of tousled curls, like organized chaos, and sexy beyond anything he'd encountered, at least since moving to Havenport.

"Get off mommy's pants, baby," she scolded while giving Rambo a gentle push off. She continued to pet and coo at the dog. Huh? Rambo's owner, he recalled, was Augusta's boyfriend, Evan's, niece, Brielle. No sign of the teen. Had the Washburns gotten a new housekeeper?

"Who *are* you?" he blurted, like an ass.

She crossed her arms and deadpanned, "Are you always this blunt?"

"Not usually," he admitted, and gave her his best smile. A grin he used for the occasional irate pet owner. Perhaps flashing the pearly whites on this pet owner might calm the storm, which may be about to hit. "I guess I left my manners in the OR. Long morning."

She nodded tightly.

Plan B.

"I haven't seen Rambo since this past summer. I guess I expected Brielle or Evan, instead of…" He left the last word dangling with the hope she'd introduce herself and ease him out of this embarrassing, backpedaling misery.

Before he realized what was happening, Rambo pumped into *his* shin like a jackhammer. It was her turn to blush or, more specifically, appear horrified. She gasped then jumped into action by tugging on Rambo's collar. However, in the process she grabbed *his* leg above his knee.

"Oh my goodness. Stop. You horny thing," she cried.

He tilted his head, staring at her hand planted on his thigh, and couldn't help grinning like the village idiot.

"I didn't mean you." She snatched her hand away like it was on hot coals, then rolled her eyes.

Why did that gesture seem familiar?

"How embarrassing," she mumbled. "I apologize."

She continued in vain to pry Rambo's front paws away from around his scrubs. He bent forward to help. *Wham.* They clunked heads like two coconuts. She reared back at the same time he straightened.

Were those stars or dust particles floating around? The room tilted. He closed one eye and swayed. By some miracle he had the good sense—thank God—to shoot out a hand and stop her from taking a tumble, too.

"Ouch," they said in unison. Her bony elbow pressed into his palm. Amid the wave of pain radiating across his temple, he tried to not squeeze her delicate appendage.

"Are you okay?"

She'd grabbed the exam table to use as a leaning post. "I think so." She rubbed the left side of her temple and winced. Beneath the wisps of her curls the soft tissue over her eyebrow appeared red and swelling.

"Let me get you an ice pack," he offered, and turned in slow motion because the ride on the Tilt-A-Whirl hadn't ended yet.

She waved a hand absently in his direction. "That's not necessary. Really. I'll be fine."

Rambo, blissfully unaware of the considerable damage he'd caused, sat back on his hind legs and barked. Dylan's focus narrowed on the pooch. "Sure, *now* you stop?"

She didn't say anything, merely shook her head gently, as if to clear cobwebs—or a concussion. Could he be more of a horse's ass?

"We O'Briens have heads made of stone, or so my mother tells me." Yeah, get the saddle. He was officially a donkey. *I mentioned my mother?* He stared at his sneakers and silently berated himself. Wait, was that a chuckle? He darted a glance her way. Her lips fell into a neutral expression.

Time to get into doctor mode and salvage this appointment. He moved closer to her, purely in a medical way. She backed up and shot him a wary glace while gripping the table.

"Are you experiencing nausea? Blurred vision?" He debated whipping out his penlight to check the reactions in her pupils, but it might be too much. She blinked a few times. Her peepers were okay. More than okay. And like the rest of her, stunning beyond compare. Her irises were dark green, and standing this close, he could make out the outline of her contact lenses.

"It's only a bump." She patted him on the forearm as if to say, *Back the hell away, buddy.*

"Right," he muttered. Yeah, time to back up. But in doing so, he almost crushed the poor dog. This morning was not going well. At all. Moving to the opposite side of the room to establish an appropriate distance, he ran a hand through his hair and caught his reflection in the metal paper towel dispenser mounted on the wall. Epic fail in the hair department. No wonder she had no idea he was the doctor.

Enough.

"Can we start over?" he asked, but didn't give her a

chance to answer. Pivoting sharply, he opened the door and stepped into the hallway. "Way to impress a client and a beautiful woman," he muttered, but clammed up when Ben passed with a funny look.

Dylan sucked in a deep breath, counted to ten, and turned the knob. "Good morning. I'm Doctor O'Brien. Sorry to keep you waiting. Hey, Rambo." He held out his hand, eyebrow arched.

Her mouth flew open, then she bit her bottom lip and her shoulders quaked with silent laughter. He spied her wedding ring right before they shook hands. A stab of disappointment hit the pit of his stomach.

"I'm Meghan LaRue. If you know Rambo here, the naughty boy…" She wrinkled her nose at the dog. "…then I suspect you also know my daughter, Brielle."

Ah, so this was Evan's sister. The only thing he recalled from what Augusta had mentioned was they lived in New York City or something. Another fact filtered into his mind, but escaped him at the moment. *My head is killing me.* No time to focus on his injuries. "Pleasure to meet you, Mrs. LaRue. What brings you in?"

She swiped a lock of hair from where it had gotten stuck in her shiny lips, and he tried to remember she was married and off limits.

"Rambo needs to be fixed," she whispered.

The dog must've realized the scope of the words, for he darted under the exam table with a whimper.

"So I see." He nodded. "How old *is* he?" Rambo's chart stuck out of the holder on the wall next to the X-ray reader. He pulled it out and flipped through the pages.

"According to what Brielle knows about his background, he turned three last month."

Dylan read the chart and located Rambo's pertinent information. "Yep. I take it you have no plans to breed him? His pedigree is pure, from what I can tell."

A vee creased her eyebrows. They were more auburn than the dark brown of her hair. He couldn't help himself and took in her features, trying to place where she resembled Evan. It was obvious where Brielle got her height.

Meghan shook her head. "No, no. One dog is about as much as either myself or Brielle can handle at the moment. Not that Rambo's trouble," she added quickly, and shifted on her feet. Dylan looked down at her high-heeled boots and gulped.

Unless he was mistaken, they were Chanel, and cost a pretty penny. Why did he know this? One word: Augusta. More than once, Augusta had roped him into shopping expeditions in Newport when Evan was off doing town councilman campaign stuff.

Jeez, he really needed a night out with the guys, drinking single malt at Royce Tavern, not knowing the brand of women's boots.

"He's very lovable." Meghan pushed away from the table and started pacing. Those Chanel heels clicked a steady staccato on the tiles. Guess her head felt better. "You see, we've recently moved back, and I think it's time he calmed down. I've read it helps males to live longer, right?" she asked, and stopped. "But you probably know that."

Well, that was news, the moving back part. She spun and reached into her bag, also designer—*stop it*—and pulled out her smartphone.

"Welcome, err...welcome *back* to Havenport. I'm glad Rambo will be my patient again." God, did he sound like an idiot or what? First mention Mom, now this lame comment? Good going.

When Augusta got wind of this disaster—he suspected Meghan would inevitably tell Evan the town vet nearly knocked her out—he'd never live it down.

She nodded absently and scrolled the screen. "When can you do the procedure?" Her tongue darted to wet her lips.

Of course he'd have to meet someone who made his abs twitch and palms sweat, and *of course* she'd have to be married. He scribbled a quick note in Rambo's chart to redirect, snapped the folder shut, and returned it to the holder. Time to get into doctor mode again.

"Have the receptionist make an appointment next week." At her nod, he continued, "It's a relatively simple procedure for a male dog. Should be same day, or maybe a quick overnight at the clinic."

Her shoulders relaxed. "My schedule is booking up, but you don't need to know that." She smiled before clicking off the phone. "I'm grateful you can help Rambo. Thank you."

He spied Rambo still hiding behind the leg of the exam table and tilted his head to the pooch. "I'm not so sure *he'll* be grateful. But you're right. Males and bitches live longer if they're neutered. Sorry, no girlfriends for you." Rambo whined again. *I can relate, pal.*

Dylan bent for Rambo to sniff his hand, palm down. The little guy had grown more trusting since Brielle had adopted him from the Havenport Animal Shelter this past summer.

Speaking of which…he checked his watch and let out a breath. It was closing in on eleven thirty. Augusta expected him at the shelter this afternoon. But for some unexpected reason, he didn't want to leave the room. Meghan LaRue, with her curls, slender curves, and nervous energy, drew him in, and he didn't want to end their conversation.

Head. Back. In. Game. The other patients in the waiting room needed his attention. He straightened with a groan and made a mental note to stretch better tomorrow morning. "I guess we're all set then. See you next week." He held out his hand again. Professionalism was the way to go, despite his stupid T-shirt.

"Thank you again, Doctor O'Brien." Their hands met and he swore he heard her suck in a breath.

"It's Dylan. Sorry about the collision. I assure you I do not make a habit of clocking my patients' owners on the head."

There went that tongue peeking out to lick her lips. She pushed a piece of hair away from her eyelash and smirked. "I have a hard head, too." She gasped as if she'd forgotten something. "Oh, how rude I am. I didn't even ask if you're okay?"

Soft fingertips brushed his temple. He froze. "Your eye looks puffy. Does it hurt? I should be getting you an ice pack."

What the hell was he supposed to do? Stare at her long lashes, the bridge of her nose with its hint of freckles, or at her lips? Anyplace he chose made him a lecher.

Eyes downward. Nope. Not a good choice, either. The soft curve of her breast under the jumpsuit thingy clung in the right places. The neckline was not risqué, nor revealing in the least. She may as well be covered like a nun.

Sexy didn't need to be naked to exist.

Peaches, mixed with some kind of musk scent, wafted into his nose like sunshine and sex wrapped into one. He almost groaned.

"Nothing to concern yourself." He croaked like Jimmy French's African dwarf frog, who'd come in last week covered in ick.

Meghan pulled away. A sense of abandonment crept into his chest.

"Oh good. Can't go injuring the infamous vet Brielle has raved about for months." She winked then bent to clip on Rambo's leash.

Infamous? He took a step back before he embarrassed himself further by doing what he craved and taking a long sniff of her delicious-smelling neck. "Tell Brielle I said hello, and I won't let anything happen to Rambo."

"I will. She'll be thrilled." She gave him a brilliant smile, and a twinge he recognized as the start of full-blown desire shot to the base of his skull and traveled along the nerve endings of his spine.

Meghan and Rambo exited the room, and Dylan braced against the exam table. His pulse skyrocketed. Her subtle scent lingered, which only made control harder.

Married ladies were off limits. Shaking his head, he grabbed the stethoscope from where he'd left it on the table and turned to the door.

Chapter Two

Twenty minutes later, Meghan strapped Rambo into his doggy car seat, something Brielle had insisted they get for the SUV, and made her way to the new office on Jefferson Avenue. Rambo lay resting his precious little head on his front paws, and she couldn't help smiling. So serene and calm now, given what a horndog he'd been. The sting in her temple reminded her of his doomed appointment. Crazy dog.

And that poor vet, Dr. O'Brien, or Dylan—cute. *If* she were inclined to take note of his cuteness, or the subtle blush on his chiseled features after their heads bumped, or his ridiculous T-shirt.

Rambo let out a snort, as if he could read her thoughts.

"It's all your fault."

His doggy eyebrows rose. He was either asleep or playing possum.

Who knew she'd get so attached to a dog? Growing up a Washburn in Havenport and owning a pet were not mutually exclusive. Evan's setter named Rusty was the only other animal barely tolerated in her parents' palatial estate. Until last year.

Yes, last summer when Evan had agreed, without her permission, to allow Brielle to adopt a puppy. She'd been annoyed, to say the least. The last thing they'd needed, or wanted, at the time was another responsibility. Bad enough Brielle was forced to spend the entire summer with her grandparents while Jacques…

She blew out a breath and gripped the steering wheel. A prism of light reflected off her solitaire, casting rainbow colors on the dash. God knew why she still wore it. Some days she couldn't wrap her mind around the fact that Jacques was gone.

The diamond bordered on magnificent. Belonged to Grandmother Washburn. Perhaps she'd have it removed from the setting and the stone put aside for Brielle. Or maybe give it to Evan if he ever proposed to Augusta.

"Time for a fresh start, huh, baby?" At that, Rambo whined. Their move back to Havenport would prove fruitful. She knew it in her heart. And restarting the profession she loved in interior design and decorating helped her stay focused and masked the grief of her crumbled marriage.

Evan and his girlfriend, Augusta, were terrific. They'd helped them in so many ways, been the support system she and Brielle needed over the past month.

More so than ever lately while she'd set up Haven on Earth Designs. Running a business sucked the majority of her free time.

Plus, the bubbly brunette made her brother happy. Finally. She softened his stiff, military, by-the-book exterior. Augusta made Evan whole again, despite his combat injury.

And then there was Mom and Dad. Meghan let out a long breath, trying to locate a parking spot. Time would uncover how that relationship could improve, or not.

She parallel parked between a Smart car, which resembled a giant sneaker, and a beat-up pickup truck, not an easy feat being out of practice. Rambo woke as she cut the engine. She unstrapped his harness and he climbed into her lap, perching his front paws on the dash and barking out the window at a couple walking by hand in hand. Quite a few people milled about town. Locals on lunch hour and, of course, tourists enjoying the New England colors of autumn.

The gazebo in the center of town, decorated to reflect the current season, held a multitude of shades of yellows and red. She'd love to have the job of decorating it. Maybe the town would accept a bid from her for Christmas.

The structure was her favorite in Havenport, and especially lovely this time of year. So Halloween being her favorite holiday made her biased, but last night when they'd walked Rambo, Brielle reveled at the hundreds of twinkling lights hanging off the structure. Yes, Brielle also loved Halloween. Had since she'd been in diapers.

Visions of many years sewing Halloween costumes came to mind. This year Brielle requested a costume for Rambo. "How about Dracula?" He cocked his head to the side thinking about it, and she grinned. "You'd be adorable in a cape."

That bachelor's in fine arts from Parsons School did have its advantages, not that she'd use it professionally. Sure had come in handy during Brielle's elementary school years and the numerous Halloween costumes she'd whipped up on a moment's notice.

Time to put it to good use in Havenport. No more living off a rich husband—or ex, as it were—or a father who had too many opinions on how she and Brielle should live their lives.

New life. A new way.

She snapped on Rambo's leash, closed the car door after he jumped onto the sidewalk, and pulled the cashmere pashmina higher on her shoulders. Autumn in Rhode

Island was in full swing. Winter wasn't far behind. "We're a duo today, my little love."

Rambo barked his version of affirmation and led the way in a trot, stub tail wagging. He stopped and sniffed a lamppost, then gnawed the fringe of her scarf. "Stop that. We'll get you a sweater." Maybe Augusta could order him a cute vest from the many catalogs in her store, Wags and Walks.

Havenport had grown and continued to every day, it seemed. It was evident by the amount of new stores and houses on this street alone. She'd missed the growth by being away, but no more. Being back and living close to Evan gave her a sense of home and rightness.

She couldn't be more proud he'd thrown his hat in the ring for town councilman come November. If elected, she knew he'd do a stellar job, no doubt. His platform: making Havenport a town where small business, tourists, and families could thrive—a wonderful idea.

She hoped—no, planned. She needed to remember to think positively, for positivity bred success, to make Haven on Earth Designs a success. Designing made her happy. Colors, textures, fabrics, all of it kept her sane and with creative juices flowing.

Rambo continued the route to her office, stopping every few feet to sniff some nonexistent doggy scent. At this rate she'd never get any work done, but he deserved the fresh air.

Taking a deep breath, Meghan looked around the town she'd grown up in, left, then returned to, hopefully better than before. The stress of the summer had washed away the minute they'd driven past the Havenport sign, like waves crashing in the ocean, steady and furious, then back out to sea. Now it was time for a long low tide, settle in with Brielle, and take one day at a time sans the drama that had been her life for as long as she could remember.

She'd vowed to stop playing the high-society Barbie when they'd moved back, too. That way of thinking hadn't gotten her anything but heartache. Brielle made it perfectly clear she was *not* moving into Washburn Estate. Their sunny condo overlooking the harbor suited them perfectly.

"Who're you kidding? You love the high life. You've got the Washburn blood. What's one little indiscretion?"

Sure, to Dad—or as Evan called him, "the old man," and Havenport's resident tycoon and hard-ass—one little *anything* could be overlooked if money was involved.

Except things weren't that simple, and Jacques hadn't had *one* indiscretion in their sixteen-year marriage.

Dad fumed after she'd dropped the bombshell about leaving Jacques and arranging a quick divorce last summer. Jacques was damned lucky she didn't have his ass deported then, or brought up on charges. She might have been a young trophy wife, but she wasn't an imbecile, nor in the dark about his shady restaurant dealings.

Heck, she'd ensured his green card by marrying him. Becoming pregnant before they'd married was a huge *oops*, but Brielle was the only good thing to come out of their relationship.

Didn't matter. That part of her life was on the way to becoming ancient history.

Someone waved and smiled as Rambo trotted along the sidewalk. Felt good to encounter friendly faces again. People who actually said hello instead of daring to make eye contact. Havenport had a warm, friendly atmosphere. Something she hadn't realized she'd missed. Living in New York City wasn't always dreadful, except maybe it *had* been for Brielle, and she'd been too blind to see.

Talk about being a crappy parent.

She'd turned into her mother, fixating on the Washburn business and the gobs of money to be made. The rotten apple hadn't fallen far, that was for sure. With building Jacques's restaurant, the lack of quality time for Brielle—her daughter, for crying out loud—was something she regretted. Terribly.

But now all that would change. Havenport held possibilities. Family, support, the feeling of belonging had been nonexistent in the high society and parties of New York.

A lunch cart with the Corky's Café logo stamped on its umbrella was parked on the sidewalk a few doors from her new offices. The aroma of fried onions and cheese steak made her stomach grumble. Lunch would have to wait. Too much time spent at the animal hospital put her behind schedule.

Dr. O'Brien's T-shirt popped into her mind, along with what she imagined as his lean physique underneath. Her heel caught on the sidewalk and she almost stumbled. Goodness, what was wrong with her?

Reaching for the key, she unlocked the door to the old warehouse building, pulled Rambo's leash, and led him inside. Her boots crunched on the mail scattered where the mailman had pushed the letters through the slot. She shut the door, bent, and picked up the few pieces while Rambo sniffed a manila envelope. It was postmarked from France. A knot coiled into her stomach.

Maybe Jacques needed advice on how to handle a slutty twenty-two-year-old sommelier? Not a chance. Ginny was welcomed to Jacques's cheating, stinking, perfume-wearing BS. If she never smelled Clive Christian again, it would be too soon. What man wore perfume anyway?

Men were not in the cards for her in Havenport, or anywhere. No, thank you. Brielle and the new business were the top priorities.

The smell of textiles, cloth, and dye lingered in the air. The prewar building had been a mill. Jane, the nice woman who owned Royce's tavern, hinted the building might be haunted.

Not that she believed in that sort of stuff. But sometimes she had to admit when working late, the faint sounds of creaking and footfalls gave her the willies. Must be the old building settling, or the wind.

The faded lettering of Havenport Textiles painted on the chipped brick face of the hallway gave the place an authentic, Old World feel. Back in the day, when the men of Rhode Island went off to war, the women of Havenport were left behind to run this mill. But then, the finery of silks and chamois for upholstery, ladies' gowns, buttons, and embroidery changed to making war materials.

Still, the building held history and an ambience worth keeping. But it hadn't been occupied in a dog's age. Talk about dust, cobwebs, and, *eww*...more than enough spiders to last a lifetime. It was now clean and functional—thanks to Evan and Augusta, as well as her sister, Savannah, and her boyfriend, Mac, who owned a garage in town.

A narrow hallway led to the large room she'd claimed as her office. The battered tin ceilings complemented the sage-colored walls and glossy white molding. A new oak desk and high-backed leather chair occupied the corner adjacent to a window. The other wall housed a cream chenille love seat and small sofa with multitextured throw pillows and a glass-and-wrought-iron coffee table. Casual, yet chic, it relayed a sense of home and comfort for client consultations.

High ceilings and large picture windows let in lots of natural light. Perfect for picking patterns and shades of wall coverings, upholstery, and paint colors.

Rambo bounded to his favorite spot, his extra-plush dog bed in the corner. Plopping the mail and her purse on the desk, she sank into the desk chair and pulled off her boots. Designer or not, they hurt. *Ah, bliss.* Squirreled under the desk was a pair of plush slippers. The message light on the phone blinked. She pushed play and winced at the voice.

"Meghan, it's your mother. Your father inquired about your attendance at the Halloween eve ball. Please return my calls. I've tried your cell phone numerous times, and now I'm forced to resort to your business phone. Your behavior is bordering on rude."

"Press seven to save and nine to delete," the machine's robotic speech instructed. No-brainer there.

Laptop opened, she fired up the calendar and email then scrolled the list of appointments and call-back notes, an invoice from a lighting place in Newport, as well as that Aubusson weave scheduled for shipment from her contact in New York. Lots to do.

The cell phone rang from inside her purse. Reaching in, she smiled at the screen and swiped. "Hi, Elle. Are you on your lunch period?"

"Yeah, I have ten minutes left. Did you arrange for Rambo's procedure? It's not today, is it?"

They'd both decided it was best for the little guy to get fixed. Once Rambo had graduated into full-blown adult male dog, none of their pant legs or throw pillows had been safe. God, he was worse than a hormonal teenager. Worse than Evan ever had been trying to hide his porn magazines.

"I scheduled it for next Wednesday morning." Meghan watched the subject at hand hump his favorite stuffed giraffe. "Although maybe I should have done it today. Doctor O'Brien said he'd be fine. Might have to stay overnight, though."

"I want to be there when you drop him off," Brielle said. Rambo and Brielle were inseparable, the bond between them tangible. Brielle had trained him. She had a talent with animals. Another reason why Havenport was a perfect fit. Augusta's training school at the shelter gave Brielle the opportunity to pursue her career dreams.

"I know, honey, which is why I booked it at eight a.m., so you'll have plenty of time to get to school."

The African violet on the windowsill—a congratulations gift from Mom—looked half-dead. Better get to watering the brown leaves, or never live it down if Mom ever graced Haven on Earth with her presence. She padded to the small restroom next to her office and flipped on the light. Balancing the cell phone on one shoulder, she filled a bottle with water, thanks to the sensor faucet Evan had installed last week.

"I'm supposed to help Augusta at the training center after school. I can get a ride home if you're not around," Brielle said.

Meghan dumped the whole thing into the plant. Was it too much? "Hang on and let me check my appointments."

Her stomach did a little flip at the name on her five o'clock slot—250 Maple Street, Dylan O'Brien. Come to remember, a woman had booked the consultation. His wife?

"Mom? Can you pick me up at five?"

She shook her head. "Um, sorry, I can't. I have an appointment. Ask Augusta to drive you home."

"Or I *could* get a ride from Jacob."

There was a wistful tone in Brielle's voice. Jacob worked for Augusta, and appeared to be a good kid, though eighteen didn't exactly qualify as a kid. "Brielle, I don't…"

"Please, Mom." Brielle cut off the rest of her sentence. "He's a great driver. Uncle Evan told Jacob if anything happens to me he'd geld him."

An overbearing helicopter mom wasn't healthy, she knew. However, Brielle riding in a car with a boy didn't sit well, either. "I'll be sure to thank Uncle Evan later, although I'd guess Augusta didn't appreciate him threatening her employee."

"Oh, no." Brielle laughed. "Augusta threatened first, but not nearly as barbaric. So? Can I get a slice of pizza with Jacob, then have him drive me home?"

"Oh, now it's pizza, too?" Something dawned. A lump formed in her throat. "Are you dating Jacob?"

Meghan tipped her head back against the high-backed chair. The tin ceiling stared back at her. *God, no. Not yet.* Then came the sex talk, birth control talk, and crap...venereal disease. Being a single parent and dealing with this stuff wasn't going to be easy.

Brielle chuckled, and it made her stomach unclench a bit. "We're friends."

"All right then, you can go. Text me when you leave the shelter, get to the restaurant, and when you're on the way home."

"So at least three times? Maybe I should do it every fifteen minutes?"

"Very funny," she said with a huff. "I know. I'm being overprotective. I worry. And I love you, and...it's just us now."

"I'll be fine," Brielle said, matter-of-fact, then hesitated. "And, Mom, I'm glad it's just us now."

The words made her want to cry. A tiny spark of hope blossomed. Could there be a hint of a chance she'd build a great relationship with Brielle as not only a mother but as a friend?

"I'll see you at home. Be safe," Meghan whispered, then hung up, not wanting to let on how sappy she'd become. Emotions seemed to bubble up at the worst times. Time to focus.

"Guess we're on our own all day before I drop you off later."

Rambo barely stopped abusing the poor giraffe to acknowledge her. Definitely neutering time.

For some unexplained reason, nervous anticipation about meeting Dylan O'Brien again sent flutters into her empty stomach. Must be hunger pains. Brielle raved about him after last summer, as if she'd had a crush on the doctor. No doubt as to why. Despite his nerdy way, Dylan O'Brien probably turned more than a few heads in town. But if Dr. O'Brien was indeed popular in Havenport, it might be a good idea to make a great impression on him about her professional abilities as a designer. Another glance at the calendar and she hopped up. "Better get lunch then, Rambo. We've got a long day ahead."

Chapter Three

At half past two, Dylan finally arrived at the animal shelter. He pushed open the glass doors, newly etched with Havenport Animal Shelter, and walked toward the reception area. "Sorry I'm late. Been a long morning."

Augusta sat at the reception desk manning the phones, but didn't glance up from the computer screen. "More like afternoon, Doctor O'Brien."

"Couldn't be helped." He shoved his cell phone into the pocket of his windbreaker and adjusted the shoulder strap to his medical bag.

She shrugged. "I know, I know. You're super vet. Let me guess, your female pet owners couldn't keep their hands to themselves." She constantly teased him about his popularity with the women of Havenport.

He shot her a death glare. No reaction, as usual.

"Were they fighting over you?"

"Huh?"

She gestured to his eye. "The shiner."

"Hit it on an open cabinet," he lied on the fly. Not one mention of his disastrous meeting with Meghan, and if Augusta knew about it, she'd never keep it quiet. "And yes, the fan club detained me." May as well keep it that way.

She sneered. "Thought so. Now get in the back and get to work. There are pets waiting for their forever homes."

"Slave driver," he muttered, and headed around the high desk, then through the double doors to the exam area. Thanks to Evan acquiring the historic waterfront building, saving it from being sold for luxury condos, Augusta was able to expand the animal shelter. With her expertise, Augusta was on her way to turning the place into a stellar training school.

"Who do we have today?" Dylan approached the cages and peeked in. A black tabby with copper eyes hissed and cowered in the corner. Food and water bowls lay untouched.

Augusta came up behind him. "She's a handful. Got the scratches to prove it. Owner dropped her off this morning. Allergies."

He sighed and regarded the poor, scared kitty. "Then why get a long-haired? Some people have no concept of how much diligence and responsibility it takes to own a pet, especially a pedigree cat."

August nodded. "Preaching to the choir, Doc."

"Looks like she's been a bit neglected." Matted hair, especially around its hind legs, had to be painful. "She'll need a good grooming. But I'll check for ear mites and fleas first. Might need to be dipped."

"Oh, joy. Cats and water go so well together."

He chuckled at Augusta's frown. "What, Bridget doesn't like baths?" Augusta's menagerie of pets was a collection to behold, and her cat held the title of queen.

"She's a diva." Augusta rolled her eyes, a gesture she'd picked up from Evan. Meghan LaRue popped into his head and he swallowed. He had to stop thinking about the unavailable, married, gorgeous Mrs. LaRue. There was no way in hell Augusta could find out about his sudden and unwanted attraction for her boyfriend's sister.

Together they wrestled the cat out of the back of the cage, and he performed the exam. "Open up," he cooed, while trying to check her teeth, and nearly lost an index finger.

"Easy, sweetheart." Gently he listened to her heartbeat with a stethoscope to the underbelly. "You're beautiful. Yes, that's it. See, not so bad." The cat calmed. A faint purring commenced.

Augusta snorted.

He gave her a sideways glance. "Jealous?"

"Hardly."

"Does our girl have a name?" he asked, wiping gunk from its face. Eye crust was typical of a Persian cat. With their flattened faces, the breed was notorious for tear duct issues.

Augusta carefully checked around its neck. "The collar says Esmeralda."

He chuckled. "Appropriate for Halloween."

"Speaking of which—and not *that* witch," Augusta began, and he flinched.

Dumb-ass. Why did he have to go and mention it?

"The masquerade ball is this weekend."

"Is it?" Wonder if any of his employees wanted his tickets. He made busy with tossing the used gauze into the trash before putting Esmeralda back in her cage. A sting hit his left shoulder.

"Ouch. That's abuse. Remember, I volunteer my time here." He rubbed the sore spot. Jeez, her punch packed a wallop. "Evan has you hitting the gym, I see." Yes, deflection. Effective.

"Don't try and change the subject." She crossed her arms high against her Wags and Walks T-shirt. Oh boy,

Augusta in fixation mode. There might be no getting around this conversation. "What are you planning to dress up as, and who do you plan on taking?"

"Myself, and myself. Maybe." With that, he turned and hunted in the mounted cabinets for flea and tick bath. "I stocked a bunch of Four Paws last week. Ms. Essie here will need it." Sorting through the jumble of stuff, he shook his head. What a mess.

Augusta brushed past him with a twirl of long hair, which always smelled like coconut, and pulled two bottles from the top shelf.

"Here." One bottle landed in his outstretched palm. "That won't do."

He regarded the bottle. "Says here for cats."

Her turn for the death glare, to which *he* ignored. "I meant you going alone. Isn't there anyone you can ask? You're reasonably attractive."

"Gee, thanks."

"Come on, Dyl. It'll be like a double date. Me and Evan, you and…" Eyebrows raised, she waited.

"No one comes to mind," he said flatly. Except Mrs. LaRue. *Shut it down.*

"What about that new receptionist you hired?"

He moved about the room, opening the cage where the beagle who'd come in last week lay. No takers yet. Such sad eyes met his before the dog sniffed his hand.

"Vanessa?" He scratched his chin, considering the suggestion. "She's a bit young." Barely twenty-five. Ten years' difference wasn't too bad. *Nah.* Dating an employee—not a good idea. What if they hated each other after twenty minutes?

Augusta shook her head in disgust.

"What?"

"Her name is Dana. You're pathetic. No wonder you can't find a woman. Helps if you remember their name."

She approached and patted his shoulder as if he were a child, or an imbecile.

He shrugged and gathered his stuff, putting it in the right order in his medical bag. It was closing in on four, and there was that interior design person coming to his house. A shower had to happen as soon as he got home.

"All the more reason to go it alone. Wouldn't want to subject any poor woman to my early-stage dementia." Satisfied he'd dodged a bullet, he smiled. Halfway to the door, he realized he'd forgotten his windbreaker. The afternoon had turned windy. Plus, the sun set around 5:45 in the evening. Winter was on its way.

"I'll find you a date," she announced as he turned to grab the jacket off the table.

Trepidation rose into his scalp. Not matchmaking Augusta. "Please," he pleaded. "If you value our friendship, don't."

That excited sparkle in her eye fizzled, and her mouth turned down. *Aw, hell.*

"Fine. Don't accept my help for your pitiful love life." She pouted while putting away supplies in such disarray it made him twitchy. "Let me remind you," her voice rose and she crossed her arms, "how well my efforts with Mac and Savannah worked."

He leaned over and pecked her on the cheek. "They're happy and in love; you're happy and in love. Does not mean everyone in Havenport needs to be. Thanks, but no thanks."

"You'll be, too. I'll call you."

He turned the corner and beelined for the door.

Chapter Four

Meghan shut the car door and smoothed out her hair. Gone were the instruments-of-torture boots, and instead she'd thrown on a pair of tan flats to go with her navy jumpsuit.

Rambo slept safely at home on Brielle's bed, waiting for her to get home, too. Evan would be proud. She'd refrained from actually going into the pizza restaurant, merely driving by to spy on Brielle and Jacob.

She squared her shoulders and considered 250 Maple Street. Situated halfway down one of the more residential streets in Havenport, the split ranch had a manicured front yard with perfectly shaped boxwoods lining under the low-hung windows, and stone steps leading to a solid oak front door. Looked like a long, high deck jutted from the side of the house around to the backyard as well. A stone chimney shot out from opposite the other side of the roof. Given the house next door's faded, ugly cedar shingles, the white vinyl siding on Dr. O'Brien's house appeared new. The whole house had been refurbished. And done well.

Except the atrocious mailbox near the sidewalk and the Red Sox banner flying on a post by the front door.

Deliberately, Meghan considered the hockey mailbox. Reminded her of Brielle's elementary school art projects. Nailed together with blades at the top facing outward, the long parts of the sticks constructed the post. A small, metal box with a *B* in black and yellow mounted onto a shelf.

That might have to go. Replaced by a nice flower planter type, or brass to match the hinges around the front door. Perhaps in a pale blue, complementing the dark gray of the wooden shutters.

Make the front less ESPN. But then again, perhaps his wife was a sports fan. For some reason the thought made her...what? Envious?

"Work time, Meghan," she muttered, and gazed up and down the road.

The tree-lined street gave a cozy and inviting vibe with its hodgepodge of different structures. Many homes had been rebuilt or had additions. White PVC fences surrounded most of the yards, and the occasional striped jungle gym tents poked into view. This particular area of Havenport housed year-round residents.

Stick mailbox aside, she wondered what kind of guy Dr. Dylan O'Brien would turn out to be. Obviously handsome, physically fit, and smart—had to be, to graduate vet school—but what about his home? More importantly, did the inside reflect his personality?

Was he married? Maybe his girlfriend booked the appointment?

Stop that.

Whoever it turned out to be, at least somebody needed a decorator. And as a designer, her job wasn't to care about the marital state of a potential client. Nor was it to administer change all at once—sometimes not much at all—but to help her clients uncover their true selves when it came to their homes. Making havens on earth—hence the business name.

Haven on Earth Designs' motto was comfortable, peaceful, with subtle sophistication. Oh boy, she'd become an ad for a Hallmark commercial.

Perhaps a few pictures would be a good starting point, although *technically* Dr. O'Brien wasn't her client. Yet. Nonetheless, better do it now or lose daylight. Retracing her steps to the front gate, she turned and snatched the Nikon from her computer bag.

The wide-angle lens easily captured the entire front of the house. She made sure to zoom in on the color of the shutters and stone on the steps for later reference. May as well take a few of that mailbox, too, in case Dr. or *Mrs.* O'Brien insisted on keeping it. Personally, she'd opt to convert the hideous thing to a planter.

Her feet crunched up the stone walkway and onto a flagstone. It was cracked, as well as some of the surrounding ones. They'd need to be replaced. Eyeballing the mailbox, Meghan decided that if the planter idea sold, finding the correct size replacement to fit next to the fence would be important.

One more picture should do it. Maybe if she leaned in a bit. Her back strained from the odd angle of squeezing between the fence and box, when suddenly her toe smashed into something hard.

"Ouch!" She squinted at the ground. A patch of gerbera daisies hid a stray rock protruding from the dirt. Her big toe burned. She tried to sidestep the rock, but another stone next to it proved as jagged. The soft leather soles on her flats held no defense against these stupid boulders. Her ankle turned.

She grabbed on to the nearest thing.

Crack.

Like a slow-motion movie, Meghan had no way to halt the disaster. One minute she'd tried to avoid dropping and breaking a five-hundred-dollar camera, and the next she held remnants of the blade of the hockey stick in her hand.

Oh, no. Her heart stopped then pounded fast and furious. Two considerations entered her mind: the ugly-ass mailbox had broken, and no one witnessed. She hadn't rung the doorbell yet. Best scenario, stuff the piece of splintered wood in her bag, quickly drive off, and no one would be the wiser.

No harm, no foul, right? Except foul existed. Broken foul. In her hand.

"Crap."

Dylan's jaw dropped. *She broke my Bruins mailbox.* "I made that in the seventh grade," he muttered, incredulous. So what? It'd busted about twenty times in the past twenty years, but still.

When he'd first spied Meghan LaRue in her fancy SUV, Dylan thought he'd fallen into a coma or in the midst of an erotic dream. A delicious subliminal fantasy struck of her knocking on his door, wanting to hook up or check on his swollen eyebrow. In reality, he'd merely observed her antics through the curtains, kind of creepy like a Peeping Tom, only in reverse, since he was the one inside the house. Then his phone reminder beeped about the five o'clock appointment, and he realized *she* might very well be the design consultant. Explained the picture taking.

Meghan bit her lip and glanced between his front door and her car. Ah, so she's planning a hit-and-run, or a break-and-run, huh? He waited. She squared her shoulders, adjusting some kind of blanket thing around them, and marched toward his front steps.

He reared back from the window. Taking the stairs two at a time, he almost dropped the freaking towel around his waist. He'd stepped out of the shower and caught movement in his front yard, and the rest unfolded. Not a good idea to come to the door naked.

In his bedroom, he threw on a Navy T-shirt and nylon running shorts. Why was it that every time they met, he dressed like a slob? The doorbell rang a split second after he shoved bare feet into a pair of kicks. After a quick glance at his wet hair in the dresser mirror—no salvaging that catastrophe—he hopped downstairs. He opened the door and fought to keep a neutral expression.

She cleared her throat and licked her lips. *Here it comes again.* Desire, wanting, attraction, despite the curved wood in her hand.

Poor choice of image, you idiot.

"Mrs. LaRue? Hello." She held up the broken hockey stick, and he frowned.

"I will fix this," she announced. "And if you don't want to keep our appointment, I totally understand."

"Appointment?" *Yeah, play dumb and see where this goes.*

It was her turn to frown, before a blush invaded her cheeks. Made the green in her eyes pop. "I'm here for an interior design consultation," she clarified. "Haven on Earth Designs? Your wife booked it."

Wife? "No, no, no. I'm not married. It was my secretary," he lied. "Must have forgotten the date."

A vee creased her brow. "If this is a bad time…" She pivoted to leave.

Do not go.

"You make it a habit of breaking mailboxes as part of your business strategy?" He couldn't help teasing her. Augusta and her sister, Savannah—heck, his own sister—

could give it as good as they got. *Uh-oh.* Meghan LaRue might not be that kind of woman, if her silence was any indication.

She turned back. The delicate muscles in her throat contracted. "Of course not. Perhaps we're even now."

She fidgeted with the strap on her computer bag and wouldn't meet his eyes.

"Oh? Funny, I don't remember breaking your mailbox." His shoulders shook. So much for playing it cool.

Her gaze narrowed, then a slow grin invaded her face, and he had a feeling he'd met his match in wits. "Funny, *I've* had a splitting headache all day."

Touché. "Acetaminophen should help," he said with a grin he couldn't control. "But I'm afraid my Bruins mailbox might be out of commission."

"Well," she said with a dramatic sigh, and juggled the remnants of his old hockey stick between her palms. Let's hope he didn't get beaned with it. "I'm sure I can come up with a solution. Being I'm a designer and all." Her eyes twinkled and he almost had to sit down, right there in his entranceway.

The tension emanating between them made his head buzz. It'd been too long since he'd enjoyed banter with an intelligent, beautiful woman who he wasn't either related to, or was a would-be sister.

He scratched the stubble on his chin. Great, forgot to shave again. She must think him a Neanderthal. "I get the distinct feeling you don't like my box."

She sucked in a breath and bit her bottom lip. "My professional opinion? It might be time for a new box. Something attractive, yet sturdy, bigger, longer lasting." She tilted her head and smirked.

Score one for the sexual innuendo department. Dylan rubbed the back of his neck. Not that he wasn't used to ladies in Havenport throwing themselves at him. Yet this didn't seem right. Was Meghan LaRue, an obviously married woman, a seriously hot married woman, someone he wanted so bad the running shorts might have been a bad choice, flirting with him?

Did no one believe in monogamy? Besides, Augusta would kill him. *Cut it out. Now.*

"I'm being rude, leaving you on my porch. Please, come in." Opening the door wider, Dylan gestured inside. Time to redirect the conversation, and either salvage the appointment, keep things professional, or cancel it. Either way, Mrs. LaRue deserved to be asked to come inside.

Her smile faltered, like she realized he'd shut down their flirt session. "Thank you. This is lovely."

His house wasn't huge by any stretch. The rooms, though not fully furnished, were spacious. Hardwood floors, resanded and stained, covered the entire first floor.

"The previous owners renovated it shortly before I bought," he informed her. "This area used to be two smaller rooms." He pointed to the open layout of the living room. "I found the original plans in the attic."

A big-screen TV he'd mounted on the wall above the fireplace acted as the focal point downstairs. A cushioned, brown leather sectional with two long ottomans sat against one wall. A slate-topped coffee table rested on a decent area rug. He'd liked the geometric pattern, and it was easy to keep clean.

In the other corner, his pride and joy: the infamous foosball table, an official Boston Red Sox full-size, mean-ass machine. Many memories from college days happened on that table. All sorts of high-stakes challenges won and lost.

Augusta suggested he name it Bea and make it his girlfriend.

Meghan stilled the minute she turned to the table. Here was the moment of truth. She'd either hate it, like

Mom did, or…*nah*…she'd probably hate it. Being a fancy-schmantzy designer and all.

"I. Love. Foosball."

Huh?

She glided across the room and began stroking, *actually stroking*, the polished mother-of-pearl custom handles. Running her palms along the red-and-blue sides of the table with the Sox and MLB logo. Was that an exclamation of joy or a *wow*?

"*You* play?"

She crossed her arms and her foot tapped under a pants leg. She'd ditched the sexy boots. "You think women can't play foosball?"

This is a test. Mom finally prayed hard enough so St. Patrick stuck it to him for not going to confession in, like, fifteen years. Dylan chose his words carefully. "I've met a few girls in college who played. I didn't envision a mature woman would."

Her eyebrows shot up. "Mature. Are you implying I'm old, Doctor O'Brien?"

Sunday mass, on the calendar. "Pfft…what? I…no," he stammered. "Mature, as in a sophisticated woman like yourself would not appear to partake in such childish games."

She blew a lock of hair away from her eyelash. "Diplomatic. Care to make a little wager?"

His face must've shown his surprise. "What?" she asked, innocently—almost. He'd heard Augusta adopt that tone. "You afraid to lose?"

Oh, ho. This was his territory. Veterinary school textbooks cost a fortune, and he'd paid for none with his own money. "Are you in a position to wager? I mean, remember my mailbox?"

She cracked her knuckles and removed the poncho thing, leaving it and her computer bag on the floor against the wall. "I'll take my chances."

She grazed past him, and he caught a whiff of her peachy musk. Hot damn, he needed to step back. She bent over to reach into the hole in the table where the balls were stored, and he froze before swallowing hard.

He cleared his throat. "Tell you what—I'll give you a few minutes to warm up. Do not say I wasn't a gentleman. Can I offer you anything to drink?"

"I'm good. But I'll tell you what," she countered, before deftly handling the rods. He grew a little nervous. "If you win, I'll replace your mailbox with a better version of a Boston Bruins creation, free of charge. And if *I* win…" A positively mischievous smile followed, and he swallowed. "It gets replaced with a pretty flower-planter-type mailbox. More fitting of your lovely house."

"Agreed." No way he would lose. He stuck out his hand, and they shook on the deal.

A half hour later, Dylan needed another shower. Damn, the woman could play. They were neck and neck, four all.

A bead of sweat formed on her upper lip. She bit it to concentrate. The defined muscles of her biceps flexed under that formfitting jumper thing, but she seemed to have unlimited stamina.

"Argh," he groaned and missed an easy shot. Distracted much?

Meghan laughed and her whole face lit. "Better work on those midfielders, Doctor O'Brien."

He pulled a rollover shot, which she easily blocked with her goalie. "Nice block, Mrs. LaRue."

"Meghan, and it's actually not," she said, and he nearly got caught up, but deflected her pull kick.

"Say again? That was a great block." And it was.

She shook her head and front-pinned the ball. "What's 'say again'?"

He shrugged. "Navy talk. I was a Corpsman. You play like—and don't throw stones—a guy."

She pursed her lips. "I'm not sure that's a compliment, but I'll take it. No, I mean it's actually not *Mrs*. At least not anymore."

His hand slipped off the rod, but he quickly recovered. Holy! "I'm sorry," he said, because he didn't know what else to say. Thank you, God?

"I'm not." She pegged him with a stare, and he was toast. *Wham*. She'd won. "Pale blue, with an appealing flower box attached."

His throat dried like the Kabul desert. "This calls for a celebration drink. I admit, begrudgingly, I haven't lost to so beautiful an opponent, ever." Crap. Way to slip and call her beautiful.

Meghan walked over and plopped on the couch. "You were more than worthy." She rubbed a bicep. "Ow. My arms got a workout."

No response to his stupid slip, although her cheeks tinged pink. "Be right back." Time to exit and pray for libation-induced tact.

"Doctor O'Brien," she called when he reached the threshold to the kitchen. "Don't think compliments will change my mind. I'll have that drink. Then come back and we'll discuss your favorite shade of blue."

The corner of his mouth lifted. Yeah, the entire house needed a makeover.

What in the world is wrong with you? Throwing caution to the wind and challenging Dylan to foosball. She hadn't had this much fun since the early days living in the city while attending college. When all she'd cared about were weekends out and blowing off steam in dive bars, which had made her pretty damn good at the game. Until Jacques, his debonair persona, and getting pregnant.

Past mistakes. Tonight's match and flirty teasing with the cute vet made her feel young again. Once his hair had dried, it changed from midnight to dark brown and curled around his ears. He resembled a frat boy—the hot ones she used to like.

Plus, there was no ignoring his muscular forearms and manly hands around the spinning foosball rods. Jacques paid for weekly manicures, his nails buffed to a shine. He'd insisted she wear fake gel claws in a French manicure. First thing she'd done after Jacques moved out was soak them all off.

Dylan had a natural way about him. No nonsense, no fancy clothes. Stupid T-shirts. When he laughed, the creases deepened around his eyes. Icy-blue irises contrasted with his pale skin and dark hair. O'Brien was an Irish surname, the shamrock light fixture over the foosball table and leprechaun gnome statue in the corner a dead giveaway to his heritage.

She leaned back against the plush blanket with the US Navy emblem thrown over the back of the couch, and sighed. A picture sat on the nearest end table. It showed Dylan and three others in their Navy uniforms. He'd probably witnessed horrible sights overseas while in the Navy. Although Evan rarely talked about it, she knew he'd battled his own demons after coming home.

Thank goodness they were both home, safe, and out of the fray. Reaching over, she picked up the frame and stared at the three gorgeous men in the photo. All were tall, two mammoth in the shoulders compared to Dylan. Of the three he took the honor of most handsome. There was something just right about the way he filled out his uniform. Yep, he was definitely stud material, yet in an intellectual way.

Sometimes a mind proved sexier than anything.

She placed the frame back in its place, and a second later he swaggered back into the room, his running shorts showing the hard, cut muscles of his thighs.

The room temperature rose about ten degrees. She debated grabbing the copy of *Veterinary Digest* from the table to use as a fan. Instead, she arranged the geometric pattern throw pillows on his couch that matched the rug, and gave him her best neutral expression. He held a bottle of wine in one hand, and two glasses in the other.

"The vintage is better than the stemware, I assure you." He placed all on the table with a grin.

She glanced at the label. "Pétrus?"

He winked. "My secret; costly indulgence. However, as much as I'd like to think I could afford the six-thousand bottle, this isn't it."

The bottle had been uncorked. Good man, to let it breathe properly.

"You're probably used to real crystal, but like I said, they're what I have." He poured a generous amount in each glass, a set of no-stemmed goblets with Red Sox logos. Thank goodness she'd eaten dinner earlier. Meghan placed her nose to the rim of the glass. The aroma, a mixture of Asian spice coupled with the tartness of cherries, invaded her senses.

Dylan folded his frame into the opposite end of the couch and stretched long legs on the other ottoman. He had on a good pair of Nikes. A hint of hair covered his legs, lighter colored than on his head.

Jacques had olive skin and was god-awful hairy, with a barrel chest covered in dark curls like a rug—and on his arms and legs, too. At one time, she'd found it sensual, kind of caveman-ish. But the subtle color of Dylan's skin and long lines in his muscles gave her a new appreciation for a runner's body. He stretched one arm overhead. "I'm sore, too." His shirt rode up his torso. A line of light hair disappeared into the low-slung waistband of his shorts. She tore her gaze away.

He took a sip of wine, then regarded his glass with a grimace. "Maybe we should discuss your ideas for revamping my housewares collection."

"Are you hiring me as your designer, or trying to impress me?"

He dipped his head and shrugged. "Since my foosball skills are clearly lacking, is that possible?" His gaze held hers for a few seconds—playful, yet appearing uncertain.

"The hiring part or the impressing part?" Her heart sped, waiting for his answer.

"Depends on which you prefer."

Heat, which had nothing at all to do with the lovely bouquet in her glass, shot to her cheeks. Was she ready for this kind of flirting? Unexpected, out-of-the-box, heart-pounding attraction? Before she knew it, her glass was empty.

Their easy conversation had completely taken her by surprise. Dylan spoke about his Navy days, and why he'd moved to Havenport. She relayed a little bit about the marriage fiasco, but not much. Besides, being close to Augusta, as he'd mentioned, he'd hear about it eventually. Small town and gossip went hand in hand.

Amazingly, the persona she put up when meeting with a client didn't exist here. It was the strangest consultation ever. Felt remarkable to let go of trying to be super businesswoman, or super mom.

Right here, right now, shoes kicked off at Dylan's insistence, sat plain old Meghan LaRue—designer, divorcée, and single mother.

"Earth to Meghan," came Dylan's voice, breaking her out of the reverie.

She shook her head. "I'm sorry."

He chuckled. "Glad I'm not the only person who gets lost in thought. Are you already calculating ways to change my decor?"

Before she could respond, a loud grumble came from his stomach. "Cripes," he muttered. "Are you hungry? Apparently I am."

She glanced at her phone. Almost seven o'clock. No text from Brielle.

"Or do you have someplace to be?" He rose and placed his empty glass on the coffee table.

"No, no, it's…Brielle promised to text, which she hasn't done yet. She went out for pizza with Jacob. I'm a little worried." *Now why go and tell him that?*

His eyebrows reached the curl falling in a sexy, yet boyish way over his forehead. "She's on a date?"

Where were her flats? She stood, searching the floor and around the base of the ottoman for them. "God help me. I hope not. At least not yet."

"Augusta told me Brielle's sixteen?" At her nod, he continued. "Yup, that's the right age. I remember my sister, Shannon, and her first 'boyfriend.'" His fingers formed air quotes on the last word. "I followed them to the movies in my shitbox car, like James Bond." He crossed his arms and grinned. "You drove by the pizza place."

Meghan blinked. How had he known that? Her mouth opened and closed a few times, thinking of the correct response, or denial.

He nodded. "Thought so. Don't worry, your secret's safe." He retrieved her shoes from under the ottoman, handed them over, then headed toward the kitchen. "Best I can do is BLTs if you're interested?"

"I have to go." As much as sharing a meal with Dylan sounded heavenly, and she so wanted to flirt and ogle his butt, she needed to make sure Brielle got home safe.

He stopped short and turned. His easy smile fell. "Oh, okay."

See now, this is why dating didn't mix with being a single mom. Her first choice would always be Brielle.

"Well, thanks for the match and the company," he said a little too quickly, and she sensed he was covering up disappointment. Unfortunately, there wasn't much she could do about it.

Grabbing her pashmina and bag off the floor, she ambled to the front door. "It was my pleasure." For some reason, the need to relay how awesome this night had been proved important. She turned to face him. "Really, I mean it. I haven't had this much fun in forever."

He leaned in, and she froze. Was he going in for a kiss? A peck on the cheek for foosball well played? But he merely reached behind her to turn the knob. *Stupid.*

"Me, too." His voice was low and deep next to her ear. She shivered.

Time to go. Adjusting the strap on her bag, she let out a breath and stepped over the threshold.

"Um, wait."

"Yes." She turned, a little breathless, to be honest. The wine had made her mellow and more talkative than usual. He made her feel sexy by listening intently to her blabbering, never losing eye contact. Jacques ignored her on a good day. Yet those comparisons were no reason to throw more caution to the wind and stay. Right? Not for BLTs, or a view of the rest of his house, like his bedroom?

Now where had that come from?

Dylan shifted and examined his sneaker before glancing up. "I'd like to hire you, err…Haven on Earth. That is, if you're still interested?" He rubbed the back of his neck. "Given I'm on the hook for a new mailbox anyway, I'm thinking perhaps the rest of the house should be changed. Can we reschedule the consultation?"

She couldn't help smiling at how adorable and uncertain this former Navy man and super vet appeared. "Is tomorrow morning too soon to discuss my ideas?"

He seemed skeptical. "Will my sports stuff need to find a new home?"

She smirked. "Well…not the table."

"Promise?"

"Uh-huh."

His shoulders relaxed, and he gave her that frat-boy look again. "Then you've got yourself a new client. I don't have to be at the clinic until eleven a.m. How about nine-ish?"

"I'll see you then." A sizzle started low in her belly, and she knew her face was a flaming fireball, thinking about tomorrow morning. She meandered down the flagstones and to the car, resisting the urge to turn around.

Chapter Five

Dylan turned the lock with a soft click and leaned a hand against the door for a few moments, trying to get a handle on his emotions.

Foosball, wine—Meghan LaRue?

He wanted to review the facts, but not on an empty stomach. In the kitchen, he surveyed the sad state of his refrigerator, then opted for the piece of leftover cold pizza.

Back in the living room, the half-full bottle of Pétrus remained, along with the recollections of her smile, their conversation, an amazing and clearly unplanned evening. Damned near perfect, except when Meghan had to leave. He understood why. Brielle was her responsibility.

She's divorced. Plus column. *She's Evan's sister.* Slide that over to the minus column. *She'd probably flirted on the rebound.* Debatable.

Their conversation seemed genuine, but what the hell did he know? He couldn't recall his receptionist's name. As much as finishing the bottle and maybe, maybe trying to decipher what had transpired, he'd never get up for a run in the morning if drunk, so he recorked the Pétrus and rinsed out the glasses in the kitchen.

Too much nervous energy left his skull buzzing. He couldn't get the image of Meghan's sexy legs stretched out on his ottoman out of his mind. Or the way she'd brushed her riot of curls away from her lashes. The clank of her bracelets when she'd raised and lowered her wineglass. They covered her left wrist. She mentioned the maker, but he couldn't recall—no surprise there. All sorts of charms hung from thin silver bands, apparently each having significance in her life. He'd commented that he'd liked the silver dog one, especially. Then, when she'd savored the Pétrus by licking her lips and letting out a faint moan, his abs twitched and his toes tingled.

She's coming back in the morning.

Anticipation hit his gut worse than running the Boston marathon last April. If he didn't blow off some of the steam engine going on in his body soon, he'd be toast. Yet running five miles wasn't on the table. His calves couldn't take it, nor was he up for a cold shower.

Mindless sports on TV? *Yeah, definitely in order.* No more pondering feelings or desires, or new paint colors.

Dylan flipped the channels until he found a repeat of the Islanders versus Rangers on ESPN. He sat back and tried to concentrate on the score. No use. Meghan stretched out on the very spot where he sat negated the effort. Food would help. That pizza wasn't near enough. How about delivery from the new Italian place in town? The menu had to be around somewhere.

A shrill bell penetrated a delicious dream of silky, dark curls and soft lips opening for a deep kiss. Why was he on the couch? Right. Food coma brought on by the large meatball sub.

The house phone rang.

Strange, it never rang. He'd kept the landline only for emergencies. Mom insisted, in case all the cell towers were ever blown up. No arguing with Peg. Groaning like a ninety-year-old, he forced himself upright and reached for the cordless. "Hello."

"Dyl, are you home?" Augusta's voice sounded funny.

"You called my house phone. Have you been drinking at Royce's again?" The last time she'd gotten piss-drunk over woes when she'd first met Evan she'd sent some pretty provocative texts by mistake—damned funny that auto correct.

"Oh, shoot. I hit your house number. Listen, I need you to come to the shelter, pronto. We've got a dog. Dyl, it's in pretty bad shape." Her voice cracked.

"On my way." He vaulted from the couch and grabbed his jacket and keys by the front door. "Sitrep?"

Her sigh blasted in his ear. "You're lucky I'm in love with a former Marine. The *situation report* is German shepherd, a bit on the mangy side, in that his coat is horrendously filthy."

"Who dropped him off?"

"Dunno," Augusta said. "Something compelled me to swing by to check on Essie and I found him."

What time is it? The hall clock showed 11:00 p.m.

"Someone either left him on the steps," she continued to explain, "or he collapsed here. I'll check the security cameras tomorrow. He's breathing, though not awake, and I cannot lift him."

"Any blood, or visible injury?" Anger rose to his scalp. Why would someone leave it? Why not call the number noted on the shelter door? He and Augusta, as well as the other volunteer staff, were notified via text when someone left a message. That way, anytime day or night, there'd be someone to intake a new animal. He'd been called in many, many nights to open the shelter and help a furry friend. He heard shuffling followed by a bark, then a low growl.

"Easy there, big guy." His stomach lurched at Augusta's warning. "Looks like he's awake but unable to get up. Lucky me."

"Back away. I'll be there in a flash."

Dylan found Augusta sitting cross-legged beside an enormous tan-and-black shepherd, stroking its mammoth head. Remnants of powdered sugar and flakes of dough covered the dog's big snout.

"Is that a doughnut?"

Augusta rose to her feet and wiped her hands on her Wags and Walks sweatshirt. "Mellie's apple pie," she clarified. "You're lucky I like you, buster," she said to the dog, who licked his chops. "I never share my pie."

Dylan blinked. "Might have waited until I examined him first," he said drily. "I pictured you maimed, or worse. Way to give me a heart attack."

Augusta rolled her eyes and unlocked the door. "Would you miss me?"

"Hardly." Although he offered up small thanks nothing had happened to her. He eyeballed the dog lying on its abdomen, gigantic paws outstretched.

"Did you, by any chance during the dessert course, see if he had any identification?" A beat-up, slightly rusted chain encircled the dog's neck. Hard to glimpse if there was a tag attached.

Augusta propped open both glass doors by their top hinges. "I did. Tag says EDD, 104th Battalion. And he's got a tattoo, left ear. Dylan, this big boy's a MWD."

He stilled and studied it more closely. *Military working dog?* All sorts of scenarios careened into his mind. He didn't know too much about MWDs, but he did know they were valuable.

"He's an explosive detection dog," she relayed. "I've personally never trained one, but I've spoken with a few of Mac's EOD buddies. They don't usually have tags. How did you end up here, big guy?" The dog merely rested his head on his paws, looking sad and tired. "Could be someone's lost pet."

"It's possible." Somehow he doubted that was the case. Those types of dogs didn't get lost. Time for action, not speculations, and to find out if the "big guy" had anything seriously wrong. "I'll need a transport stretcher. Do we have one here, or should I swing by the hospital?"

Augusta smiled and wrapped her hair so it jutted atop her head like a palm tree. "We're in luck. Got one donated the other day. It's in the back storage closet. I hope it holds his weight." She rubbed her chin. "He tried to stand, but the right hind leg gave out."

He crossed his arms high on his windbreaker. "Was that before or after you offered him a treat?"

Augusta shrugged. "*I* sensed he wasn't violent, and *he* sensed I wasn't a threat."

"Still, a risk, given his training," he muttered. "Since you two are besties now, stay here and I'll get the stretcher." He strolled inside, flipping on the fluorescents on his way to the back.

Meow.

"And hello to you, too, Ms. Essie." She blinked at the bright light, then gave him a view of her rump. Diva.

Once outside with the stretcher, he and Augusta wrestled with trying to keep it steady. One of the wheels was busted, which was probably the reason for the donation.

Dylan surveyed the situation. "We can't lift him onto the table, so let's keep him right here."

He spoke in low tones, trying to sooth the dog, and started the exam. "Phew, he smells like a sewer. Fleas for sure. Visible signs of loss in skin elasticity, lethargic, enophthalmia."

Dylan ticked off the list of symptoms. He also took note of the wicked-long canine teeth. Yeah, not going there. He needed all his digits. Some sign of dry gums, and evidence of pie.

"What's that last term?"

"Sunken eyes. He's definitely dehydrated."

"Yeah, I know." Augusta handed him a wet rag to clean off the dried dirt from his back paw pads. The dog barely moved. "He downed two of my water bottles in two-point-three seconds."

He palpated the dog's hind leg and got a faint whimper in return. "That hurt, buddy? Looks like a sprain or maybe a ligament tear. There's swelling and inflammation. I suspect nothing's broken, although I can't be sure without an X-ray."

"Can't help you there, sadly. You want Evan to bring the Jeep and we can all get him to the animal hospital?"

The idea had merit. Between his and Evan's combined strength, they could easily lift the dog. Yet the movement might trigger more pain in that leg, which might trigger a big, angry, military-dog-type reaction. Not worth Augusta or him getting bitten. Right now the dog was calm and didn't appear too distressed.

"No. I think we should clean him up, ice the leg, and wait it out. Since his vitals are okay and he drank a bunch without vomiting, and, yep, just peed." Dylan jumped back from the puddle making its way toward his sneaker. He grabbed a stack of paper towels from the countertop. "I'd make him comfortable here and check him in the morning."

Augusta rummaged through the cabinets, handing him flea bath and shampoo. "Glad you're in shorts. I think we're both gonna get soaked." He grimaced, and she laughed. "I know how much you love getting sloppy, Doctor Immaculate."

An hour later, three lathers, rinses, and repeat, Augusta had worked her magic. "Look how handsome you are." She clucked and smoothed the dog's whiskers.

He chuckled. "Why, thank you."

She merely shook her head in disgust and went back to her ministrations on the dog. "You certainly smell better." The dog licked her hand in thanks. "But my back is done for." She stretched with a groan.

He glanced around the room. "He'll need a crate."

She bit her lip. "I don't have one big enough to keep him comfortable. I'm not sure, Dyl. Perhaps he shouldn't be left by himself. What if he becomes aggressive? There's Essie, and that beagle." She nodded to the cages across the room.

She had a point. They didn't know how the dog had come to arrive on their doorstep. Although the ice pack helped with his mobility a bit, he still needed assistance and a big enough area to ensure the safety of the other animals. "Call Evan so we can get this big guy to the clinic tonight."

Augusta had that look on her face, and he was sure he wasn't going to like her suggestion. "Why don't you take him home?"

"Seriously?"

She threw up her hands. "I certainly can't. Zeus would smother him wanting playtime, and Bridget would plan a coup."

Zeus, her bloodhound, still had horrible puppy tendencies. This poor dog did not need to be traumatized by an overenthusiastic toddler.

"You're the town vet, for crying out loud. You need a pet."

"I have plenty of patients who may as well be my pets." People wondered why he didn't have a pet. Not even a goldfish or a hamster. Guess the aversion to being responsible for anyone other than himself came down to raising Shan and Dan for most of his teens and early twenties.

Dylan had a feeling Augusta wasn't budging on this. "All right. You're coming to the O'Brien castle." The dog's ears perked and he let out a short bark.

They both blinked.

"See, he thinks that's a great idea." Augusta smirked.

"How's that great idea now?" Dylan muttered and punched his pillow. It was going on four thirty in the morning and the damn dog wouldn't stop scratching and crying at the attic door. Heart-wrenching cries and whimpers. Annoying as all hell. Maybe the dog hated being inside? In combat and on patrol, he'd spent innumerable nights sleeping out in the desert. This dog had, too. Maybe he hated being cooped up in the house. Although that did not explain scratching at the attic door. The front door, perhaps. But this?

Like nails on a chalkboard, the dog scraped the narrow four-panel next to his bedroom door, which he'd kept cracked in case the dog needed him. There was no way he'd allow it to share his bed, even if he were able to jump up onto the mattress.

The house, built in the early sixties, included a narrow staircase leading up to the attic. Great for storage, but a bit tight on the incline for someone of his height. Mostly, he kept old sporting gear up there, and the odd piece of luggage. What in the world could the dog want? Had a squirrel gotten in the easement again? He'd blocked those destructive little bastards last month.

More whimpers. "Okay, okay. I'll get up. You hungry?" Earlier, the dog hadn't touched a bite of kibble from the shelter. There was half a meatball sub left over in the fridge. Might as well try and see if he'd eat it.

Swinging his legs over the side of the bed and onto the floor, he stood, stretched, and exited his bedroom. The dog looked over one muscular shoulder, and Dylan's heart lurched. Way too much sadness reflected in his soulful eyes. His tail wagged as he pressed against the door, sniffing and nudging.

Strange. Dylan placed his hand on top of the dog's furry head. "Hey, buddy, nothing up there but dust bunnies and squirrels." The dog pressed into his palm with a whine. Knees creaking like an old man, he sat cross-legged and they regarded each other, nose to snout. The leathery black nostrils flared and a pink tongue hung down.

"Dude, you're clean." Dylan twisted his head to one side. "Well, your breath needs work. No dust bunnies for you, or Augusta will have my hide. I'll deal with those squirrels tomorrow."

As if the dog understood the repartee, it plopped paws against Dylan's knees and laid his heavy head on the carpet. "Whatever happened, it's okay now. I'm here, boy."

One heavy paw slumped down on his bare leg. Yeah, those nails might need to be clipped. "Nothing to fear. No IEDs. I bet you were constantly on alert, huh? On patrol, sniffing out really bad things that do really bad shit to good people." The dog heaved a long sigh out his nostrils and his huge body gave a shudder. Seemed the cadence in his voice calmed the poor thing's agitation. So he continued to speak in a low and steady rhythm. If it eventually fell asleep, there'd be hope for a few hours of shut-eye.

"Your work saved a lot of our troops. I know firsthand. I patched up wounds and held hands when there wasn't anything I could've done."

Hell, he hadn't talked aloud about this stuff…ever.

While vocalizing his recollections of the sights, sounds, smells, and experiences of combat he'd locked away for so long, he stroked the dog's thick coat. At some point, Dylan stretched out on the carpet, because he was too damned tired to get up and back into bed. "You need a name. Can't keep calling you bud or boy. How about Ed?" Why not—his tag said EDD, right?

Chapter Six

"Were you sleepwalking?" came a soft, feminine voice. A pair of Vera Wang rhinestone boots settled into view. He knew the brand because of one person.

Augusta.

Dylan groaned and realized two things: he was in his underwear, and he'd slept on the floor. *She does not need a view of my ass*. He rolled over and shielded his front as best as possible. "Why are you in my house?" he grumbled and tried to sit. God, his body ached like it'd been run over by a tank.

"Jeez, how ungrateful." She held a foam coffee cup.

Nails *clickety clacked* in a steady rhythm on the wood stair treads, and pointed ears shot into eyesight. "Ed? You're walking up steps? Nicely done." Once at the top, although a slow go and with a slight limp, the dog stopped at his side, sat, then licked his nose.

He laughed. "Good morning to you, too." Progress was a great thing.

"Ed?"

He shrugged and patted the dog's ribs. "It fits."

"Babe, you upstairs?" Evan's voice called out, and

Dylan jumped to his feet. No freaking way would he be caught half-naked by Augusta's Marine Corps boyfriend. Notwithstanding his one leg, Evan could kick most people's ass, hands down.

"You surprise me, Doctor O'Brien." She tilted her head and clucked her tongue.

He grabbed the cup, motioned for Ed to enter his bedroom, then kicked the door shut. "Why?" he asked through the wood, not sure he desired to hear the answer.

"Pegged you more of a boxers kind of guy. And you're welcome for the coffee, by the way."

"Go. We'll be down in a few." He hunted through the clean clothes pile on the chair for a pair of sweats and a Navy sweatshirt. "She's annoying, you'll see." Ed's head tilted to the side, his furry eyebrows bunching as if he understood.

Dylan took a large gulp of caffeine and opened the door, waiting for Ed. "Nice and slow there, bud," he said as they both went downstairs.

Evan sat on a stool at the kitchen island reading the *Havenport Herald* and sipping an extra-large cup of coffee. Augusta made herself busy cleaning up Ed's food bowls in the sink. "I brought wet food, which he devoured. Nice shirt." She eyeballed his covered-up body with a quirk of her eyebrow.

"That's debatable," Evan said wryly.

No secret where Evan's loyalty lay—the corps. However, since Dylan had been a Navy Corpsman, they'd come to a friendly sort of adversarial truce. Plus, Evan totally respected his and Augusta's friendship.

Evan folded the newspaper and set it on the granite. "Augusta filled me in on last night's events. What do you make of him?" He nodded toward where Ed lay wedged into the corner under the kitchen window, with his nose pressed against the baseboard molding.

Dylan downed his coffee. "Not sure. I do know that all MWDs are microchipped. When I bring him to the hospital later, I'll check with the scanner. Find who he belongs to and, I guess, find his real home." He frowned down at Ed, who'd raised his head to stare at him. Why did the idea of handing him over create a hollow feeling in his stomach? Probably just hunger pains. He spied the paper bag on the counter from Led Zeppoli.

"Did you guys bring anything besides coffee? I seriously need to buy food."

Evan shook his head in disgust. "You're as bad as she is"—he raised his chin toward Augusta—"with her empty refrigerator. Chocolate croissants in the bag."

"You like PB and J, admit it," Augusta said.

"Only yours," Evan teased, but the smolder in his eyes relayed something entirely different.

Dylan couldn't help it, and rolled his eyes, a signature Washburn gesture he'd apparently picked up, too. Speaking of Washburns...*crap, it's already 8:15 a.m.* Good God, what kind of fiasco would greet Meghan when she showed up in forty-five minutes? A stray dog, his nosy-hole best friend, and most likely a pissed-off brother when Evan found out Dylan had the hots for her. Which was truer than true. That delicious dream Augusta interrupted after finding Ed had continued right where he'd left off, and more. Surprising Augusta hadn't gotten herself a stiff morning eyeful, instead of a mere glimpse of his boxer briefs.

Talk about a *shitstorm*.

But for the first time in a long time, he wanted—no, yearned—for a woman to be impressed by the real Dylan: sports-loving, foosball-playing, wine-drinking Dylan. And not because he was some mother's idea of the hot, young, and single town vet they'd land for their daughter. The marrying kind, or so Augusta mentioned was the buzz around the Garden Club.

Jeez, last week, Mrs. Wilson practically gave out her daughter's ring size, along with her cell number.

Perhaps Meghan would agree to go out to dinner. Better, he'd make dinner so none of the hens in town could gossip. Now that was a first. Helped to buy food, of course. Otherwise how in the hell would he pull off any kind of meal?

Hell, he didn't know. His mind was jumping all over the place.

Evan and Augusta didn't seem to notice his making mental plans with Meghan as they stared moon-eyed at each other like he wasn't in the room. How in the hell was he going to get those two lovebirds out of his kitchen and on their way? Fake feeling sick? Hungover? Insist Ed and he bond by themselves?

"Doc, I might have a contact at Lackland Air Force Base willing to investigate buddy boy over there." Evan's comment interrupted his game plans.

Augusta stood behind Evan and rubbed his shoulders. "Dylan calls him Ed. You guys bonded last night, I see." Ed lifted his head. "Look how he knows his new name."

"Lackland's in Texas. You think Ed's from there?"

Evan shrugged. "Likely he'd been trained there, but he could have been what they call excessed." Evan explained what happened when dogs were no longer needed for active duty. "The majority are adopted by their handler after their service ends."

"Still doesn't explain how or why he appeared at our door," Augusta said. "Let me show you something." She hopped off the stool and grabbed her laptop out of her large satchel bag.

He discreetly glanced at his watch. 8:25 a.m. *Hope this doesn't take long.*

"Dyl, take a look at this. Evan insists I'm seeing things."

He examined the screen over her shoulder. "I saved the footage from the entrance security camera." She clicked into her downloads and a black screen popped up, followed by an image of the front of the shelter. It showed an overview of the front door, including the concrete slab on the top step where Ed was found.

"It's stationary. Does not pan the area like the side camera will. Look at the film jump. Like it shorted out for a split second, then this happened." He followed her index finger and squinted.

"Can you rewind it?"

She did. Clearly, Ed had been placed on the steps by someone, given he was unconscious and couldn't walk. Yet nobody visible had been recorded on the tape. "Wait, freeze it," he said. "There, see? What is that?"

Augusta and Evan leaned in for a closer look. "What's with the haze? It wasn't foggy last night. Could the camera be dirty?" Dylan asked.

"That's what I suggested," Evan said.

Augusta shot Evan a glare. "It's possible."

"Slow the video down." There had to be some kind of explanation for the fog. Could the person have been smoking? Wearing a white scarf? Where was his logical, deductive doctor reasoning when he needed it?

"I'll try." She clicked the mouse and made a few keystrokes. "I'm no expert on computers, as everyone knows."

"Is that a boot?" Evan peered at the screen.

"It's not clear. Might be, or at the very least the heel of some sort of shoe."

Evan harrumphed. "If I didn't know better…hmm."

"What are you thinking?" he asked.

Augusta glanced up from the screen. "You have a theory, babe?"

"Looks like a combat boot. I know because I've had

plenty of pairs. And that there"—he touched the screen—"it's fuzzy, but it's in the right place. I think it's an eagle, globe, and anchor. I missed it before."

The video suddenly cut. Nothing but white static.

"Damn," they all said in unison.

How frustrating. "So someone wearing combat boots drops off an unconscious dog? Makes no sense."

Augusta clicked out of the application and closed the computer. "Well, whoever this person was, we'll figure it out eventually. I'm extremely glad we found Ed, or I suspect he may not have made it. He's better today, so that's all that matters."

Dylan observed Ed, who'd curled into a ball on the tiled floor. Physically, the dog had improved. His mental state proved more worrisome.

The Red Sox clock on the wall chimed. Eight forty-five. *Shit.* Time to get Evan and August outta here. "I've got to hit the head and start the day. Any news from Lackland, call me," he told Evan. "Thanks for stopping by, and for the coffee." He crumpled the paper bag and tossed it into the trash. Way to give a hint, huh?

Evan hopped off the stool and, despite his prosthetic leg, the man maneuvered steadier than most of the athletes Dylan knew. "Let's get going, babe. I've a ten thirty with the Emerson Foundation about their donation match and the restoration plans for Havencroft Manor. The mayor wants my input," he told Dylan.

Augusta circled behind Evan and snaked her arms around his back. "So when you're elected to town council in November, they'll be ahead of the game. Speaking of Havencroft, you still need a date, Dyl." August winked at him around Evan's shoulders. "Never fear, my friend. I'm working on it."

"Please go," Evan practically begged. "I could use someone to converse with besides potential constituents.

Other than my buddy, Dean, and his brother, Jeremy, I think you're the only guy under the age of seventy who'll be there, and you're normal."

Augusta snorted.

He shot her a death glare, to which she merely chuckled before grabbing her bag.

"And," Evan added, "your friend here." He turned and kissed Augusta on the lips. "Has me dressing up as a pirate. Peg leg and all."

"That's wrong on so many levels."

Her mouth flew open. "What?" She gasped before punching Evan's bicep. *Glad it's not me for a change.* "It was all your idea. It was all his idea. And conveniently he forgets to mention his suggestion I go as a wench."

"Yeah, no. Not touching that," Dylan said, earning a glare from Augusta.

"Find a date, man." Evan slid the newspaper across the granite to him. "Preferably someone we know and like so she doesn't whine."

"I do not whine." Augusta did actually what she'd protested, and Evan snorted, then sauntered toward the hallway.

A date? Dylan's hands froze on the copy of the *Herald*. Meghan LaRue, perhaps? Somehow, he suspected Evan's idea of finding a date didn't constitute his sister. Besides, she probably already had someone to go with. The Washburn family was one of the oldest and wealthiest in town. No doubt they'd been invited as VIPs or something.

Augusta and Evan bickered for a few more seconds. Crisis averted. They would be on their way out the door with ten minutes to spare. Suddenly, Ed shot up and barked, then swiftly—or as swiftly as possible with his limp—made a beeline for the front door.

"Where's he off to?" Augusta asked with a puckered brow.

The bell rang and Dylan silently grumbled. It was probably too much to hope Ronnie, the paperboy, had come to collect on a Saturday morning.

Despite Evan's and Augusta's presence, a flutter of eagerness latched on to his gut. He concentrated on putting one foot in front of the other to answer the damn door and not embarrass himself.

Ed stopped, nose touching the doorknob, and stared. At least his tail wagged. That was a good sign Meghan wouldn't be eaten for breakfast.

Dylan plucked aside the pleated curtains on the door's sidelight. Meghan LaRue and her daughter, Brielle, stood on the porch.

This should prove interesting.

Dylan opened the door with a smile. "Good morning, ladies."

"See, Mom, I told you." Brielle pointed to Ed, who'd stepped forward to investigate their new guests. Dylan's palms grew sweaty. Given Ed's background—more importantly, their considerable lack of information about his background—he'd no idea what would or would not trigger aggression.

If he attacked Meghan or Brielle, they'd be in for serious shit.

"Hi, Doctor O'Brien." A deep blush invaded her stunning features. Yep, easy to see where Brielle got her beauty as well as her height. Brielle topped five feet eleven by at least half an inch. The alabaster-like skin and wide-set eyes matched Meghan's. Though Meghan's features were softer with curls framing her face, rather than Brielle's supermodel-high cheekbones and arm's-length straight hair.

Any way one sliced it, both were spectacular. Meghan stood outside armed with a pile of material in every shade of blue he'd ever seen. Were those paints sample cards in her hand?

"Told her what?" Evan said behind him.

Great. Brother and protective uncle in the foyer, along with an MWD with possible signs of PTSD. Why hadn't he stayed in the bedroom with Ed?

"That you and Augusta were coming here to visit the new dog." Brielle rolled her eyes dramatically before putting her hand palm down for Ed to sniff.

Dylan shot forward. "I'd be careful if I were…"

"Oh, he won't hurt me."

He certainty was dubious at best. "We don't know where he's from, or his behavior traits yet," he said, not wanting to scare Brielle, yet wanting to avoid a serious complication, like her losing a limb or being badly bitten.

Surprisingly, Ed sniffed Brielle's hand, then licked it. Furry body slowly inched closer to Brielle, rubbing her legs with his gargantuan head.

"Would you look at that," Augusta exclaimed. "I've always said you have the magic touch when it comes to animals, Elle."

The tension eased out of his chest. He cleared his throat, then laughed. "It seems Ed likes you. Thanks for the almost heart attack." He clutched his chest, and Brielle laughed. Last summer, when she'd adopted Rambo, he hadn't spent much time with her, but Augusta raved about the teen. Whenever in his company, and that mostly happened at the animal hospital, Brielle portrayed herself as mature and courteous. But then again, he hadn't been around teenagers since Shannon, which was almost ten years ago. A lot went along with keeping a sixteen-year-old, especially a girl, in line. He didn't miss those days.

"Well I, for one, am glad Doctor O'Brien gave you a warning, although a fat lot of good it did, Elle." Meghan glowered.

Brielle knelt beside Ed, scratching his torso. "Relax, Mom. I sensed he was fine."

"Spoken like you spend way too much time with this one." He pointed to Augusta, then sidestepped another punch to his arm.

Motionless, Meghan stood outside. *Invite her inside, idiot.* "I'm sorry. Please come in," he said, moving sideways to open the door. "Let me help you."

He grabbed for the bundle in her arms. She plucked a lock of hair away from her eyelash, and he was forced to swallow hard. The croissant lodged in his throat before he closed the door.

God, those curls of hers made messy and sexy simultaneous.

Wonder if she's as sexy straight out of bed. Whoa.

She'd swept up her hair with some sort of clip thingy on the back of her head. Inadvertently, his nose twitched, remembering that titillating peachy musk which had lingered on the throw blanket on his couch.

"What is all that stuff?" Evan asked, breaking him out of horny-toad mode.

Meghan smirked at her brother. "Nothing you care about one iota, I'm sure. But for your information, these are swatches and paint color palettes for my new client."

Augusta stepped forward, too, offering to help Meghan since it appeared she'd brought over her entire repertoire of choices. They placed the bundles on top of the foyer table.

"Dylan's your client? For a minute I thought you'd come to make him a costume for the Halloween Ball tomorrow night." She winked not quite discreetly, and he gnashed his teeth.

There it was. The wood burning in Augusta's matchmaking head. First, he didn't need help asking Meghan to the ball, *if* he'd decided to do it. And if she didn't already have plans.

"Shoot. Is that tomorrow night?" Meghan bit her lip.

"It is. You are going, right?" Evan asked and stood behind Augusta, nodding yes and mouthing *please go.*

Meghan sneered at her brother's antics. "I had wanted to buy a ticket, or actually I had hoped to lend the organizers my decorating expertise to try and drum up business. However, with setting up the office, and the new clients, it slipped through cracks of my calendar. I guess it's too late now."

Dylan wondered why Meghan LaRue, the daughter of the Washburns, would need to drum up anything in this town. Her family had a monopoly, for crying out loud.

He sensed a story there. Perhaps she and the parental figures weren't on the best of terms? Evan mentioned how challenging his father could be. Maybe if the entourage would finally leave he'd get time alone to pose the question to Meghan. And then gather courage to ask her to the ball.

Wow, talk about a definite decision.

"Dylan needs a date," Augusta blurted. "You guys can go together."

Jeez, was he seventeen again?

Meghan's eyes grew wide. "I couldn't impose on Doctor O'Brien."

Suddenly he'd transformed to a bumbling mute. His brain refused to move in sync with his mouth.

Brielle popped up from the Ed pet-fest. "It'll be great, Mom." She faced him. "Hey, can I watch Ed?"

"Sure…I guess that would work."

Meghan flinched. What an asinine response. He wanted to crawl up the stairs and suffer a slow, painful, lonely existence in his bedroom. Where a beautiful, confident woman like Meghan could avoid his pathetic shortcomings.

"You guys are going to have such fun." Brielle clapped her hands. Ed gave a short bark. "Halloween's Mom's favorite holiday, you know," Brielle announced, and yet he still couldn't find a lick of sense in his dimwit brain to reply.

Augusta pivoted, placing her back to the others with a get-your-head-out-of-your-ass expression.

"Plus, his fan cl...err..." Augusta stuttered when he tapered his gaze with a minute shake of the head. He knew the exact moment the lightbulb came on in Augusta's head and she realized he minded what Meghan thought of that bullshit "fan club" label. Her expression grew amazed. *Ah shit, been found out.* "That is," she said, turning to Meghan, "many of his patients' owners are attending. I spoke to quite a few at the store this week. This works out perfectly. He gets a date, and you can network."

Augusta was in so much trouble.

Time to get his head out of his ass. Hell, if the whole crew here suggested it, he'd be a freaking idiot to lose this opportunity, right?

Dylan turned to face Meghan. He hoped his expression relayed the interest and playfulness they'd shared last night, and not the awkwardness which had invaded the entire convoluted family affair conversation going on in his foyer.

She licked her lips, and he couldn't help but fixate on the wet spot at the fullest part of her bottom lip, begging for him to taste. Had it been only last night that they'd shared an amazing connection? When the stirrings of something he couldn't define had invaded his chest? "I'd love to take you to the ball. You know, to help network for your business, and it's for charity, too, so there's that." Yeah, so much for being debonair.

"Slick," Augusta whispered under her breath, but he ignored it.

A slow grin invaded Meghan's face, reminiscent of the one after her foosball victory. His insides unclenched. The connection he hoped she'd remember from last night returned with her chuckle.

"Only if you'll let me decide the costumes." She tilted her head to the side and perused him from head to toe.

"He can be the horse's-ass side, and you can be the horse's head," Augusta suggested. Evan chortled along with Brielle.

Ignoring the whole lot of knuckleheads seemed prudent.

"Deal."

Dylan held out his hand, and Meghan shook on it. Not the most romantic of gestures. No missing the electric current sizzling between them, though. Was that a short gasp? Having an audience and doing what he really wanted to with Meghan LaRue didn't mix. At least not at the moment.

"Well, that's all settled," Evan said in his usual precise military way, and checked his watch to break the tension. "I've got that appointment at ten hundred, so let's vamoose. Elle, you staying or hitching a ride to Wags with Augusta?"

"I've got the grooming mobile and a few stops. You game?" Augusta asked Brielle.

Brielle gave Ed one last pet on the head. "I'll come with you. What time should I watch Ed tomorrow night, Doctor O'Brien? And," she said, shifting on both sneakered feet, "can I bring company?"

His face must have shown the shock of her question.

"Brielle," Meghan warned.

"As in a party?" he asked cautiously, not wishing to sound like a wimp, but the idea of teenagers having a party here…yeah, his bachelor pad and teenagers didn't mix.

Shaking her head rather forcefully, Brielle replied, "Oh, no. Only Jacob."

Meghan's sigh shifted her entire chest cavity up, then down. Not a good sign. "Elle, I'm not comfortable with you and Jacob being here alone together." It was clear from the tension in Meghan's body that Brielle would be disappointed.

"Come on, Mom. I told you we're friends." Brielle crossed her arms, looking defiant, and he had to stop from flinching. Yeah, Shannon pulled that stuff whenever Mom had worked nights and he'd refused let her stupid guy friends in the house.

Nothing good came of a teenage tantrum.

Hoping to diffuse a potential situation, especially since Meghan had explained last night that she yearned to rebuild a good relationship with Brielle, he bit the bullet. "Tell you what," he began, and they all faced him again. "I'd actually be more comfortable with Jacob coming over to watch Ed, too." When Meghan started to protest, he reached for her hand. "Hear me out, please?" At her nod, he continued. "We still don't know where Ed came from, and Jacob knows how to handle animals from working in Augusta's place."

Meghan didn't seem convinced, if her wary glance was any indication. Hell, he knew it was tough balancing wanting to be a friend and a parental figure. But he had to make his point, if only for purely selfish reasons—if Meghan refused, they couldn't go to the ball. He'd have to stay home and be with Ed, at least until they found out where he belonged. No way could he leave Ed alone or at the shelter.

Meghan's frown deepened. Uh-oh, wrong suggestion?

"Is the dog disturbed?" Meghan broke their contact and took a step back, hand to her throat.

Augusta, bless her soul, earned a bit of redemption by quickly piping in. "Ed's a good dog. But Dylan's right. And believe me, I don't admit that often." He snorted. "Brielle could use the help, and I can absolutely vouch for Jacob. Even my sister's boyfriend, Mac, knows he's a good kid.

Besides," she said in a whisper, "your brother already threatened him bodily harm of the worst kind."

Said brother cleared his throat. "I heard that. Meggy, he'll be fine. Jacob knows what's expected of him. Hey, as long as you're cool with it, Doc?"

He nodded, but wasn't sure Meghan was cool with it.

"Sorry to break up our breakfast party, but I've got to boogie." Evan opened the door and stepped onto the porch.

Augusta followed, but not before giving him a discreet thumbs-up. "Meet you out front, Elle."

"So? What's the answer, Mom?" Brielle tapped her sneaker on the wood floor.

Meghan blew the hair away from her forehead. "I guess I have no choice. You and Jacob can stay and watch the dog," At that, Brielle headed to the door. "Provided you don't mess up Doctor O'Brien's house, no alcohol, and you check in every half hour."

A bit excessive, but who was he to complain?

Brielle stopped short and nodded tightly. "Fine. Time?" she asked, and it took him a moment to realize the question needed his answer.

"Eight. I can come and get your mom and drop you back here." How was this arrangement going to work itself out?

"Oh no, I'll drop off Brielle and bring your costume."

"Please, not Augusta's suggestion."

Brielle didn't wait around to hear her mother's reply. "Gotta go. See you later, Mom. Love you."

Mother and daughter embraced, the war between them forestalled at least for now, although the costume question stood unanswered.

Brielle turned to leave, and Ed whined. She laughed. "Don't miss me too much. See you tomorrow night." She bent and patted his head before shutting the door with a click. Ed promptly lay at the foot of the stairs, staring at the closed door.

Dylan turned to face Meghan. "Well, that was something, huh? Don't know about you, but I need coffee. You want some?"

Alone at last, Meghan looked ready to spit nails. "You're upset," he said, posed as a statement more than question, but not sure he wanted the answer.

She crossed her arms.

"You're not upset?"

Shit, possibly whiskey instead of coffee. "Look, I confess, I'm not good with gauging reactions in women." *Why in the hell admit that?*

She simply pursed her lips, brushed passed, and headed to the kitchen. Today she wore nice jeans—and by nice, he meant formfitting—with a fluffy pink sweater. He swallowed hard at the back view and the subtle sway of her hips.

"Doctor O'Brien, this might constitute another victory in the Meghan column."

The Meghan column? Feet fixed to the floor, he pondered how this might play out. One, she'd be pissed, or was pissed, or two…hell, she'd brought an arsenal of paint colors. Bye-bye, Red Sox red.

He dragged himself into the kitchen. "How so?" he asked, trying to make it sound a mere innocent question, versus coming off as stupid. Ed had followed, for moral support, he hoped. Meghan searched his cabinets, located the cups and coffee pods, and stuck one in the single-brewer machine. Then she opened his refrigerator door, sniffed the milk, which he knew wasn't expired yet, and added it to her cup.

"Sugar?" she asked, exploring the countertops.

"Packets on the top shelf where you found the cups." He pointed and sat on a stool at the island.

Once she'd fixed the brew to her satisfaction she, too, sat in silence.

He rubbed the back of his neck and eyeballed Ed, who eyeballed him back. *A little help here?*

"Meghan," he began, and she glanced over the rim of her cup. "If I put you in a shitty, err, strange situation by suggesting Brielle and Jacob watch Ed here together, I didn't mean to. Look, if you want to nix going to the charity ball, I'd get it, totally." That suggestion sucked.

She took a long gulp and regarded him. "You do know I'm on my own here in Havenport?" He sensed an answer wouldn't be necessary. Seemed like she needed to unload.

"Besides the occasional call from my mother…" She rolled her eyes, a gesture he'd learned recently translated to different things in the Washburn dictionary. Impatience, embarrassment, and in this case emphasis on something unpleasant, perhaps. "…or a stupid congratulations plant, there's been no support whatsoever since I divorced Jacques." She toyed with the corner of the *Herald*, folding it back into a triangle, and hesitated. "Dylan, it's not that I am angry with your suggestion about Brielle, as much as upset I couldn't think logically like that, too."

He contemplated either placating her or speaking his mind. "Some people can't think logically when faced with a difficult or scary situation with their kids. They're too emotionally attached. I understand it. Raising Brielle by yourself can't be easy."

One eyebrow arched. "No offense, but you wouldn't have a clue."

"You'd be surprised," he said, although this was not the time to explain his ancient history. "And, to be perfectly frank, I don't envy your situation. She's a good kid, but you can't stop nature from happening, or time from passing. Being responsible for making all the decisions, I imagine, isn't easy."

She opened her mouth to either argue or agree when a loud thump, as if his roof had collapsed, made them jump. Ed shot to his feet and growled, then bounded out of the room. "What the hell…"

"Sounds like it came from upstairs." In a flash, they followed Ed, who'd made it to the top step before disappearing around the corner of the upstairs hallway. Once upstairs they found him scratching at the attic door.

"You don't let up." Dylan pet Ed's head as the dog nudged the brass doorknob.

"Is that an attic," she asked from behind. Ed pawed at the door, his long nails gouging into the wood.

"Cut it out," he scolded Ed.

Another thwunk preceded what could only be deciphered as footsteps. He and Meghan both squinted at the attic door.

Dylan took a hold of Ed's collar, pulled him away, and opened the door. "It is. Problem was, last month Rocky and his girlfriend, Sandy Squirrel, decided to claw their way in through the easement and make a nest."

She wrinkled her nose. "Eww. Those little critters can do damage."

"You're telling me," he said. "Had an exterminator in and I *thought* all was clear, until last night. Ed did the same thing." He rubbed at his chin, wondering what the hell the dog sensed up there. Strange. "I'll check it out. You okay staying here with him?" He only asked because Meghan didn't seem super at ease around the dog. Not surprising. Hey, Ed was a military machine and probably pushing almost a hundred pounds of solid muscle and aggressive canine.

"Um." She hesitated and bit her lip. "I'll go, too. Who knows, you may have hidden treasures up there, besides the squirrels, of course." She laughed, the sound a bit on the nervous side.

He snorted. "Don't count on it."

"I'm serious. I've found many an attic to be a wealth of good reusable decor."

He opened the door leading to the low-lying ceiling, praying to elude being scalped by its slanted rafters for the umpteenth time. "Whatever you say. First, let's investigate that sound. Would hate to have to get rabies shots." He shuddered.

"Are you afraid of needles, Doc?" she teased.

He smirked. "No. You're more than welcome to hunt once I know it's clear. Will warn you, though, not much stored besides dust bunnies."

She shook her head, and the curls at the back danced. "Sounds like you're afraid to me. And I'll be the judge of what's valuable. There a light up there?" She brushed passed him and bounded up the steps before he had a chance to react.

At least her slight frame fit a hell of a lot better than his, as he had to maneuver the sideways crunch to ascend to the top. The steps weren't steep, but they also weren't finished—merely crappy pine, a bit rickety. Particles of dust kicked up from her footsteps stung his nose and throat. He coughed. She located the switch, and the naked bulb fixture came to life. He blinked as his eyes adjusted to the brightness.

Ed woofed. Dylan craned his neck and glanced down. "Not sure you'll make it up here, bud." He should've known better than to underestimate a military dog's abilities. Ed wasn't your run-of-the-mill pooch. The dog was highly trained to deal with any type of terrain and challenge, like a workhorse. He wasn't surprised when he heard nails clicking on the pine treads. Once at the top, Ed's nose hit the deck and he sniffed at the floorboards, then made a loud doggy sneeze.

Meghan chuckled, and he shook his head in amazement. "You're determined, I'll tell you that much, pal."

"Dylan, look." Meghan carefully treaded to the wall where the round window was housed near the top of the rafters. "You neglected to mention this." She gestured to an old and hideous dark-colored wooden chest with ugly claw-foot legs.

He knit his brow. "That old thing? I forgot it was up here. I assume the previous owner left it behind." He shrugged and made his way to her side. That delightful peaches fragrance of her skin was infinitely better than the musty, stale smell which had crawled up his nostrils.

"I haven't had a chance to dump it. Don't come up here much, except during hockey season to get my gear to bring home—err, well, *home*—to Boston when I visit for the holidays. I play a lot with my old team buddies." *Way to ramble.*

"Sounds like fun." She investigated the lock, but her answer sounded sincere. Maybe she didn't think him such a hockey dork after all—mailbox notwithstanding.

Meghan turned away from perusing the trunk, and their eyes met. She smiled shyly, and he dipped his head. God, he could easily get lost in her green depths. This intensity of reaction—hammering heart, sweaty palms, half a boner whenever he stood within a foot of her general vicinity—had never happened before. Never entered the equation of his dismal dating life. It was exciting and scary.

"You get embarrassed easily," she said. Her soft fingertip gently brushed across his cheek, and he froze. "Dirt smudge."

"Not with everyone I don't," he said in response to her earlier statement, his voice raspy. Must be the damn dust. He moved in closer. She sucked in a breath with opened lips, then swallowed hard enough for her throat to shift. They were alone in the attic. Hmm, a perfect opportunity.

"I'm only embarrassed when a beautiful woman beats the pants off me in foosball and plans to wreak havoc on my bachelor pad."

Her green eyes twinkled like the shamrock sun catcher hanging against the window. "I promise it won't hurt a bit."

Something crunched from the opposite corner, breaking their moment. Then, a muffled thump came from the other corner of the attic—the dark area. Meghan recoiled.

Ed whined, his ears twitched, and he made a beeline toward the sound, but Dylan jumped into action in time and seized his collar. "Whoa. The floor over there sucks, dude. Don't want anyone falling through the ceiling."

His biceps burned from the strain of Ed towing on them like a sled dog.

"Heel. Stay," he said with force, hoping at least one of the two freaking commands proved effective. Ed finally ceased pulling, then sat on his haunches. *Thank you, God.*

Dylan pet Ed and murmured an endearment, then happened to glance over to see Meghan's eyes big as saucers. "It's probably nothing. Stay here. I'll check it out."

He left Ed and grabbed a hockey stick from the collection against wall.

"I had no plans to follow you. No offense, but I hate rodents." Her face had grown pale and she shuddered.

That thump was no mere rodent, but he wasn't about to voice his speculation. If a raccoon made its way up here, and out in daylight, they'd be in deep doo.

"I need a light. Damn," he muttered.

"Here." She handed him her cell phone after turning on the flashlight.

Slowly he approached, stick in one hand, shining light aimed at the corner of the room. No masked black and furry face peered back at him from the corner. *Good sign.*

No signs of excrement or anything besides dust and vet school books. Blankets stacked on top of boxes he also forgot he'd stored.

Guess the squirrels were gone. But he really needed to clean out the attic.

"Just a bunch of my old textbooks and blankets. DVDs." The entire Sean Connery James Bond collection haphazardly piled and knocked askew. "James Bond collection." He held up the plastic jackets.

"Good taste," she said. "Connery or Moore?"

"Pfttt…Connery, of course," he said. "Something in this mess pile probably fell when we were moving around or walking up the stairs." Stepping across the loose boards like walking through a minefield, he returned to Meghan, injury free.

Ed let out a bark and, before Dylan knew it, moved forward and snatched the top blanket off the pile and dragged it back to them. Ed pounced on it like he was guarding a prisoner or holding down prey.

"Guess he likes your blanket," Meghan said as they watched Ed paw and sniff the coarse wool.

"Yeah, but why?" he wondered aloud. Could be Ed smelled the vermin who'd most likely put their skittish little destructive paws all over it.

"Maybe he likes dust," she suggested and wrinkled her nose.

"It's possible he's latched on to a scent. We found out Ed's MWDs, a military working dog," he explained. "They have a heightened and honed sense of smell. Ed was also a bomb-detection dog." Didn't explain the footsteps they'd heard earlier. The whole of last night and this morning had taken a strange turn when it came to his attic.

Meghan shivered beside him and rubbed at the soft material covering her arms. "Phew, is there a draft up here?"

A chill skated across the back of his neck and down his forearms. Like an icy blast, as if you'd put your head into the freezer to cool off on a hot summer day, which he'd frequently done since their ancient colonial in Boston didn't have central air. He could hear Peg yelling in his mind.

The sensation lingered a few seconds before traveling across the back of his neck.

"Guess I need more insulation," he said with a shake of the head. "I say we head back downstairs. Without that ugly-ass chest."

"It is not ugly."

"Says you," he said with a laugh. "Face it, there's nothing here of value I'd recommend using for a makeover. You agree?"

Meghan shot him a to-be-argued-later look. For some reason, he couldn't wait to banter with her again. But it was time to end this dust bunny visit and go back downstairs…

He approached the steps and held out his arm. "After you, ma'am."

She swaggered toward the steps. "Although I know it's polite, and Evan lapses into his 'ma'am this' and 'ma'am that' from time to time, it makes me feel like an old maid."

Could she be any further from the truth? "You're hardly that," he said. "You'd give any Bond girl a run for her money."

Meghan stopped short.

Uh-oh. Had he overstepped again? He hadn't the skill to decipher if she wanted him to be flirty, or if it was too soon since…hell, they'd only met yesterday.

"Thank you, Doctor O'Brien. I've had a brainstorm." Her face lit up and she clapped. Ed rose at the smack of her palms and dragged his blanket to the steps.

He blanched. "Do I want to hear it?"

She shot him an impish grin. The same one Augusta

adopted whenever she planned something he knew he wouldn't like. Meghan was up to something.

"It's a surprise." She left it at that, stomping down the steps without a backward glance.

Why wasn't there a manual on women? Like the guide on intestinal obstruction repair he referenced last week? Ed, sensing his angst, whined and nudged his leg, blanket clenched between his teeth. "Leave that dusty thing up here." He tried pulling. Yeah, that amount of force per inch of jaw made it impossible.

"Leave it," he commanded, hoping another directive worked as well as the previous. Nope. Ed didn't budge.

"Suit yourself." He shrugged. "Don't take a tumble with that crusty thing."

Making sure Ed followed, Dylan went down the stairs backward and they both got to the bottom in one piece. Stupid blanket, too.

Meghan sat in the living room waiting for Dylan to return from the kitchen. It was a lot warmer down here. His creepy attic far surpassed her spooky office building. What were those thumping noises?

She spread bolts of sample materials and paint color palette cards across the surface of his coffee table. Would he react to her ideas positively? She'd considered how to create a haven for his home. How would his comfort-zone pieces, like the plush leather couch and manly sports-entertainment-themed prints he seemed to gravitate toward, mix with a feminine subtle touch the house sorely lacked?

She certainly didn't know him well enough to judge the good doctor's reactions. Except those adorable flushes, which started at his ears and turned his Adam's apple crimson when he'd gotten embarrassed. Or the long curl which had a mind of its own. Her fingers itched to brush it away from his brow.

You're going with him to the charity ball.

Jeez, was that a good idea? As soon as Augusta voiced her suggestion, the urge to run out the door almost took over, despite the flutters in her stomach and twinges in other parts at the idea of being Dylan's date.

Who wanted to face the cronies in town? It was the reason she hadn't bought a ticket. That excuse about it slipping her mind was a lie. Her parents undoubtedly had their hooks in the charity committee and would want her to play the dutiful daughter. Not the way she envisioned spending an evening. But now it might be okay. For some reason, Dylan and his quirky cuteness would make it enjoyable.

A real date.

It'd been forever. Perhaps she needed to lighten up. Be witty and fun again. *Like you used to be.*

Her costume idea might render the good doctor speechless. Excitement filled her head, along with the list of what she needed for tomorrow night.

A swatch of fabric slipped off the table, and she bent to pick it off the floor. She eyeballed the front window. The robin's-egg linen would make a great valance. Not too much fluff, maybe a few pleats along the bottom. Paired with—she hunted through the cards—the beeswax, color number one hundred and twenty-eight in a flat paint? Yes, they'd work well with the dark-brown couch.

Smart, yet simple. Dylan was certainly smart. He'd caught on to her discontent with Brielle's bullying to get her way. He'd also made a valid point. Time wouldn't stand still, and the apron strings needed loosening. Not cut entirely, but let out an inch.

She glanced around the room, ticking off ideas for prints, maybe a plant stand and some metal decorative pieces to complete the guy theme. There were photos on the far wall. Last night, she'd been too engrossed in their fun banter to take notice. Pushing off the couch, she approached where he'd mounted the TV above the fireplace. On either side of the brick were photos matted in a beaded wooden frame.

One showed a woman, she assumed his mother, smiling at the camera from the middle of three sets of arms surrounding her. What a loving family. A lump formed in her throat and the taste of coffee followed. Thinking about her family gave her stomach a dull, hollow pain. Her scalp tingled with envy.

The Washburns' idea of a family portrait consisted of a professional hour-long sitting, with Dad in the center, of course. They'd all be required to dress in the same colors, usually white. *Monochromatic* being Mom's favorite word. Plug in *stark* and *sterile* in a search engine, and the Washburn Estate popped up in the results. She'd been forced to don elegant gowns, Evan in his monkey suits, for staged, phony, and miserable portraits year after year.

This family photo portrayed candid joy, like they'd shared a secret joke. Meghan recognized the dark-haired guy on one side of the woman as a younger Dylan. Not much had changed, except his shoulders were wider. The young girl, no older than Brielle's age, had straight blond hair and blue eyes enhancing her freckled face. The other boy, maybe a tad older, sported shocking red hair, a true ginger. All striking. All had similar features to their mother.

Where was the father?

Dylan broke her reverie by trudging back into the room. "Needed to let Ed out in the backyard. I wanted to make sure the back gate had latched. It sticks." He took in the array of samples on the coffee table with an arched eyebrow and strolled to her side.

"That's the rest of the O'Brien clan." He motioned to the photo.

Meghan swallowed hard. Standing this close, she detected the scent of the dryer sheets she used at home on his cotton sweatshirt. Manly, yet clean, and stirring to her insides.

Back in the attic, she fantasized of kissing him, reaching up and wrapping her arms around his neck to see how soft she knew his hair had to be. God, she wished she'd had the courage to act on her urges.

Granted, Dylan put the *H* in *hot*, but she'd tingled to her toes. Who knew a bit of friendly foosball competition could bring her back to wanting a man again, feeling true desire, versus being a robot wife?

Her heart sped. *Focus on the picture, not Dylan.*

It was hard to do. He pointed out the members of his family. She tried not to stare at his thick wrist and his cool sports watch. He had manly hands. Nails cut square, his fingers long with a hint of hair on the knuckle. Hands she knew had saved many lives, both human and animal. Okay, so maybe her dreams about *where* his hands had caressed her body didn't help.

"My brother, Danny," he said, then gave her a funny look.

Her face flamed. *Crap.* His shoulders shook with laughter. "I'm sorry, I was contemplating paint colors," she lied.

He cocked his head. "Never thought I'd meet someone as focused as I am. Listen up, Ms. LaRue. There'll be a quiz later," he teased, and touched the tip of her nose. She laughed.

"I'll pay attention. I promise."

He smiled and turned back to his lesson. "My mother, Margaret. We call her Peg, which she hates. Don't try it yourself. Bugs the crap out of her."

Was he planning for her to meet his family? *Don't read into his words.*

"My brother. He's an attorney in Boston. Aspires to be an ADA, God help him. And there's Shannon," his said, his voice softening. "She's a pediatric nurse. Lives in Colorado. I don't see her often."

"Father?" she blurted, then shot a palm over her mouth when his lips thinned. "I'm sorry. It's none of my business."

He regarded her a moment, and she silently regretted her slip. *Stupid.*

"The sperm donor to my mother split a long time ago," he said, grounding out the words with a cynical half laugh. "We did fine without him."

Her stomach dropped. "I'm sorry." God, what could she say? Her father was difficult, but he hadn't left her mother, was devoted to their family, albeit in his own warped way. And Jacques, that slimy philanderer, would've left things as they'd stood if she hadn't kicked him out.

But to abandon three kids was unthinkable.

"Mom had a burly Irishman brother. My uncle Sean was a merchant marine. He was the best." His face lit in remembrance. "We didn't see him often, but when he was in port, he made sure Dan and I behaved, and had fun, too. He settled more than one fight. My point is, we did fine without a father figure. I know you might be worried about that with Brielle and all, but she's got Evan, right?"

How the hell did he identify one of the gazillion worries churning in her mind?

"Am I that transparent?" Her brow creased and she stepped away without waiting for his answer. Time to get a grip on the old fears threatening to choke the air out of her lungs. Why ruin this wonderful moment of Dylan sharing his family?

She rolled her shoulders and walked back to the couch. It was tough to avoid the fears. They cropped up at the worst times. Tough to think she'd made the wrong decision by imagining she'd be able to handle raising Brielle by herself.

She turned to face him. "You need to stop reading my thoughts, Doctor. Now, let's talk about my decorating ideas."

He nodded tightly, perhaps sensing her abrupt change of subject.

"That pile of samples is damned intimidating." He glanced at his watch. "I have maybe another half hour before I need to bring Ed to the hospital and try to see who he belongs to."

"Well then, let's get to it. Sit," she ordered, and he plopped down with a grimace at the blue linen. "Keep an open mind. This won't take long, then I'll be on my way."

Not that she wanted to go, but she still needed to plan their Halloween Ball costumes.

Chapter Seven

A few hours later, Augusta loomed over his shoulder and peered at his office computer. "Any luck?" She grabbed a chocolate-wrapped pumpkin from the candy dish on his desk, another surprise piece of decor he'd noticed upon arriving this morning.

He shook his head and hit the backspace again. "I'm filling out the form. They need tons of information. Chip number, which I have, then the tattoo, and all kinds of stuff. Any word on Evan's end?" They'd been at this for hours. It was pushing after five.

Saturday patients and exams were completed. Now the only thing pressing was to find out who the heck Ed turned out to be and why he'd ended up in Havenport.

She gave a negative shake. "He said he'd call if anything came up. I have faith he'll find out."

Dylan was sure of it, so why then did he have a bad feeling? Why was Ed seemingly happy one minute, playful with the staff, and the next, he'd sit and stare into space like a bipolar pup? The crusty blanket sat on the floor underneath him, too. Yeah, that had been a pleasurable attempt to leave the house without it. Growling and tugging ensued. In the end, might had right. Ed sure had might.

"Soooo," Augusta said next to his ear. Dylan sighed. Didn't take a doggy brain surgeon to figure out the next question.

"So, what?" He glowered, knowing what the *what* was.

"You and Meghan?"

"Me and Meghan?" He loved playing dumb. It frustrated her, if the look of impatience crossing her features was any indication. He tightened his arm. *Wait for it.* Yep, there went her jab. "That left a black and blue."

"When were you going to tell me?" Pissed-off, annoyed Augusta was one thing he could handle. Hurt Augusta, an entirely different universe.

He pretended to be engrossed in updating the chart on his desk. "Nothing to tell."

"I totally call bullshit."

He tsked and minimized the Lackland AFB main site. "Is that language appropriate?"

She plopped herself on top of his desk, blocking the chart.

"Do you mind? I have chart updates." He yanked the file folder away, and blood pooled in the paper cut on his middle finger. "Ouch." He grimaced and sucked on the bleeding digit. Stung like hell.

"She's newly divorced," she said.

"She told me about Jacques." He liked tripping her up. That did it, for her eyes widened before narrowing.

"I'm glad she trusted you to open up about the scummy French-tard." She wrinkled her nose. "Dyl, I'm thrilled about it. I've grown to love Meghan like a sister. Don't tell Savvy or she'll be jealous, but are you ready for this?"

Ready? Just what did he need to be ready for? "Let me get this straight. You set her and me up for this charity ball—which, by the way, I have no idea what kind of costume I might be forced to wear—and you've been on me to find someone I like in forever."

"Aha. You do like her," she exclaimed.

He lifted one shoulder in a half shrug. "I'd either be dead or senile not to, ya think? She's lovely, and funny, and can whip my ass at foosball." He chortled before realizing what had slipped out.

"And she's raising a daughter alone."

"All things I know."

She huffed and chewed on her lip. "What if it came down to choice?" At his blanch, she continued, "No, hear me out. You fall for her, and I suspect you already have, and she falls for you, which from the looks you two exchanged, phew. I thought Evan and I were bad. Where does that leave Brielle?"

Dylan totally understood Brielle and Augusta shared a special bond, more than a friendship. It was Augusta's new mission in life to protect the teen from any emotional distress. Had been like that since last summer.

"It leaves Brielle right where she is, with her mother."

Truth in that statement.

"Can you raise another teenager?"

That gave him pause, his pen hovering over the chart. The idea hadn't occurred…wait, maybe it had? Maybe Ms. Nosy-Hole Augusta uncovered something he'd already considered in his subconscious? What if they did hit it off and things progressed? Dating anyone, let alone anyone with a child, hadn't entered the equation in a dog's age. Could he do it? Would he even want to?

"I…guess," he mumbled, and spit out the top of the felt-tip he hadn't realized was in his mouth.

Her face screamed skepticism. "Come on, Dyl, you won't even own a pet. What makes you think you're ready for a woman who is the sole custodian for her daughter, and a pet. Let's not forget Rambo."

Who could forget that horndog? For some reason, the forecast of having Meghan and Brielle, and a sexually frustrated dog, in his life didn't make him want to vomit, run for cover, or escape. Would you look at that? Peg had probably prayed a dozen novenas for this type of realization.

However, he'd keep that refreshing bit of illumination to himself for now. The last thing he wanted was someone blabbing to Meghan. Hell, how did she feel?

"We're going to the ball, for crying out loud. It's one date. You think too much. Have some faith."

Her cell phone rang. "It's Evan."

Dylan watched as she listened intently. A myriad of emotions crossed her face before she ended the call. "What?"

"They found Ed's info. His handler was killed last month. Get this. Ed was all set for adoption by him, which explained the tags." Tears filled her eyes. "The handler was hit by a drunk driver. They sent Ed back to Lackland, but then he went AWOL. Dyl, his handler lived here. His name was David Prentice. Evan knew him. His parents live on the other side of town."

Ah, shit. Poor Ed. "Wow. So he followed his handler home. Was there a wake or something?"

"Dunno. Um, maybe you should take Ed over there today? You know, to where he belongs. The parents might want to keep him, if that's allowed?"

Anxiety hit his gut. On one hand, to finally understand Ed's background was a good thing, but pondering giving him over to someone else, even after one day, did make him want to vomit.

What the hell was going on? What happened to his boring life, going for a ten-mile run each morning, getting to work, no responsibility, frat-boy decor? One day, and all of that shot to shit.

For some reason, meeting Meghan, taking in Ed, redecorating his house—the most obscure events to happen—all felt right, like this was the next chapter about to unfold.

"Let's look up the address, and I'll take him over."

The Prentices' house sported an American flag hanging half-staff on a pole, and a multitude of yellow ribbons tied around each tree in their yard. As soon as Dylan pulled up in front and cut the engine, Ed went wild. He pawed at the window, his barks piercing into Dylan's eardrums like bullets.

"Hang on and let me open the door." He snapped on a heavy-duty leash and wondered why he'd bothered. The dog could probably haul a car if he had to. He was incredibly strong.

Ed yanked on the leash, heading up the wood steps and stopping at the front door before he turned and followed an undetectable scent, performed a quick pivot and bounding back down the steps. Dylan had no choice but to comply with his navigation. No wonder he'd served as a bomb-sniffing canine. Jeez, he honed in on a target like a heat-seeking missile.

Ed whined at the closed gate, and Dylan hunted for the latch over the top of the wood. He pulled a corded string, and as soon as the door swung open, Ed pulled again. They trudged through a wooden arch where red roses still bloomed overhead. A small white bench sat in one corner of the yard with an iron patio set.

Ed sidestepped, heading to the opposite end of the yard for a dilapidated tree house. The faded boards had long seen better days, and hung down from a huge oak. He stopped at the base and sat, then sniffed and wagged his tail furiously. Ed panted and danced around the spot, sticking his nose into the dirt.

The swoosh of sliders opening sounded from behind. A white-haired man came out looking confused, followed by a woman Dylan assumed was his wife. She had on an apron. The smell of pot roast wafted out the open door, and Dylan's stomach growled. Last time he'd eaten was that chocolate croissant this morning.

"Can I help you?"

Dylan kept a tight hand on Ed's leash. Again, he had no idea what the hell would happen next. "Mr. and Mrs. Prentice?"

"Yes," the man answered, and frowned at Ed, who was still digging up the dirt next to a bunch of newly planted flowers. He'd be replacing those tomorrow.

"I'm Dylan O'Brien, the vet in town. This is going to sound crazy, but I think Ed…err, this dog here belonged to your son. David?"

The woman clutched her throat. "Robert, it can't be."

"Can I come closer?"

Wise question. And if these indeed were David-the-handler's parents, they knew a thing or two about Ed.

"Sure, but do it slowly," he said. They weren't old, but Mrs. Prentice couldn't be more than ninety pounds soaking wet.

The pair came forward. One glance at the woman's tear-streaked cheeks and Dylan almost broke down.

"Marian, it's him." The man's voice faltered. "How in the world did he get here?"

Dylan swallowed hard before replying, "I'm not entirely sure. He's been with me for the past day. By the way, I'm very sorry for your loss."

They both flinched, and he knew he needed to help them understand. "In investigating him…" He nodded to

Ed. "…it led me here. He came to the animal shelter last night and, well, he was in pretty bad shape." No use in telling them that unsolved mystery. They were in too much shock as it was. Ed whined and finally sat down on the upturned dirt, as if he'd somehow calmed.

"So you took care of him?" Mrs. Prentice asked, pointedly.

Dylan nodded. "I took him home. He's better now. Although I'm sorry about the flowers." The heads were popped off every one of the pansies with roots upturned. "I'll replace them. Don't understand why he did that. Must have followed a scent."

The woman gasped. "David."

"Huh?"

"This is where we scattered his ashes, under his favorite tree."

A chill ran down Dylan's spine. Blood rushed away from his head. He shot out a hand and leaned on the weathered bark. The dog had followed his handler's ashes halfway across the country. "That's incredible." Dylan cleared his throat, dipping his head, embarrassed. "Ed's…err…that's the name I gave him last night."

"My son wrote his name is Apollo," the father said.

"I see." Dylan nodded. "Apollo, come," he ordered. Ed's ears barely twitched at that name. *Strange.* "Apparently he left the Air Force base in Texas, and it's my guess he followed David's remains."

Mr. and Mrs. Prentice's jaws hit the grass. "Why, that's amazing."

The sun dipped low in the sky. Must have been close to 5:45 p.m. What a long day.

"Son, would you like to come inside? We're about to sit for supper." It seemed like they needed to tell their story, or merely needed to grieve with company. "There's plenty. You like pot roast?"

With that, Ed jumped up and barked.

"It was David's favorite," Mrs. Prentice said. "Guess he wants some, too."

"Oh, I wouldn't want to impose," he answered, and his stomach cursed at him. Reheated leftover meatball hero, or homemade dinner? *Dumb-ass.* "I figured, well, would you want him to stay with you until we figure out what to do?"

Trepidation invaded his gut, waiting for their answer.

"Son, as much as we loved our son," Mr. Prentice explained, "we can't keep him. Marian is highly allergic. Which is why David chose the K9 duty after joining the Marines. We'd never allow him to have a dog."

He frowned. Now what? "Oh, I see. Wait, David was a Marine?"

"Yes, why?"

Another chill, reminiscent of the one in the attic, spanned across his forehead. Dylan held his tongue. *Nah.* The idea that David's ghost left his dog on the steps to be rescued? Might explain the boots, but talk about nuts. "I just wanted to know."

"So you'll stay?" Mr. Prentice asked, expectantly.

"I'd love to." He glanced back at Ed lying on the dirt, happier than he'd seen in the past day. "He'll be fine outside. He's used to it."

"We can give him a doggy bag to go," Mrs. Prentice said.

They laughed, and Ed agreed with a bark.

Guess he'd finally own a pet after all, even if temporarily.

Chapter Eight

"Hi, Doctor O'Brien." Brielle and Jacob stood at the front door the next evening, earlier than expected. Meghan had called to say she needed to deliver the costume, which he still had nightmares about.

"Doc." Jacob nodded in his usual succinct teenager way.

"Where's Ed?" Brielle didn't wait for his answer when the pooch in question turned the corner and headed for them. "He looks scary, but he's really a softy," she told Jacob, and all three disappeared into the kitchen. "We're taking him outside."

"Um, okay," he answered like a fool. He stood stock-still at the vision on his porch. Gone was the dark hair, and in its place a long, blond wig and gown that could stop traffic. Meghan held a hanger with a black tuxedo.

How the hell was he going to get through the evening without everyone knowing his state of arousal? For there was no doubt it would be that way for hours.

She frowned and blinked beneath insanely long eyelashes. "Tell me you don't get it?"

"You're stunning," he finally said, finding his voice, albeit it dry and crackly.

She blushed beneath her makeup. "Thank you, but…" Her eyebrows rose and fell waiting for his reply. "You're no Connery fan, then," she said with a huff.

He split into a dumb grin. "You're a Bond girl."

Her lips flattened. "Which one?"

He rubbed his chin trying to guess.

"*Dr. No?* Ursula Andress? You like?" She twirled on the porch with a laugh.

"Not the way I remember her. Where's your tiny white bikini?"

"Very funny." She smirked. "Too cold. Speaking of which, why am I always left on the porch?" she teased.

"So sorry, ma'am. Please come in, Ms. Bond."

She shoved the hanger into his hand. "Get dressed, James."

Hours later, they stood in the grand ballroom of Havencroft Manor, the masquerade ball in full swing. Dylan pulled his collar away from his throat. She'd almost gotten the size right.

"Can I ask you a question?"

"Sure." He handed her a glass of champagne and looked out over the patrons. Most couldn't hold a candle to Meghan, but no doubt the gossip hens would be in full armor as soon as they were spotted. He nodded politely at one of the fan club, and turned his attention back to where he longed to be.

"Do you ever get scared?"

At first, he couldn't fathom where her question originated. Then he followed her gaze to Evan and Augusta on the dance floor. Their pirate costumes were a hit, but more important was the way they gazed at each other, how Evan moved, despite his prosthetic leg, which made some people stop and gawp.

Smoothly, deftly, Evan epitomized a survivor, like Ed.

Dylan hunted for the right answer. "I do."

She toyed with the stem on her goblet. "I do, too. After sixteen years of marriage, life on the other side is terrifying. He's an entrepreneur. Jacques, that is. High-society Frenchman. It was easy to look the other way when the penthouse was mine and I wanted for nothing, like my mother."

He stayed quiet and let her continue.

"But then things changed. I knew I couldn't live like that and be that kind of example for Brielle. She'd been rebelling. Not eating."

"I noticed," he said, and she seemed surprised. Her mouth opened and closed a few times before she tilted her head to regard him.

"You did?"

"I'm a doctor," he said quietly, not in a condescending way. "She seems to have gained weight."

She nodded. "Evan commented over last Christmas and I ignored it. Makes me a crappy mother."

How could he make her see what he saw in a mere few short days? "Mothers come in all degrees of strength. Don't beat yourself up about things that don't matter now. Don't let your fear get in the way of moving forward. Brielle adores you."

She reached up and pushed a lock of hair away from his eyelash. "You're pretty wise, Mr. Bond. And I'm glad we came here together."

"Cheers." They clanked glasses. He flagged the waiter, placed the glasses down, and led her onto the dance floor.

⚜ ⚜ ⚜

Later that night…before the stroke of midnight…

Jacob promised to bring Brielle home safely, and she promised to call as soon as she let herself into the house. Dylan was surprised Meghan agreed to stay for a bit after the ball.

He extended an arm, motioning for Meghan to step across the threshold onto his back deck. Ed bounded down the wood steps and galloped onto the grass, ecstatic to be out.

Sparkles in the material of her gown twinkled in the soft glow coming from the dome-shaped light fixture. Her back was bared down to the soft curve at the end of her spine above her butt, and he had to bite his cheek.

God, it was almost too much to take. He itched to place his palm there. Augusta had laughed at their James Bond and Bond girl costumes, but holy St. Patrick, it was all he could do to keep his hands to himself.

Time to calm it. Ed gave a growl somewhere in the darkened yard. Probably found a squirrel or a possum. Nice to have a live-in exterminator. *Less of them for the attic.*

Meghan stopped at the railing. "He seems happier," she said with a glance back over one shoulder.

"Yeah. Things have certainly calmed down."

Ed also had a new doggy collar courtesy of Mr. and Mrs. Prentice. They'd delivered it this afternoon. And hanging from it, a small vial of his handler's ashes. David Prentice, Sergeant EOD, unit: US Marine Corps.

Dylan came to stand next to her and gripped the railing so their hands almost touched. What he wanted to do was pull her body against him and kiss her senseless.

She glanced over and arched an eyebrow. "Will you keep him?"

They observed Ed circle the yard, sniffing the ground every few feet. "I hope so, but it might take time." He was a powerhouse of a dog, and Dylan couldn't imagine not having him around. Realistically, though, the process could turn out to be a disappointment.

She faced him, licking her lips, and he got lost in the fullness of the bottom one, which now glistened. Wonder if it tasted like the peach martini she'd drank right before they'd left the bar.

"Why?"

He cleared his throat. "Well, even though Ed was found here," he explained, "all adoptions have to go through the Military Working Dog School at Lackland Air Force Base in Texas. Since his handler and adopter died, I don't know what will happen."

"Oh no." She frowned. "He won't be sent back there, will he?"

He shrugged. "I doubt it. Especially since he'd made the journey from there already. Crazy dog. Traveling across country."

"I think it's amazing." Ed jumped onto the steps and nudged Meghan's hand. She petted his enormous, furry head, and damn if the dog didn't look positively blissful.

Yeah, I wish she'd caress me like that, buddy.

"Ed and his owner must have had a miraculous kind of bond," she said, cooing and earning a grateful whine. "I truly can't imagine what we'd do without Rambo now that he's become part of our family. Many people in Havenport are part of our family now."

"Even me?" Time to throw caution to the wind. Either that, or he'd never know her true feelings or how she viewed where they might be heading.

She stopped her massage therapy session on his four-legged roommate and opened and closed her mouth a few times. "I already have a brother," she said.

His heart nearly stopped. *Take your cue, idiot.* Reaching under her chin with his fingertips, he gently tilted her head back so that the soft column of her neck was exposed. He wanted to see how that creamy bit of skin tasted. Again, that scent that sent him over the edge rose into his nose.

"Is that so? And should I be worried your brother will beat me with his bionic leg?"

She laughed and moved in closer. "Not if he wants to keep it." Then she leaned in and kissed him. With those Cinderella-like heels they were practically lips-to-lips level.

Shooting stars of pleasure, more vibrant than the night sky, headed straight to the top of his head. Her lips were soft and plump and opened just a tad, but not nearly enough.

"Let me in." It came out as almost pleading, but hell, he didn't care. He'd wanted her all night, and damn, she did as he asked. Holy…

His palm found that indent at the base of her spine and his stomach twitched at the smooth softness of her skin. He pressed her closer so that their bodies were flush. He plundered her mouth and earned a soft moan from the back of her throat. He felt her fingers at his neck, pulling him more fully into their kiss.

Peaches, vodka, and that Tic Tac she'd popped in her mouth on the car ride invaded his senses. Tongues meshed, and he knew he could literally kiss her for the rest of his life.

Ed's bark made her stiffen. They broke the kiss, but he kept his arms around her. He gave a quick sideways glance into the darkened yard, but there was no sign of Ed. Guess that possum had bit the dust.

She sighed and rested her head on his shoulder. They fit together perfectly. "That was lovely, but…" She paused and his stomach plummeted. "Dylan, I'm not into the casual stuff."

He pulled away an inch and with soft pressure raised her chin with his fingertips. "I'm not, either. And I don't want this to be casual."

Her lips parted. "What do you want?"

"You, Brielle, us, together as a family." And there it was, out loud and so comfortable and right something inside his chest shifted.

Her smile made the corners of her eyes crinkle. "I hoped you'd want that. And what about Ed? Can he be part of our family?"

He cleared his throat, for it was filled with emotions he'd never dreamed would enter his world. "I have to do the adoption suitability test, which is basically a way for me to tell he's okay to be around civilians, et cetera."

"Can you do that?"

"I can, being former military and a vet. It's a process." He breathed in the night air. The sky held hues of deep blue smattered with the twinkling of the Big Dipper.

"It's chilly tonight." She crossed her arms and rubbed at her biceps.

He slid his tuxedo jacket off and placed it around her shoulders. It was criminal to cover that gorgeous dress, but it was more criminal to have her succumb to hypothermia in his backyard.

"Halloween is here," she said, and snuggled into the long sleeves. "I hope you have enough candy for the trick-or-treaters."

He leaned his back against the wood deck railing, crossed his ankles, and faced her. "It's my first Halloween since moving to town. I have zero idea how many kids or teenagers will come knocking. I imagine it's a crowd, though. God, back in Boston we'd prowl the streets making mischief."

She laughed. "You? Straitlaced Doctor O'Brien? I do not believe it."

"You'd be..." She grabbed his wrist, cutting off his words. Icy fingers clamped on to the hairs above his fitness band. What the hell? Her face paled to scary. "Meg? Are you okay?"

"I—I," she stuttered. The slender curl touching her cheek from her sexy updo danced with the negative shake of her head. She lifted her index finger. It shook a bit. "Dylan, look."

What in the world? He blinked. Several times.

"Ed? Come. Apollo?" The dog didn't acknowledge either, which was puzzling, since he usually came running in a heartbeat and mostly by the former name. Instead, the dog remained perfectly still; not even his tail wagged while he sat facing them. He seemed to be looking right through them. Kind of creepy.

"What's up, buddy?" God, his voice sounded hoarse. Maybe he'd imbibed too many glasses of champagne. The vintage had been stellar. His head felt fuzzy, too. Either that, or bubbles had suddenly caused hallucinations.

Ed's handsome snout shot up and his nostrils flared, sniffing the air, perhaps searching for a scent. His pointed ears twitched and one flopped over a bit. Something that happened whenever Ed concentrated on listening to those sounds undetectable by human ears, quite amazing. Or when he was issued a command, or...*no way.* Dylan gulped. When someone was petting him. But none of the above was happening.

Strange.

A swirl of light and a fog-like image floated into a faint outline next to Ed, and Dylan did a double take. A man stood in profile, in full combat gear, boots, helmet, and an M4 strapped to his back.

Dylan's jaw slid open. A chill passed through his sternum, and he shivered.

"Christ. It can't be."

The handler touched the dog on the head, and his tail wagged. Ed tilted his head with a whine and the look of dog bliss in his chocolate eyes was unmistakable.

"What?" Meghan squeezed his forearm again. He'd forgotten she'd been standing next to him, probably taking it in as well. Or maybe not, and he'd finally lost his mind.

"Meghan," he said, slow and deliberate, and stayed as still as death, "are you seeing what I am?"

Eyes glued to Ed, in his peripheral he saw Meghan give him a quick sideways glance, then stare back to the two figures. Almost like she didn't want to make any sudden moves, either.

"The soldier?" she whispered.

He let out a shaky breath. Good that he'd not turned totally bat-shit crazy.

"Marine," he clarified, not sure why he felt the need. If the ghost could hear, he wanted to make sure he showed respect. "Army is soldiers; Marines are just that. Marines. Phew. I thought I was going crazy."

"Maybe we both are?" she asked, and her voice wavered.

Dylan didn't want to move closer. His feet were rooted to the spot, but he had to know. He had to put an end to what he'd suspected was going on. On the shelter surveillance camera. Sounds in his attic.

"Sergeant Prentice, sir," he called out.

The man's head turned.

Dylan saluted.

The spirit of Sergeant Prentice returned the gesture, nodded to Ed, then disappeared into the night air.

Read more about Dylan, Meghan, and their combined family and love of dogs in the next installment of the Havenport series.

About the Author

NICOLE S. PATRICK has always loved to read, and in her teenage years, she "borrowed" her mom's books to sneak away and become lost in the world of romance. After more than ten years in the corporate world of tech recruiting and HR management, she decided to stay home and raise children. But with so many romantic stories and characters floating around in her head, when the kids napped, she was compelled to put those words on a page and pursue this crazy dream of becoming published. Nicole writes romantic suspense and her heroes are those alpha males in uniform. She lives in New Jersey with her real-life hero, her husband, and her two sons.

For more information about Nicole, please visit her website at www.NicoleSPatrick.com

Also by Nicole S. Patrick

Kindred Spirits

by Lita Harris

It's been five years since Lauren Bishop lost her husband, Carl, to a ski accident. Unable to let go of her grief she casts a spell to help her along, and moves to the family home she inherited in Havenport, Rhode Island.

On her first night in town, she runs into her husband's best friend, Cooper Smith, who she hasn't seen since Carl's funeral. Each excited to be around someone familiar, they resume the friendship they once shared.

Has enough time passed, where they can get beyond the emptiness of the loss of Carl? Will Lauren and Cooper's relationship become more than the memory of their friend? Will Lauren find happiness in Havenport?

Dedicated to ~

Ruth, Emma, Nicole, and Desi. Thank you.

Chapter One

Lauren Bishop had to purge the negative energies coursing through her body. It was time to find a way to deal with the death of her husband.

For five years her heart ached and kept her from moving forward with her life. Five years of waking up alone in her bed, running her hand over the spot where Carl used to lie. If she closed her eyes and wished hard enough, she could feel the heat from his body.

So many times she relived the call from Cooper to tell her about the accident. Her breath caught and her chest constricted, a slow, steady vise grip on her heart. She was supposed to be on that ski trip, but she stayed in Brewster and let work come before spending that weekend with her husband. Instead, Cooper went in her place. She hadn't seen or heard much from her husband's best friend since the funeral. But she often thought of him. Up until Carl's death, Cooper had been a close friend of hers. It was like she lost two people she cared about that fateful day.

The brisk night air had a bite of frost. Darkness closed in behind her while she walked to her sacred space deep in the forest behind her home. Moonlight guided her safely along the well-worn path. Though alone, she didn't fear the night. Whispers from the trees comforted and welcomed her into the heart of her sanctuary. The woods were quiet, far from the incessant noise of life. She needed to escape this day—real life was too much to deal with.

She came upon a tree stump, tipped her head back, and stretched her neck, releasing tension that ran down her spine.

Her hands stretched wide beside her, fingers to the ground, directing energy back into the dirt to neutralize.

Slowly she opened her eyes. Her shoulders relaxed. Calmness swept over her. From the east, she stretched her hand before her and slowly walked clockwise around the old tree stump.

Her circle securely cast.

No one knew of her altar protected in the woods behind her house, not even her mother, who had taught Lauren the old ways.

The full moon embraced her and illuminated the flat surface of a hollowed tree stump. She slid the top aside and uncovered a worn wooden box she'd hand-decorated at fifteen. It contained the magickal tools given to her by her mother and grandmother.

She removed the box from its home and replaced the slab of wood on her altar. She draped a black velvet cloth, adorned with a silver-embroidered pentacle, across the top of the stump, gently smoothing the material. Next, she inserted a red candle into a pewter holder, one that had belonged to her grandmother. A swift breezed kicked up, just long enough to remind her where she stood.

Lastly, Lauren pulled rose petals from her pocket. "Be still, wind. Please let me finish," she whispered.

The wind obeyed, allowing her to place the rose petals at the base of the candle holder.

She shouldn't prepare such a spell, but her heart ached for too many years. If only she had gone away with him, he might still be with her. The one time she stayed home because of work. A job she despised and soon left. Opening her own graphic-design business was the best decision she'd ever made. Too bad she realized it too late.

She lit the candle and cupped the flame. Staring into it, she could see Carl's face. She smiled. His smile was so full of love—she missed that. Lauren turned her palms to the sky, drawing the moon's rays into her soul.

"This night I remember you,
Your love forever in my heart.
I release your soul from mine tonight,
So I may move forth, though torn apart."

Feet planted on the ground, eyes closed, she forcibly willed away her guilt for resorting to a spell to bury her pain.

She shouldn't proceed, especially since her spell casting was rusty. If her intention wasn't strong enough, the results could be disastrous—but the pain had to go away.

With the candle still burning and the rose petals fresh, she removed a raw chunk of rose quartz from her pocket and laid the gemstone on her private altar.

The full moon slid partially behind clouds. Her eyes adjusted to the night.

Who-hoo-ho-oo.

A great horned owl perched on a tree limb above. She looked up. "Hello there. Nice night, isn't it?"

The owl tilted its head and locked eyes with her. Was he giving her a sign? Her grandmother considered her spirit animal an owl. Lauren didn't buy in to that line of thinking much.

Hesitation of casting the next spell set in, but the moon would shift soon, and she needed to take advantage of its most powerful state. She needed to make sure she worded her spell carefully so it wouldn't affect another's free will. Not that she had anyone in mind, but she had to be careful anyway.

Reluctance cast aside, she continued.

"Relieve my pain of a broken heart,
Heal the open wound so right.
To open the path with a new start,
May new love find me tonight."

Leaves swirled around her feet. Lauren's arms floated down, resting heavily by her sides. Her magick was stale, but she had to try. Time hadn't made her miss Carl less. In fact, it was harder as each day passed.

Lauren sat on the ground. Two spells in a row drained her. Her arms fell to her sides. It'd been so long since she'd practiced magick. She wasn't strong enough to conjure the amount of energy she'd amassed tonight.

Carl never knew about her secret. He'd caught little things like crystals and candles used throughout the house, but he thought of them as decorations. Once she had fallen in love with him, she'd lost interest in practicing magick.

Tired, but she felt good. The heaviness in her heart lightened, so the spell must be working. Even if wishful thinking, she had to believe in the magick she'd spun beneath the full moon.

She pulled her shawl tighter around her shoulders, watching the flame fade into the night.

"Ewww." A fox ran past her and nearly knocked her over as the determined animal continued on its quest. She was never one to be afraid of the dark, or the woods. As a young girl, she practically grew up in the forest behind her family home. She named each tree along the beaten-down path while her mother held her hand and taught her the rules of nature.

Yes, her mother would be proud of her, continuing to practice the Bishop family traditions long after she'd moved on to the next realm. Everybody left her. At least that was how she felt. Her loneliness brought her to the woods tonight. She couldn't doubt the power of the spells she set out into the universe. No, she would be okay. Though she cast a love spell, she didn't seek out a particular individual, so she wasn't manipulating another's free will. She had been careful with her intention and words. She simply let the universe know she was available for love should someone find her.

With the candle burned to the nub and the rose petals scattered by the wind, Lauren folded up her altar cloth and returned her tools to the storage space within the tree stump. Something brushed against her as she bent over to replace the tree slab.

Fox?

She finished sliding the slab onto the stump. The air shifted. Different, thicker, heavy as pea soup. She glanced at the moon. No clouds. The sky was clear, yet the darkness heavy.

"Who's there?" Lauren clutched for the flashlight she forgot to bring. As a child she would seek solace in the woods to get away from her nagging grandmother, though she would appreciate her company at the moment.

Could it be?

"Gram, is that you?"

One never knew what magick would bring.

Again, leaves shuffled around her a few feet away. Her lips trembled. She peered into the darkness. She couldn't see anything. A hereditary witch should welcome the unknown. Not her. Once, she'd encountered a spirit after one of the family séances. Leave it to her mother and grandmother to conjure up spirits for fun.

Sure, she felt the presence of spirits, and even caught a few disembodied voices over the years, but she always fought against an actual ghostly encounter since she was ten years old. One night, a man appeared before her while she read in bed. He'd stood next to her a mere few seconds. He wasn't threatening, and she didn't sense danger, but the incident scared her. His semisolid appearance unsettled her. From that day, she shut down from interacting with spirits.

Her mother and grandmother thought her fear was silly, but to her, the fear was real.

Dark clouds eclipsed the moonlight as she pulled her shawl tighter, more for comfort than warmth against the night air.

Her mother and grandmother treated spirits like regular guests, always able to see and chat with them like company. Lauren couldn't, and would not, allow herself to be that open, even when her grandmother teased and challenged her to converse with the other side. A part of her wanted to accept the spirit realm, but her fear was stronger than her desire to welcome. Maybe one day. But she wasn't ready.

Snap. She jumped, spooked from her own thoughts. Surely it was just an animal rustling about. Her pace quickened to leave the woods. It was movie night, and Charley waited. No theater tonight, just a DVD with homemade popcorn, and wine.

Thank God for her best friend. She wouldn't have made it through Carl's death if it wasn't for Charley.

She thought back to the day they'd met on the beach in Havenport. Both their families had been there for vacation. Charley stumbled over Lauren, who'd been stretched out on her blanket taking in the crash and roll of the waves.

"Oops. Sorry. You must think I'm an ass."

Lauren shielded her eyes from the sun and peeked between the blinding rays. "No, but I'd appreciate you paying more attention to where you're going."

"I'm Charley. Charlotte's what my birth certificate says." She stuck out her hand. "Pleased to meet you, even if it was in the most offending way."

"Lauren." She sat up and accepted the peace gesture. "You're not from here."

"Nope. How can you tell?"

"Have you ever heard yourself talk?"

"I try not to."

"New York, right?"

"Nope. Jersey."

"Same difference." Charley flashed a cynical smile.

"Not even close. You really need to get off this beach and venture out into the world."

The memory warmed her heart. A fluke they had met that day. Her family had a house in Havenport and were regular summer residents. Charley's family ended up there that day because her father had gotten too tired to continue driving to Martha's Vineyard.

They'd kept in touch and became best friends. Eventually Charley started spending the occasional summer at the Bishop summer home.

Time to visit the beach house. She'd ignored it since Carl's death. She meant to go. Wanted to. But she had spent her honeymoon there, and since Carl's death, well, it hadn't been easy to walk around the empty home.

She rented it out the past few years, even thought of selling. She had no one to enjoy it with. Except for Charley, but she didn't get to Rhode Island much. Too busy working in the city. Havenport couldn't compete with Manhattan with its Broadway plays, concerts, restaurants, basically anything one desired anytime of the day.

Just one of the things they couldn't agree on. Charley craved the fast-paced life of the city. And Lauren liked to have the space around her filled with trees and animals. That's why she gave up the Manhattan apartment soon after Carl was gone.

She looked back at her sacred stump. Shoulders slumped, sadness gnawed at her, as if this would be the last time she would be here. She dug her toe in the dirt and drew a small circle, a nervous habit.

It was getting late.

"I miss you, Carl. You'll never know how much I still ache for you." She tossed her words into the universe, hoping he'd somehow know.

She pulled her shawl tighter around her shoulders, imagining a hug that had been gone too many years. Charley had to be at the house waiting to delve into wine, chocolate, and popcorn. She could do without the extra calories, but she'd have to burn them off another day.

Shadows followed her along the path back to her house.

She stopped short of the edge of the forest.

"In a hurry?" a man's voice spoke at her back.

She whipped her head around. No one. The hairs on the back of her neck prickled. Phantom fingers touched her ear.

"No! Do not appear to me." She ran out of the woods, struggling to not faint from fear.

❖ ❖ ❖

Lauren flung the front door open and clutched her chest.

"What the hell?" Charley rose to her knees and peered over the back of the couch.

"Nothing, just spooked." She tossed her shawl onto a freestanding wooden coatrack.

Hearing things. Again.

"Catch your breath. *Steel Magnolias* is loaded and I'm halfway through this bottle of fumé blanc. It goes best with popcorn."

She joined her best friend on the couch. "I should have known better than to go out there."

"Playing in the woods again by yourself?" Charley emptied her wineglass with one swig.

"How can you tell?" She hadn't told anyone what she was going to do.

"This gave you away." Charley picked a small maple leaf stuck in her hair.

"You got me. I needed to clear my head. I told you I've been thinking about moving. Getting away from here."

"I know, sweetie. Too many memories. I mean, you still have your grandmother's stuff lying around this house."

"My mother couldn't bring herself to get rid of any of her belongings, either. I just left them, as well. Carl didn't seem to mind."

They were rarely home after they married. His job as an international money manager took him around the world. She was able to run her graphic-design business from wherever they traveled.

"It might be time to clean out the place." Charley split the rest of the wine in the bottle into two glasses.

"I'm not ready for that. Three deaths in five years is a lot to process. I've decided to go to Havenport, at least for the summer."

"It's been years since I was there. Want some company?"

Having Charley there would be comforting, but it was time to move forward. She even committed to renting the house in Brewster. But she wasn't in the mood to be managed by her best friend so it was best that she didn't go to Havenport. At least not so soon.

Plus, the job at Serendipity would keep her busy. She always wanted to open her own metaphysical shop, but liked the idea of making her own hours, not tied to a regular schedule. She liked to be able to take off and travel when she got antsy and bored of her routine.

"How could you? Isn't this your busy time of year?"

Charley pulled her legs onto the couch and hugged her knees, while deftly holding her glass without spilling a drop.

"I might be leaving."

"Why?" She broke off a piece of almond bark.

"Because I'm probably getting fired."

She sat back, shocked at her friend's nonchalant manner. "What?"

"Well, maybe not technically fired, but let go. It's all the same to me. There's talk of downsizing. I'm sure I'm on the list. Seniority and all that bullshit."

She popped open a bottle of red wine. She wasn't picky—whatever was near suited them. "I'm glad to see you're okay with this. It doesn't bother you at all?"

"Hey, what can I do?"

Lauren had been there herself. After eight years of loyalty to her former company, she was let go with nothing more than a "sorry-but-we-had-to-make-cuts" speech. That had been the catalyst to open her own company. Perfect timing. When Carl's job started shipping him all over the world, she needed only an Internet connection to stay in business. She was grateful for the few clients she picked up through his connections.

"I'd love for you to be there, but I need to do this by myself. I've been hiding too long. Maybe you can visit for Christmas."

"Have you decided how long you're going to stay?"

"Not really. The house is rented for six months starting January, so I don't have to rush out of here. I haven't confirmed a lease yet."

"What? You can't rent this place without a lease."

"Maybe so, but I had a good sense of the guy I will be renting it to. Plus, it'll be a corporate rental, so I'm not worried."

"Do you have someone to watch the place until then?"

"Yes, the Realtor will manage it. Havenport isn't that far from here. What, an hour?"

"Okay. I'll be back in the city so I won't be close by to run here if you need me."

Lauren hugged Charley. "You've done enough over the years. I'll be fine."

She could always count on a phone call at the right moment, or unexpected visit when she felt low, which had been often since Carl's death.

"Okay, enough of this bonding crap. Movie time." Charley hit play.

Lauren leaned back. "I love this movie. It's been years since I watched it."

"Yeah, I think the last time was with you." Charley stretched her legs across the couch, squishing Lauren into the arm.

"Stop." She laughed. "You're so annoying."

The lights went out.

"Damn! How am I going to refill my glass without spilling the wine?"

"I'm sure it won't be long until the electricity comes back on." She lit a candle on the coffee table.

"Did you make that one?"

"Of course. I never buy store-bought candles. My grandmother would freak if she knew I did that."

"Do you think she's here?" Charley looked around the room.

"Don't start with that. You know it spooks me."

"Even if it's someone you know?" Charley laughed.

The fear from the woods resurfaced. She was sure she'd heard a man's voice. Maybe it was the wind—it could do strange things.

She pulled a blanket from the top of the couch and spread it over her, tucking it under her chin.

"When are you leaving for Havenport?"

"Next week."

She removed her wedding ring and pressed it into her palm. It was her first step in letting go of Carl.

Chapter Two

The tourist-free streets on a crisp October day soothed her as her car rolled into Havenport.

As much as she loved the ocean and summer nights at the shore, nothing pleased her more than the pumpkins, cornstalks, and Halloween ghouls adorning each streetlight post. Ever since she could remember, the local high school students made spooky figures out of clothing and stuffed the bodies to look like real people. A serious competition she almost participated in, but found she couldn't because she didn't attend the Havenport schools.

She felt like an outsider, even though her grandparents owned the house as long as she could remember. Even though she'd spent most of her summers, Halloween, and Christmas vacations in Havenport, she still wasn't a local.

The house had been closed up since the summer. Fortunately, she got Liz to find someone trustworthy to open and air it out before she arrived. She was glad she held on to the family properties. Havenport provided her a steady second income. Even renting in the fall was lucrative, but she wouldn't this year. She needed the house for herself more. She planned to spend at least Halloween through Christmas in Havenport.

She didn't want to miss the fund-raiser masquerade party at Havencroft Manor, but she shuddered at the idea of going alone. Except for peeking into the house as a kid, she'd never been inside. Stories of the place being haunted with the ghost of an Emerson kept her from tackling her curiosity.

Charley was relentless with trying to get Lauren to break in to the manor. The summers her best friend stayed in Havenport were the worst. Especially once they'd met up with Jason, a local boy that Charley flipped over. He brought nothing but trouble, but while her best friend didn't care, Lauren did. Even though she didn't live in Havenport, her grandparents spent more time there and she worried how her actions affected them.

She didn't have Charley's wild, don't-care attitude.

The sun set on the horizon, nearly blinding her as she drove down Main Street.

She pulled up to Serendipity and parked on the street. The store had curb appeal. She could see why it was doing well. The dark-brown-stained, weathered wood was a nice contrast to the hunter-green sign and its gold-burnished lettering. The store welcomed even the casual window-shopper with its orange mini lights that lined the window's edge, which was the entire front of the building. Real pumpkins were tucked in and around books on display.

She had felt bad that she'd delayed starting at the store, and Olivia had been an angel understanding Lauren's situation. The job could have been given to anyone. Olivia held a loyalty to her aunt, Susan, and the friendship of Lauren's grandmother, Gertie.

It would take some getting used to, but living in a small town could be what she needed to get back into circulation. Her graphic-design job kept her in the house at her desk. Human interaction was necessary for her to get engaged with society once again.

She tapped on the window before entering the store.

"You're here!" Marcie spread her arms wide and wrapped them around Lauren.

"Yes, finally. I like the feel of this place."

"Really? That soon? You just got here." Marcie backed away and smoothed her shirtsleeves.

"I know, but sometimes I have an instinct, and it's very strong right now. Is Olivia here?"

"Of course. She practically lives here. Well, she kind of does. Upstairs apartment, for the most part." Marcie walked over to the doorway between the bookstore and metaphysical shop.

"Olivia. Guess who's here?" Marcie called out, then turned back to Lauren. "I feel like I know you already."

She smiled. "Yes, technology can be good sometimes."

"I'd never done a video chat before. I didn't know what Olivia was talking about when she suggested it for your interview. Cool stuff."

They'd spent most of the summer communicating that way. What started as an interview quickly became a way to get to know each other.

In her grief-induced solitude, she'd gotten very comfortable dealing with people by phone or computer. Working at Serendipity, having to talk to people face-to-face, would be a challenge. The only person she spent any time with was Charley, and that wasn't very often.

"Hi." Olivia dropped a box on the floor next to the counter as she came into the room. "I'm so glad you're finally here. We've been so busy."

"I would imagine so. Halloween has a special eeriness that makes it different from the other holidays. I see the schoolkids are still painting storefront windows." Lauren placed her purse on the counter.

The spirit of the store space overwhelmed. Her body lightened and she smiled. It'd been years since she felt that familiar surge of electricity. It was strongest when her grandmother was with her. They never classified themselves as witches, though most people would. The Bishop women considered themselves to be more sensitive and aware of their surroundings. Intuition, they called it.

Supposedly, they were descendants of Bridget Bishop, or so they believed. A cousin of Lauren's started researching the family tree a decade ago, but as far as she knew, hadn't finished.

But her grandmother insisted they were from that Bishop line, and that's why the women in the family never changed their surname when they married.

Whatever the truth, there was no denying the sensations Lauren felt and worked hard to keep under wraps.

"Do you want me to put this away?" Marcie asked Olivia.

"No, it's heavy. Max will be here soon, and he can lift it for you. It's books."

Lauren walked the edges of the store. "Do you have unusual happenings here?"

Marcie looked at Olivia. "Go ahead. Tell her."

"Well, nothing I can substantiate, but I get weird vibes when I'm alone. Not on the bookstore side." Marcie wrinkled her nose.

"That's not true," Olivia interjected. "Remember the one time…"

"I don't want to talk about it. It's nothing, really." Marcie's eyes widened, as if she'd seen something strange.

Olivia held Marcie's hand and squeezed it lovingly.

"Don't worry. She'll tell you, and once she does, she won't shut up about it." Olivia let go. "Why do you ask?"

"Oh, nothing. I was getting a sense of sadness. I could be tired."

"Hello?" a deep voice called from the other side.

"In here." Olivia smiled.

Lauren wished she could be that happy again.

"Ran a little late today. We finally got the slate shingles for the tower room."

He had to be talking about Havencroft Manor. No other building in town had a need for a shingle like that.

"Hi. I'm Max. You're…?" He held out his hand.

She shook his hand. "Lauren—"

Kelly Fielding. Her shoulders cringed at the vision. She couldn't make out the face. The girl was blond. Her signature on a piece of paper.

"Nice to meet you, Max." She slowly pulled her hand away and grabbed her purse. "Um, sorry. I have to run. I'll be in early tomorrow."

Lauren ran out of the store and rushed to her car. Heat rose from her hands. She cupped and rubbed her palms together.

She still had it—and it scared her. If only she'd been more persistent about her premonition when Carl went skiing.

She should have stopped him.

She'd hugged him before he left and she saw him crashing into a tree in a vision, but brushed it off as her own transposed fear.

She worked so hard to squelch her premonitions, because with them came spirits, and nothing scared her more than being face-to-face with one.

But Kelly was alive.

She couldn't rely on her own intuition. Too unsure if what she saw was real. She'd give it a day or two and research the name to see what she could find out.

She turned the ignition and pulled away. Maybe it was time to face her fears.

Her curiosity compelled her to take a short ride out of town. Havencroft Manor loomed before her as she drove down Manor Road.

Scaffolding detracted from the beautiful stonework on the tower. That had to be what Max talked about. She decided to park.

If only Charley were with her, she might be brave enough to go in. A faint light leaked through the front door.

She got out of the car and walked up to the marble entryway. A sign caught her eye.

COOPER SMITH
HISTORIC HOME RESTORATION
CONTRACTOR

It couldn't be.

She looked behind her. This was the furthest she'd ever gotten onto the manor property. It didn't seem as scary now as it did when she was a teen. The grass was well kept and bushes trimmed. A few of the oak trees needed to be cut back, but overall the grounds were beautiful.

She tiptoed closer to the manor and peeked through the window next to the door. Canvas drop cloths covered the floor. Definitely construction going on. A sampling of sawdust was evident on the cloth.

How would the house be ready in time for the masquerade ball?

"Can I help you?" a familiar voice spoke at her back.

She turned her face to him. Crow's-feet etched the corners of his eyes. That was new. His hair was longer, and his face was scruffier than she had ever seen on him. The last time she'd seen him was at the funeral. Her heart sank a bit, yet she was happy to see Cooper, her husband's best friend. "It is you."

"Lauren? What are you doing here?"

"Me? I have a history here. You?"

He pointed to the sign.

"I see that. I didn't know you did this type of work."

It had been too painful to keep in touch. She never forgave herself for not going on the ski trip. And she knew Cooper well enough to know he carried some guilt of the accident even though he had nothing to do with it except being there. Neither of them could get past the pain. The few ill attempts to get together after Carl was gone never happened.

"A lot of things have changed." He folded his arms across his chest, as if holding in the pain of losing his best friend.

She knew Cooper well enough to know how hard it was for him to have been with Carl when the accident happened. She'd heard the pain in his voice when she got the call.

Maybe they could be friends again. Up until five years ago they were. She swallowed hard, pushing the hurt down so she wouldn't cry.

"Yes, they have. Was carpentry a latent trait?" She fought to stay focused on their conversation and not their memories.

"My dad taught me a lot when I was a kid. He felt I should have a trade in case the college thing didn't work out." He smiled.

"I guess that was good advice. And what are the chances of us running into each other like this?"

"Not likely, but I'm glad we did."

She smiled.

"Do you want to see what the place looks like inside?"

An invite into her childhood summer nightmare. *Gulp.*

Her childhood fear from years ago was being realized. But Cooper was with her. How bad could it be?

"Sure," she said with more certainty in her voice than her gut.

He reached out to her. "Careful, there's stuff lying around. We're almost done. It's mostly cleanup at this point."

She went no farther than the Great Hall. Impressed by the high ceiling and stained-glass skylight. The room made her feel shorter. Heavy oak woodwork followed the contour of high ceilings that met marble walls.

Exquisite as the manor was, she preferred her old New England home with its plaster walls, which gave a warm and inviting embrace.

"It's lovely." She meant that. Not scary like she envisioned. The larger rooms made her uncomfortable, but didn't have poorly lit shadows dancing around the rooms.

Then again, she was quite a few years older and didn't upset as easily. And having Cooper take her on the tour of the house helped to stifle her fear of spirits. She would beg her mother and grandmother to stop with the séances, but they never listened to her. They would laugh that Lauren was silly and dramatic. But her fear was real.

She followed Cooper, lightly holding on to the back of his shirt. A flash of him kissing her stopped her cold. She let go of his shirt and stepped back.

"Would you like to see the rest of the place?"

"No, that's fine. I need to be getting to my house." Her voice quivered slightly.

"I heard you were coming to town. You'll be working at that New Age store next to the bookshop?" He picked up a heavy-duty orange extension cord and wrapped it around his hand and elbow with the precision of a professional.

"It's true." She almost sang her response. "I wanted to, you know, get back out in the world. Stop hiding in my office."

"I get that. That's one of the reasons I started doing this. After the…"

His eyes glistened with tears.

"I know. It's hard for me, too." She stiffened her core. She was past this.

Pull it together.

"I thought losing myself in woodworking would help me gain some perspective. It did. I realized that I needed more out of life. I called my dad and asked him if he had any contacts for historical restorations. His connection to the Emerson's put me here." He placed the extension cord on top of a wooden toolbox. "I have to tell you I enjoy this so much better than the world of finance."

She glanced around the room trying to pick what was original and what had been restored. She couldn't tell. His work was that good.

"I guess you can say I'm on the same path. It's taken me longer to get there, but better late than never, right?"

He nodded. "Hey, I don't know if you've eaten yet, but Royce's has some good meals on the menu. Want to stop in for a bite? You don't have to if you don't want to. I planned on going there anyway, and it's nice to have company. You can only listen to so many fish stories before you run out of polite ways to tell people to shut up. I don't want to hear about the one that got away."

Her thoughts ran to Carl and the last time they had dinner in Havenport. The last walk they took on the pier.

She smiled. "I'd like that."

✤ ✤ ✤

Royce's was packed. Every bar stool occupied. She couldn't tell through the sea of people if there were available tables. The clanking of beer bottles on the bar and throaty fishermen voices filled the restaurant with intense energy that made her flinch for clarity.

She looked at Cooper. "Maybe we should have called ahead for reservations?"

He shook his head. "No problem. Liz, over here."

She recognized Liz immediately, though she was older and wore even more makeup. What did she hide underneath the heavy foundation?

She bit her lip, trying not to be judgmental. She didn't mean to be. Sometimes it slipped out. Fortunately, her thoughts stayed in her head more often than not. She never understood why people didn't love who they were.

But who was she to talk? She'd spent the past five years barely leaving her home. If it wasn't for Charley being a pain in the ass, she never would have.

A large window across the room filled with the nearly full moon. It was a special time for her when the full moon fell on All Souls' Night. She'd release a kicker for her spell at the stroke of midnight at the ball to help her spell gain momentum.

"Over here, sweetie." Liz waved them to the other side of the bar.

"Thanks, Liz. Are you working here permanently now?" Cooper held out a chair for Lauren at a table along the water.

"About as permanent as I can get. With my other jobs, well, I make it work."

She found Liz interesting and would love to get into a conversation with her, away from everyone. She could tell that Liz had stories to tell. Personal in-depth discussions fascinated Lauren. It helped to keep her intuition sharp. And in that area she sorely lacked confidence.

"You're the Bishop girl, aren't you?" Liz lit a mason jar candle on the table.

"Yes, I recognized you." Though nearing forty, she didn't feel like a girl. "You still look the same."

"Aw, aren't you a sweetie? What'll you have?"

"Do you have birch beer on tap? Frosted mug?" She'd been craving a cold one since she walked into the restaurant.

"Yep. You, Coop?"

"Whatever Sam you have on tap."

"Okay, I think he's got the pumpkin something-or-other."

"That's fine."

Liz handed them menus and went to get their drinks.

"I'm not in the mood for anything heavy. Ooh, lobster roll. Corn on the cob and coleslaw." Her stomach growled at the anticipation of being fed.

"You know what? That sounds good. It's been a while since I've had a lobster roll." Cooper closed his menu and took hers, placing them on the edge of the table.

It was weird but comfortable sitting across the table from him after not seeing him for so long. She wasn't sure what to talk about. It's not like she could ask him about his family. He always said he would never marry, and traveled too much to have kids.

"So how long have you been working on the manor?" *Safe conversation.*

"About six months. It's in pretty good shape considering how old it is and with the salt air and harsh winters. It's held up."

"Why is it taking so long if it's in decent shape?" She spread her napkin across her lap, nervously smoothing out the wrinkles to keep from thinking about Carl.

"Because the work is so intricate. It can take hours to replicate a six-inch piece of wooden scroll."

"From what I saw, the woodwork is beautiful."

"You should stop by to see the rest of the house in the daylight. It really is a wonderful example of craftsmanship."

"Here you go. What'll you have to eat?" Liz placed the mug and pilsner glasses on the table.

"Two lobster rolls with corn on the cob and coleslaw." Cooper held his beer.

"Fries?" Liz asked.

Lauren shook her head.

"No, thanks. We're good."

"Is this place always this crowded?" Lauren picked up her mug.

"Seems to be. I don't come here much. I usually grab something from Corky's or his dad's hot dog truck right outside on the pier."

"I don't remember a hot dog truck." She rested her chin on her hand and leaned in closer. The noise made it hard to hear him.

"He's only had it a few months. Beginning of summer. It annoys Corky to no end. His dad retired from fishing and decided a hot dog truck would give him something to do with his time. It's Corky's fault. He's the one who encouraged his dad. Nothing like direct competition from your old man."

His laughter made her smile. She thought back to a New Year's Eve when she, Carl, and Cooper stayed at their office in Times Square. They watched the ball atop the Allied Chemical Building slowly descend, and just before the new year rang in, a rat ran across her foot and she smashed her champagne flute on the floor.

That year became known as the rat ran at midnight.

She'd never seen a man laugh so hard, and she thought of that moment every time he laughed.

But there hadn't been much of that in the past five years. She relaxed her shoulders and rested her elbows on the table, her chin on her fists.

"So what have you been up to?" He pushed his empty glass to the table edge.

"Not much. I'm sure you heard my grandmother and mother passed away."

He nodded.

She understood the sorrow in his eyes at the mention of her losses.

"Anyway, um, it's been years of settling estates and deciding what to do with the properties. Charley's been a big help."

"You never went back to the city, did you?" He twirled his empty glass.

"No. There wasn't any need to. I sublet the apartment until the lease ran out and let the landlord take it from there. I knew I wanted to keep the house in Brewster. I wasn't sure about the Havenport place. My time here will decide that. Don't get me wrong—I love the house and the town, but I don't need two places to take care of."

"I can understand that. I still have my co-op in the city. I wasn't sure how this business would take off. The work is limited. Not many people are interested in restoring old buildings. They'd rather knock them down and build new."

Her stomach relaxed and she glanced at the moonbeams lighting up the ocean. She was happy she decided to come to Havenport.

Chapter Three

He couldn't believe Lauren sat across the table from him. He missed her, but could never bring himself to call her after Carl's funeral. The few times he did talk to her, she had initiated the phone conversations. It was too easy to unleash his emotions at that time, and that wasn't the time.

After all, he was Carl's friend.

"How's your lobster roll?" He wiped his mouth, trying not to be rude. It had been a while since he had dinner with a woman. Easy to forget table manners when he was used to grabbing fast food for most of his meals.

"It's very good. They use real lobster, not that fake imitation crab stuff. Not that I'd expect them to. This place seems too upscale for that sort of thing."

"Do you still have your graphic-design business?" He wanted to keep the conversation light.

"Yes, but it has slowed down a bit. It seems anyone who has a computer can put up a website or create a print campaign. I'm trying to find my niche."

She took dainty bites of the overstuffed sandwich. He was almost done and wanted another, but didn't want to make a pig of himself. He opted for another beer instead.

"Liz?" He held his glass in the air to get her attention.

Either the crowd got quieter or he was so into Lauren that background noise wasn't as distracting as it was when they'd first arrived.

"Thanks. Do you want another drink? This is my last beer of the night." He took his drink from Liz.

"No, I'm good. Thanks. I should be getting to the house. I haven't stopped there yet. Plus, I have to get up early to get to the store."

"Is that something you really want to do? It doesn't seem like a job for you."

"It's something for me to do now. It's an easy way to get back into circulation. I've been hiding away too long. Don't you think?"

He swallowed his desire to tell her what she meant to him. He wanted to rush to her side years ago, but didn't. He wasn't going to do that now, either, and risk scaring her away.

He felt like an awkward sixteen-year-old boy. Had he sabotaged his love life waiting for her?

"You took the time you needed to. Everyone deals with tragedy in their own way."

"I guess. I felt sorry for myself. Anyway, when I was thinking about moving here, I reached out to Susan Chadwick because she was good friends with my grandmother. When I called the bookstore, I found out that she had sold it to her niece and was looking for help with the new store adjoining the bookstore. I didn't want to say no because she sounded desperate. Anyway, I figured I would give it a try. At least through the holidays."

"You plan on spending Christmas here?" He waved his hand for the check.

"I do. There's something comforting about holidays in a small town. Maybe because it's easy to contain the excitement because everything is concentrated within a small community."

He smiled. The Havencroft project would carry him through Thanksgiving if the job stayed on course, possibly longer if he encountered unforeseen delays. He didn't like running over budget. He wouldn't like it done to him if he were the homeowner.

"I haven't been here during the winter. Just the few times you and Carl…" His stomach clenched at the mention of the name. He didn't want to upset Lauren by bringing up her dead husband.

She reached across the table and took his hand. "Listen, it's going to come up. Maybe it's best not to ignore him. He was a part of our lives and in some way I still think he is a part of mine. It's not your fault what happened."

He squeezed her hand gently. "I know. I mean, seeing you, I…"

"Didn't expect to."

"Right."

"It was a surprise for me as well. It's strange how things work out."

He smiled as she squeezed his hand again, and slowly pulled hers away. "I'm glad you're here. Now I have someone around who knows me."

The thought of her being around made him happy and nervous. His feelings for her never changed. He had hoped that with the passing of Carl and the time gone by, his unrequited love for Lauren would fade. Having her near proved that time hadn't made him forget.

"There must be some people you know around here." She pushed her plate away and finished her beer.

"Not really. I hired some guy who's pretty new to this place also. I use him when I need an extra hand. Young guy. Max."

She nodded. "Unless there's another Max in town, I met him when I stopped at the store earlier today."

"That's probably him. He dates the owner, Olivia."

"Yep, same person."

She pulled back, crossed her arms, and seemed to escape into thought. She pursed her lips. He didn't think he said anything to upset her, but it was an odd reaction. Maybe it was too much being around each other.

But they'd always gotten along.

"Did you enjoy your dinner?" He placed money in the check holder and leaned in closer to her. "Hello? Are you still here with me?"

She shook her head. "Sorry. Just lost in thought. Nothing personal."

"Care to elaborate?"

"How about we take a walk on the beach? It's a little cool, but it's a clear night."

He wasn't going to push her. If she wanted to tell him about it, she would.

"I'd like that. I don't enjoy the shore as much as I'd like to."

"That's a shame. Havenport has one of the most beautiful beaches on the east coast."

"I'm too busy working. I get lost in what I'm doing and then I'm too tired to do anything else."

"Would you rather not go?"

"No, we're going."

He wasn't about to lose the opportunity for a walk on the beach with her, no matter how tired. He opened the door and led her down to the sand.

The roar and rumble of the ocean soothed as much as frightened in the dark. It took about five minutes for his eyes to adjust.

Lauren walked with her arms across her chest, her shoes dangling from her fingers.

Was he wrong to think about holding her?

He thought back to the night he knew he was in love with her. It was a year into her marriage to Carl. He had heard his best friend talk about his wife. How pretty she was. Smart. Independent.

Then, one night Carl invited him over for dinner. The chicken was dry and the mashed potatoes resembled wallpaper paste. He didn't care about the dinner, though. Instead, her voice captivated him. As if she sang when she spoke. A light lilt to her speech.

They spent more time together—summers in Havenport; nights in the city—but it was the night they'd met for dinner when Carl got stuck at the office that he'd always remember.

The waiter brought a bottle of red wine sent by Carl with his apologies for being late but that he would be there as soon as he could. Start dinner without him.

It was that night, when she twirled her wineglass and laughed at his joke, that he fell for her. She'd asked him why he didn't have a girlfriend. He hadn't known until then...

"Who's lost in thought now?" She tugged on his shirtsleeve.

"Just enjoying the view." He smiled and warded off the pang of guilt in his gut. "Will Charley be coming out to visit?" *Why did he ask that? Stupid.* Lauren had been trying to fix them up for years. He liked Charley as a friend, but she was too brash for his taste. Fun to hang out with, but he could only take her in small doses.

"I'm sure she'll be coming to visit when she can. Not that you care to see her." She laughed.

She knew?

He thought he did a good job of hiding his opinion about Charley. Apparently he wasn't as slick as he thought.

She stopped at the lifeguard stand. "What's that?"

He stopped next to her. "What?"

"Over there. There's something wiggling around next to that rescue boat."

He narrowed his eyes to look through the darkness. The clear night had given way to clouds, making it harder to see. A small overturned wooden boat came into view.

A whimper came from the boat.

Lauren walked toward the cry.

"Maybe you shouldn't…"

Too late. He caught up with Lauren. She reached down and rested her hand on a long-haired dog that quieted from her touch.

"He's caught. His collar is wrapped on the oar hook. Release it while I keep him calm."

He was amazed how quickly the dog responded to her. "How do you know it's a he?"

"Just a sense I have." She scratched the dog behind his ear, and his whimper stopped.

He dug around the oar hook stuck in the sand. The collar unlatched once the dog relaxed. "He must belong to someone."

She pulled out her cell phone and turned on the flashlight. "There was a tag, but it's ripped off the collar. It looks like it hasn't been missing for too long. The spot where it was isn't as faded as the rest."

"What do you want to do?" He ran his hand down the dog's back. The stray buried its nose in Cooper's knee.

"He must smell your dinner. We can't leave him here."

"You keep calling it a he."

The dog lifted its leg and peed on the boat.

"Told you." She laughed. "I have a knack with animals."

"Apparently. Seriously, what are you going to do with him?"

"Hmm, I guess I'll take him to my place tonight and check around town tomorrow. He must belong to someone."

He sat on the boat and patted the dog's head. She sat next to him.

The tide had calmed from when they'd first walked onto the beach. He grew even more tired, though he enjoyed her company and didn't want the night to end. But he had to get the main floor of Havencroft done in time for the masquerade party. He still had a few weeks, but he liked to build in a buffer of at least ten days.

She played with the dog. Its scruffy hair needed to be brushed, possibly cut. There were some mats of hair around its haunches.

"You might want to clean him up before setting out to find his owner. I hear that place in town is good, Wags and Walks, near the bookstore."

"I think you're right. I'll bring him over in the morning when I get to work."

"It's getting late. I'm sure you want to get a good night's sleep for your first day."

"I'm a bit tired. I haven't even stopped at the house yet."

He was concerned about her walking into the house at night by herself. How would she react to being alone? Had she been there since Carl's death?

"How about if I go with you and help get him settled?"

She hesitated.

Not the response he looked for, but he understood if she needed to be alone.

She stood and brushed sand off the seat of her pants. "I'd like that."

He smiled, happy he could do at least that much. "What about if he takes off on us?"

"No problem." She held out her hand. "Give me your belt."

"What?" He laughed.

"Come on. Give it up." She held her hand out in front of her.

"Okay. I want it back."

"You'll get it back. Don't worry."

He handed her his belt. She slipped the end under the dog's collar and then through the buckle. "See? Instant leash. No running after him through the dark streets of Havenport."

"Genius. I knew there was always something special about you."

Damn. Stupid thing to say.

This was going to be impossible. He had to get his feelings under control. With Carl gone and not seeing her for so long, then showing up... Well, this was not how he expected his day to go.

"I think we should be going. Work tomorrow."

He pulled into her driveway behind her car.

Pull it together, Cooper. Be cool.

He walked up to Lauren waiting on the front porch. He liked this house. It had simple lines, but the shutters and scrollwork gave it character, along with the stained-glass window over the front porch. He appreciated the skillful details of the waves and seagulls embedded in the artwork.

The hair on his nape stood. It felt like someone was sitting in one of the chairs to the right on the porch.

It had to be his nerves. He had never been to the house without Carl. He thought he saw a chair rocking—just once.

"Would you hold your belt while I get the lock?" She smiled and handed the makeshift leash to him. He relaxed a bit as the watched feeling dissipated.

It must be his mind playing tricks because he was tired.

"You coming?" She waved him into the foyer.

The house smelled stale. Clean, but like it hadn't had fresh air moving about for months, maybe years. How long had it been since she'd last been there?

He wanted to ask. Had many questions, but wasn't going to be nosy, so he waited for her to offer up information.

"Do you want the dog inside the house or in the yard?"

"In the house. Why would I keep him outside?"

His mother never allowed pets in the house. One time he found a turtle, and even that he had to keep outdoors. He grew up with a love for animals, but didn't know how to take care of them properly.

"Just checking before I let him off the leash. He's going to run through your house and scratch up your wooden floors."

That was his mother talking. So typical of what she would say. It was easier for him to never own an animal. Especially with him moving around since starting his restoration business.

"I'm sure he'll be fine for the night. He's probably tired anyway. Looks beat up from struggling to get loose." She tapped her thigh, and the dog followed her into the kitchen. "Would you like some coffee or tea?"

He followed her into the room. "No, thanks. I should get going. Early day tomorrow." As much as he wanted to stay, it was time for him to go. He turned and set out to leave.

"I want you to know that I never blamed you for the accident," she said.

The elephant in the room was finally being addressed.

He stopped and turned to her. "I always felt like I had contributed somehow. Mainly because I suggested the resort."

He put the water bowl she had filled on the floor next to the empty garbage can and leaned against the sink. She clutched her upper arms and looked at the floor.

"That's no reason to blame yourself. It was merely a suggestion. It's not like you planted the tree in his way."

A gust of cool air blew through the kitchen.

"Do you have windows open?"

"No, I haven't been through the house yet. I tried getting Sonia to open it for me, but she's on vacation with her family. She's the only one I trust with the place."

"Mind if I check the rooms?" A chill ran through his shoulders. It wasn't like him to spook easily, but something felt off.

"Sure, have a look around. I don't mind."

He looked in the dining room off the kitchen. The furniture was dusty, but that was to be expected. The living room was clear, and the little side-library room was as dusty as the dining room.

Thud!

The noise came from upstairs. He turned on the stairway light and made his way to the second floor. The air was stale and hot. His throat began to close and he fought to breathe. It felt like an asthma attack, but he'd never had asthma.

He pushed open the stained-glass octagon window at the top of the staircase. A soft breeze of sea air filtered into the stagnant wall of air.

The watched-over feeling crept up behind him. Not a threatening sensation, but he wasn't alone. He swallowed hard and mustered up courage to search the three bedrooms.

He peeked into the small bedroom on the left. The atmosphere was light, like the white wicker furniture it held.

He made his way to the second bedroom and slowly opened the door, finding nothing but more white wicker furniture and quilted bed coverings.

He turned to the master bedroom. Beads of sweat collected on his forehead and nape. He wiped away the perspiration stinging his eyes.

The doorknob didn't turn as easily as the last. The room was hotter, the air heavy. The oppressive feeling followed him. Same as what he'd felt when he'd stepped onto the front porch.

The room was dust free. A picture of Carl and Lauren stood on the dresser.

Was he betraying his dead best friend? Nothing except dinner happened between him and Lauren.

It wasn't a decision he thought he would ever have to make. Could he be friends with her? Could they be more to each other? Was something in their way that wouldn't let it happen?

He made up his mind to spend the night.

Chapter Four

"Come here, you." Lauren tapped her thigh to get the dog's attention. Weird not having a name to call him by, but he had to answer to something. Food was a safe bet to get him to listen. He liked the tuna fish and expired macaroni and cheese she'd found in the pantry. The first thing on her list, after dropping off the dog and her first day of work, was food shopping.

She needed basic necessities. She didn't even have coffee to offer Cooper. She walked up the stairs with a hot cup of green tea and knocked on the small bedroom door.

"Are you awake?" She listened through the door. It was the room he had stayed in numerous times before when he visited Havenport. "Hello?"

She knocked again. No answer.

"Hmm. Oh well, this cup is for me, I guess."

She went downstairs to the kitchen and watched the dog lap up the last of his water. "I can't keep calling you dog, so until I find out what your name is, you will be referred to as Sandy. Original, huh? I found you on the beach digging in the sand to get loose, so Sandy it is."

The kitchen door flung open. Her nose took in the caffeine-fueled aroma. "Good morning."

"Morning. I got up early and you didn't have a grain of coffee in this place. I can't function without it, so I ran to Mellie's and got us some cups. Milk and sugar are on the side because I don't remember how you drink your coffee."

She wrapped her hands around the cup like it was the last she would ever drink. She poured three sugars and the slightest drop of milk.

"Why bother putting any milk in your coffee?" He mixed his cup.

"You drink yours your way. I have my preference."

He shook his head. "Did you sleep okay last night?"

"Yes. You?"

"Fine."

"Thanks for staying. That wasn't necessary."

"It was late and it was your first night back here in how long?"

She savored her coffee before answering him. "The summer before."

"I figured. That explains why the house is so dusty."

"Dusty?" Her brows knitted together. Sonia cleaned before she left for vacation. She just wasn't around to open the windows to let the place air out.

He narrowed his eyes. She wasn't going to push him. It was late when they'd gotten back to her place. And the lighting wasn't the best. She always said the house needed more ceiling lights. That was something she'd take care of this time. Cooper must know an electrician to recommend.

"Staying over was a sweet thing to do. Thank you again. By the way, I named the dog Sandy, at least until I find out otherwise."

"Cute. I have to get going. Are you okay this morning?"

She stood with her back to the sink and a second cup of coffee cradled in her hands. "Yeah. I'm okay. It was strange to be here, and at one point I felt like something else was in the room with me, but that could have been wishful thinking."

His breath stalled and he rolled his shoulders. "I'm glad."

"I'm heading out early so I can drop Sandy off at that place you mentioned."

"Wags and Walks, and if they can't hold the dog, someone there will be able to help you. They'll at least be able to clean him up."

"Thank you again for the coffee. I don't know how I would have started my day without it. I should have asked Sonia to stock up the pantry with canned goods before she left. Have a good day."

She watched him get into his car before she left for work. She didn't dare tell him about the uncomfortable feeling she'd experienced in her bedroom. She shrugged it off as having been away from the place for so long. But there was something familiar in what she felt. She had the impression that Carl was near, but couldn't reach out. She was relieved it wasn't a malevolent presence.

Whatever it was, she didn't want to see it. The twinge in her chest and stomach was enough proof of something. Just like that last night in the woods in Brewster.

Her spells!

Could her words have found their way through the universe so fast? She wasn't used to her spells working so quickly. She'd been lax with her magick.

Did Cooper know her secret? It took years for Carl to figure it out, and that was an accident. He came home early one day and caught her casting a spell.

Coming to Havenport for All Hallows' Eve was important this year. The stroke of midnight would give her spells the extra boost they needed. If she was to break through to her dead husband, that would be the time when the veil was the thinnest.

She peeked into the dining room. Cooper must have been more tired than he thought. There wasn't a speck of dust to be found.

"Come on, Sandy." She found an old leash from her dog, Tate, long passed. "You're going to the doggy spa. I promise you're going to have a more relaxing day than I am."

Besides the fear of a spirit showing up in her bedroom last night, she worried about her new job. Afraid she'd screw up by saying the wrong thing or not be able to figure out the register.

Being much older than the owner and her staff, would she have the patience to take instruction from people younger? She had her own business for so long, could she meld into a team player? Was that the correct lingo?

It would be whatever it was. She'd have to go with the flow.

"Good morning! What can I help you with?" The clerk practically sang her morning greeting, and it got under Lauren's skin. She was not a morning person. No matter how hard she tried to be one, and no amount of magick could change that.

"I'm hoping you can help me. First, he needs a bath. Whatever it'll take to get the mats out. Next, do you recognize this dog? I'm Lauren."

"Augusta. Nope, don't recognize him at all. Sometimes we get tourists who forget their pets, either intentionally or not." She ran her fingers through his coat and checked his teeth. "He looks like he might have been on his own for a while."

"Possibly. I found him on the beach last night. His collar was caught on the rescue boat."

"Hmm, probably looking for food. I can clean him up for you and notify the shelter and police department to see if anyone is looking for him."

She half smiled. "He's very kind and gentle. I hope we can find his owner."

"How can I reach you?"

She handed August a business card.

"You're from out of state?"

"Sort of. I have a house on Franklin. It was owned by my grandparents. My grandmother was Dee Bishop."

"I knew her. Nice lady. Sorry for your loss. Dee always gave donations to the shelter and supported our pet adoption program. She's missed by many."

Her heart swelled with love for her grandmother. Could that be the presence in the house? Nah. If it was, Dee was sure to make an appearance no matter how afraid Lauren would be.

"I start work today next door at Serendipity."

"Nice store. Olivia's done a lot with the bookstore, but the other one has some cool stuff, too. I usually just buy soaps and shampoos, but I'm intrigued by the mystical stuff she carries. I don't know how to use any, but it's fun to look at."

Lauren handed the leash to Augusta.

"Why don't you stop in one day when you have time to spare and I'll go over what some of the things are?" She meant it. She enjoyed teaching people. It was hard to admit to being a witch. She wasn't sure if she was one, or if she was someone who simply liked the culture.

Her ancestor, Bridget, wasn't proved to be a witch,

though she was executed as one. That alone was reason to keep quiet about her practice.

Her mother also told her to never let anyone know. It wasn't their business. It was a private belief just as anyone's religion.

Carl wasn't too happy when he found out her magickal secret, but he came around once she explained. He didn't have to believe like she did, and he was cool with that. Though she wished he would have listened to her the day of the accident.

Augusta hesitated. "I'd like that. There's not much new to learn about in this town. I'll give it a try."

"I think you'll find some interesting things besides soaps and shampoos on the shelves. I hear Marcie is also running classes. Stop in."

"I will. I'll let you know what I find out about this little guy as well. Have a great day."

She left the doggy spa feeling comfortable that Sandy would be taken good care of and enjoy his day of wash, fluff, and dry.

She walked down to Serendipity. She was fifteen minutes early. The bookstore wasn't even open. The scent of fresh-baked goods invited her across the street to Led Zeppoli.

"Awesome. Something to wash down my coffee."

The bakery was crowded as she expected. It had to be, with an aroma so rich it coaxed people into the building even if they weren't hungry.

She scanned the selection of sweet confections and spotted a chocolate frosting rose cupcake, but that would be too messy to eat at the store. She didn't want her first day to be marred by her insatiable desire for chocolate.

"Can I help you?"

"Chocolate mousse bomb with a cherry. And a coffee—three sugars, drop of cream." She had her morning coffee gratis Cooper, but needed another cup to accompany her unhealthy breakfast.

The clerk handed over her order, and she passed the girl a ten-dollar bill. "Keep the change."

A generous tip, but she liked to give to people. She liked making someone else's day a little bit better. She turned to leave.

"Oops, sorry." Max spilled his coffee, narrowly missing her.

"Hi. Busy in here."

"Yeah. Thought I'd try something else instead of Corky's too-strong brew."

"Will you be stopping in the store later?" She had to tell him about Kelly, but the bakery wasn't the place to do it. She got the same mental image of Kelly as the last time she ran into him.

"I'll probably be there around five when Liv is getting off work."

"Good. I'll see you then. Have a good day."

She hurried out of the store. She went from being too early to just making it to work on time.

She stopped outside the door to collect herself. Kelly was definitely alive. The impression was as if they were standing next to each other. It was that strong. The connection to Max was unclear, but she would do what she could to help him.

That would have to wait until later in the day when she could talk to Max without people around.

She flipped her hair behind her shoulder, moved her chin up, and strolled into Serendipity like she owned the place.

❧ ❧ ❧

Marcie was at the register, counting the opening till.

"Sorry I'm late. I actually got here early and went across the street to kill time. That bakery is a busy place."

"Yep, and overpriced. That's why I never go." Marcie closed the cash drawer and walked around the counter, carrying a book ledger.

"I'm sorry that I took the extra weeks before starting…"

Marcie put her hand up. "No worries. The universe had other plans for you. I get it. Plus, as long as Olivia was okay with the arrangement, what do I have to say? Not my business. But this is yours."

Lauren placed her food and coffee on the end of the counter.

Marcie plopped the oversize book in Lauren's hands.

"This is your baby. Did Olivia tell you about the special events? How she will be renting out the room upstairs for sacred circles, séances, drumming, and Wicca classes, mainly herb, candle, and crystal education?"

"She ran through it quickly."

"Good. I hope you listened as quickly because this is your baby. I don't think Olivia anticipated such a demand. I guess there're a lot of closeted witches in this town." Marcie laughed.

"Did you say séances?" Lauren gripped the edges of the book tightly.

"Yep. And, boy, will you be busy this month. Especially as Halloween gets closer."

She was fine with sacred circles, Wicca tool education, and appreciated the occasional drum circle, but séances scared her. As a child, she would hide in the stairs and watch her mother, grandmother, and their friends try to conjure up old friends long passed. She blamed them for antagonizing the spirit in her room who scared her.

She might have to talk to Olivia.

"Am I expected to mediate the séance?"

"Oh, no. It's purely to rent out the space. Make sure it's set up with what they need and they clean before they leave."

"Okay." She could do that. A healthy dose of white sage would clear the space quickly. Like nothing ever happened.

She hoped.

"The contact is listed next to the event. I'm sure you'll be fine. Oh, in some cases, Olivia also rents out a spot in the store if the event has less than ten people and it's after closing. Times like that are usually for meditations."

Marcie ripped open a box of rose-and-sandalwood soap and placed it in the wicker basket resting on a ledge that ran the length of the wall.

A bell over the door rang, and a woman walked in.

"Showtime. Have fun. Any questions, just ask. I'm busy with inventory today. But I'll help you with the register, so don't panic."

Lauren walked behind the counter and opened the book for a quick glance. The days were filling up. Most of the events she'd like to attend. Maybe she would learn more at the job than she anticipated.

She walked around the store, familiarizing herself with the merchandise and checking if the inventory was practical for her magickal needs.

Lavender, of course. Rosemary—protection—yes, she needed some for home. A quick glance showed that Serendipity was sufficiently stocked and becoming more of a metaphysical shop instead of a bath, soap, and shampoo store.

She went up to the woman browsing the shelves.

"Can I help you?" Lauren asked in her most professional voice.

"I'm just looking around. Nothing special." The woman averted eye contact and walked away, toward the bookrack.

She followed. Something was wrong. Her ability to read people was taking hold and draining her empathic nature. Taking on the emotions of others exhausted her. Her eyes were getting heavy.

She needed to get distance until she got a handle on being in that situation again and around so many people. She was still reeling from the high-energized environment of the bakery. This was why her graphic-design job suited so well. Easier to control the emotional drain over the phone. She could cut the call short if she needed to. People weren't in her face making it difficult to get away.

Heaviness engulfed her and her throat got tight. She stepped away to release the vibrational pull from the woman.

"I'll be at the counter if you need help." As she walked away, the air grew lighter. *Wow! Intense.* She grabbed the edge of the wood counter to release the bottled-up energy. Her grandmother taught her that trick when she was a teenager. Worked every time.

She straightened the business cards in the holder next to the register.

"Good morning, Lauren. I didn't hear you come in." Olivia dropped a small box on the counter.

"I got caught up talking to Marcie."

"Where is she?" Olivia ripped the packaging tape from the sealed box.

"Upstairs, doing inventory."

"You can let her know about these tickets. They're for the Havencroft masquerade ball. The sales don't get rung up in the register. Just take down the name of the person who bought them, how many, and put the money in the envelope inside the box."

"It sounds like it's going to be a nice function." She took the box and placed it in the drawer underneath the counter.

"I think so. There is always something going on in this town that brings everyone together. Cooper's been doing a wonderful job restoring the manor. I was hoping my aunt and uncle would come up for the party, but it doesn't seem like they will." Olivia frowned.

"You miss them?"

"Yeah, I do. Though I talk to my aunt Susan just about every night. I'd like her to see what I've done with the bookstore."

The woman still walked aimlessly around the store. "This lady has been in here for about a half an hour, but it doesn't seem like she wants anything."

Olivia smiled. "She doesn't. That's Hazel. She comes in here just about every day. Looks around, but never buys anything. I don't think she has money or even wants anything that we sell. She's harmless. Just let her look around and she'll be on her way."

"Okay. I..." She almost told Olivia about the foreboding feeling she got next to Hazel. It wouldn't matter if she said anything, so she didn't.

"I'll be in the bookstore if you need anything," Olivia said.

Chapter Five

Cooper couldn't think of anything but Lauren all morning. He barely slept, knowing she was across the hall from him last night. He spent the long hours convincing himself that enough time had gone by and he wouldn't be out of line asking her out on a date.

Why else would they have shown up in the same town?

He didn't believe in fate, but even he had to admit their meeting had happened for a reason. He'd have to be careful how he played this out.

One p.m.

He needed a break. The paint wasn't due to be delivered until later that afternoon, and his stomach growled. He pulled out his phone and started to text her. All those years he hadn't used her number. Would she recognize his? He erased the text, fearing it too impersonal, and dialed her number instead.

Ring.

Ring.

Ring.

No answer. Maybe she did recognize his number and opted to ignore his call. She seemed okay when he gave her coffee. Maybe she rethought the idea of them being friends with so much history between them.

It wasn't like him to worry. To give so much thought to something he had no control over. He put down his hammer and got into his car. He was going to handle this like he would any other situation. Straightforward and in person.

He pulled up to Serendipity and caught a glimpse of her through the window. *Beautiful.* She was alone. He turned off the ignition and headed into the store.

"Good afternoon. How's the first day going?"

Her eyes grew wide and she smiled.

That's a good sign. At least she's not annoyed.

"It's been interesting. Slow, but that's giving me time to get familiar with the stock and events scheduled for later this month."

"Do you get lunch?"

"You know, I never asked. I'm sure I do, but let me find out what time. Be right back." She left the counter and went into the bookstore.

He browsed the selection of goods. Nothing that he would buy, but having three sisters, he could understand the attraction.

A large purple amethyst caught his eye. He picked it up and watched the sun bounce off the deep-purple points.

"Looking to enhance your magickal abilities?" Lauren snuck up on him.

He put it down and chuckled. "No. It's different. Something my sister Simone would like. She's into stuff like this."

"And what is 'stuff like this'?" She ran her fingertip along the points of the stone.

"New Age, metaphysical. Weird stones and music."

"Some people think this stuff makes them feel better. It helps them focus."

All he could focus on was her. She could recite the entire encyclopedia, and he'd stand there captivated by her voice. But he was hungry and would have to settle for lunch.

"What's the verdict?"

"I get an hour. What did you have in mind?" She walked to the staircase. "Marcie, I'm going to lunch. You got the store?"

"Enjoy," Marcie responded. Lauren waited for her to come downstairs before they left.

"Something quick, like a burger, or some type of sandwich," Lauren suggested.

He nodded. "How about Mellie's? I haven't been there in a while."

"Works for me."

"Wow, it's one already?" Marcie brushed dust from the front of her jeans. "You need to check out the new books."

"Maybe later. Ready? I'm starving." Lauren grabbed her purse.

He held the door open. "How did Sandy make out?"

"I haven't checked. Augusta was really sweet, though. She's going to give him a good cleaning up. Part of me hopes his owner isn't found. Selfish, I know."

"I wouldn't consider it selfish. You connected to the dog. But you do have to be prepared to give him back." He kept a comfortable distance as they walked down the street to the diner. As much as he wanted to hold her hand, he couldn't.

"I know I do. But you're right, my first hope is that Sandy is reunited with his owner." She pouted. She was becoming attached to the dog too soon.

"Hey, if it doesn't work out, you can always get another dog. The shelter usually has animals looking for a home."

"I miss him, you know." She put her head down as they made their way to the diner.

He missed his best friend, too. Here he obsessed over her, when it was apparent she hadn't finished grieving.

His heart broke for her.

The diner wasn't crowded, so they were seated immediately, which was good because they'd get served fast and she could get back to work. Max should be finished installing the trim back at Havencroft. And he wanted to get his work prepped so he could start painting first thing in the morning.

"What would you like?" He handed her a menu.

"I'm paying for my own lunch today. Thank you for dinner last night, but you can't expect to pay for me every time we go out to eat."

Every time? Did she mean they would be spending more time together? He wasn't going to get his hopes up and expect her to want him the way he wanted her. She needed time to move on from Carl. The move to Havenport was her first step into a new life. He had to be patient and follow her lead.

"Are you insisting that we go dutch?"

"Yes." She closed the menu. "Hamburger, lettuce, tomato, onion, french fries, and root beer."

"That sounds good, except I'm adding cheese to mine."

A young girl, barely eighteen, took their order.

"Oh, and mayonnaise on the side for mine, please," Lauren added.

"I took you for a healthier eater," he said.

"Sometimes. There's something about the sea air that makes me hungry for heavier foods." She opened her mouth again like she was going to say something, but changed her mind.

"Here you go. Enjoy." The waitress put the food on the table and turned away.

"Um, our drinks?" Lauren pointed to the empty spot on the table where her drink would be.

"Sorry. Be right back."

"She's young." Lauren lifted the top of the hamburger bun and spread a healthy dose of mayonnaise, then doused everything with ketchup.

"I'll take the ketchup if you're going to leave some."

She handed him the bottle and smiled.

"I've been meaning to ask you something." She dipped a fry.

"Shoot."

"Did you hear or see anything out of the ordinary at my house last night?"

It wasn't just me. So there *was* something odd going on. The feeling he'd experienced on the front porch happened again when he had gotten up to use the bathroom during the night. He wasn't afraid as much as uneasy.

"I did feel a presence, but thought it was because I was tired. I first felt it on the porch before we went into the house, then again later during the night." He grabbed a fry. "Why? Did you witness anything?"

She hesitated, took a bite of her hamburger, swallowed, then picked up a french fry to use as a pointer. "I didn't see anything." She ate the fry and hesitated again. "Do you believe in ghosts?"

He didn't know what to say. He never thought about it, but last night made him question his belief and whether other things existed that couldn't be seen.

"I'm not sure. I never thought I did, but hey, some

people say ghosts do exist. Who am I to tell them they're wrong?"

"I have to tell you something and I hope you don't think I'm crazy." She sat back with her hands in her lap.

"Go ahead. I won't make fun of you."

"Even if you do, what I'm going to tell you is true and that's why I asked if you experienced anything at the house."

"Go ahead. I'm listening." Even if he didn't believe her, he didn't want to make her feel silly.

"I'm petrified of ghosts and I know they exist because I saw one when I was a kid. My mother and grandmother used to conduct séances, and I saw a man in my bedroom after they finished. There, I said it. You are the third person I've told—well, except for my mother and grandmother. I told them as soon as it happened. They told me not to worry. But ever since then, if I've felt like someone was near I would close my eyes and will them to not show themselves."

Fascinating. Sweat beaded on her brow. He didn't want to make fun of her, but he didn't believe in that kind of stuff.

"Maybe it was an illusion."

"No, it wasn't. I've even heard voices over the years. They're called disembodied voices. From what I know, it's a spirit trying to reach out that can't materialize."

Was the woman he was in love with losing her mind?

"Forget I said anything." She stabbed a fry into the ketchup.

"No, no, don't stop. You can tell me. It's a lot to take in. I've never known anyone who had a paranormal experience. Please don't feel that you can't talk to me about stuff like this, or anything."

Her phone rang. "Do you mind? I think it's Augusta."

"No, go right ahead." It gave him a chance to absorb

what she said. How could he think she told him some wild story after what he felt at her house? He finished his meal, even the pickle, which he usually left on the plate.

Taken aback with her story, he couldn't wholeheartedly believe her. Maybe they were too different and he wasn't meant to be with her.

"No owner yet. Augusta let the people at the shelter know I'm looking. She also checked with the police department and no one reported a missing dog."

"It looks like he's going home with you. At least for today."

"That would be nice." She slid out of the booth and grabbed her purse. "You think I'm crazy, don't you?"

"About the dog?" He laughed.

"No." She smiled. "About my teenage ghost sighting."

"I can't dispute what you saw." He tried being as understanding as he could.

"Well, I have to get back to work. Will I see you later?"

He wasn't expecting to hear that, but he could use some company. Maybe stop at her house again to figure out what was going on.

"Do you like Chinese food?" He had been craving steamed dumplings and barbecue spareribs.

"Love it! We never had very good takeout in Brewster. How is it here?" She walked with him back to the store.

"Decent. Text me what you want, and I'll pick it up." She started to say something. "I know. You'll pay for your portion. You can give it to me later."

"Good."

It was nice having someone around that he knew, even if there were some tense moments. Nothing to do with her. Just the situation.

"Thanks for walking me back. You didn't have to do that."

"I know, but I needed some exercise. Fixing plaster keeps me in one spot for too long. My back starts seizing up."

What a stupid thing to say.

She stopped at the door and smiled. "I'll bring the wine."

"I think I like that." For the first time since they'd run into each other, Carl wasn't standing between them. Cooper slid his hands into his pockets and turned away so she didn't see his big grin.

He kept thinking about the ghost story Lauren told him. He knew her to be a smart woman. Lauren wouldn't make up a ghost story if it didn't happen. She was too skeptical and direct. Not one for what-ifs, but what is. Facts were what formed her decisions.

A quick stop at her place might give him some answers.

He turned onto Franklin and pulled into her driveway, then walked onto the front porch.

And waited.

Nothing out of place like the previous night. Could it have been his nerves at being alone with her in the house without Carl there?

He walked around the house and looked into the basement windows. It wasn't creepy like he expected. A few boxes were placed on shelving and the cellar looked clean and painted recently.

She did mention she had considered selling the place.

Nothing seemed odd to him.

"Oh well."

Back to the manor so he could get the work done for the day. He took off, convinced their imaginations were playing tricks. Tonight would give him another opportunity for a closer inspection inside.

"Hey. I finished the trim. Anything else you need me to do before I take off? Claude has some lobsters for me to off-load. His back's been killing him, so he called and asked if I could run down to the dock and help out." Max loaded his toolbox into his pickup truck.

"Thanks. That's good for today. I need to button things up so the Historical Society can get the rooms set up."

"The party's a few weeks away, isn't it?"

"Yeah, but I'm going to get the painting finished, then take some time off. Everything that needs to be done for the event, is done."

"Thanks for giving me work. Call if you need me again." Max drove away, leaving Cooper to finish on his own.

He'd get the painting done in a week. He thought about hiring someone, but had grown attached to the house and wanted to give the finishes touches. Working on old buildings had given him the satisfaction his former career as a financial advisor hadn't.

To carve a plain piece of wood into an intricate work of scroll gave him a sense of accomplishment. To take a building in disrepair and restore it to its original splendor was his way of keeping the past alive. They were homes people had lived in. Buildings where they had worked.

The occupants were no longer alive to enjoy their homes—or were they? Lauren's confession stuck with him. He couldn't imagine a spirit appearing out of nowhere. It would be easier to dismiss her statement, but in doing so, he'd be dismissing her.

He shook his head and cleared his thoughts, only to start thinking about the original owners of Havencroft. It was supposed to be a job that made him some money and help build his résumé. Instead, the project had sucked him in with the history behind the place.

The job brought Lauren to him. An unexpected bonus. Each day he learned something new about himself. How had he lived so long being clueless to where he found happiness?

He thought about his years in the city and the shallow relationships he'd forged. Living a life that others expected. Denying himself the pleasure of being happy.

"Sorry, Carl." He looked up to the sky. "I know you loved her, but so do I. And I can't wait anymore."

His phone vibrated. He checked the message. *Shrimp toast, fried dumplings, BBQ ribs, and vegetable lo mein.*

"Damn, the girl can eat."

He slid his phone into his pants pocket and went upstairs for the first time in Havencroft.

There weren't any immediate plans to work on the second floor. Money needed to be raised to continue the restoration.

The hallway was in terrific shape. Smooth plaster and tight to the furring strips. Good. Though he was good at it, plaster was not one of his favorite processes. It was tedious and required a steady and firm, but flexible, touch to get the spread just right.

Scrollwork was less prominent in the bedrooms than the rooms downstairs. It wasn't unusual to find less of an investment in craftsmanship higher up. Focus of decor concentrated on rooms used for entertaining or gathering.

An oak handrail followed the curve of the stairs and length of the hall. He opened each closed door and peeked into the rooms. Freestanding wardrobes took the place of closets. Four-poster bed in each room, typical of the time the house was built.

He'd have to talk to the head of the Historical Society to find out what their plans were after the masquerade ball. He hadn't bought a ticket yet, wasn't sure if he was going. He wasn't into dressing in costume, and until Lauren arrived, he didn't have anyone to bring.

Damn! Lauren. He glanced at his phone. Almost five— she'd be getting home soon. He hadn't realized how much time he'd wasted wandering around the manor.

He started to type a text to her, but was interrupted by a text from her.

Be home at 6. Have something to do.

Good. That gave him some time to clean up without rushing to get to her place. His stomach growled, and he could taste the spareribs with hot mustard.

He made his way down to the Great Hall.

Hmm. "Max, are you still here?"

He waited.

No answer. The room was swept and a broom stood in the corner. *He must have come back and cleaned.*

He could have sworn he'd stepped around sawdust when he'd come back from lunch. Well, whoever it was saved him, giving him an opportunity to run home and shower before picking up dinner.

Chapter Six

"Does it always get busy at the end of the day? Seems like I spent most of the afternoon straightening shelves." Lauren locked the door.

"It seems to be that way most times." Marcie dropped a box of books in front of the counter. "I guess most people work and try to get here on their way home. In the summer, we're busy all day. Tourists seem to like us."

A tap on the door caught her attention. "Marcie, would you let Max in, please?"

"Hi. Waiting for Olivia?" Marcie let him into the store.

"Ah, no. I'm here to see Lauren."

"Oh, okay. I'll let you two be. I promised Olivia I'd help her finish stacking. I'll be back before I leave to make sure everything is closed up, so you don't have to hang around waiting for me." Marcie left through the archway.

"Thank you. I'll see you tomorrow."

She turned to Max. He looked relaxed. Good. She had no idea how he would react to what she told him.

"Thanks for stopping by. Cooper tells me you're a big help."

"I like that kind of work. I did a lot of carpentry back home. We didn't live close to much of anything, so we had to learn how to do it ourselves or do without."

"I know he appreciates it. You're probably wondering why I asked to see you."

He nodded. "Considering we don't know each other, yes."

"Okay, what I'm about to tell you may seem strange, but when I ran into you earlier, a name came to me that I know is connected to you."

He scratched his head and narrowed his eyes. "Who would that be?"

"Kelly Fielding."

His mouth dropped open and he stepped back.

"So you do know that name." Her shoulders relaxed. Her premonition was correct. Kelly Fielding was connected to Max.

"I've heard of it."

"The information I'm getting is that she is searching for you."

He rubbed his eyes, then put his thumb and index finger under his chin and stared at her.

Confidence welled inside her. The image of the woman and her name was too strong to be wrong. But she didn't want to scare him. She didn't know who Kelly was, but it was something huge. The intensity of the message she'd received was too intense to ignore.

"I have to sit." He sat on the edge of the potpourri table.

"I hope I haven't frightened you." She walked to him, stopping short of arm's reach.

"How do you know about her?" He crossed his arms across his chest.

"I don't know anything about her. The name and a vision came to me when you were here this morning.

Occasionally, I have visions." She weighed his apprehension and kept her distance.

"This is too weird."

"I understand if you don't believe me…"

"How can you know? I barely know anything about her."

"Like I said, I'm sorry if I've upset you in any way. But it seemed like something you needed to know."

"She's looking for me?"

"Yes, that's the sense that I got."

"Then she must be alive. Thanks, I guess. Nice meeting you, but excuse me if I seem a little put off."

"I understand. No problem."

He left the store, and she locked the door. "Phew."

Her phone buzzed. *On my way*, the text from Cooper read. She walked to the archway between the stores.

"Marcie?"

"Be right there," Marcie responded. She sounded rushed.

Lauren straightened books and soap and rifled through crystals.

Hmm, this one is calling to me. She picked up a clear quartz point. The gem began vibrating. *Yep, it's mine.*

She loosened her grip, and energy from the stone reverberated through her hand, up to her shoulder. She'd never held a stone so powerful, and she hadn't even cleansed it.

"Phew, what a busy day. How'd you make out?" Marcie came up behind her, silent as a mouse.

She spun around. "Good. Mostly cash transactions so that's why I didn't have to bother you."

"I'm glad you did okay. I'm usually available. We normally don't receive inventory for both stores on the same day. Weird how that worked out. But it's done."

"Oh, I did get a call to schedule a séance a few days before Halloween."

"Good. Got a minute? Let me show you where that space is." Marcie waved her to the stairs. "This is the space Olivia is reserving for classes and séances."

Except for a pile of empty boxes in the opposite corner, the room was clear of unnecessary furniture and clutter. A large round maple table took the center of the room, accompanied by twelve chairs. A matching podium stood in a corner, and a side table adorned with candles and holders waited to be used. Oak bookcases held books on the Craft.

"This is lovely. One thing: I don't need to sit through the séance, do I?" Spirits still weren't her thing. Even though her intuition surfaced and her energy field was high, she wasn't ready to deal with the afterlife.

"No, you won't need to sit in. Just get the attendees set up, and we can always make arrangements for one of us to stay close after they're done. Whoever stays can hang downstairs."

"Thanks. Good to know. See you tomorrow. Oh, by the way, I'm purchasing this crystal." She gave Marcie the money and put the crystal next to her heart in her bra and left.

Cooper was waiting on her porch when she arrived.

"Sorry I'm late. We got busy at the end of the day." She thought of telling him about her visit with Max, but Cooper'd had a difficult time with her spirit story. Another thing she could sense: how people felt around her.

All this stimulation was becoming too much. The spells she'd cast stirred up more than she'd bargained for.

She only wanted to stop hurting and to be open to love again. Instead, it was like the universe awakened every nerve and emotion in her, making her susceptible to being overwhelmed.

"No problem. Food's still hot." He stood as she came up the stairs. "How was your first day?"

"Okay." She turned the key and threw open the door. Mail was scattered on the floor.

"You may want to replace that mail slot with an actual mailbox." He bent to pick up her mail.

"I know. We never got much mail here. Usually just junk mail. Everything else for the house gets sent to Brewster."

Cooper put the bags of food on the kitchen counter. "If you pick out a mailbox, I'll put it up for you."

"You know what I never liked about the mail slot?"

"What?"

"Someone can peek into the house. They could be looking at you and you wouldn't even know."

"All the more reason to get a mailbox and remove the slot. Consider it done."

He unloaded the bags and placed the takeout containers in an orderly fashion on the counter. Rice on the left, and entrees to the right, then the bags of spareribs and shrimp toast. An assembly line of food just as she would have laid it out.

"It's nice having you around." That came out of nowhere. Even though she thought it, she didn't plan on telling him.

"Ditto. It's difficult moving to a new town. I was surprised when my dad suggested looking for work here. He didn't know I knew of Havenport. I guess New England is the mother lode of historic restoration."

She took two glasses from the cabinet beside him, catching a whiff of his scent. "Makes sense since it's the oldest area of this country."

He handed her a plate and waited for her to choose her food. A nice guy. She never understood why he didn't have a girlfriend. She opened a bottle of red wine and poured two glasses.

"Are you in a hurry to go anywhere?" She took a sip.

"No."

"Okay. I didn't want to keep you from anything." She ripped open a pouch of hot mustard. She wasn't shy about enjoying spicy food.

"Did you hear any more about Sandy?" He sipped his wine.

"Augusta has him all cleaned up. He looks like a different dog. She said she would keep him another day to see if anyone claims him. I'll bring him home tomorrow if no owner shows up."

She leaned over her plate, twirling vegetable lo mein on her fork, and snuck a look at Cooper. He looked a little older. Crow's-feet slightly etched the corners of his eyes, something she'd never seen before. A lot could change in five years.

"How about some music?" she said.

"Sure."

She went into the living room and turned on the radio. "Classical okay?"

"Works for me," he shouted from the kitchen.

He'd refilled her wineglass by the time she returned to the kitchen. "I wanted something for background noise. I'm not really a fan of classical, but sometimes the music is soothing."

"My grandfather used to listen to Mozart."

She joined him at the table. "Thanks for the refill."

"No problem."

Having him there was nice. She'd forgotten how big the house was, and the echoes could be unnerving. She missed the house in Brewster, small rooms that made her feel safe and cozy. The move was going to be an adjustment, but one she wanted to make.

The first thing to focus on was making friends. She missed Charley, but Manhattan was too far away for weekend visits. She didn't want to rely solely on Cooper, either.

"How's your dinner?"

"Good. I mean, the takeout isn't as good as the city, but it's passable."

"My opinion exactly." He brought their dirty plates to the sink and washed them.

"Nice. Are you always such a lovely guest? Come to think of it, I don't remember you washing a dish after dinner, never mind all of them."

"Things change."

Yes, they do. She never thought Cooper would become a part of her life after Carl died. But something stirred within her. The pain she carried all these years lessened.

Cooper was in her life for a reason.

She reached past him and grabbed a dish towel, brushing his arm.

Oh, no!

Maybe she was mistaken. He couldn't be in love with her. Could he? Maybe her premonitions were wonky. She had successfully suppressed her ability, and now that she unleashed her will—

Smash!

"What the hell?" Cooper ran into the living room.

She followed behind.

"What happened?" She walked over to a shattered vase on the floor. "How could this be?"

Cooper checked the windows. All were closed. He put his hand up to the heat vent. "There's no air coming out of this. Can't be here."

"No, I haven't put the heat on yet. It's been warm enough." She left to grab a broom and dustpan. "Maybe the music vibrated it off the cabinet."

Cooper took the broom and swept up the shards of glass. "Could be."

That's what she said, but the cold feeling swirling inside her stomach told her differently. The same churning, chilling feeling she'd had the night she saw the spirit at the foot of her bed as a teen.

"Could you stay the night? I'm a little scared to stay by myself."

He hesitated. His stare looked through her. "Okay."

The dishes were clean and put away. Slivers of glass long gone from the living room floor. Uneasy and bothered by the vase incident, she didn't want to stay alone. The energy of the house was off. Not threatening, just lively. Like the air had an underlying force as it moved throughout.

"I'm going to bed now. Thank you for picking up dinner." She yawned, aching to go to sleep, but afraid to be alone.

"I'm calling it a night also." He went into the guest room.

Once his bedroom door closed, she went into the living room, stood in the center of the room, and closed her eyes.

Her new crystal vibrated in the palm of her hand.

There's something here.

Acid churned in her stomach. She planted her bare feet firmly to the hardwood floor and cleared her mind.

She focused on the house and imagined each room. The living room, the kitchen, the bedrooms. Sometimes she was able to visualize the energy moving around her.

Nothing.

She closed her eyes tighter.

Again, nothing.

She hummed quietly to block out the sounds of cars passing by the house. Slowly, a blur of soft white light came into view.

Her heart beat faster and a wave of warmth shot through her chest. Her breathing softened. She couldn't make out the image, but it felt loving.

She shook her hands to disperse pent-up energy and opened her eyes. A white haze filled the room, but she wasn't scared. She took a seat by the window.

The vase.

It was the one Carl had sent filled with an arrangement of sunflowers one summer. She had started her graphic-design business and needed a logo. He had walked through town and saw the arrangement on a cart outside the flower shop. It made him think of her. He always said she was his sunshine.

A tear slid down her cheek as she remembered. The last time they were all together. Her grandmother, mother, her, and Carl.

She slung her legs over the chair arm and leaned back, resting her head against the overstuffed cushion. "I miss you. All of you."

Times like this, she hated being an only child. Loneliness a thought away. Holidays were lonely. A hole in her heart would not heal.

She pulled out her cell phone and dialed.

Ring.

Ring.

"Come on. Answer."

"What's up?" Charley let out a yawn when she answered the phone.

"I'm bored." She sat a little taller in the chair.

"You just got there. How can you be bored already? You haven't even had time to unpack."

"Did you get fired yet so you can come visit?" Lauren chuckled at Charley's snarky attitude.

Sigh. "No, not yet. Though I try my best."

"Guess who's upstairs in my guest room?" she whispered into the phone.

"Hmm, no one I can think of. Give me a clue."

She wanted to let her stew a minute or two, so she stayed silent.

"Lauren, who is it?" Charley's voice raised a pitch.

She enjoyed playing with her friend. "I tried setting you up with him."

"Cooper?"

"Yep." She stretched out across the chair, having fun annoying Charley.

"How? Hold on while I get a drink."

Lauren decided to grab a drink also. Many of their late-night conversations were accompanied by a glass of wine. She went into the kitchen and finished off the little bit left in the bottle from dinner. She held the bottle upside down until the last drop dripped out into her glass.

Lauren looked up the staircase on her way back to the living room. Something was there. The air was thicker at the foot of the stairs.

"Charley, hold on," she whispered into the phone.

She put one bare foot on the bottom step and reached for the banister. The cooler air touched her arm deeper into the stairway.

She went to her left foot to start up the staircase.

Creak!

She backed down. "Cooper?"

No answer.

She raised the phone to her ear with her shaky hand. "Charley, there's some crazy stuff going on here."

"Aw, don't worry. It's been a while since you were there, and it's an old house."

Always the logical one. She narrowed her eyes to focus through the darkness. "Cooper?"

"He up?" Charley's voice rose with anticipation.

"I don't see his door open, but then again, it's so dark up there. And if he doesn't have a light on, I don't know."

"Why is he there again?"

"Because I'm afraid to stay here. I feel that I'm not alone."

"Well, you're not. You have that gorgeous, but shy as hell, guy in your house."

"Didn't you ever wonder why he doesn't have a girlfriend?" Talking kept her mind off being afraid. She could chat all night.

"Wonder? No." Charley laughed hysterically.

"Why do you think it's so funny?" She ignored the staircase and went back into the living room, flopping back into her favorite chair.

"You know what, lady? For all your intuition and insight, you miss what's right under your nose."

"What are you talking about? The wine is hitting me and it's late."

"Remember when you tried to fix me up with him?"

She remembered the disaster date. They didn't like each other. "Yeah, it didn't work out. So?"

"Why do you think that was?"

Lauren ran through a myriad of reasons Cooper wouldn't like Charley, who was brash, made it clear she didn't need a man to take care of her. And was much happier alone.

"Well, why do you think?"

"You two weren't compatible?" Lauren spun her wineglass on her knee.

"You could say that. I'm not you."

"What? That's ridiculous." She looked up the stairway to make sure he wasn't standing there.

"Maybe so, but I could tell the man had the hots for you since the first time I saw him around you. All those years it was the three of you. He never had a date—never. A man in his position could have had any woman he wanted."

"This is nonsense." She started shaking. How could her husband's best friend want her?

"Think what you will, but that man is in love with you. And that, my dear, is why it didn't work out between me and him."

"Why didn't you ever say anything to me?" Her voice softened. She didn't want him to hear.

"It wasn't my place, and I had nothing other than my instinct to prove it. You were hurting so much that I didn't want to put that on you. And I could have been wrong."

She nodded. "I understand. I need to get some sleep. Thanks for the talk. Love you."

"Love you, too. I'll be out there as soon as I can. Good night."

She hung up the phone and curled up into the chair. This was going to be one night she wouldn't sleep.

Chapter Seven

"This is my favorite week of the year. I love Halloween." Lauren wrapped a sage/lemongrass candle, slipped it into the bag, and handed it to her customer.

"I'm so glad you're staying open late this week." The lady handed her credit card to Lauren to finish the sale.

"Doesn't the town look nice lit up in orange lights, and the stuffed monsters, scarecrows, and ghosts that are tied to the lampposts? I'm tossing in a sample of our newest soap. Neroli orange blossom."

"Why, thank you. Have a nice evening. You're such a doll, Lauren."

Helen was the last customer of the night. It was a long day, but it went by fast. Sandy lay patiently at the side of the counter. Olivia was a wonderful boss and allowed Lauren to bring Sandy to the store when she worked a long day.

She hadn't seen Cooper the past three weeks, except for the occasional brief encounter. She used the excuse that the store kept her busy, but the truth was she was falling for him and it scared her.

Ever since she'd brought Sandy home, the uneasy moments and crashing vases had stopped. She never allowed Cooper to stay over again.

Charley!

"Marcie, I have to go. I forgot my friend at the airport." She grabbed Sandy's leash and rushed out of the store. *Oh, no. I'm late.*

She was so excited about Charley coming to visit and yet she forgot about picking her up. *Yeesh.* She opened the back door, and Sandy spun in a circle before sitting in the spot he always did.

She tossed her purse into the car. The contents spilled across the passenger seat "Okay. Breathe."

She closed her eyes, took a deep breath, and pulled herself together. Ignition on. She turned the wheel and pulled—

Crash!

Her head flew against the back of the seat.

"What the hell are you doing?"

It was him.

She rolled down her window. "Cooper, I'm so sorry. I was in a hurry to get Charley at the airport. I'm running extremely late."

He walked to the front of his truck where her car had rammed into his. "It looks okay. You have a small dent on your fender, but you can drive the car."

"So, so sorry. Can I catch up with you later?"

"Sure." He walked back to his truck. "Don't pull away until I do."

She waited for him to drive away. Her funds were starting to get tight. Not many graphic-design jobs coming, but then again, she wasn't pursuing any. Her store salary wasn't enough to support both properties.

With light traffic, she zipped up Route 1 to 95 and arrived at the airport in under forty-five minutes. She pulled up to Arrivals.

Charley yanked open the door. "It's about freakin' time. Do you know how boring it is standing in this place?"

"Well, hello to you, too, cranky ass."

"Rough flight." Charley shoved her duffel bag over the passenger seat into the back.

Lauren headed for 95 south. "Turbulence?"

"Nah, that wasn't it. I had this guy sitting next to me who wouldn't shut up. You know how I am around people I don't know."

"Not much different than when you're around people you do know. Love ya anyway." She smiled and hit the gas pedal. It was getting late, and she was tired and hungry. Pizza would take care of her hunger. Good thing they delivered so she could get right home.

"Have you been spending time with Cooper?"

She hesitated and turned up the radio. "How about we listen to some music until we get home? You can unwind from your flight. I can decompress from work."

"Fine. You can ignore the topic all you want, but that doesn't mean it doesn't exist." Charley closed her eyes and leaned the seat back.

Lauren had a feeling Charley would stir the pot with her and Cooper. The truth was, she did find herself thinking about him, and loved being around him. He was easy to talk to and kind. But he represented her past, and she felt she would betray Carl's memory if she got involved with Cooper.

Charley's snoring kept Lauren alert, and she was able to drive faster with her friend asleep and not complaining. She looked forward to spending the long weekend together. Wine-and popcorn-induced conversation. Where their lives headed.

Where?

How does a woman her age meet someone new? Especially in a new town? She wasn't the type for online dating or hanging in a bar.

This opening herself to finding love was going to be difficult.

She pulled into her driveway and nudged Charley. "Hey, we're here."

Yawn. "Thanks for letting me catch a nap. I didn't get much sleep last night."

"Anxious about the flight?"

"Yep."

Sandy barked as they walked up to the front door.

"Who's that?" Charley pointed to the chair on the porch.

"Who? No one." She crinkled her nose, confused by the question.

"Okay. I must be super tired. I could have sworn I saw someone in the chair."

"Nope. It's just me and the dog. Must have been a shadow. The weeping willow casts all kinds of crazy shadows with the wind." She was a little spooked, but wasn't going to say anything. That someone else sensed a presence at the house told her she wasn't crazy.

At least she wouldn't be alone.

"What a cute store. You like working here?" Charley stopped into Serendipity after spending the day cruising Havenport while Lauren worked.

"It's different, but I'm enjoying it. Come upstairs with me. I have to make sure everything is set up for the séance tonight."

Charley followed her. "Are you conducting a séance?"

"No. I only book them and set them up."

"Like providing spirits?" Charley laughed.

"Of course not. The standard table, chairs, candles, sage, crystal ball, if requested, and any other special requests." Everything looked to be in order. Her stomach rumbled. She was starving. "Marcie said she would close tonight so I could spend more time with you. Where do you want to eat?"

"Royce's. I've been dying for fried scallops and clams on a half shell."

Her stomach tightened. She hadn't been to Royce's since the night she went to dinner with Cooper. It was difficult trying to stay away from each other in such a small town. She worked later than him, so that helped, but she never knew where she would run into him at dinnertime, so she made most of her dinners at home.

But today was special. She and Charley were celebrating new beginnings. Careers, men, and all the other unfulfilled dreams they uncovered in a wine-induced haze the night before. They stayed up until three in the morning.

"Marcie, I'm leaving." She grabbed her purse behind the counter.

"What are these tickets for?" Charley picked up one from the register. "Masquerade ball?"

"Yes. It's at the house Cooper has been restoring."

"Are you going?" Charley held the door open for them to leave. "Walk there?"

Lauren nodded. "I'm not going."

"Why not?"

"I don't have anyone to go with."

"What am I? Not party worthy?"

She laughed. "No, not that. I decided not to go before you said you'd come. And when you decided to visit, I didn't think about it."

"I think it'll be fun to go. We both like Halloween."

"No, you like Halloween. I *love* Halloween." Lauren smiled. Staying up a little past midnight was her ritual. That moment made her feel her most grounded. When she was young, she'd stay up with her grandmother and mother. She continued the tradition after they'd left. It was a night she felt close to them again.

"I love the smell of the ocean. I'd be walking on this beach every day if I lived here." Charley opened the door for Royce Tavern. "Did they redo this place?"

"Yes, Adam wanted to spruce it up a bit."

"Nice job. A little dark, but nice."

There were plenty of empty tables so they chose a booth along the window where they could see the whitecaps as the moon illuminated them.

"Red or white?" Lauren placed the linen napkin across her lap.

"Red. It helps me sleep better. Cheeseburgers and fries?"

"No cheese. Plain burger."

"Okay, and it's my treat." Charley raised her hand, her sign for no comments or argument.

"Fine." She waved away the menus and gave their order. "Fast service tonight. I've never been in here when it was this slow."

Charley lit the table candle. "She must have forgotten this one. So what have you been doing with yourself after work?"

"I have a few small design jobs. I think the business is shrinking. A lot of people do their own graphic work now." A glass of wine was placed before her. "There are so many free premade web design programs available. What I've been getting are mainly orders for book covers."

"There's a demand for that?" Charley's eyes grew wide and she tipped her head to sip her wine. She pointed to the bar.

Lauren turned. Cooper sat with Max, having a beer. She'd done so well avoiding him, for the most part. Always polite, but effectively able to keep her distance. She sensed he was doing the same.

"I should say hi." Lauren dipped a fry in ketchup and shoved it in her mouth. Her growling stomach needed attention more than Cooper.

"I don't think he saw me. I'm going to say hi." Charley got up.

"Wait. Don't. Never mind." She sighed and raised her burger to her lips, bit into the bun, and swallowed the angst that Charley was sure to stir.

She sat back, picking at her fries, while her best friend got comfortable next to Cooper. Max walked over to her.

"Your friend—Charley?—is quite the conversationalist."

"Her real name is Charlotte, but everyone calls her Charley." She motioned for Max to join her.

He sat across the table. "I've been meaning to stop in and see you. I haven't been able to get over you telling me that Kelly is looking for me."

"Sorry if I spooked you with that information. It just comes to me."

"She's my birth mother. I've known for a few months, but haven't acted on the information until you mentioned her name to me."

She smiled. "I don't want to give you false hope."

"Don't worry. It's been a journey. I discovered who my father was a few months ago and haven't approached him yet. I don't want to upset his family. I mean, they may not know about me. I'm more interested in knowing who my mother is."

"I wish you happiness in your search." She squeezed his hand.

Nothing this time. Just a peaceful feeling. That was good enough.

"Good night. I'm sure I'll run into you at the store."

"Night."

She dug into her cold burger, enjoying each bite. The fries were beyond edible, but at least her stomach stopped growling. It didn't look like Charley would end her conversation anytime soon.

"Miss, would you please wrap up her meal to go? Thanks."

She finished her wine and Charley's. It was getting late, and she wanted to crawl into bed. There wasn't going to be any girl talk tonight.

"Tonight is our time. Sorry about last night." Charley stood in front of the bathroom mirror finalizing the heavy black eyeliner with flecks of purple.

"You make a great witch. You know that?" Lauren laughed and shimmied past Charley to get a bottle of hairspray. "This was a good idea, putting in the double sink. Carl was clever that way."

Charley wrapped her arms around Lauren's shoulders. "You still miss him like it was yesterday, don't you?"

She lowered her head. "Yeah, I do. But life goes on, doesn't it?"

"Yes, and tonight will be proof of that." Charley held Lauren's hand and swung away from her, as if dancing. "We are going to enjoy ourselves. Sister witches."

Lauren smiled to herself. She hadn't practiced any magick since arriving in Havenport. She wanted to see if the spells she cast had any power.

So far nothing.

Except for—

"I have to tell you something. You might think I'm crazy, but…"

Charley stood in the bathroom door, arms crossed and sincere. "Proceed. I'll weigh in on the crazy after you tell me."

As annoying as Charley could be, she was more loving than anything else. She didn't let it show much, except with Lauren.

"I sense Carl in this house. It could be wishful thinking, but I swear sometimes I feel him near me when I'm lying in bed."

"I don't think you're crazy at all. I told you the first night I came here I felt something was on the porch." Charley sat on the bed, face serious.

"You're not the only one to say that. Cooper felt it also. And because of that, I've been keeping my distance from him. If Carl's spirit is here, I don't want the wrong energy to be conjured."

"Do you believe that Cooper loves you?"

She put down the hairspray and set her pointed hat on her over-teased hair. "I do. I've felt it."

"Is that the real reason you're staying away from him?"

"Partly. It's a tough situation. I'm not sure how comfortable I am knowing that. I enjoy being with him. We get along well. And you know me. I'm not good at meeting new people. There's a certain level of comfort knowing a person and not having to go through the discovery process."

She glanced at the clock. Eleven thirty. "Come on, we need to get going. I want to be there before midnight."

They ran down the stairs where Sandy greeted them. He paced back and forth and scratched at the door. "I have to let him run a minute."

"It's a good thing we took a nap before the party. I don't have the energy anymore for these late nights." Charley sat in the porch chair. "What the…"

"Sandy, come on. We have to go. Come here, boy." She patted her thigh to push him along. "What are you complaining about?"

"Nothing. I caught my dress on the wood. That's all."

She knew that wasn't all. Charley's eyes gave her away. She was spooked.

"That's a good boy." Lauren let him into the house. "Be good. I'll be back soon."

It was a perfect night. The air had just enough crispness to make her feel alive. The moonlight cast swaying shadows in the soft breeze. Driving with the windows down was the perfect compromise.

"You don't drive anymore, do you?" She started the car and headed to Havencroft Manor.

"No need to. I have any means of transportation outside my door in the city." Charley hung her head out the window, the breeze blowing her hair around. "Plus, I couldn't do this if I drove."

"Don't you ever think about leaving the city?"

"Oh, no. I know what you're working on. I'm not moving here. Visiting is fine, but I don't think I could do this as a steady diet."

She wondered if she could. The few days Charley had been there were fun, and the house didn't feel empty. Then there was Cooper.

Yeah. Cooper. She missed having him around. The past three weeks felt like years. She could talk to him all night. He was comfortable to be around.

Who was she kidding? She missed the familiar, and it wasn't going to be recreated in Havenport no matter how much she wanted it to be. She needed to get out and meet people. She could have gone to the ball earlier, but didn't want to be bothered wasting time forcing small talk. Charley would be leaving soon, and she wasn't going to misuse their time together. It could be months before they saw each other again.

The party was still going strong as they pulled up to the manor. Cars took every available spot. Music wafted from the parlor. Orange lights dotted the outline of the veranda. Jack-o'-lanterns grinned with the help of candles.

"Okay. You happy? We're here." She pulled her witch hat onto her head and fluffed her hair to frame her face.

"We look adorable. Like we're teenagers." Charley adjusted her cape. "Ready, sister witch?"

She nodded.

The front door stood open. Music weaved its way through her soul. Relaxing. Almost welcoming her into another dimension. The lighting calmed her—enough to see, but low enough to not be distracting.

It neared midnight.

A passing waiter offered a flute of champagne. Charley wandered off the minute they stepped into the entrance hall.

Lauren walked along the perimeter of the room, admiring Cooper's precision work. He was a man of detail. He put time and thought into what he did.

"Care to dance?"

Cooper.

Her cape flowed around her as she turned to him. He took her glass and placed it on a side table.

"I don't really know how."

He took her hand and walked backward, never losing eye contact as she followed him to the center of the room. He slid his hand onto the small of her back and pulled her close enough so she could feel the heat of his body, but not too close to make her uncomfortable.

His fingers intertwined with hers, and she smiled. The noise fell away, except for the music. The tempo slowed, and so did they. She closed her eyes and let her body follow Cooper. It came naturally. It felt right.

He's a good man, Lauren. Go with him.

The music softened.

I want you to be happy.

She opened her eyes to Cooper. She looked past him. Her heart beat faster. A tear rolled down her cheek.

Carl.

Be with him, Lauren. I love you.

She rested her head on Cooper's chest and surrendered to his arms.

About the Author

LITA HARRIS spends her time between New Jersey and the Endless Mountains region of Pennsylvania, where she writes most of her books. She also lived in Alaska for a short time just for fun. An avid crafter, unused supplies clutter her basement and attempts at making pottery, jewelry, and stained glass are proudly displayed in her house, usually behind a picture or holding a door open. She also makes candles and homemade soap. With enough books to stock a small library she may need to construct a building to store her literary obsessions.

She writes in multiple genres, including women's fiction, contemporary romance, paranormal, and cozy mysteries.

For more information about Lita, please visit her website at www.LitaHarris.com or at Twitter.com/LitaHarris and Facebook.com/LitaHarrisAuthor.

Also by Lila Harris

Timeless Tales – Short Stories

Christmas Spirits featured in Timeless Keepsakes

Chasing Fireflies featured in Timeless Escapes

Trusting Kindness featured in Timeless Treasures

Till Death Do Us Part featured in Timeless Vows

Havenport – Novellas

Winter Wonderland featured in Christmas in Havenport

New Beginnings featured in Welcome to Havenport

Wishful Thinking

In Days Past

If you enjoyed your time in Havenport, please spread the word by leaving a review on the site where you purchased your copy or on a reader site such as Goodreads or Shelfari. Thank you!

To receive up-to-date information on future Timeless Scribes publications, please sign up for our mailing list at www.TimelessScribes.com.

Timeless Scribes
Publishing